WITHDRAWN

D1015721

WHITE
RIVER
BURNING

PREVIOUS BOOKS IN THE *DAVE GURNEY* SERIES

Wolf Lake
Peter Pan Must Die
Let the Devil Sleep
Shut Your Eyes Tight
Think of a Number

WHITE RIVER BURNING

A DAVE GURNEY NOVEL

JOHN VERDON

COUNTERPOINT
Berkeley, California

White River Burning

Copyright © 2018 by John Verdon
First hardcover edition: 2018

All rights reserved under International and Pan-American Copyright Conventions. No part of this book may be used or reproduced in any manner whatsoever without written permission from the publisher, except in the case of brief quotations embedded in critical articles and reviews.

This book is a work of fiction. Names, characters, places, and incidents are the product of the author's imagination or are used fictitiously. Any resemblance to actual events is unintended and entirely coincidental.

Library of Congress Cataloging-in-Publication Data
Names: Verdon, John, author.
Title: White River burning : a Dave Gurney novel / John Verdon.
Description: Berkeley, CA : Counterpoint Press, [2018]
Identifiers: LCCN 2017057561 | ISBN 9781640090637
Subjects: LCSH: Detectives—New York (State)—New York—Fiction. | Serial murder
    investigation—Fiction. | GSAFD: Suspense fiction. | Mystery fiction.
Classification: LCC PS3622.E736 W48 2018 | DDC 813/.6—dc23
LC record available at https://lccn.loc.gov/2017057561

Jacket designed by Jarrod Taylor
Book designed by Jordan Koluch

COUNTERPOINT
2560 Ninth Street, Suite 318
Berkeley, CA 94710
www.counterpointpress.com

Printed in the United States of America
Distributed by Publishers Group West

10 9 8 7 6 5 4 3 2 1

For Naomi

I

HIDDEN FURY

1

Dave Gurney stood at the sink in his big farmhouse kitchen, holding one of Madeleine's strainers. He was carefully emptying into it what appeared to be several dirt-encrusted brown pebbles from a very old tinted-glass jar.

As he washed away the soil, he could see that the pebbles were smaller, lighter in color, and more uniform than they'd first appeared to be. He laid a paper towel on the sink-island countertop and eased the contents of the strainer onto it. With another paper towel he carefully patted the pebbles dry, then carried them along with the glass jar from the kitchen to his desk in the den and placed them next to his laptop and large magnifying glass. He started the computer and opened the document he'd created with the archaeological graphics program he'd acquired a month earlier—shortly after discovering the remnants of an old laid-stone cellar in the cherry copse above the pond. What he'd found in his examination of the site so far led him to believe that the cellar may have served as the foundation of a late-seventeenth- or early-eighteenth-century structure—perhaps the home of a settler in what then would have been a wild frontier area.

The archaeology program enabled him to overlay a current photograph of the cellar area with a precisely scaled grid, and then to tag the appropriate grid boxes with identifying code numbers for the items he'd found at those locations. An accompanying list linked the codes to verbal descriptions he'd provided along with photos of the individual items. Those items now included two iron hooks that his internet research told him were used for stretching animal hides; a tool fashioned from a large bone, probably a flesher for scraping hides; a knife with a black handle; the rusted remains of several iron chain links; and an iron key.

He found himself viewing these few objects, barely illuminated by his scant knowledge of the historical period with which they seemed to be associated, as the first tantalizing bits of a puzzle—dots to be connected with the help of dots yet to be discovered.

After recording the location of his newest find, he then used his magnifier to examine the bluish, slightly opaque glass jar. Judging from the pictures on the internet of similar containers, it seemed consistent with his estimate of the foundation's age.

He turned his attention to the pebbles. Taking a paper clip from his desk drawer, he unbent it into a relatively straight wire and used it to move one of the pebbles around, turning it over this way and that under the magnifier. It appeared relatively smooth except for one facet that consisted of a tiny hollow spot with thin, sharp edges. He went on to a second pebble, in which he saw the same structure; and then on to a third, a fourth, and the remaining four after that. Close examination revealed that all eight, while not quite identical, shared the same basic configuration.

He wondered about the significance of that.

Then it occurred to him that they might not be pebbles at all.

They could be teeth.

Small teeth. Possibly human baby teeth.

If that's what they were, some new questions came immediately to mind—questions that made him eager to get back down to the site and dig a little deeper.

As he stood up from the desk, Madeleine came into the den. She gave the little objects spread out on the paper towel a quick glance along with that slight flicker of distaste that crossed her face whenever something reminded her of the excavation now blocking the little trail she liked so much. It didn't help that his approach to the site reminded her of the way he would have approached a murder scene in his days as an NYPD homicide detective.

One of the persistent sources of tension in their marriage was the gap between her desire for a clean break with their past lives in the city, an unquestioning embrace of their new lives in the country, and his inability or unwillingness to shed his career-long mindset, his persistent need to be investigating something.

She put on a determinedly cheerful smile. "It's an absolutely glorious spring morning. I'm going to hike the quarry trail. I should be back in about two hours."

He waited for the next sentence. Usually, after informing him that she was going out, she would ask if he wanted to come along. And usually he would make some excuse, involving something else that needed doing. The simple fact was that walking in the woods never gave him the same sense of inner peace it gave her. His own sense of peace, a sense of strength and self-worth, came not so much from enjoying the world around him as from trying to figure out what exactly was going on and why. Peace through investigation. Peace through discovery. Peace through logic.

This time, however, she didn't offer him an invitation. Instead, she stated with a conspicuous lack of enthusiasm, "Sheridan Kline called."

"The district attorney? What did he want?"

"To talk to you."

"What did you tell him?"

"That you were out. He called just before you came back up to the house with those *things*." She pointed at the pebble-teeth. "He refused to leave a message. He said he'd call again at eleven thirty."

Gurney looked up at the clock on the den wall. It was now a quarter to eleven. "He didn't give you any hint of what he wanted?"

"He sounded tense. Maybe it's about the trouble over in White River?"

He thought about that for a moment. "I can't imagine how I could help him with that."

Madeleine shrugged. "Just guessing. But whatever he really wants from you, he'll probably be less than truthful about it. He's a snake. Be careful."

2

While Madeleine was lacing up her hiking boots in the mudroom, Gurney made himself a cup of coffee and took it out to one of the Adirondack chairs on the bluestone patio next to the asparagus patch.

The patio overlooked the low pasture, the barn, the pond, and the little-used town road that dead-ended into their fifty acres of woods and fields. It was a long time since the place had been a working farm, and what he and Madeleine liked to refer to as "pastures" were now really just overgrown meadows. Disuse had made them, if anything, more naturally beautiful—especially now in the early days of May with the first burst of wildflowers spreading across the hillside.

Madeleine emerged from the French doors onto the patio wearing a fuchsia nylon windbreaker half open over a chartreuse tee shirt. Whether it was the exuberant sense of life in the spring air or the anticipation of her outing, her mood had brightened. She leaned over his Adirondack chair and kissed him on the head. "Are you sure you'll hear the phone out here?"

"I left the window open."

"Okay. See you in a couple of hours."

He looked up at her and saw in her soft smile the woman he'd married twenty-five years earlier. He was amazed at how rapidly the tenor of their relationship could shift—how fraught small events and gestures could be and how contagious were the feelings they generated.

He watched as she made her way up through the high pasture, her jacket shining in the sun. Soon she disappeared into the pine woods in the direction of the old dirt road that connected a series of abandoned bluestone quarries along the north ridge. He suddenly wished that she had invited him along, wished that Kline's call would be coming to the cell phone in his pocket rather than to the landline in the house.

He checked his watch. His thoughts about the objects he'd found in the old buried cellar were now fully eclipsed by his efforts to imagine what was on the district attorney's mind. And how obscure the man's intentions would be.

At eleven thirty Gurney heard the distant sound of a car coming up the narrow town road below the barn. A minute later a gleaming black Lincoln Navigator passed between the barn and the pond, hesitating at the point where the gravel surface ended, before lumbering up the rutted farm track through the wild pasture grass to an open area beside the house and coming to a stop by Gurney's dusty Outback.

The first surprise was that it was Sheridan Kline himself who emerged from the big SUV. The second surprise was that he emerged from the driver's seat. He'd come in his official car but without the services of his driver—a notable departure, thought Gurney, for a man in love with the perks of his office.

Sharply dressed, Kline gave a couple of quick tugs to straighten the creases in his pants. At first glance the man seemed to have gotten smaller since their last meeting, ten months earlier, in the messy legal aftermath of the Peter Pan case. It was an odd perception, as well as an unpleasant reminder of the occasion. A lot of people had died in the horrendous finale of the Pan investigation, and Kline had appeared quite willing to have Gurney indicted for reckless homicide. But as soon as the media's preference for portraying Gurney as the hero of the case had become clear, Kline had supported that narrative—with a cordial enthusiasm that Madeleine had found nauseating.

He approached the patio now with a fixed smile, taking in the immediate area with a series of assessing glances.

Gurney rose to meet him. "I thought you were going to call."

The smile remained in place. "Change of plan. I happened to be in White River, meeting with Chief Beckert. Just forty miles from here, forty-five minutes with no traffic. So why not do it face-to-face? Always better that way."

Gurney inclined his head toward the Navigator. "No chauffeur today?"

"*Driver*, David, not *chauffeur*, I'm a public servant, for Christ's sake." He paused for a moment, radiating restless energy. "I often find driving relaxing." A small tic was playing at the corner of his determined smile.

"You drove here directly from White River?"

"As I said. From a meeting with Beckert. Which is what I want to talk to you about." He nodded toward the Adirondack chairs. "Why don't we have a seat?"

"Wouldn't you prefer to come inside?"

He made a face. "Not really. Such a beautiful day. I spend too much time indoors."

Gurney wondered if the man was afraid of being recorded and considered the patio safer than the house. Perhaps that was also his reason for avoiding the phone.

"Coffee?"

"Not right now."

Gurney gestured toward one of the chairs, sat down in the one facing it, and waited.

Kline removed the jacket of his expensive-looking gray suit, draped it neatly over the chair back, and loosened his tie before perching on the edge of the seat.

"Let me get right to the point. As you can imagine, we're facing a hell of a challenge. Shouldn't have been totally unexpected, given the inflammatory statements coming out of that BDA bunch, but something like this is always a shock. You spent twenty-five years in the NYPD, so I can only imagine how it feels to you."

"How what feels to me?"

"The shooting."

"What shooting?"

"Christ, how cut off from the world are you up here on this mountain? Were you even aware of the demonstrations going on all week over in White River?"

"For the one-year anniversary of that traffic-stop fatality? Laxton Jones? Hard not to be aware of all that. But I haven't checked the news yet this morning."

"A White River cop was shot dead last night. Trying to keep a racial mess from getting completely out of hand."

"Jesus."

"Jesus. Goddamn right."

"This happened at a Black Defense Alliance demonstration?"

"Naturally."

"I thought they were a nonviolent group."

"Hah!"

"The cop who was shot. Was he white?"

"Of course."

"How—?"

"Sniper. Fatal head shot. Somebody out there knew exactly what the hell he was doing. This was no coked-up idiot with a Saturday-night special. This was planned." Kline ran his fingers nervously back through his short dark hair.

Gurney was struck by the emotional intensity of the district attorney's reaction—natural in most people but noteworthy in such a coldly calculating politician, a man Gurney had come to believe evaluated every event by how it might facilitate or obstruct his own ambitions.

There was the obvious question—which Kline addressed on cue as Gurney was about to ask it. "You're wondering why I'm bringing this problem to you?" He shifted on the edge of his chair to face Gurney squarely, as though he believed that direct eye contact was essential to communicating an attitude of forthrightness. "I'm here, David, because I want your help. In fact, I *need* your help."

3

Sheridan Kline stood silently at the open French doors, watching as Gurney prepared two mugs at the coffee machine in the kitchen. Neither man spoke again until they were back outside on their chairs—the district attorney still looking stiff and uncomfortable, but perhaps feeling assured from his own observation of the coffee-making that Gurney hadn't taken the opportunity to slip a recording device into his pocket. He took a few sips from his mug, then set it down on the flat wooden arm of the chair.

He took the deep breath of a man about to dive into a cold pool. "I'll be perfectly frank with you, David. I have a huge problem. The situation in White River is explosive. I don't know how closely you've been following it, but there've been outbreaks of looting and arson all this past week down in the Grinton district. Constant stink of smoke in the air. Sickening. And it could get a hell of a lot worse. Keg of dynamite, and these BDA people seem to be trying to set it off. Like this latest attack. Cold-blooded assassination of a police officer." He fell silent, shaking his head.

After a few moments Gurney tried to nudge him toward explaining his visit. "You said that you drove here directly from a meeting with the White River chief of police?"

"Dell Beckert and his number two, Judd Turlock."

"About how to respond to the shooting?"

"Among other things. A discussion of the whole situation. All the implications." Kline made a face as if he were regurgitating something indigestible.

"Is there some connection between that meeting and your coming here?"

Another pained expression. "Yes and no."

"Tell me more about the 'yes' part."

Before answering, Kline reached for his cup, took a long sip from it, and replaced it carefully on the chair arm. Gurney noted a tremor in his hand.

"The situation in White River is delicate. Feelings are running way too high on all sides. I called it a keg of dynamite, but that's not right. It's more like pure nitroglycerin—tricky to handle, unpredictable, unforgiving. Stumble, whack against it the wrong way, and it could blow us all to pieces."

"I get that. Racial sensitivities. Ugly emotions. Potential for total chaos. But—"

"But how do you fit into this?" He flashed an anxious politician's smile. "David, never in my career have I encountered a greater need to marshal all our available resources. I'm talking about brains—the right kind of brains. The need to understand the angles. See around the corners. I don't want to get blindsided because we didn't look into things closely enough."

"You think Beckert's department might not be up to the job?"

"No, nothing like that. You won't hear any criticism of Beckert from me. The man's a law-and-order icon. Hell of a record of achievement." He paused. "There's even a rumor about a run in the special election for state attorney general. Nothing definite, of course." Another pause. "He could be the perfect candidate, though. Right image. Right connections. Not everyone knows this, he certainly doesn't advertise it himself, but his current wife happens to be the governor's cousin. Right man in the right place at the right time."

"Assuming that everything goes well. Or at least that nothing goes terribly wrong."

"That goes without saying."

"So what exactly do you want from me?"

"Your investigative instincts. Your nose for the truth. You're very good at what you do. Your NYPD homicide record speaks for itself."

Gurney gave him a puzzled look. "Beckert's got the whole White River Police Department at his disposal. You've got your own investigative staff. If that's not enough, you could leverage the racial element of the situation and bring in the FBI."

He shook his head quickly. "No, no, no. Once the FBI comes in, we lose control. They talk a cooperative game, but they don't play one. They've got their own agenda. Christ, you ought to know how the feds operate. Last thing we want to do is lose our ability to manage the process."

"Okay, forget the FBI. Between your staff and Beckert's, you've still got plenty of manpower."

"Might seem like we do, but the fact is my staff is at an all-time low. My right-hand guy, Fred Stimmel, hit his magic pension number six months ago and headed for Florida. My two female investigators are both on maternity leave. And the rest of the crew are locked into assignments I can't pull them away from—not without a major prosecution going down the tubes. You may think I've got ample staff. Fact is I've got zip. I know what you're thinking. That the investigation belongs to the White River PD in any event, not the county DA. The ball is in Beckert's court, so let him handle it through his own famously effective detective bureau. Right? But I'm telling you there's way too much at stake to play this game with anything other than a full-court press. That means with all I can muster on my side as well as Beckert's—period!" A small vein in Kline's temple was becoming more prominent as he spoke.

"You'd like me to join your staff as some sort of adjunct investigator?"

"Something like that. We'll work out the details. I have the authority and contingency funds. We've worked together before, David. You made huge contributions to the Mellery and Perry cases. And the stakes in this case are sky-high. We need to get to the bottom of this police killing fast—and we need to get it right, so nothing comes back later to bite us in the ass. Get it wrong and it's chaos time. What do you say? Can I rely on you?"

Gurney leaned back in his chair, watching the vultures soaring lazily above the north ridge.

Kline's smile tightened into a grimace. "Do you have any concerns?"

"I need to sleep on this, discuss it with my wife."

Kline chewed on his bottom lip for a moment. "Okay. Just let me repeat that there's a hell of a lot at stake here. More than you might think. The right outcome could be enormously beneficial for all concerned."

He got up from his chair, straightened his tie, and put on his jacket. He pulled out a business card and handed it to Gurney. The politician's smile reappeared in full force. "My personal cell number is on the card. Call me tomorrow. Or tonight if you can. I know you'll do the right thing—for all of us."

Two minutes later the big black Navigator passed between the pond and the barn, heading down onto the town road. The crunch of the tires on the gravel surface soon faded into silence.

The soaring vultures had disappeared. The sky was a piercing blue, the hillside a painter's palette of greens. Next to the patio, in the raised planting bed, the day's growth of asparagus was awaiting harvest. Above the tender new shoots the airy asparagus ferns were swaying in an almost imperceptible breeze.

The overall picture of spring perfection was tainted only by the slightest hint of something acrid in the air.

4

Gurney spent the next hour visiting various internet sites, trying to get a broader view of the White River crisis than the perspective Kline had presented. He had the feeling that he was being manipulated with a carefully arranged account of the situation.

Countering an impulse to go to the most recent news of the shooting, he decided to search first for coverage of the original incident—to refresh his recollection of the fatal shooting that occurred the previous May and that the Black Defense Alliance demonstrations were commemorating.

He located an early newspaper report in the online archive of the *Quad-County Star*. The front-page headline was one that had become disturbingly common: "Minor Traffic Stop Turns Deadly." A brief description of the incident followed:

> At approximately 11:30 PM on Tuesday White River Police Officer Kieran Goddard stopped a car with two occupants near the intersection of Second Street and Sliwak Avenue in the Grinton section of White River for failing to signal prior to changing lanes. According to a police spokesman, the driver of the vehicle, Laxton Jones, disputed the officer's observation and refused several requests to present his license and registration. Officer Goddard then directed Jones to switch off the ignition and step out of the vehicle. Jones responded with a series of obscenities, put the vehicle in reverse, and began backing away in an erratic fashion. Officer Goddard ordered him to stop. Jones then placed the vehicle in drive and accelerated toward the officer, who drew his service weapon and fired through the windshield

of the approaching vehicle. He subsequently called for an ambulance as well as appropriate supervisory and support personnel. Jones was declared dead on arrival at Mercy Hospital. The second occupant of the vehicle, a twenty-six-year-old female identified as Blaze Lovely Jackson, was detained in connection with an outstanding warrant and the discovery of a controlled substance in the vehicle.

The next relevant article in the *Star* appeared two days later on page five. It quoted a statement issued by Marcel Jordan, a community activist, in which he claimed that the police version of the shooting was "a fabrication designed to justify the execution of a man who had embarrassed them—a man dedicated to uncovering and publicizing the false arrests, perjury, and brutality rampant in the White River Police Department. The officer's claim that Laxton was attempting to run him down is an outright lie. He posed no threat whatever to that officer. Laxton Jones was murdered in cold blood."

The *Star*'s next mention of the event appeared a week later. It described a tense scene at Laxton Jones's funeral, an angry confrontation between mourners and police. The funeral was followed immediately by a press conference at which the activist Marcel Jordan—flanked by Blaze Lovely Jackson, out on bail, and Devalon Jones, brother of the deceased—announced the formation of the Black Defense Alliance, an organization whose mission would be "the protection of our brothers and sisters from the routine abuse, mayhem, and murder carried out by the racist law-enforcement establishment."

The article concluded with a response from White River Police Chief Dell Beckert. "The negative statement issued by the group calling themselves the 'Black Defense Alliance' is unfortunate, unhelpful, and untrue. It demeans honest men and women who have dedicated themselves to the safety and welfare of their fellow citizens. This cynical grandstanding deepens the misconceptions that are destroying our society."

Gurney found little in other upstate papers and virtually nothing in the national press regarding the shooting of Laxton Jones or the activities of the Black Defense Alliance for the next eleven months—until the BDA's announcement of demonstrations to mark the one-year anniversary of the shooting and to "raise awareness of racist police practices."

According to the ensuing media coverage, an initial peaceful demonstration was followed by sporadic instances of violence throughout the Grinton section of

White River. The unrest had been going on for a week, becoming more confrontational and destructive with each passing day and generating increasingly dramatic media coverage.

The fact that he'd been only partially aware of this was the result of his and Madeleine's decision to leave their TV behind when they moved from the city to Walnut Crossing and to avoid internet news sites. They felt that "news" was too often a term for manufactured controversy, superficial half-truths, and events about which they could do nothing. This meant he had some catching up to do.

There was no shortage of current coverage of what one media website was calling "White River in Flames." He decided to make his way through the local and national reports in the sequence in which they'd been posted. The rising hysteria evident in the changing tone of the headlines as the week progressed suggested a situation spinning out of control:

UPSTATE CITY DEBATES YEAR-OLD CONTROVERSY

BDA PROTEST OPENS OLD WOUNDS

WHITE RIVER MAYOR CALLS FOR CALM IN FACE OF PROVOCATIONS

BDA FIREBRAND MARCEL JORDAN CALLS POLICE MURDERERS

DOZENS INJURED AS DEMONSTRATIONS TURN UGLY

JORDAN TO BECKERT: "YOU HAVE BLOOD ON YOUR HANDS"

WHITE RIVER ON THE EDGE OF CHAOS

ROCK-THROWING, ARSON, LOOTING

PROTESTERS BEATEN, ARRESTED IN CLASH WITH POLICE

SNIPER KILLS LOCAL COP—POLICE DECLARE WAR ON BDA

Gurney's reading of the articles added little to the information in the overheated headlines. His quick perusal of the comments section after each article reinforced his belief that these "reader involvement" features were mainly invitations to idiocy.

His main feeling, however, was a growing sense of unease at Kline's eagerness to pull him into the gathering storm.

5

When Madeleine returned from her hike, radiating the satisfaction and exhilaration she derived from the outdoors, Gurney was still in his den, hunched over his computer screen. Having moved on from the internet news sites, he was exploring the physical reality of White River with the help of Google Street View.

Although it was only an hour's drive from Walnut Crossing, he'd never had a compelling reason to go there. He had a sense that the place was emblematic of the decline of upstate New York cities and towns, suffering from industrial collapse, agricultural relocation, a shrinking middle-class population, political mismanagement, the spreading heroin epidemic, troubled schools, eroding infrastructure—with the added element of strained police relations with a sizable minority community, a problem now vividly underscored.

The image of White River was further clouded, ironically, by the looming presence of the area's largest employer and supplier of much of its economic lifeblood: the White River Correctional Facility. Or, as it was known locally, Rivcor.

What Gurney could see, as Google Street View led him along the city's main avenues, supported his negative preconceptions. There was even a clichéd set of railroad tracks dividing the good section of town from the bad.

Madeleine was standing next to him now, frowning at the screen. "What town is that?"

"White River."

"Where all the trouble is?"

"Yes."

Her frown deepened. "It's about that traffic-stop shooting of a black motorist last year, right?"

"Yes."

"And some statue they want removed?"

Gurney looked up at her. "What statue?"

"A couple of people were talking about it at the clinic the other day. A statue of someone connected to the early days of the prison."

"That part I wasn't aware of."

She cocked her head curiously. "Does this have something to do with your call from Sheridan Kline?"

"Actually the call turned out to be a visit. By the man himself."

"Oh?"

"He said something about not being that far away and preferring face-to-face meetings. But I suspect that coming here was always his plan."

"Why didn't he say that from the beginning?"

"Knowing how manipulative and paranoid he is, I'd guess he wanted to take me by surprise to keep me from recording our meeting."

"The subject was that sensitive?"

Gurney shrugged. "Didn't seem so to me. But it would be hard to know for sure without knowing what he wants from me."

"He came all this way and didn't tell you what he wants?"

"Yes and no. He says he wants my help investigating a fatal shooting. Claims he's short-staffed, running out of time, with the city on the verge of Armageddon, et cetera."

"But . . ."

"But it doesn't add up. Procedurally, the investigation of homicides is strictly a police matter. If there's a need for more personnel, that's a police command decision. There are channels for that. It's not up to the DA or his investigatory staff to take this sort of initiative—unless there's something he's not telling me."

"You said there was a fatal shooting. Who was killed?"

Gurney hesitated. Law-enforcement deaths had always been a sensitive subject with Madeleine, and more so since he himself was wounded two years earlier at the end of the Jillian Perry case. "A White River cop was hit last night by a sniper at a Black Defense Alliance demonstration."

Her expression froze. "He wants you to find the sniper?"

"That's what he says."

"But you don't believe him?"

"I have the feeling I haven't gotten the whole story yet."

"So what are you going to do?"

"I haven't decided."

She gave him one of those probing looks that made him feel as if his soul were on display, then switched gears. "You remember that we're going to the big LORA fund-raiser tonight at the Gelters', right?"

"That thing is tonight?"

"You might actually enjoy it. I understand the Gelters' house is something to see."

"I'd rather see it when it isn't full of idiots."

"What are you so angry about?"

"I'm not angry. I'm just not looking forward to spending time with those people."

"Some of *those people* are quite nice."

"I find the whole LORA thing a little nuts. Like that logo on their letterhead. A goddamn groundhog standing on its hind legs and leaning on a crutch. Jesus."

"It's an injured-animal rehabilitation center. What do you think their logo should be?"

"Better question: Why do we have to attend a fund-raiser for limping groundhogs?"

"When we're asked to take part in a community event, it's nice to say yes once in a while. And don't tell me you're not angry. You're obviously angry, and it has nothing to do with groundhogs."

He sighed and gazed out the den window.

Her expression suddenly brightened in one of those transformations that was part of her emotional wiring. "Want to take the pasture walk with me?" she asked, referring to the grassy path they kept mowed around the perimeter of the field on the slope above the house.

He screwed up his face in disbelief. "You just got back from a two-hour trek on the ridge, and you want to go out again?"

"You spend too much time bent over that computer screen. How about it?"

His first reaction went unvoiced. No, he didn't want to waste time trudging pointlessly around that old pasture. He had urgent things to think about—the protests verging on all-out riots, the cop killing, Kline's not-quite-believable story.

Then he reconsidered—remembering that whenever he took one of Madeleine's annoying suggestions, the result always turned out better than he'd anticipated.

"Maybe just once around the field."

"Great! We might even find a little creature with a limp—for you to bring to the party."

As they reached the end of the path, Gurney suggested they go on to his archaeological project in the cherry woods above the pond.

When they reached the partly exposed foundation, he began pointing out where he'd uncovered the various iron and glass artifacts he'd catalogued on his computer. As he was indicating the spot where he'd found the teeth, Madeleine broke in with a sharp exclamation.

"Oh my God, look at that!"

He followed her gaze up into the treetops. "What do you see?"

"The leaves, the sun shining through them, the glowing greens. That light!"

He nodded. He tried not to let his irritation show. "What I'm doing here bothers you, doesn't it?"

"I guess I'm not as enthusiastic about it as you are."

"It's more than that. What is it about my digging here that annoys you so much?"

She didn't answer.

"Maddie?"

"You want to solve the mystery."

"What do you mean?"

"The mystery of who lived here, when they lived here, why they lived here. Right?"

"More or less."

"You want to solve the mystery of what brought them here, what kept them here."

"I suppose so."

"That's what bothers me."

"I don't understand."

"Not everything has to be figured out . . . dug up, torn apart, evaluated. Some things should be left alone, in peace, respected."

He considered this. "You think the remains of this old house fall into that category?"

"Yes," she said. "Like a grave."

At 5:35 PM, they got in the Outback and set out for the LORA fund-raiser at Marv and Trish Gelter's famously unique residence, located on a hilltop in the chic hamlet of Lockenberry.

From what Gurney had heard, Lockenberry was close enough to Woodstock to attract a similar crowd of artsy weekenders from Manhattan and Brooklyn, yet far enough away to have its own independent cachet, derived from the poets' colony at its core. Known simply as the Colony, it was founded by the town's eponymous whale-oil heiress, Mildred Lockenberry, whose own poetry was revered for its impenetrability.

Just as the value of property within Lockenberry was affected by how close it was to the Colony, the value of any property in the eastern part of the county was affected by how close it was to Lockenberry—a phenomenon Gurney noted in the postcard perfection of the nineteenth-century homes, barns, and stone walls lining the last few miles of the road leading into the hamlet. The restoration and maintenance of these structures could not be inexpensive.

Although the natural endowments of the land and buildings in the immediate vicinity of Lockenberry had been groomed and highlighted, the entire route from Walnut Crossing, winding through a succession of rolling hills and long river valleys, was, in its uncultivated and unpolished way, amazingly beautiful—with wild purple irises, white anemones, yellow lupines, and shockingly blue grape hyacinths scattered among the delicate greens of the spring grasses. It was enough to make him understand, if not feel as deeply, Madeleine's enthusiasm for the display of sunlit leaves over his excavation by their pond.

When the GPS on the dashboard of their Outback announced that they would be arriving at their destination in another five hundred feet, Gurney slowly pulled over onto the road's gravelly shoulder and came to a stop by an antique iron gate in a high drystone wall. A freshly graded dirt-and-gravel driveway proceeded from the open gate in a wide curve up through a gently rising meadow. He took out his phone.

Madeleine gave him a questioning look.

"I need to make a couple of calls before we go in."

He entered the number of Jack Hardwick, a former New York State Police investigator with whom he'd crossed paths a number of times since they'd met many years earlier pursuing in different jurisdictions a solution to the sensational Peter Piggert murder case. Their unique bond was formed through a kind of grotesque serendipity—when they discovered, separately, thirty miles apart, on the same day, the disconnected halves of Piggert's last victim. Who happened to be Piggert's mother.

Gurney and Hardwick's subsequent relationship had had its ups and downs. The ups were based on an obsession with solving homicides and a shared level of intelligence. The downs were the product of their conflicting personalities—Gurney's calm, cerebral approach versus Hardwick's compulsive need to debunk, irritate, and provoke—a habit responsible for his forced transition from the state police to his current role as a private detective. The recording on the man's phone was, for him, relatively inoffensive:

"Leave a message. Be brief."

Gurney complied. "Gurney here. Calling about White River. Wondering if you know anyone there who might know something that's not already in the news."

His second call was to the cell number Sheridan Kline had given him earlier that day. Kline's recorded voice was as oleaginously cordial as Hardwick's was curt. "Hello, this is Sheridan. You've reached my personal phone. If you have a legal, business, or political matter to discuss, please call me at the number listed on the county website for the office of the district attorney. If your call is personal in nature, when you hear the beep leave your name, number, and a message. Thank you."

Gurney got directly to the point. "Regarding your description earlier today of the situation in White River, I came away feeling that some critical factor had been left out. Before I decide whether to get involved, I need to know more. The ball's in your court."

Madeleine pointed at the dashboard clock. It was 6:40 PM.

He weighed the pros and cons of making a third call, but making it now in Madeleine's presence might not be a good idea. He restarted the car, passed through the open gate, and headed up the spotless driveway.

Madeleine spoke without looking at him. "Your security blanket?"

"Excuse me?"

"I got the impression you were touching base with the reassuring world of murder and mayhem before having to face the terrifying unknowns of a cocktail party."

Half a mile into the Gelters' property the driveway crested a gentle rise, bringing them suddenly to the edge of a field planted with thousands of daffodils. In the slanting sunlight of early evening the effect was startling—almost as startling as the massive, windowless, cubical house overlooking the field from the top of the hill.

6

The driveway led them to the front of the house. The imposing dark wood facade appeared to be perfectly square, perhaps fifty feet in both height and width.

"Is that what I think it is?" asked Madeleine with an amused frown.

"What do you mean?"

"Look closely. The outline of a letter."

Gurney stared. He could just barely make out the distressed outline of a giant *G*—like a faded letter on a child's alphabet block—imprinted on the house.

While they were still gazing at it, a young man with chartreuse hair, wearing a loose white shirt and skinny jeans, came running toward the car. He opened the passenger door and held it while Madeleine got out, then hurried around to the driver's side.

"You and the lady can go right in, sir." He handed Gurney a small card bearing the name "Dylan" and a cell number. "When you're ready to leave, call this number and I'll bring your car around." Flashing a smile, he got into the dusty Outback and drove it around the side of the house.

"Nice touch," said Madeleine as they walked across the patio.

Gurney nodded vaguely. "How do you know Trish Gelter?"

"I've told you three times. Vinyasa."

"Vin . . ."

She sighed. "My yoga class. The one I go to every Sunday morning."

As they reached the front door, it slid open like the pocket door of an enormous closet, revealing a woman with a mass of wavy blond hair.

"Mahdehlennnne!" she cried, giving the name an exaggerated French inflection that made it sound like a jokey endearment. "Welcome to Skyview!" She grinned, showing off an intriguing Lauren Hutton gap between her front teeth. "You look fabulous! Love the dress! And you brought the famous detective! Wonderful! Come in, come in!" She stood to the side and, with a hand holding a frosted blue cocktail, waved them into a cavernous space unlike any home Gurney had ever seen.

It seemed to consist of a single cube-shaped room—if anything so big could be called a room. Cubical objects of various sizes were being used as tables and chairs on which clusters of guests perched and conversed. Sets of cubes pushed together served as kitchen counters at each end of a restaurant-sized brushed-steel stove. No two cubes were the same color. As Gurney had noted from the outside, the five-story-high walls had no windows, yet the whole interior was suffused with a sunny brightness. The roof was constructed of clear glass panels. The sky above it was a cloudless blue.

Madeleine was smiling. "Trish, this place is amazing!"

"Get yourself a drink and have a good look around. It's full of surprises. Meanwhile, I'll introduce your shy husband to some interesting people."

"Good luck with that," said Madeleine, heading for a bar that consisted of two four-foot-high cubes, one fire-engine red, one acid green. Trish Gelter turned to Gurney, moistening her lips with the tip of her tongue. "I've been reading all about you, and now I get to meet the supercop in person."

He grimaced.

"That's exactly what *New York* magazine called you. It said you had the highest homicide arrest and conviction rate in the history of the department."

"That article ran more than five years ago, and it's still an embarrassment."

His NYPD record was a distinction he didn't mind having, since it occasionally had the practical value of opening a few doors. But he also found it embarrassing. "Magazines like to create superheroes and supervillains. I'm neither."

"You look like a hero. You look like Daniel Craig."

He smiled awkwardly, eager to change the subject. "That big letter out there on the front of the house—"

"A postmodern joke." She winked at him.

"Pardon?"

"How much do you know about postmodern design?"

"Nothing."

"How much do you want to know about it?"

"Maybe just enough to understand the big *G*."

She sipped her blue cocktail and flashed her gap-toothed grin. "Irony is the essence of postmodern design."

"The *G* is an ironic statement?"

"Not just the *G*. The whole house. A work of ironic art. A rebellion against humorless, boring modernism. The fact that this house and everything in it was designed by Kiriki Kilili says it all. Kiriki loves to stick it to the modernists with his cube jokes. The modernists want a house to be an impersonal machine. *Pure efficiency*." She wrinkled her nose as if *efficiency* had a foul odor. "Kiriki wants it to be a place of fun, joy, pleasure." She held Gurney's gaze for an extra couple of seconds on that last word.

"Does the big *G* stand for something?"

"Giddy, goofy, Gelter—take your choice."

"It's a joke?"

"It's a way of treating the house as a toy, an amusement, an absurdity."

"Your husband is a playful fellow, is he?"

"Marv? Omigod, no. Marv's a financial genius. *Very* serious. The man shits money. I'm the fun one. See the fireplace?" She pointed to one of the walls, at the base of which was a hearth at least ten feet wide. The flames across the width flickered in the full spectrum of a rainbow. "Sometimes I program it for all those colors. Or just green. I love a green fire. I'm like a witch with magic powers. A witch who always gets what she wants."

Mounted on the wall above the hearth was a TV screen, the largest he'd ever seen. It was displaying three adjacent talking heads in the divided format of a cable news program. Several of the party guests were watching it.

"Trish?" A loud male voice from a corner of the room broke through the general hubbub.

She leaned close to Gurney. "I'm being summoned. I fear I have to be introduced to someone horribly boring. I feel it in my bones." She managed to make her bones sound like a sex organ. "Don't go away. You're the first homicide detective I've ever met. An actual murder expert. I have so many questions." She gave his arm a little squeeze before heading across the room, sashaying through an obstacle course of cubes.

Gurney was trying to make sense of it all.

Postmodern irony?

The big *G* was a symbol of absurdity?

The whole house was a multimillion-dollar joke?

A witch who gets whatever she wants?

And where the hell were the other rooms?

In particular, where was the bathroom?

As he looked around at the chatting guests, he spotted Madeleine. She was talking to a willowy woman with short black hair and catlike eyes. He made his way over.

Madeleine gave him a funny look. "Something wrong?"

"Just . . . taking it all in."

She gestured toward the woman. "This is Filona. From Vinyasa."

"Ah. Vinyasa. Nice to meet you. Interesting name."

"It came to me in a dream."

"Did it?"

"I love this space, don't you?"

"It's really something. Do you have any idea where the restrooms are?"

"They're in the companion cube out back, except for the guest bathroom over there." She pointed to an eight-foot-high pair of vertically stacked cubes a few feet from where they were standing. "The door is on the other side. It's voice-activated. Everything in this house you either talk to or control with your phone. Like it's all alive. Organic."

"What do you say to the bathroom door?"

"Whatever you want."

Gurney glanced at Madeleine, searching for guidance.

She gave him a perky little shrug. "The voice thing actually does work. Just tell it you need to use the bathroom. That's what I heard someone do a few minutes ago."

He stared at her. "Good to know."

Filona added, "It's not just the bathroom. You can tell the lamps how bright you want them. You can talk to the thermostat—higher, lower, whatever." She paused with a half-somewhere-else sort of smile. "This is the most fun place you could ever find out here in the middle of nowhere, you know? Like the last thing you'd expect, which is what makes it so great. Like, wow, what a surprise."

"Filona works at the LORA shelter," said Madeleine.

He smiled. "What do you do there?"

"I'm an RC. There are three of us."

All that came to mind was Roman Catholic. "RC?"

"Recovery companion. Sorry about that. When you're in something, you forget that not everyone else is in it."

He could feel Madeleine's *be nice* gaze on him.

"So LORA is . . . pretty special?"

"*Very* special. It's all about the spirit. People think taking care of abandoned animals is about getting rid of their worms and fleas and giving them food and shelter. But that's just for the body. LORA heals the spirit. People buy animals like they were toys, then throw them out when they don't act like toys. Do you know how many cats, dogs, rabbits are tossed out every day? Like garbage? Thousands. Nobody thinks about the pain to those little souls. That's why we're here tonight. LORA does what no one else is doing. We give animals friendship."

The voices of the TV talking heads had gotten louder, more argumentative. Occasional words and phrases were now clearly audible. Gurney tried to stay focused on Filona. "You give them friendship?"

"We have conversations."

"With the animals?"

"Of course."

"Filona is also a painter," said Madeleine. "A very accomplished one. We saw some of her work at the Kettleboro Art Show."

"I think I remember. Purple skies?"

"My burgundy cosmologies."

"Ah. Burgundy."

"My burgundy paintings are done with beet juice."

"I had no idea. If you'll excuse me for just a minute . . ." He gestured toward the cubical structure housing the bathroom. "I'll be back."

On the far side of it he found a recessed door panel. Next to the panel there was a small red light above what he guessed was a pinhole microphone. He further guessed that the red light indicated that the bathroom was occupied. In no hurry to get back to the discussion of burgundy cosmologies, he stayed where he was.

The variety of people with whom Madeleine cultivated friendships never stopped surprising him. While he tended to be attuned to the dishonesty or loose screw in a new acquaintance, her focus was on a person's capacity for goodness, liveliness, inventiveness. While he found most people in some way warranting caution, she found them in some way delightful. She managed to do that without being naïve. In fact, she was quite sensitive to real danger.

He checked the little light. It was still red.

His position by the bathroom door gave him an angled view of the wide screen above the hearth. Several more party guests, drinks in hand, were gathering in front of it. The talking heads were gone. With a fanfare of synthesized sound effects, a swirling jumble of colorful letters was coalescing into words:

PEOPLE—PASSIONS—IDEAS—VALUES

THE AMERICAN DREAM IN CRISIS

The list then contracted into a single line to make room for three statements covering the width of the screen, accompanied by a martial-sounding drum roll:

EXPLOSIVE CRISIS—HAPPENING NOW

SEE IT ON *BATTLEGROUND TONIGHT*

NOTHING'S AS REAL AS RAM-TV

A moment later these statements burst into flying shards, replaced by a video of a nighttime street scene—an angry crowd chanting, "Justice for Laxton . . . Justice for Laxton . . . Justice for Laxton . . ." Demonstrators with signs bearing the same message were thrusting them up and down to the rhythm of the chant. The crowd was being contained by waist-high movable fencing, backed up by a line of cops in riot gear. When the video source was switched to a second camera angle, Gurney could see that the demonstration was taking place in front of a granite-faced building. The words WHITE RIVER POLICE DEPARTMENT were visible on the stone lintel above the front door.

At the bottom of the video screen, the words *BATTLEGROUND TONIGHT*—ONLY ON RAM-TV were flashing in a bright-red stripe.

The video shifted to what appeared to be another demonstration. The camera was positioned behind the demonstrators, facing the speaker addressing them. He spoke in a voice that rose and fell, paused and stretched in the cadences of an old-time preacher. "We have asked for justice. Begged for justice. Pleaded for justice. Cried for justice. Cried so much. Cried so long. Cried bitter tears for justice. But those days are over. The days of asking and begging and pleading—those days are behind us. Today, on this day that the Lord hath made, on this day of days, on this day of reckoning, we DEMAND justice. Here and now, we DEMAND it. I say it again, lest there be deaf ears in high places—we DEMAND justice. For Laxton Jones, murdered on this very street, we DEMAND justice. Standing on this very street, standing in the place anointed by his innocent blood, we DEMAND justice." He raised both fists high above his head, his voice swelling up into a hoarse roar. "It is his sacred RIGHT in the sight of God. His RIGHT as a child of God. This RIGHT will not be denied. Justice MUST be done. Justice WILL be done."

As he spoke, his dramatic pauses were filled with loud *amen*s and other cries and murmurs of approval, growing more insistent as the speech progressed. An identifying line was superimposed on the video like a foreign-film subtitle: "Marcel Jordan, Black Defense Alliance."

The group standing in front of the Gelters' TV, holding colorful cocktails and little hors d'oeuvre plates, had grown larger and more attentive, reminding Gurney that nothing attracts a crowd like aggressive emotion. In fact, that one nasty truth seemed to be propelling the race to the bottom in the country's political discourse and news programming.

As the demonstrators began to sing the old civil rights anthem "We Shall Overcome," the video scene changed again. It showed a crowd outdoors at night, but very little was happening. The people were loosely assembled with their backs to the camera on a grassy area just beyond a treelined sidewalk. The illumination, evidently coming from overhead streetlights, was partly blocked by the trees. From somewhere out of sight came bits and pieces of an amplified speech, its rhythms indistinctly captured by the camera's microphone. Two patrol officers in modified riot gear were moving back and forth on the sidewalk, as if to continually vary their lines of sight around the trees and through the crowd.

The fact that nothing of significance was happening in a video selected for broadcast could mean only one thing—that something was *about* to happen. Just as it occurred to Gurney what it might be, the video frame froze and a statement was superimposed on it:

WARNING!!!

A VIOLENT EVENT IS ABOUT TO BE SHOWN

IF YOU WOULD PREFER NOT TO WITNESS IT

CLOSE YOUR EYES FOR THE NEXT SIXTY SECONDS

The video continued, with the two officers again moving slowly along the sidewalk, their attention on the crowd. Gurney grimaced, his jaw clenched in anticipation of what he was now sure was coming.

Suddenly the head of one of the officers jerked forward, and he fell facedown onto the concrete, hard, as though an invisible hand had slammed him down.

There were cries of shock and dismay from the guests around the TV. Most continued watching the video—the panicky movements of the second officer as he realized what had happened, his frantic attempts at first aid, his shouting into his cell phone, the spreading awareness of trouble, the confused milling and retreat of many of the nearest onlookers.

Two key facts were clear. The shot had come not from the crowd but from somewhere behind the victim. And either the shooter was far enough away or the weapon was sufficiently silenced for the shot not to be picked up by the camera's audio system.

Gurney was aware of the bathroom door sliding open behind him, but he remained focused on the video. Three more officers arrived on the run, two with weapons drawn; one of the other officers took off his own protective vest and placed it under the man's head; more cell phone calls were made; the crowd was breaking apart; a distant siren was growing louder.

"Goddamn animals."

The voice behind Gurney had a rough scraping quality that sharpened the contempt conveyed by the words.

He turned and came face-to-face with a man of his own height, build, and age. His features were individually normal, even ideal; but they didn't seem to go together.

"Gurney, right?"

"Right."

"NYPD detective?"

"Retired."

A shrewd look entered the eyes that seemed a bit too close together. "Technically, right?"

"A bit more than technically."

"My point is, being a cop gets in the blood. It never goes away, right?" He smiled, but the effect was chillier than if he hadn't.

Gurney returned the smile. "How do you know who I am?"

"My wife always lets me know who she's bringing into the house."

Gurney thought of a cat announcing with a distinctive meow that she was bringing in a captured mouse. "So you're Marv Gelter. Nice to meet you."

They shook hands, Gelter eyeing him as one might examine an interesting object for its potential utility.

Gurney nodded toward the TV. "That's quite a thing you have over there."

Gelter peered for a moment at the big screen, his eyes narrowing. "Animals."

Gurney said nothing.

"You had to deal with that kind of shit in the city?"

"Cops being shot?"

"The whole thing. The circus of bullshit. The *entitlement.*" He articulated the last word with vicious precision. His eyes narrowed as he stared at Gurney, apparently waiting for a response, an endorsement.

Again Gurney said nothing. On the screen, two talking heads were arguing. One was contending that the current problems were part of the endless price being paid for the moral disaster of slavery, that the destruction of families had wrought irreparable damage, carried from generation to generation.

His opponent was shaking his head. "The problem was never the enslavement of Africans. That's a myth. A politically correct fairy tale. The problem is simpler, uglier. The problem is . . . Africans! Look at the facts. Millions of Africans were never enslaved. But Africa is still a total disaster! Every country, a disaster! Ignorance. Illiteracy. Lunacy. Diseases too disgusting to describe. Mass rapes. Genocides. This isn't the result of slavery. This is the nature of Africa. *And Africans!*"

The talking heads froze in place. Jagged triangles of color came swirling in from the edges of the screen, forming the letters of the words that earlier had blown apart:

EXPLOSIVE NEWS—HAPPENING NOW

SEE IT ALL ON *BATTLEGROUND TONIGHT*

THERE'S NOTHING AS REAL AS RAM-TV

Gelter nodded appreciatively before speaking, his eyes still on the screen. "Killer point about all the slavery bullshit. And he nailed the truth about the African cesspool. Refreshing to hear a man with the balls to tell it like it is."

Gurney shrugged. "Balls . . . or a mental disorder."

Gelter said nothing, registering the remark only with a sharp sideways glance.

The three-line statement on the screen blew apart again, and a single line coalesced from tumbling shards of color—THE CONTROVERSY CONTINUES—then it, too, broke into pieces that cartwheeled out of the frame.

A new talking head appeared—a young man in his early twenties, with fine features, a fierce gaze, and thick reddish-blond hair pulled back in a ponytail. His name and affiliation crept across the bottom of the screen: "Cory Payne, White Men for Black Justice."

Payne began in a strident voice, "The police claim to be defenders of the rule of law."

Gelter grimaced. "You want to hear a mental disorder, listen to this asshole!"

"They claim to be defenders of the rule of law," repeated Payne. "But their claim is a lie. It's not the rule of law they defend, but the laws of the rulers. The laws of the manipulators, the ambition-crazed politicians, the dictators who want to control us. The police are their tools of control and repression, enforcers of a system that benefits only the rulers and the enforcers. The police claim to be our protectors. Nothing could be further from the truth."

Gurney suspected, from the practiced flow of Payne's accusations, that he'd made them many times before. But there didn't seem to be anything rehearsed about the anger driving them. Or the intense emotion in the young man's eyes.

"Those of you who seek justice, beware! Those of you who trust in the myth of due process, beware! Those of you who believe the law will protect you, beware! People of color, beware! Those who speak out, beware! Beware the enforcers who use moments of unrest for their own ends. This is such a moment. A police officer has been shot. The powers that be are gathering to retaliate. Revenge and repression are in the air."

"You see what I mean? Unmitigated garbage!" Gelter was seething. "You see what civilization is up against? The rabble-rousing crap that spews out of the mouth of that self-indulgent little shit—"

He broke off as Trish came up to him looking hurried and anxious. "You have a call on the house phone."

"Take a message."

She hesitated. "It's Dell Beckert."

There was a shift in Gelter's expression.

"Ah. Well. I suppose I should take it."

After he'd disappeared through one of the doors in the back wall, Trish put on a bright smile. "I hope you like vegan Asian cuisine. I found the cutest young Cambodian chef. My little wok wizard."

7

They said little during the drive home. Madeleine rarely spoke when they were in the car at night. For his part, he'd been making an effort not to be critical of social events she'd involved him in, and he could think of little positive to say about the party at the Gelters'. As they were getting out of the car by the mudroom door, Madeleine broke the silence.

"Why on earth would they keep that television on all evening?"

"Postmodern irony?" suggested Gurney.

"Be serious."

"Seriously, I have no idea why Trish would do anything. Because I'm not sure who she is. I don't think the packaging is particularly transparent. Marv might like to keep the TV on to keep himself angry and right about everything. Bilious little racist."

"Trish says he's a financial genius."

Gurney shrugged. "No contradiction there."

It wasn't until they were in the house and Gurney was starting to make himself a cup of coffee that she spoke again, eyeing him with concern. "That moment . . . when the officer . . ."

"Was shot?"

"Were you . . . all right?"

"More or less. I knew it had happened. So the video wasn't a *total* shock. Just . . . jarring."

Her expression hardened. "*News,* they call it. *Information.* An actual murder on-screen. What a way to grab an audience! Sell more ads!" She shook her head.

He assumed that part of her fury was indeed provoked by the profit-based hypocrisy of the media industry. But he suspected that most of it arose from a source closer to home—the horror of seeing a police officer, someone like her own husband, struck down. The price of her deep capacity for empathy was that someone else's tragedy could easily feel like her own.

He asked if she'd like him to put on the kettle for some tea.

She shook her head. "Are you really planning to get involved in . . . all of that?"

With some difficulty he held her gaze. "It's like I told you earlier. I can't make any decision without knowing more."

"What kind of information is going to make—" The ringing of his cell phone cut her question short.

"Gurney here." Though he'd been out of NYPD Homicide for four years, his way of answering the phone hadn't changed.

The raspy, sarcastic voice on the other end needed no identification, nor did it offer any. "Got your message that you're looking for insider shit on White River. Like what? Gimme a hint, so I can direct you to the type of shit you have in mind."

Gurney was used to Jack Hardwick's calls beginning with bursts of snide comments. He'd learned to ignore them. "Sheridan Kline paid me a visit."

"The slimebag DA in person? Fuck did he want?"

"He wants me to sign on as a temporary staff investigator."

"Doing what?"

"Looking into the cop shooting. At least, that's what he says."

"There some reason the regular White River PD detective bureau can't handle that?"

"Not that I know of."

"Why the hell's he getting involved in the investigation? That's not his turf. And why you?"

"That's the question."

"How'd he explain it?"

"City on the verge of chaos. Need to make solid arrests fast. Pull out all the stops. No time for turf niceties. Full assets into the breach. The best and the brightest. Et cetera."

Hardwick was silent for a bit, then cleared his throat with disgusting thoroughness. "Odd pitch. Distinctive odor of horseshit. I'd be careful where I stepped, if I were you."

"Before I step anywhere, I want to know more."

"Always a good idea. So what do you want from me?"

"Whatever you can find out fast. Facts, rumors, anything at all. About the politics, the shot cop, the department, the city itself, the old incident with Laxton Jones, the Black Defense Alliance. Anything and everything."

"You need all this yesterday?"

"Tomorrow will do."

"You don't ask for much, do you?"

"I try not to."

"Very fucking kind of you." Hardwick blew his nose about an inch from the phone. Gurney wasn't sure whether the man had a perpetual sinus problem or just enjoyed producing unpleasant sound effects.

"Okay, I'll make some calls. Pain in my ass, but I'm a generous soul. You free tomorrow morning?"

"I'll make myself free."

"Meet me in Dillweed. Abelard's. Nine thirty."

Ending the call, Gurney turned his attention back to Madeleine, recalling that she'd been in the middle of asking him something.

"What were you saying before the phone rang?"

"Nothing that won't wait till tomorrow. It's been a long day. I'm going to bed."

He was tempted to join her, but the questions on his mind about the situation in White River were making him restless. After finishing his coffee, he got his laptop from the den and set it on the table in the breakfast nook. He pulled up a chair and typed "White River NY" into the browser. As he scrolled through the results, looking for articles he might have missed earlier in the day, a few items caught his eye:

An article in the *Times*, emphasizing the ongoing nature of the problem: "Police Officer's Death Deepens Upstate Racial Divide."

A shorter, punchier *Post* article: "Cop Gunned Down at BDA Rally."

A muted approach in the *White River Observer*: "Mayor Shucker Calls for Calm."

And then there was the all-out RAM promotional screamer: FIRST BLOOD DRAWN IN RACE WAR? COP SHOT DEAD AS ACTIVIST INCITES CROWD. SEE IT ALL ON *BATTLEGROUND TONIGHT*—STREAMING LIVE AT RAM-TV.ORG.

After skimming the articles attached to these headlines and finding nothing that he didn't know already, he scrolled on. When he came to a link to the official

White River municipal website, he clicked on it. It was a predictable presentation of city departments, budget data, upcoming events, area attractions, and local history. A section on "Career Opportunities" listed a job opening for a part-time waitress at the Happy Cow Ice Cream Shoppe. A section titled "Community Renewal" described the conversion of the defunct Willard Woolen Socks Factory into the Winter Goose Artisanal Brewery.

There were pictures of clean but deserted streets, redbrick buildings, and a tree-shaded park named after Colonel Ezra Willard, of the sock-manufacturing family. The first of the two Willard Park photos showed a statue of the eponymous colonel dressed in a Civil War uniform astride a fierce-looking horse. A biographical note below the photo described him as "a White River hero who gave his life in the great war to preserve the Union."

The second park photo showed two smiling mothers, one white and one brown, pushing their giddy toddlers on adjacent swings. Nowhere on the website was there any reference to the fatal shooting or the hate-driven violence tearing the city apart. Nor was there any mention of the correctional facility that provided the area with its main source of employment.

The next item that attracted Gurney's attention was a section devoted to White River on a site called Citizen Comments Unfiltered. The site seemed to be a magnet for racial attacks posted by individuals with IDs like Truth Teller, White Rights, American Defender, and End Black Lies. The posts went back several years, suggesting that the city's overt racial animosities were nothing new. They brought to mind a wise man's comment that few things on earth were worse than ignorance armed and eager for battle.

He returned for a moment to the section of the White River website that showed the park and the statue of Colonel Willard, wondering if that might be the statue that Madeleine had told him was one of the objects of the current protests. Finding nothing there that answered the question, he decided to do an internet search—trying various combinations of terms: "Ezra Willard," "Civil War," "statue," "New York State," "White River," "racial controversy," "Correctional Facility," "Willard Park," "Union," "Confederacy." Finally, when he added the term "slavery" to the mix, he was led to the answer in the journal of one of the Civil War historical societies.

The article was about the federal fugitive slave laws that legalized the capture in the North of slaves fleeing from slave owners in the South. Among the examples given of this practice was the "establishment in 1830 by the mercantile Willard family of upstate New York of a detention facility to house captured runaway slaves while payments were negotiated for their return to their Southern owners."

A footnote indicated that this lucrative practice ended when the war began; that at least one family member, Ezra, ended up fighting and dying on the Union side; and that after the war the former detention site became the core of what was gradually rebuilt and expanded into a state prison, now the White River Correctional Facility.

Pondering the ugly nature of the seed from which the institution had grown, Gurney could understand the impulse to protest the memorialization of a Willard family member. He searched the internet for more information about Ezra but could find nothing beyond brief news references to BDA demands for the removal of his statue.

Putting the historical issue aside, he decided to return his focus to getting as up to date as he could on the current turmoil. He revisited the RAM website in the hope that he might be able to extract some useful information from the opinionated noise they retailed as "news and analysis."

The site was slow in loading, giving him time to consider the irony of the internet: the world's largest repository of knowledge having become a megaphone for idiots. Once it appeared, he clicked his way through a series of options until he reached the page titled "*Battleground Tonight*—Live Stream."

He was puzzled at first by what he saw on the screen—a close aerial view of a police car with siren blaring and lights flashing, speeding along a thoroughfare. The angle of the shot indicated that the camera was above and behind the cruiser; when the cruiser made a fast right at an intersection, so did the camera. When it came to a stop in a narrow street behind three other cruisers, the camera slowed and stopped, descending slightly. The effect was similar to a tracking shot in a movie chase scene.

He realized that the equipment involved must be a sophisticated drone equipped with video and audio transmitters. As the drone maintained its position, its camera slowly zoomed in on the scene the cruiser had been racing to. Helmeted cops were standing in a semicircle around a black man who was leaning forward with his open hands against the wall of a building. As the two cops from the cruiser joined the others, the man was handcuffed. A few moments later, after he was pushed into the back of one of the original cruisers, a line of text crawled across the bottom of the screen: 10:07 PM . . . DUNSTER STREET, GRINTON SECTION, WHITE RIVER . . . CURFEW VIOLATOR TAKEN INTO CUSTODY . . . SEE DETAILS ON NEXT RAM NEWS SUMMARY.

As the cruiser pulled away, the video switched to a new scene—a fire engine in front of a smoldering brick building, two firemen in protective gear holding a hose and directing its powerful stream through a shattered ground-floor store window. A worn sign above the window identified the burned-out remains as Betty Bee's BBQ.

The camera's elevated point of view was similar to that of the first camera, indicating that its source was a similar high-end drone. It would seem, Gurney noted with interest, that RAM was applying significant resources to its coverage of White River.

The next video segment was a street interview between a mic-wielding female reporter and a large fireman whose black helmet displayed in gold letters the word CAPTAIN. The reporter was a slim dark-haired woman whose expression and voice projected great concern. "I'm Marilyn Maze, and I'm talking to Fire Captain James Pelt, the man in charge of the chaotic scene here on Bardle Boulevard." She turned toward the big man, and the camera zoomed in on his jowly, ruddy-skinned face. "Tell me, Captain, have you ever seen anything like this before?"

He shook his head. "We've had worse fires, Marilyn, worse in terms of the heat and the combustion of toxic materials, but never in conditions like this, never this wantonness of destruction. That's the difference here, the wantonness of it."

She nodded with professional concern. "It sounds like you've concluded that these fires are the intentional work of arsonists."

"That's my preliminary conclusion, Marilyn—subject to analysis by our arson investigator. But that's what I would say the conclusion would be."

She looked appropriately appalled. "So what you're telling us, Captain, is that these people—*some* of these people, I should make that clear right now, that we're talking about just a percentage, the law-breaking percentage of the population—some of these people are burning down their own neighborhood, their own stores, their own homes?"

"Doesn't make a darn bit of sense, does it? Maybe the whole idea of sense isn't part of the thinking here. It is a tragedy. Sad day for White River."

"All right, Captain, we thank you for taking the time to talk to us." She turned to the camera. "Interesting comments from Captain James Pelt on the insanity and tragedy of what's happening in the streets of this city. I'm Marilyn Maze, reporting live for *Battleground Tonight*."

The scene shifted back to the earlier talking-heads format. As before, the video was partitioned into three sections. A female newsperson now occupied the center position. She reminded Gurney of a certain kind of girl on a cheerleading squad—blond hair, straight nose, wide mouth, and calculating eyes—every word and gesture a tactic for success.

She spoke with a cool smile. "Thank you, Marilyn, for that thought-provoking exchange with Captain Pelt. I'm Stacey Kilbrick in the RAM News Analysis Center, with two high-powered guests with colliding points of view. But first, these important messages."

The video went black. With key words flashing in bold red type against the dark background, an ominous voice intoned over the rumble of distant explosions, "We live in dangerous times . . . with ruthless enemies at home and abroad. As we speak, conspirators are plotting to strip us of our God-given right to defend ourselves from those out to destroy our way of life." The voice went on to offer a free booklet revealing imminent dangers to American lives, values, and the Second Amendment.

A second commercial promoted the unique importance of gold bullion—as the most secure medium of exchange "as our debt-ridden financial system approaches collapse." An ancient anonymous authority was quoted: "Wisest of all is the man whose treasure is in gold." A free booklet would explain it all.

The commercial faded out and the video cut back to Stacey Kilbrick, in the center section of the screen. On one side was a thirtysomething, strong-featured black woman with a short Afro. On the other side was a slightly wall-eyed, middle-aged white man with short sandy hair. Kilbrick's voice projected an artful balance of confidence and concern. "Our subject tonight is the growing crisis in the small city of White River, New York. There are conflicting points of view on what it's all about." A bold line of type moved across the bottom of the screen:

WHITE RIVER CRISIS—PERSPECTIVES IN COLLISION

She continued, "On my right is Blaze Lovely Jackson—the woman who was in the car with Laxton Jones one year ago when he was killed in a confrontation with a White River police officer. She's also a founding member of the Black Defense Alliance and a forceful spokesperson for the BDA point of view. On my left is Garson Pike, founder of ASP, Abolish Special Privileges. ASP is a political action group promoting the repeal of special legal protections for minority groups. My first question is for Ms. Jackson. You're a founding member of the Black Defense Alliance and an organizer of the demonstrations in White River—

demonstrations that have now led to the death of a police officer. My question: Do you have any regrets?"

Since they were evidently in different studios and responding to each other via monitors, each participant was addressing the camera head-on. Gurney studied Blaze Lovely Jackson's face. Something inside her was radiating an almost frightening determination and implacability.

She bared her teeth in a hostile smile. "No surprise that you have that a little back to front. Nothing new in that, with young black men getting killed all the time. Streets are full of black men's blood, going back forever. Poison water, rats biting babies, rotten houses full of their blood. Right here in our own little city, there's the big nasty prison, full of black men's blood, even back to the blood of slaves. Now one white cop is shot, and that's the question you have? You ask how much regret *I* have? You don't see how you have that all back to front? You don't think to ask which came first? Was it black men shooting white cops? Or was it white cops shooting black men? Seems to me you have a little sequence problem. See, my question is, where's the regret for Laxton Jones? Where's the regret for all them black men shot in the head, shot in the back, beat to death, year after year, forever and ever, hundreds of years, for no good reason on God's earth? Hundreds of years and no end in sight. Where's the regret for that?"

"That may be a subject for a larger discussion," said Kilbrick with a patronizing frown. "Right now, Ms. Jackson, I'm asking a reasonable question raised by the senseless assassination of a community servant trying to maintain public safety at the BDA rally you organized. I'd like to know how you feel about the murder of that man."

"That *one* man? You want me push aside hundreds, thousands, of young black men murdered by white men? You want me push them aside so I can fill up with regret about this *one* white boy? And then tell you all about that regret? And maybe how much I regret being responsible for a shooting I didn't have nothing to do with? If that's what you want, lady, I'll tell you something—you have no idea what world we're living in. And there's something else I'll tell you right here to your pretty face—you have no damn idea how damn crazy you are."

Along with Stacey Kilbrick's ongoing frown there was satisfaction in her eyes—perhaps the satisfaction of achieving the RAM goal of maximizing the controversy in every situation. She moved on with a brief smile. "Now, for a different perspective, Mr. Garson Pike. Sir, your viewpoint on the current events in White River?"

Pike responded with a shake of his head and a long-suffering smile. "P-perfectly predictable tragedy. Cause and effect. Chickens coming home to roost. It's the p-price we all p-pay for years of liberal permissiveness. P-price for political correctness." His accent was vaguely country. His gray-blue eyes blinked with each small stutter. "These jungle attacks on law and order are the p-price of cowardice."

Kilbrick urged him on. "Could you elaborate on that?"

"Our nation has been on a p-path of reckless accommodation. Giving in again and again to the demands of every minority race—black, brown, yellow, red, you name it. Lying down like doormats for invading armies of mongrel freeloaders and terrorists. Giving in to the demands of the cultural saboteurs—the atheists, the abortionists, the sodomites. It's the terrible truth, Stacey, that we live in a country where every vile p-perversion and every worthless segment of society has its champions in high places, its special legal protections. The more detestable the subject, the more protection we give it. The natural result of this surrender is chaos. A society turned upside down. The maintainers of order are attacked in the street, and their attackers pretend to be victims. The inmates, Stacey, have taken over the asylum. We're supposed to be politically correct while all they do is complain about their *minority disadvantages*. Hell, like what? Like being p-put front of the line for jobs, promotions, special minority protections? And now they complain that they're disproportionately represented in p-prisons. Simple reason is that they're disproportionately committing the crimes that put them there. Eliminate black crime, and we'd have pretty much no crime in America at all."

He concluded with an emphatic little nod and fell silent. The emotional momentum that had been increasing through his speech left little tics tugging at the corners of his mouth.

Kilbrick limited her reaction to a thoughtful pursing of her lips. "Ms. Jackson? We have about a minute left, if you'd care to offer a brief response."

Blaze Lovely Jackson's gaze had hardened. "Yeah, I'll be brief. That Pike babble's the same fascist crap you RAM folks been feeding all these years to your trailer-trash fans. I'll tell you what it really is—what you're doing is disrespectful. The white man is always making the black man feel small, feel like he's got no power at all, feel like he's no kind of man. You don't give him any decent job, then you tell him he's worthless cause he ain't got a decent job. I tell you what that is. That's the sin of disrespect. Hear me now, even if you don't hear another thing. Disrespect is the mother of rage, and rage is the fire that's going to burn this country down.

Laxton Jones had no drug, no gun, no warrant. Hadn't broken any law. Hadn't done any crime. The man hadn't done nothing to nobody. But he got shot anyway. Got shot dead in the face. How often do police do that to a white face? How often do they kill a white man who hasn't done a crime? You want to understand the true place we're at, you want to understand what BDA is all about, you think on that."

Kilbrick's eyes were alive with excitement. "Well, there you have it! Two sides of the White River crisis. In head-on collision. On *Battleground Tonight*. We move now to our cameras on location—your eyes on the tense streets of White River. I'm Stacey Kilbrick, on the watch for breaking news. Stay with us."

The studio scene was replaced by an aerial shot of the city. Gurney could see smoke pouring from the roofs of three buildings. Orange flames shot up from one of them. On the main boulevard he noted a procession of police cars, a fire engine, and an ambulance. The aerial camera was picking up the sounds of sirens and bullhorns.

Gurney eased his chair back from the table, as if to distance himself from what he was seeing on his computer screen. The cynical conversion of misery, anger, and destruction into a kind of reality TV show sickened him. And it wasn't just RAM. Media enterprises everywhere were engaged in the continual promotion and exaggeration of conflict, a business model based on a poisonous insight: *dissension sells*. Especially dissension along the fault line of race. It was an insight with an equally poisonous corollary: *nothing builds loyalty like shared hatreds*. It was clear RAM and its host of vile imitators had no qualms about nurturing those hatreds to build loyal audiences.

He realized, however, that it was time to put aside grievances about which he could do nothing and focus on questions that might have answers. For example, might Blaze Lovely Jackson's rage at the police have been sufficient to involve her in actions beyond staging protests? Actions such as planning, abetting, or executing the sniper attack? And why hadn't Kline gotten back to him? Had the query he'd left on the man's voicemail concerning the missing ingredient in their conversation scared him off? Or was the potential answer sensitive enough to demand long consideration or perhaps even discussion with another player in the game?

That thought led by a crooked route to another question that had been in the back of his mind ever since Marv Gelter had abandoned his party to take a call from Dell Beckert. What sort of relationship did the racist billionaire have with the White River police chief?

"Do you know if the upstairs windows are closed?"

Madeleine's voice startled him. He turned and saw her standing in her pajamas in the hallway that led to the bedroom.

"The windows?"

"It's raining."

"I'll take a look."

As he was about to shut down his computer, an announcement appeared on the screen in bold type:

CRISIS UPDATE

LIVE-STREAMING PRESS CONFERENCE—9:00 AM TOMORROW

WITH CHIEF BECKERT, MAYOR SHUCKER, DISTRICT ATTORNEY KLINE

He made a mental note of the time, hoping the event would be concluded before he had to leave for his meeting with Hardwick.

Upstairs he found only one window open, but it was enough to fill the room with the flowery aroma of the spring night. He stood there for a while breathing in the soft, sweet air.

His racing thoughts were replaced by a primitive sense of peace. A phrase came to mind, something he'd once read—just the phrase, emerging from an unrecalled context and attaching itself to the moment: *a healing tranquility.*

Once again, as so often in the past, a pleasant and totally unanticipated consequence had followed from his doing a simple thing Madeleine had asked him to do. He was sufficiently logic-driven to avoid attributing any mystical significance to these experiences. But their occurrence was a fact he couldn't ignore.

When the wind shifted and the rain began to spatter lightly on the sill, he closed the window and went downstairs to bed.

8

Tranquility, unfortunately, was not his natural state of mind. During several hours of fitful sleep his innate brain chemistry reasserted itself, bringing with it the low-level anxiety and uneasy dreams to which he was accustomed.

At some point during those hours he awoke briefly, discovering that the rain had stopped, a full moon had appeared behind the thinning clouds, and the coyotes had begun to howl. He went back to sleep.

Another round of howling, closer to the house, woke him once more—from a dream in which Trish Gelter was ambling around a white cube in a field of daffodils. Each time she circled the cube she announced, "I'm the fun one." A blood-covered man was following her.

Gurney tried to clear the image from his mind and doze off again, but the persistent howling and the need to go to the bathroom finally got him out of bed. He showered, shaved, put on his jeans and an old NYPD tee shirt, and went to the kitchen to make himself some breakfast.

By the time he'd finished his eggs, toast, and two cups of coffee, the sun was rising above the pine-topped eastern ridge. When he opened the French doors to let in the morning air, he could hear the chickens making their morning clucking noises out in the coop by the apple tree. He stepped onto the patio and for a while watched the goldfinches and chickadees visiting the feeders that Madeleine had set up next to the asparagus patch. His gaze moved across the low pasture to the barn, the pond, and the site of his exploratory dig.

When he'd discovered the buried foundation—accidentally, while clearing large rocks from the trail above the pond—and had exposed enough of it to get a sense of its antiquity, it had occurred to him that he might invite Dr. Walter Thrasher to have a look. In addition to being county medical examiner, Thrasher was an avid historian and collector of Colonial artifacts. At the time, Gurney had wavered on whether to involve him, but now he was inclined to do so. The man's insights into the remains of the old house could be interesting, and having a personal avenue of access to him might prove useful if Gurney decided to accept Kline's invitation to step into the White River investigation.

He went back into the house, got his phone, and returned to the patio. He scrolled through his list of numbers, found Thrasher's, and tapped on it. The call went to voicemail. The recorded announcement was nearly as short as Hardwick's. Rather than gruff, though, the tone was refined. It invited the caller to simply leave a name and number, but Gurney decided to include some details.

"Dr. Thrasher, this is Dave Gurney. We met when you were the medical examiner on the Mellery homicide. Someone mentioned then that you were an expert on the Colonial history and archaeology of upstate New York. I'm calling because I've uncovered a site on my property that may date back to the eighteenth century. There are a variety of artifacts—a flesher tool, ebony-handled knife, iron chain links. Plus possible human remains—a child's teeth, if I'm not mistaken. If you'd like to know more about this, you can reach me on my cell anytime." Gurney added his number and ended the call.

"Are you talking to someone out there?"

He turned and saw Madeleine at the French doors. Her slacks-and-blazer outfit reminded him it was one of her workdays at the mental health clinic.

"I was on the phone."

"I thought maybe Gerry had arrived. She's picking me up today."

She stepped out onto the patio, raising her face into the slanting morning sunlight. "I hate the idea of being cooped up in an office on a day like this."

"You don't have to be cooped up anywhere. We have enough money to—"

She cut him off. "I don't mean it that way. I just wish we could see our clients outdoors in weather like this. It would be better for them, too. Fresh air. Green grass. Blue sky. Good for the soul." She cocked her head. "I think I hear Gerry coming up the hill."

A few moments later, as a yellow VW Beetle made its way up the weedy lane through the low pasture, she added, "You're going to let the chickens out, right?"

"I'll get to it."

She ignored the edge in his voice, kissed him, and headed out past the asparagus patch just as her exuberant fellow therapist, Geraldine Mirkle, lowered her car window and cried, "*Andiamo!* The maniacs await us!" She winked at Gurney. "I'm referring to the staff!"

He watched as they drove, bumpily, through the pasture, around the barn, and out of sight onto the town road.

He sighed. That resistance in his response to Madeleine's chicken reminder was childish. A silly way of trying to be in control when there was no reason for delay. His first wife had complained that he was a control freak. In his early twenties he couldn't see it. But now it was obvious. Madeleine generally had no reaction to it other than amusement, which made it feel even more childish.

He went out to the henhouse and opened the little door into the fenced-in run. He tossed some commercial chicken feed, corn kernels, and sunflower seeds onto the ground, and the four hens came running out and started pecking at it. He stood there for a moment observing them. He doubted he would ever be as fascinated by them as Madeleine was.

A few minutes before nine he sat down at the breakfast table, opened his laptop, and went to the "Live Stream" section of the RAM website. As he was waiting for the promised press conference to begin, his phone rang. The number on the screen was vaguely familiar.

"Gurney here."

"This is Walter Thrasher. You've discovered something of historical importance?"

"Your judgment on that would be sounder than mine. Would you be interested in taking a look at the site?"

"Did you say something about teeth? And a black-handled knife?"

"Among other things. Pieces of chains, hinges, a glass jar."

"Pre-Revolution?"

"I think so. The foundation is Dutch-style laid stone."

"Not dispositive by itself. I'll take a look. Tomorrow. Early morning. That work for you?"

"I can make it work."

"See you then, assuming nobody else on my turf gets shot in the meantime."

Thrasher ended the call first, with no good-bye.

As the RAM news anchor was announcing that the press conference was about to begin, a line of bold type crawled across the bottom of the screen:

OFFICIALS REVEAL SHOCKING NEW DEVELOPMENTS

The scene shifted from the anchor, with her hybrid expression of steadiness and concern, to three conservatively suited men at a table facing the camera. In front of each was a tent card bearing his name and title. Mayor Shucker, Chief Beckert, District Attorney Kline.

Gurney's attention was drawn to Beckert, a casting director's fast-tracked Marine general. In his midforties, lean and square-jawed with an unblinking gaze, salt-and-pepper hair in a crisp military crew cut, he was the group's clear center of gravity.

Mayor Shucker was a corpulent man with pudgy lips, suspicious eyes, and a comb-over dyed the color of rust.

Kline, on the other side of Beckert, looked more conflicted than ever. The determined set of his mouth was belied every few seconds by tiny tremors that reminded Gurney, rather fancifully, of those minuscule vibrations along the San Andreas Fault that create shimmers of unease on the surface of still water.

CRISIS UPDATE began to flash repeatedly on the screen, and the camera moved in on Beckert. When the blinking phrase disappeared, he began to speak. His voice was clear, dry, unaccented. There was also something familiar about it that Gurney couldn't quite place.

"One hour ago the White River Police Department Special Weapons and Tactics Unit carried out a successful assault on the headquarters of the Black Defense Alliance. Pursuant to appropriate warrants, the premises have been secured and are currently being searched. Files, computers, phones, and other potential evidentiary materials are being gathered for forensic examination. Fourteen individuals have been arrested at the location on charges including felony assault, harassment, obstruction, drug possession, and weapons violations. This process is being conducted pursuant to our receipt of credible information regarding the shooting death of patrol officer John Steele. Be assured that our full investigatory resources are being applied to the apprehension of those responsible for the heinous murder of one of White River's finest officers, a man who earned my deepest respect and admiration." He lowered his head for a respectful moment before going on.

"I have an important request. Two high-ranking members of the BDA organization, Marcel Jordan and Virgil Tooker, were observed leaving the Willard Park demonstration just half an hour prior to the shooting of Officer Steele. We are eager to ascertain their whereabouts at the time of the shooting. We also have reason to believe that these same individuals slipped away from BDA headquarters prior to this morning's raid. It's vital that we find these two men. If you know where they are, or have information that could lead us to them, please call us anytime, day or night."

An 800 number began flashing on the screen next to the words POLICE HOT-LINE as Beckert continued, "This savage attack on civilized society will be met with all necessary force. We will not allow jungle law to triumph. We will do whatever it takes to end this anarchy. I promise you—order will prevail."

Concluding with a gaze of fierce determination, Beckert turned toward Shucker. "Mayor, you have a few words for us?"

Shucker blinked, looked down at a sheet of paper in his hands, then back up at the camera. "First, Mrs. Steele, my condolences for this tragedy." He looked down again at the paper. "Those who set out to terrify our community with wanton violence and attack the heroes who protect us are the worst kind of criminals. Their reprehensible acts must be halted to restore peace to our wonderful city. Our prayers go out to the Steele family and to White River's brave protectors." He folded his sheet of paper and looked up. "God bless America!"

Beckert turned toward Kline. "Sheridan?"

The district attorney spoke with iron resolve. "Nothing challenges the rule of law like an attack on the men and women sworn to uphold it. My office is applying the full weight of its resources to a thorough investigation, the discovery of the truth, and the achievement of justice for the Steele family and for our whole community."

The video cut to the female news anchor. "Thank you, gentlemen. Now we go to our follow-up questions from the RAM Issue Analysis Team." The video cut back to the three men at the table as questions were posed by off-camera voices.

First Male Voice: "Chief Beckert, are you suggesting that Jordan and Tooker are the prime suspects in the sniper shooting?"

Beckert replied expressionlessly: "They're definitely persons of interest in our investigation."

Second Male Voice: "Do you consider them fugitives?"

Beckert, in the same flat tone: "We have a high degree of interest in finding them, they have not come forward, and their whereabouts are currently unknown."

First Female Voice: "Do you have evidence of their involvement in the shooting?"

Beckert: "As I said, we have a high degree of interest in finding them. We are focusing significant resources on that objective."

Same Female Voice: "Do you think Jordan and Tooker were tipped off prior to the raid?"

Beckert: "A reasonable person might reach that conclusion."

First Male Voice: "What's your plan for addressing the ongoing chaos? Fires are still breaking out in the Grinton area."

Beckert: "Our plan is full-force pushback. We will not tolerate disorder or anyone who threatens disorder. For anyone tempted to use political protest as a cover for looting, burning, hear this: I have instructed my officers to use lethal force wherever necessary to protect the lives of our law-abiding citizens."

Another male voice asked Chief Beckert if his SWAT team had encountered armed resistance by BDA members. He replied that weapons were present during the operation and more facts would be released after the filing of formal charges.

The same voice asked if injuries had been sustained on either side of the confrontation. As Beckert was giving another "more information later" nonanswer, Gurney noted the time on his computer screen. It was nine fifteen, meaning he needed to leave for his nine thirty meeting with Hardwick. Although he was curious about what might be revealed during the remainder of the press conference, he knew RAM programming was routinely archived for later viewing. He closed his laptop, grabbed his phone, and headed for the Outback.

9

Formerly a creaky old country store with a distinctly musty smell, Abelard's had been taken over by a transplant from the Brooklyn art scene by the name of Marika. An abstract expressionist, she was an intense thirtysomething woman with a dramatic figure she wasn't shy about showing off, numerous piercings and tattoos, and a startling array of hair colors.

When she wasn't painting or sculpting, she'd been gentrifying the place. She'd removed the live-bait cooler and the displays of turkey jerky. She'd sanded and refinished the wide-board floors. She'd installed a new cooler full of things organic and free-range; a bin for locally baked breads; a high-end espresso machine; and four funky cafe tables with hand-painted chairs. The hammered-tin ceiling, pendant-globe light fixtures, and rough-hewn shelving had been left intact.

Gurney parked next to Hardwick's classic muscle car—a red 1970 GTO. As soon as he entered the store he spotted Hardwick sitting in the back at one of the little round tables. He was wearing the black tee shirt and black jeans that had become his de facto uniform ever since he'd been forced out of the state police for offending his superiors too many times. This combative man with the pale-blue eyes of an Alaskan sled dog, a razor-keen mind, a sour wit, and a fondness for obscenity was definitely an acquired taste—one you could almost get to like if you didn't choke on it first.

His muscular arms were resting on the table, which seemed too flimsy to support them. He was talking to Marika, who was laughing. Her hair that day was a spiky patchwork of iridescent pink and metallic blue.

"Coffee?" she asked when Gurney arrived at the table. Her striking contralto voice always got his attention.

"Sure. Double espresso."

With an approving nod she headed for the machine. He took the chair opposite Hardwick, who was watching her departure.

When she disappeared behind the far counter, he turned to Gurney. "Sweet girl, not as batshit as she looks. Or half as batshit as *you* are if you're planning to get involved in that White River insanity."

"Bad idea?"

Hardwick uttered a grunt of a laugh, picked up his mug of coffee, took a long sip, and laid it down with the care one might give an explosive. "Too many virtuous people involved. All with high opinions of their own visions of justice. Nothing in this world worse than a pack of crazy fuckers who know—absolutely *know*—they're right."

"You referring to the Black Defense Alliance?"

"They're part of it. But only part. Depends on what you want to believe."

"Tell me more."

"Where should I start?"

"With anything that would explain Kline's desire to get me involved."

Hardwick thought for a moment. "That would probably be Dell Beckert."

"Why on earth would Beckert want me involved?"

"He wouldn't. What I mean is, Beckert might be Kline's problem."

Before going on, Hardwick made a face like the subject had a bad taste. "I know what the fucker was like when I worked with him ten years ago in the Bureau. That was before he became the big deal he is today. But even then he was on his way. See, that's the thing—Beckert is always *on his way* to something. Eye on the goal. He's got that win-at-any-cost fixation that has a way of turning people into scumbags."

"From what I've heard, his reputation is more law-and-order than scumbag."

"Like a lot of high-class scumbags, he's good at nurturing and polishing that reputation. Beckert has an instinct for turning everything to his advantage, even negative shit. Maybe I should say, *especially* negative shit."

"Like what?"

"Like his family life. Back then, it was a fucking mess. His son, who was maybe thirteen at the time, was a nasty little bastard. Hated his father. Did everything he could to embarrass him. Painted swastikas on police cars. Told Child Protective

Services that his father was selling confiscated drugs. Then the kid tried to set fire to a Marine recruiting office, probably because his father had been a marine. That's when Dad made his move. Sent the kid off to a super-tough behavior-modification boarding school somewhere down South—more like a prison than a school. And then . . ." Hardwick inserted a dramatic pause.

Gurney stared at him. "And then . . . what?"

"And then Dell Beckert revealed his true talent. He turned the whole stinking pile of crap into gold. Most cops try to keep their domestic problems private. But Beckert did the opposite. He spoke to parent groups. Gave media interviews. Appeared on talk shows. Got well known within the world of parents with shithead kids. The tough-love cop who did what had to be done. And when his painkiller-addicted wife died about a year later of a heroin overdose, he even turned that into a plus. He became the drug-fighting cop whose zero-tolerance attacks on drug dealers came from the heart, from his own painful experience."

Gurney was getting a bad taste in his mouth. "Sounds like a formidable character."

"Cold as they come. But he's managed to position himself as the perfect hard-ass cop every white citizen can love. And vote for."

"Vote for?"

"There hasn't been any official statement. But the blue grapevine says he'll be running for state attorney general in the special election."

"Kline mentioned the same rumor."

"It would be the perfect next star on his precious résumé."

Marika delivered Gurney's double espresso. Hardwick continued, "That résumé, by the way, is fucking impressive. Highest score in every NYSP promotion exam he took. After a few hot-shit years in the Bureau, during which he picked up a master's degree in public administration, he took over the top spot in the Professional Standards Unit. Then he moved into the private sector and set up a consulting organization to work with police departments around the state—assessing the psychological status of cops involved in violent confrontations, counseling them, and educating department brass on the nature and causes of violent incidents."

"How'd that work out?"

"Great for Beckert. Hugely expanded his contacts in the law-enforcement world."

"But?"

"Legal activists claimed the purpose of his 'consulting' was to help the police describe questionable incidents in ways that would minimize their exposure to criminal or civil actions."

Gurney took a sip of his very strong coffee. "Interesting. So how'd this rising star get to be police chief in White River?"

"Three, four years ago—just before you moved up here—there was a corruption scandal. The then-chief's phone was hacked, and a lot of embarrassing shit came out. Seems that the chief, one of the captains, and three guys in the detective bureau were on the take from a gang running Mexican heroin into upstate New York. WRPD public relations disaster. Cried out for a new team. And what better guy than Beckert—with his Professional Standards background and hardline image—to fumigate the place, reassure the citizenry, rebuild the department."

"Another success?"

"Most people thought so. After dumping the tainted guys, he brought in his own people—allies from the state police and his consulting company." Hardwick's jaw muscle twitched. "Including a particularly close ally, Judd Turlock, who he installed as deputy chief."

"How close, exactly?"

"Turlock went through the academy with him, reported to him in the Bureau, and was his number two in the consulting outfit. They'd even been in the fucking Marines together."

"You don't sound fond of this guy."

"Difficult to be fond of a sociopathic attack dog."

Gurney considered this over another sip of coffee. "Is Beckert's tenure at White River being viewed as a success?"

"Depends on your point of view. He cleaned up the streets. Put away a lot of drug dealers. Reduced the number of break-ins, muggings, violent crimes."

"But . . ."

"There've been some incidents. Right after he took over, couple years before the Laxton Jones thing, there was a traffic stop that escalated into the beating and arrest of the young black driver. Nelson Tuggle. The cop claimed he found a handgun and a bag of coke under the front seat and that Tuggle took a swing at him. Tuggle asked for a lie detector test. His lawyer got very aggressive with that, even got some media attention by publicly demanding that his client and the cop both be polygraphed. Two days later Tuggle was found dead in his cell. Heroin overdose, according to the ME. Got hold of some jail contraband, was how the COs explained it. Couple of street acquaintances said that was bullshit, that Tuggle might've done a little pot now and then, but no hard stuff."

"Anyone pursue the case?"

"Tuggle had no family. There were no witnesses. No friends. Nobody gave a shit."

"Is there a pattern? People claiming White River PD plays by its own rules?"

"Most of the convicted drug dealers claim exactly that. Course none of them can prove it. The judges and juries around here are overwhelmingly pro-cop. But the thing is, those popularity points Beckert's been winning on the white side of White River he's been losing on the black side. It isn't that they don't want to get rid of the criminal element, but they have the feeling the man is playing God and dropping the hammer extra hard on black people to make a point."

"So the pressure cooker's been heating up?"

"Big time. Unfortunately for Beckert, resentment that couldn't really be expressed in support of drug dealers found a perfect outlet in the case of Laxton Jones. The difference between Jones and Tuggle is that Jones wasn't alone. He had a girlfriend who witnessed what happened and was hell-bent to do something about it. Blaze Lovely Jackson."

"I saw her on that RAM *Battleground Tonight* program. I'd say she's an angry woman."

"Very angry. But also very smart. So there are some damn tricky days ahead for Beckert—sinkholes he needs to avoid to get where he wants to go."

"You mean the attorney general's office?"

"And beyond. Fucker might even be picturing himself in the White House someday."

That seemed a bit of a stretch. But who could say? The man did look the part—more so than a lot of nasty creeps with their eye on the top rung of the ladder. In fact, he had the kind of chiseled face that would be at home on Mount Rushmore.

"In the meantime," said Gurney, "we have a sniper on the loose. Were you able to find out anything about Steele?"

Hardwick shrugged. "Straight arrow. Everything by the book. Smart. College grad. Going to law school in his spare time. You want me to dig deeper?"

After a thoughtful pause Gurney shook his head. "Not yet."

Hardwick regarded him curiously. "So what's next? You signing up for the sniper hunt?"

"I don't think so. If Kline is worried about Beckert's methods, that's his problem, not mine."

"So you're going to walk away?"

"It seems like the sensible option."

Hardwick flashed a hard, glittery grin. "You mean you have no appetite for a clusterfuck in a dark closet? Shit, Gurney, you're saner than I thought."

10

Gurney spent the drive home from Abelard's pondering what Hardwick had told him about Beckert and convincing himself that backing away was, in fact, the sanest course of action.

As he was getting out of the car by the side of the house, he could hear the landline phone ringing. He had some difficulty opening the mudroom door, stuck as it often was in warm weather, and by the time he got to the phone a morose female voice was concluding a message with a call-back number.

He picked up the handset. "Gurney here."

"Oh . . . Mr. Gurney?"

"Yes?"

"This is Kim Steele. John Steele's wife."

He grimaced, picturing the TV image of the cop falling facedown on the sidewalk. "I'm terribly sorry, Mrs. Steele. Terribly sorry."

There was a long moment of silence.

"Is there something I can do for you?" he asked.

"Can I come and speak with you? I don't want to talk on the phone." There was another silence, followed by what sounded to Gurney like a stifled sob. "I know where you live. I could be there in twenty-five minutes. Would that be okay?"

He hesitated. "Yes, that's okay."

He ended the call, thinking immediately of three good reasons why no would've been a smarter answer.

Putting aside his inclination to speculate on why the wife of a dead cop might want to talk to him or how she even knew he existed, he decided to use the intervening time to check the internet for any stories on the shooting that provided more than the bare-bones information he'd already seen.

He went to the table in the breakfast nook where he'd left his laptop. Using the combination of "Steele" and "White River" brought up links to Beckert's press conference, media reports on the incident, and opinion pieces from every point on the political spectrum—each purporting to explain the true causes of the violence. Nowhere did he find any details on the life of John Steele beyond the fact that he had a wife, now a widow.

He decided to try entering the names "John Steele" and "Kim Steele" at various social media sites. He went first to Facebook. While he was waiting for the page to load, his attention was drawn to movement out beyond the French doors in the low pasture. He stood up just in time to see three whitetail deer bounding through an opening in the ancient rock wall that separated the pasture from the woods. Assuming something had spooked them, he looked in the direction of the barn and pond. And there, at the end of the town road, another kind of movement—a glint of light, perhaps reflecting off a car or pickup truck—caught his eye. Whatever it was, it was obscured by the big forsythia bush at the corner of the barn.

He opened the door and stepped out onto the patio. But the situation was no clearer from there. He was about to walk down to the barn to satisfy his curiosity when the landline phone rang. He went back and checked the ID screen. It was Sheridan Kline.

"Gurney here."

"Hi, Dave." Kline's voice was full of oily sincerity. "I'm responding to your message. The truth is there are some sensitive details in this situation that wouldn't be appropriate for me to discuss with someone outside the official law-enforcement circle. I'm sure you can understand that. But if you choose to step inside the tent, on day one I'll make sure you know everything I know. And you'll have the best of both worlds here—official status plus independence from the bureaucracy. You'll be reporting only to me."

That last promise was delivered as though it were a precious privilege.

Gurney said nothing.

"Dave?"

"I'm absorbing what you said."

"Ah. Well. Good. We'll leave it at that. The sooner you give me your answer, the better our chances of saving some lives."

"I'll be in touch."

"I look forward to it."

Gurney replaced the handset, aware he'd let pass an opportunity to tell Kline he'd decided not to get involved. He'd hardly begun to rationalize his foot-dragging when he remembered the possible vehicle by the barn.

He headed out through the French doors and down into the pasture. When he reached the far side of the forsythia, he had two surprises. The first was the car. It was a sleek Audi A7, a rarity in an area where "luxury vehicle" usually meant a crew-cab pickup with big tires. The second was that there was no one in it.

He looked around. He saw no one.

"Hello?" he called out.

There was no response.

He walked around the barn. The lush spring grass was moist with dew where the old apple trees shaded it, but there were no footprints.

Back by the car, he scanned the surrounding area—the pastures, the pond, the cleared swath along the edge of the woods. No sign of anyone.

As he was deciding what to do next, he heard a faint scraping sound. He heard it again—sharper this time and coming, it seemed, from the thicket above the pond. The only thing he could see up there that wasn't part of the natural flora was the tractor he'd been using to clear his little archaeology site.

Curious, he headed up the trail that led to the excavation. The scraping became more distinct. He came around a bend in the trail and the broad rectangular hole came into view. But it wasn't until he reached the excavation's edge that he discovered the source of the sound.

A man, intent on his work, was using a hand trowel to probe a crevice between two foundation stones. He was wearing beige slacks, expensive-looking brown loafers, and a tropical sport shirt garishly printed with palm fronds and toucans.

The man spoke without turning away from the ground. "Seventeen hundred, I'd say. Give or take twenty years or so. Could be as early as sixteen eighty. Interesting rust deposits along here." He tapped the area in front of him with the point of the trowel, which Gurney recognized as the one he kept at the site. "Four separate deposits, at three-foot intervals."

He straightened up now—a lanky, stork-like man with thinning hair the color of his beige slacks. As he gazed at Gurney the lenses of his horn-rimmed glasses magnified his eyes. "Those remnants of chain links you mentioned in your message? They were distributed along the base of this wall, am I right?"

Some people were put off by Dr. Walter Thrasher's mildly autistic avoidance of the social graces, but Gurney—for whom getting to the point was a virtue—was quite comfortable with the man's approach.

"Right. Directly below the rust spots," Gurney replied with a puzzled frown. "I thought you said you were coming here tomorrow. Did I lose a day somewhere?"

"No days lost. Just happened to be passing. Coming from White River, going to Albany, took a chance you might be home. Drove up to your barn, caught sight of your tractor, figured that'd be the site. Interesting. Very interesting." As he was speaking he put down the trowel and scrambled with surprising agility up the short ladder out of the excavation.

"Interesting in what way?"

"Wouldn't want to answer that prematurely. Depends on the nature of the artifacts. You mentioned baby teeth? And a knife?"

"As well as some glass, bits of rusted metal, hooks for stretching animal hides."

There was a peculiar intensity in Thrasher's magnified gaze. "No time to examine it all right now. Maybe just the knife and the teeth. A quick look?"

Gurney shrugged. "No problem." He thought of asking Thrasher for a ride up to the house, but the chance of the low-slung A7 bottoming out in the pasture ruts was too great. "Wait here. I'll be back."

Thrasher was standing by his car when Gurney returned with the knife and the tinted-glass jar containing the teeth.

Thrasher gave the knife, especially what appeared to be a fingernail-sized crescent moon carved in the black handle, a close but rapid inspection. Ending with a nod and a grunt of satisfaction, he handed it back to Gurney. He took the tinted jar with greater care, almost a kind of trepidation, at first holding it up to examine the contents through the glass, then removing the top and peering in at the tiny teeth. He slowly tipped the jar, carefully letting just one tooth slide out onto his palm. He tilted his hand this way and that to view it from different angles. Then he tipped it back into the jar and replaced the lid.

"Would it be all right if I borrowed this for a day or two? Need my microscope to verify what we've got here."

"You're not sure they're baby teeth?"

"Oh, they're definitely baby teeth. No doubt about that."

"Well, then . . ."

Thrasher hesitated, looked momentarily troubled. "There could be more than one way they ended up in this jar. Until I take a closer look, let's leave it at that."

11

There were two paths from the barn up to the house. The more direct one that they used as a driveway went up through the pasture. The roundabout one meandered through the woods below the pasture, then curved up around it to the far side of the henhouse and the bluestone patio.

Gurney chose the second route. He paid attention to the forest sights, sounds, scents—the rustlings and chirpings, the sweetness in the air, the tiny blue flowers among the lush ferns—trying to dispel a vague sense of uneasiness created by Thrasher's parting comment.

As he was heading for the house by this alternate route, he heard a vehicle approaching on the town road. Soon he saw a small white car coming around the barn. It slowed and began to make its way haltingly up through the pasture.

It came to a stop forty or fifty feet shy of the side door, where Gurney's Outback was parked. A woman emerged from the car and stood for a moment by its open door. Assuming it must be Kim Steele, Gurney started across the pasture toward her. He was about to call out when she got back in the car and tried to turn it around—an attempt that ended when a rear wheel sank into one of the pasture's groundhog burrows.

He found her sobbing, hands gripping the steering wheel. Her dark curly hair was disarranged. Her face was drawn.

Gurney blinked, confused for a second or two by the fact that the woman in the car was part African American, which didn't jibe with the mental image he'd constructed from the fact of her being married to an upstate white cop. Feeling some chagrin at the narrowness of his expectation—and the not-so-subtle prejudice lurking under it—he cleared his throat.

"Mrs. Steele?"

Her eyes had the exhausted red puffiness that comes from hours of crying.

"Mrs. Steele?"

She sniffled, her gaze fastened on the steering wheel. "Damn . . . stupid . . . car."

"I can pull your car out of that hole with my tractor. Come up to the house. I'll take care of your car for you. Okay?"

He was about to repeat his suggestion when she suddenly opened the door and stepped out. He noticed that her shirt was unevenly buttoned. She pulled a loose khaki jacket tightly around her despite the warmth of the day.

He led the way to the patio and gestured toward one of the chairs at a small metal cafe table. "Would you like something to drink? Water or coffee?"

She sat at the table and shook her head.

He sat in the chair opposite her. He saw grief, exhaustion, indecision, anxiety.

He spoke softly. "It's hard to know who to trust, isn't it?"

She blinked, looking at him now in a more focused way. "You're a retired police officer?"

"I was a homicide detective with the NYPD. I took my pension after twenty-five years. My wife and I have been up here in Walnut Crossing for three years now." He paused. "Do you want to tell me why you wanted to see me?"

"I'm not sure. I'm not sure of anything."

He smiled. "That may be a good thing."

"Why?"

"I think doubt is a realistic approach to situations where there's a lot at stake."

He was thinking of the times he had felt baffled and how only by talking something out with Madeleine had he been able to decide what to do. He wondered if that was the kind of relationship Kim Steele had enjoyed with her husband. Maybe she'd always relied on their conversations to help resolve her doubts.

Tears began to make their way down her cheeks. "I'm sorry," she said, shaking her head. "I shouldn't be wasting your time."

"You're not wasting my time."

She stared at him.

He could see in her eyes the battle in her mind—and its sudden resolution.

She reached into the pocket of her big khaki jacket—which he realized was probably her husband's, adding a poignant note to the way she wrapped herself in it. She pulled out a smartphone. After tapping a few icons, she extended it across the table so he could see the screen. When he reached for it, she pulled back.

"I'll hold it," she said. "Just read what it says."

It was a text message. "Watch ur back. EZ nite for mfs to ice ur ass n blame the BDA."

Gurney read it three times. He noted the date and time—the evening John Steele was killed, about an hour prior to the shooting.

"What is this?"

"John's phone. I found that message on it."

"How come you still have it? Didn't the crime-scene team want it?"

"It wasn't at the crime scene. On duty they use BlackBerrys. This is John's personal phone. It was at home."

"When did you find the message?"

"Yesterday morning."

"Have you shown it to the police?"

She shook her head.

"Because . . ."

"The message. What it says."

"What does it mean to you?"

Although she was sitting in the direct sunlight, she wrapped herself more tightly in the jacket. "He was being warned to watch his back. Doesn't that suggest someone who was supposed to be on his side really wasn't?"

"You're thinking someone in the department?"

"I don't know what I'm thinking."

"Your husband wouldn't be the first cop to have enemies. Sometimes the best cops have the worst enemies."

She met his gaze, nodding with conviction. "That's who John was. The best. The best person on earth. Totally honest."

"Do you know if he was doing anything that less honest people in the department might have found threatening?"

She took a deep breath. "John didn't like to talk about work at home. Once in a while I'd overhear something when he was on the phone. Comments about past cases with questionable evidence, deaths in custody, throwdowns. You know what they are, right?"

He nodded. Some cops wouldn't go anywhere without one—an easily concealed, unregistered, untraceable pistol that could be dropped next to the body of someone the cop had shot, as "evidence" that the victim had been armed.

"How did he know which cases to look into?"

She hesitated, appeared uncomfortable. "Maybe he had some contacts?"

"People who pointed him in the direction of specific cases?"

"Maybe."

"People in the Black Defense Alliance?"

"I don't really know."

She was a lousy liar. That was okay. It was the good liars he worried about.

"Did he ever tell you how high up in the department the problems might go?"

She said nothing. Her deer-in-the-headlights expression was answer enough.

"What made you come to me?"

"I read about that Peter Pan murder case you solved last year, how you exposed the police corruption behind it."

The explanation sounded real, as far as it went.

"How did you know where to find me?"

The deer-in-the-headlights look was back. It told him that she couldn't tell the truth but wouldn't tell a lie. It was, he thought, the reaction of an honest person in a difficult spot.

"Okay," he said. "We'll let that go for now. What would you like me to do for you?"

She answered without hesitation. "I want you to find out who killed my husband."

12

While Kim Steele waited on the patio, Gurney got his tractor from the excavation site, pulled her car from the collapsed groundhog burrow, and got it oriented in the right direction. He promised to look into the White River situation. As she was leaving, she shook hands with him, and for a couple of seconds a smile relieved the desolation in her eyes.

Once she was safely on the town road, he went into the house, opened a new document on his computer, and, from memory, typed in the text from her husband's phone. Then he called Jack Hardwick and left on his voicemail a summary of what Kim had told him and a request that he use his contacts to dig a little deeper into the backgrounds of Dell Beckert and his number two, Judd Turlock. Then, for good measure, he emailed Hardwick a copy of the text message.

Next he took his cell phone out to the patio where the signal was strongest, activated its Record function, and called Sheridan Kline's private number.

The man picked up on the second ring, oozing a warmth that didn't quite conceal an edge of anxiety. "Dave! Great to hear from you. So, tell me, where do we stand?"

"That depends on how accurately I understood your invitation. Let me spell out what I'm agreeing to: full LEO authority, credentials, and protections as a member of your investigation staff; investigatorial autonomy, with a sole reporting line to you personally; and compensation at the standard hourly rate for senior contract investigators. Contract is to be open-ended, cancelable by either party at any time. Have I got it right?"

"You recording this?"

"You have a problem with that?"

"No problem at all. I'll have the contract prepared. There's a CSMT meeting this afternoon at White River Police Headquarters. Critical Situation Management Team. Three thirty. Meet me in the parking lot at three fifteen. You can sign the contract, attend the meeting, get off to a running start."

"See you there."

As Gurney ended the call, a chicken in the pen by the asparagus patch let out a startling squawk. It was a sound that still struck him with the visceral impact of an alarm, even though he'd learned during his year of chicken tending that the sounds they made rarely had any decipherable purpose. Utterances that resembled cries of distress never seemed to coincide with the presence of threats of any kind.

Still, he ambled over to the pen to assure himself that all was well.

The big Rhode Island Red was standing in that perfect chicken pose, presenting the classic profile featured in country-craft art. It reminded him that he needed to sweep out the coop, change the water, and refill the feeder.

While Madeleine always seemed pleased by the variety of her roles in life, Gurney's reaction to his diverse responsibilities was less positive. A therapist had long ago advised him to actively *be* everything he was—a husband to his wife, a father to his son, a son to his parents, a fellow worker to his workmates, a friend to his friends. He insisted that balance and peace in one's life depended on participating in each part of that life. Gurney had no argument with the logic of this. As a guiding principle it felt true and right. But he recoiled from the practice of it. For all its horrors and perils, his detective work was the only part of his life that came naturally to him. Being a husband, a father, a son, a friend—all of these required a special effort, perhaps even a special kind of courage, that tracking down murderers did not.

Of course, he knew in his heart that being a man meant more than being a cop, and leading a good life often meant swimming against the current of one's inclinations. He also felt the nudging of an axiom his therapist was fond of repeating: *The only time a man can do the right thing is right now.* So, embracing a sense of duty and purpose, he got the utility broom from the mudroom and headed for the chicken coop.

With an energizing sense of accomplishment from having dealt with the dirt, the water, and the feed, he decided to go on to another maintenance task that needed doing—the mowing of the broad path that encircled the high pasture. That activity did promise certain distinct pleasures—the bursts of fragrance rising from the patches of wild mint, the view from the top of the pasture out over the unspoiled green hills, the sweet air, the cerulean sky.

At the end of the pasture path he came to the trail above the pond that led to his excavation. Although the shaded grass there was slower growing, he decided to mow it as well, proceeding under the canopy of cherry trees until he arrived at the excavation itself. He stopped there, picturing the artifacts he'd uncovered and pondering Thrasher's strange comment on the teeth. Something told him it would be best to put it out of his mind and finish the mowing job. But that idea was replaced by another—to spend a few minutes digging down a few additional inches along the foundation, just to see if anything of interest might turn up.

His tractor with the mini-backhoe attachment was still up by the house, but there was a spade by the excavation. He went down the little ladder and began prying shovelfuls of soil away from the base of the stone wall that Thrasher had been probing. Working his way along it, finding nothing but more soil and suspecting that he was becoming a trifle obsessive, he decided to return to his mowing. Then, as he turned over a final shovelful, he noted something solid. He took it at first to be just a hardened lump of reddish-brown clay, but when he picked it up and worked it in his hands he discovered embedded in the clay a rusted piece of iron, thick and curved. As he dislodged more of the caked soil, he saw that it was a circle of iron, perhaps three inches in diameter, with a thick chain link attached to the side of it.

While he realized that it could have a variety of uses, one in particular was obvious. It looked very much like some form of shackle—like half of a primitive set of handcuffs.

13

The westbound drive to White River consisted of a gradual descent from modest mountains and sloping meadows through rolling hills and broad valleys into a region of shabby strip malls. The final symbol of the area's economic depression was the abandoned White River stone quarry, made famous by the sensational news coverage of an explosion that killed six passing motorists, bankrupted the company, and led to the unnerving discovery that someone had made off with more than a hundred sticks of dynamite.

Gurney's GPS led him into the center of the cheerless city on an avenue that bordered the partly burned and looted Grinton section. At the end of the avenue stood White River's police headquarters. A world apart from the picturesquely dilapidated barns and tilting silos of Walnut Crossing, the building was constructed of gray-beige brick in the boxy style of the nineteen sixties. Its treeless, grassless setting was as sterile as its aluminum-framed windows and concrete parking lot, both the color of dust.

As he reached the entrance to the lot, a man sitting on what appeared to be a small furniture dolly rolled by, propelling himself along the sidewalk with his gloved hands. He was wearing a grimy army-surplus jacket and a baseball hat. Looking closer, Gurney could see that the man was legless below the knees, and the gloves were actually oven mitts. An American flag hung limply from the top of an old broomstick that was affixed to the back of the dolly. With each thrust of his hands the man cried out repetitively in a voice as abrasive as a rusty hinge, "Sunshine . . . sunshine . . . sunshine . . ."

When Gurney drove into the lot, the first vehicle to catch his eye was Kline's gleaming black Navigator. In a row marked Reserved, it occupied the space nearest the building's front door. He parked next to it, got out of his car, and was struck immediately by the odor of smoke, burned plastic, wet ashes.

The Navigator's tinted rear window descended and Kline peered out at him, at first with a look of satisfaction, then concern. "Everything all right?"

"Bad smell."

"Arson. Pointless stupidity. Get in. I have your contract."

Gurney slid into the back seat across from Kline—a luxuriously isolated environment of plush leather and soft lighting.

"High-class vehicle," said Gurney.

"No cost to the taxpayer."

"Confiscation?"

"Forfeiture of property employed in the facilitation of drug trafficking."

Perhaps interpreting Gurney's silence as a criticism of the controversial practice of seizing an accused individual's assets prior to trial, Kline added, "The bleeding hearts like to whine about the tiny number of cases where there's some inconvenience to a guy who ends up beating the rap. But ninety-nine times out of a hundred we're just transferring ill-gotten goods from scumbags to law enforcement. Perfectly legal and personally satisfying."

He clicked open an attaché case on the seat between them, pulled out two copies of the contract, and handed them to Gurney with a pen. "I've signed these. You sign both, give me one, and keep one for yourself."

Reading through the contract, he was surprised to find no surprises—no subtle changes from the provisions he'd demanded on the phone. Oddly, this straightforwardness aroused his suspicion. He was sure everything Kline did was some sort of stratagem. Honesty would always be a route to something more important. But he could hardly object to the contract on that basis.

"So, about this meeting, is there an agenda?"

"Just to share the known facts. Establish priorities. Application of resources. Media guidelines. Get everyone in sync."

"Everyone being who?"

"Dell Beckert; Beckert's right hand, Judd Turlock; chief investigating officer, Mark Torres; Mayor Dwayne Shucker; Sheriff Goodson Cloutz." He paused. "Word of warning about Cloutz, so you're not taken by surprise. He's blind."

"Blind?"

"As a bat, supposedly. Wily country boy who talks like a hillbilly. Runs the county jail. Always gets reelected, unopposed the last three times."

"Any particular reason he's part of this so-called team?"

"No idea."

"They all expecting me?"

"I gave Beckert a heads-up. Left it up to him to fill in the others."

"Any liaisons to outside agencies? FBI? State police? AG's office?"

"We're keeping the FBI out unless we're forced to let them in. Beckert has his own back channels to the state police, to be used at his discretion. As for the AG's office, they have more than they can handle with the new issues around the AG's death."

"What new issues?"

"Some embarrassing questions. The fact that he died in a Vegas hotel room creates speculation. Prurient suggestions." He grimaced, glanced at his Rolex, then at the contract in Gurney's lap. "It's meeting time. You want to sign that so we can go in?"

"One more question."

"What?"

"As I'm sure you know, I met with Kim Steele this morning. She gave me her perspective on her husband's death, along with the evidence she found on his phone." He paused, watching Kline's face. "I wondered who sent her to me. Then I realized it had to be you."

Kline's eyes narrowed. "Why me?"

"Because what she told me was a direct answer to the question I'd raised with you—about what you were leaving out of your description of the situation. The text message on Steele's phone and its possible implications. Kim was afraid to take it to the local police, who she didn't trust, so she took it to you. But it was too touchy a matter for you to share with me as long as I was outside the tent. But if the victim's wife told me about it on her own, you'd be clear of any blowback. Plus, a visit from a grieving widow would put pressure on me to accept your offer."

Kline stared straight ahead, said nothing.

Gurney signed both copies of the contract, handed one to Kline, and slipped the other into his jacket pocket.

The inside of White River Police Headquarters was a predictably drab reflection of the outside—with buzzing fluorescent lights, stained acoustic ceiling tiles, and the smell of a disinfectant whose ersatz pine aroma was mixing with the sourness of whatever was being disinfected.

Kline ushered him quickly through a security checkpoint and led him down a long corridor with colorless cinder-block walls. At the end of the corridor they passed through an open door into an unlit conference room. Kline felt for a light switch and pressed it. Fluorescent tubes flickered on.

The wall opposite the door was devoted mainly to a wide window over which blinds had been lowered. A long conference table stood in the center of the room. On the wall to the left was a whiteboard on which CSMT 3:30 had been printed with a black marker. According to a circular clock above the board, it was now 3:27. Looking to his right, Gurney was surprised to see the chair at the end of the table was occupied by a thin man with dark glasses. A white cane lay on the table in front of him.

Kline turned with a start. "Goodson! I didn't see you sitting there."

"But now you do, Sheridan. Course I can't see you. Bein' kept in the dark's my natural state. It's the cross I bear, to be forever at the mercy of my sighted companions."

"Nobody in this part of the world is less in the dark than you, Goodson."

The thin man cackled. The exchange had the tone of a jokey ritual that had long since lost what humor it may once have contained.

Footsteps approached in the corridor, accompanied by the sound of someone blowing his nose. A short fat man stepped into the room, recognizable to Gurney from the press conference as Mayor Dwayne Shucker, holding a handkerchief to his face.

"Goddamnit, Shucks," said the blind man, "sounds like you got yourself pollinated."

The mayor stuffed his handkerchief in the pocket of his too-small sport jacket, took a seat at the opposite end of the table, and yawned. "Nice to see you, Sheriff." He yawned again, looked at Kline. "Hey, there, Sheridan. Leaner and meaner than ever. Meant to ask you at that press affair—you still running them marathons?"

"Never did, Dwayne, just the occasional 5K."

"Five Ks, fifty Ks, all the same to me." Sniffling again, he gave Gurney a once-over. "You're our DA's new investigator?"

"Right."

The thin man at the other end of the table raised his blind man's cane in a kind of salute. "I knew there was another party in the room, just wondered when you'd make yourself known. Gurney, is it?"

"Right."

"Man of action. I've heard about your exploits. I hope our modest level of mayhem up here in the backwoods don't bore you."

Gurney said nothing. Kline looked uncomfortable.

The man replaced his cane carefully on the table and produced a lizardy smile. "Seriously, Mr. Gurney, tell me—what's your big-city impression of our little problem here?"

Gurney shrugged. "My impression is that 'little' might be the wrong word."

"Tell me, what word would you—"

He was interrupted by the energetic entry into the room of two men. Gurney recognized the tall one in a crisply tailored dark suit as Dell Beckert. He was carrying a slim briefcase. The other man, presumably Judd Turlock, in a nondescript sport jacket and slacks, combined the body of a defensive lineman with the impassive face of a mobster in a mug shot.

Beckert nodded to Kline, then turned to Gurney. "I'm Dell Beckert. Welcome. You've met everyone?" Without waiting for an answer, he continued. "We're missing Mark Torres, CIO on the homicide. He's been delayed a few minutes. But let's get started." He strode around to the other side of the table, chose the center chair, placed his briefcase squarely in front of it, and sat down. "Can we get some more light in here?"

Judd Turlock stepped behind Beckert's chair and raised the blinds, carefully and evenly. Gurney, in the seat across from Beckert, was struck by the stark composition of the view framed by the picture window.

A black macadam road, bordered by chain-link fences topped with razor wire, extended out from the police headquarters to another colorless brick building, several times larger but with narrower windows. A black-and-white sign identified it as the Haldon C. Eppert Detention Center, official name of the county lockup. Looming on a rise a few hundred yards beyond it were the massive concrete wall and guard towers of what Gurney recognized as the White River Correctional Facility, the state prison named after its city host. With this bleak tableau serving as a backdrop for the man at the center of the table, it occurred to Gurney that if someone in a fanciful moment should consider those incarceration facilities as a kind of hell, then Beckert had positioned himself as hell's gatekeeper.

"To keep us on track we have an agenda." Beckert reached into his briefcase and pulled out some papers. Turlock passed one to each man at the table. Beckert added, "Orderly process is important—especially when we're confronting an insane level of disorder."

Gurney scanned the terse list of topics. It was orderly, but revealed little.

"We'll start with the RAM-CAM videos from the Willard Park homicide site," said Beckert. "The digital files are being—"

He stopped at the sound of hurried footsteps in the corridor. A moment later a slim, young Hispanic man entered the room, nodded apologetically all around, and took a seat at the table between Gurney and the sheriff. Turlock slid a copy of the agenda across the table, which the young man examined with a thoughtful frown. Gurney extended his hand to him.

"I'm Dave Gurney, with the DA's office."

"I know." He smiled, looking more like an earnest college kid than the chief investigating officer on a major homicide. "I'm Mark Torres. White River PD."

With a flicker of irritation, Beckert continued, "The original digital files are being enhanced at the forensic computer lab. These will serve our purposes for now."

He nodded at Turlock, who tapped a few icons on a small tablet computer. A large video monitor high on the wall behind the sheriff came to life.

The first segment of the video was a longer version of the clip Gurney had seen at Marv and Trish Gelter's house. The extra length consisted of several minutes of additional footage prior to the actual shooting—the period during which Officer Steele was walking back and forth on the sidewalk at the edge of the park, his attention on the crowd. At the side of the crowd, as if preparing to charge into it on his great stone horse, was the larger-than-life statue of Colonel Ezra Willard.

Perhaps because there was less distraction here than at the Gelters', or because this portion of the video was longer, Gurney noticed something he'd originally missed—a tiny red dot moving on the back of Steele's head. The dot followed Steele for at least two minutes prior to the fatal shot, stopping when he stopped, moving with him when he moved, centering itself on the base of his skull just below the edge of his protective helmet. The fact that it was obviously the projected dot of a rifle's laser sight gave Gurney a sick feeling.

Then the bullet struck, knocking Steele facedown onto the sidewalk. Even though Gurney knew it was coming, he flinched. The reassuring words of a wise man he'd once known came back to him: *Flinching at another's injury is the essence of empathy, and empathy is the essence of humanity.*

At a gesture from Beckert, Turlock stopped the video and switched off the monitor.

The silence in the room was broken by Mayor Shucker. "The damage being done to the businesspeople of this city by that damn RAM-CAM video is just awful. They run the damn thing over and over. Makes our little city look like a war zone. A place to avoid. We have restaurants, B and Bs, the museum, kayak rentals—the tourist season about to start, and not a damn customer in sight. This media thing is killing us."

Beckert showed no reaction. He looked toward the opposite end of the table. "Goodson? I know the video's already been described to you in detail. Comments?"

Cloutz fingered his white cane with an unpleasant smile. "I do appreciate Shucks's business concerns. Natural for a man invested in the economy of the city to feel that way. On the other hand, I do see some value in givin' folks around the state a glimpse of the barbarian shit we're facin' here. Folks need to see it to appreciate the steps we need to take."

Gurney thought he detected a nod of agreement from Beckert. "Other comments?"

Kline shook his head. "Not at the moment."

"How about our new investigator?"

Gurney shrugged, his voice casual. "Why do you think it took the shooter so long?"

Beckert frowned. "Long?"

"The dot from the laser sight was on Steele's head for quite a while."

Beckert shrugged. "I doubt that it matters. Let's move on to the next agenda item, the ME's report. Copies of the full report will be available shortly, but Dr. Thrasher has provided me with the salient points."

He removed a sheet of paper from his briefcase and read aloud: "'In re John Steele, DOA, Mercy Hospital. Cause of death: catastrophic damage to medulla oblongata, cerebellum, and posterior cerebral artery, leading to immediate failure of heart and respiratory functions. Damage initiated by the passage of a bullet through the occipital bone at the base of the skull, through critical brain and brain-stem regions, emerging through the lacrimal bone structure.'"

He replaced the paper in his briefcase. "Dr. Thrasher further estimated, informally, that the bullet was probably a thirty-caliber high-energy FMJ. That estimate has now been confirmed by preliminary ballistic analysis of the bullet recovered at the Willard Park site. Any questions?"

Shucker sniffled. "What the hell's an FMJ?"

"Full metal jacket. Keeps the bullet from expanding or fragmenting, so it passes through the target intact. Plus side is that it preserves the rifling marks for ballistics, so we can match the bullet to the weapon that fired it."

"Assuming you recover the weapon?"

"Assuming we recover it. Any other questions?"

Kline steepled his fingers. "Any progress finding the shooter site?"

Beckert looked at Torres. "Ball's in your court, Mark."

The young CIO looked pleased at the handoff. "We're narrowing the possibilities, sir. Aligning the position of the victim's head in the video frame that captured the impact with the position of the recovered bullet gave us a general vector for the bullet's path. We've laid that vector out on a map of the area to identify possible sites. Priority goes to those farthest from the victim, since the shot wasn't heard at the site, and no audible traces were picked up by the RAM-CAMs. We have patrol officers out now doing door-to-doors."

Cloutz was idly stroking his cane. "And you ain't gettin' diddly-shit cooperation from our minority citizens. Am I right?"

Gurney noted that the sheriff's fingernails were nicely manicured.

Torres frowned, his jaw muscles tightening. "The level of cooperation so far has been uneven."

Kline continued. "Apart from the door-to-doors, Mark, what else is under way?"

Torres leaned forward. "We're collecting and reviewing video data from the security, traffic, and media cameras in the area. A careful examination of that data is likely to—"

Mayor Shucker broke in. "What I want to know is, do we have any real leads on them sons of bitches on the run? That's gotta have priority. Catch 'em, incarcerate 'em, and put this goddamn nightmare to rest."

There was a hard edge to Beckert's voice. "Jordan and Tooker are at the top of our list. We're going to get them. That's a personal guarantee."

Shucker seemed mollified.

Kline steepled his fingers again. "Can we tie them directly to the shooting?"

"We know from reliable informers that they were involved. And we just heard from a credible source that a third person may have been involved along with them—possibly a white male."

Kline appeared startled. "I didn't think the BDA had white members."

"They don't. Not technically. But they do have some white enablers, even financial supporters."

"Leftie loonies, need to have their goddamn heads examined," interjected the sheriff.

Kline looked pained.

Beckert exhibited no reaction at all. "We hope to identify that third person and have Jordan and Tooker in custody within the next forty-eight hours. And we expect that Mark and his people will have conclusive physical evidence very soon— from the shooter site, from BDA materials seized in the raid, and from cooperating BDA members."

"Speakin' of which," said the sheriff, "I would hope that Sheridan here will be askin' the judge to set bail high enough on our BDA detainees so they don't go flyin' out free as fuckin' birds. More time we have them in custody, better our chances of gettin' what we need."

Gurney knew what the sheriff was talking about. He'd no doubt already separated the detainees from each other and put them in cells with jailhouse snitches who might be eager to trade incriminating information for sentence reductions. It was one of the rottenest parts of a rotten system.

Beckert glanced at his watch. "Any further questions?"

Gurney spoke with bland curiosity. "Do you think there's any chance your hypothesis might not be correct?"

"What hypothesis?"

"That the Black Defense Alliance is responsible for the shooting."

Beckert stared at him. "What makes you ask that?"

"I've made some mistakes myself by getting too sure too soon. I stopped asking questions because I thought I had all the answers."

"Is this a general concern, or do you have a specific pebble in your shoe?"

"I had a visit this morning from Kim Steele, John Steele's widow."

"And?"

"She showed me an odd text that was sent to her husband's personal phone the night he was shot. I made a note of it." Gurney brought it up on his phone and slid it across the table.

Beckert read through the text, frowning. "You've seen this, Sheridan?"

"Dave discussed it with me before we came in."

It struck Gurney that wielding the truth deceptively was one of Kline's talents.

Beckert passed the phone on to Turlock, who gazed expressionlessly at the message and then passed it back.

The sheriff spoke up in an oily voice. "Could someone kindly enlighten me?"

Beckert read aloud from the screen with obvious contempt for the street-slanginess of the text. " 'Watch ur back. EZ nite for mfs to ice ur ass n blame the BDA.' "

"Hell's that all about?"

Ignoring the question, Beckert gave Gurney a long look. "Did you take possession of Steele's phone?"

"No."

"Why not?"

"Mrs. Steele wasn't ready to hand it over, and I had no standing to demand it."

Beckert tilted his head speculatively. "Why would she bring this matter to you?"

"She referred to some work I'd done on another case."

"What work?"

"I helped exonerate a woman who'd been framed for murder by a corrupt cop."

"What relevance does that have here?"

"I have no idea."

"Really? None at all?"

"I'm determined to keep an open mind."

Beckert held Gurney's gaze for a long moment. "We need that phone."

"I know."

"Will she surrender it willingly, or do we have to hit her with a warrant?"

"I'll talk to her. If I can persuade her, that would be a better route."

"You do that. In the meantime Judd will get a warrant. In case we need it."

Turlock, who had been flexing his fingers and examining his knuckles, nodded.

"Okay," said Beckert. "That wraps it up for now. Just a final word. Procedure is key. Lack of orderly procedure produces chaos, chaos produces failure, and failure is not an option. All communications will be routed through Judd here. He'll be the hub of the wheel. Everything flows in to him, and everything flows out from him. Any questions?"

There were none.

It struck Gurney as a strange arrangement, since that central role normally would be filled by the CIO, in this case Mark Torres. And the tone of bureaucratic rigidity seemed like anything but a plus. But this need for control was obviously coming from a central point in Beckert's personality, and Gurney didn't want to strain his relationship with the man any further by probing the matter. At least not for the moment.

14

Kline and Gurney left the building together, saying nothing until they reached their cars. Kline glanced around like a man wary of being overheard.

"I want to clarify something, David. I don't want you thinking I'm being less than totally honest with you. In the meeting you explained that you couldn't ask Kim Steele for the phone because at that point you had no official standing in the case. Well, that's exactly why I couldn't tell you she'd come to me. You can understand the sensitivity of the thing."

"The same sensitivity that kept you from telling Beckert about it?"

"I was delaying slightly on that—mainly out of respect for Kim's concerns. But one thing leads to another. The best of intentions can create problems."

"What problems?"

"Well, the simple fact of any delay at all. If that came to light, it could create the impression that I shared Kim's mistrust of the department. That's why I chose to handle it the way I did—not out of any desire to mislead you. By the way, how you handled the phone business in the meeting—that was ideal."

"It was the truth."

"Of course. And the truth can be very useful. The more truth, within reason, the better." There were beads of sweat on Kline's forehead.

From their first meeting back at the start of the Mellery case, Gurney was aware that there were two distinct layers in Kline's construction: the veneer of a confident politician with his eye on the gold ring and, beneath it, a frightened little man. What struck Gurney now was the increasing visibility of the fear.

Kline looked around the lot again and checked his watch. "You see or hear anything in that meeting that surprised you?"

"The possible involvement of a third person was interesting."

"What do you make of it?"

"Too soon to say."

"What's your next step?"

"I'd like more information."

"Like what?"

"You want me to email you a list?"

"Easier this way." He took out his phone and tapped a couple of icons. "It's recording."

"I'd like to see the incident report; crime-scene photos; copies of the video we just saw; ballistics report; victim bio; Jordan's and Tooker's criminal records; anything you can pry out of Beckert regarding his informants; and I'd like to know what's behind his obvious hatred for Jordan and Tooker."

Kline shut off the Record function of his phone. "That last one I can answer right now. Beckert's strengths as a law enforcer come with a passion for maintaining order. He sees Jordan, Tooker, the whole BDA organization as agents of anarchy. Dell Beckert and the BDA are like matter and antimatter—a huge explosion waiting to happen."

As he began his drive home, Gurney had two things on his mind. The first was Kline's obvious anxiety. It suggested that he mistrusted the handling of the case by the department or by Beckert himself. He wondered if the source of that mistrust ran deeper than the phone text. The second was the motorcycle that had been maintaining a consistent position about a hundred yards behind the Outback since he'd left White River.

He slowed from seventy to sixty and noted that the motorcycle did the same.

He increased his speed from sixty to seventy-five with a similar result.

A few minutes later, as he passed a sign indicating a rest stop one mile ahead, the motorcycle accelerated into the left lane, rapidly coming abreast of the Outback. The rider, unidentifiable in a helmet with a face shield, extended his hand—holding a gold detective's shield—and gestured toward the upcoming exit ramp.

The rest area turned out to be nothing more than a row of parking spaces in front of a small brick building that housed a pair of restrooms. The area was isolated from the highway by a line of overgrown shrubbery. As the motorcycle pulled in and stopped a couple of spaces away, the loneliness of the place prompted Gurney to move his Beretta handgun from his glove compartment to his jacket pocket.

When the rider stepped off the machine and removed his helmet, Gurney was surprised to see that it was Mark Torres.

"Sorry if you thought I was following you. I live out this way, my wife and I, in Larvaton. The next exit."

"And?"

"I wanted to talk to you. I'm not sure whether it's okay to be speaking to you directly, I mean privately like this. I don't like going outside channels—with everything supposed to be going through Deputy Chief Turlock—but then I decided it would be sort of okay, since we've met before."

"We have?"

"You probably wouldn't remember, but I attended a seminar you gave at the academy a couple of years ago on investigative procedures. It was really amazing."

"I'm glad you enjoyed it, but . . ."

"I should get to the point." He looked like the idea was causing him physical pain. "The thing is . . . I kind of feel in this case like I'm in a little over my head."

Gurney waited as a series of heavy trucks roared by on the far side of the bushes. "In what way?"

"I just got promoted from patrol to the detective bureau six months ago. To be put in this position on a case like this, with so much at stake . . ." He shook his head. "To be honest, I'm a little uncomfortable." The hint of an accent was creeping into his voice.

"With the responsibility? Or something else?"

Torres hesitated. "Well, it's sort of like I'm the case CIO and sort of not. Chief Beckert seems to be running it. Like this thing of staying focused on Jordan and Tooker, like he's positive they're guilty. But I don't see enough evidence to be that positive about it myself. Is this a big mistake, talking to you directly about this?"

"That depends on what you want from me."

"Maybe just your phone number? I'd love to be able to bounce things off you. Unless that's a problem."

Gurney saw no reason to refuse, regardless of how rigid Beckert might be about the flow of information. He shrugged and gave the young detective his cell number.

Torres thanked him, and then was gone—leaving Gurney to muse over the encounter. Like everything else in the case, it felt not quite right. He wondered if the secrecy surrounding the request was the product of Torres's insecurity, the White River police culture, or something nastier altogether.

His musings were interrupted by the passing shadows of a pair of vultures circling over the weedy field adjacent to the restrooms. It was interesting, he thought, that vultures, nurturing themselves only from the bodies of dead animals, harming no living thing, had become in popular parlance predators devouring the defenseless. More evidence that the popular mind was rarely distracted by the truth.

These musings were interrupted in turn by the ringing of his phone.

It was Hardwick.

"Gurney here."

"Damn! That text you sent me from Steele's phone? Could be a legit warning. Or something pretending to be a legit warning. Or some other fucking thing entirely. You know where the call came from?"

"We can pursue that when we get possession of the phone from Steele's wife. But I'm sure the pursuit will dead-end at an anonymous prepaid cell. You have anything on Beckert or Turlock?"

"A bit more than before. I called in a favor from a guy at NYSP headquarters with access to old recruitment archives—the original forms with the CV data provided by applicants. Beckert's and Turlock's applications reveal a very early connection. They both attended the same military prep school in Butris County, Virginia. Beckert was a year ahead of Turlock, but it was a small school, and they would have trained together."

"Interesting."

"Also interesting is a notation on Turlock's application indicating that he had legal problems back at that school. 'Juvenile court hearing, proceedings sealed. Applicant explanation, supported by Butris County sheriff's affidavit, deemed adequate for application to proceed at this time.' That's all the notation says."

The vulture shadows passed again across the pavement and out across the scraggly field. "Hmm. Did Beckert have any problems there?"

"If so, nobody noticed. Top of his class every year. Clean as Butris County spring water."

"Be nice to know what Turlock got banged up for."

"We'd need a hell of a good cause to persuade a Virginia judge to open the sealed juvie file of a deputy police chief. And as of now we have no cause at all."

"Be nice to find one."

"For a guy who's not sure he wants to get involved, you sound pretty damn involved."

Gurney waited for another noisy convoy of trucks to pass. "One little peculiarity seems to lead to another, that's all."

"Like what?"

"Like the relationship Kline has with Beckert. Kline describes him as a law-and-order god. Even told me in a worshipful tone that Beckert is married to the governor's cousin."

"So?"

"So why doesn't he trust this paragon of justice?"

"You don't think he does?"

"I think something about Beckert's approach to this homicide has Kline running scared."

"The fuck you think is going on?"

"I don't know. Something to do with Beckert's plan to run for attorney general?"

Hardwick let out a braying laugh.

"What's so funny?"

"Something I just heard. Latest rumor is that the former AG's passing on to his heavenly reward in a Vegas hotel was more colorful than first revealed. Seems there was a hooker trapped under the fat fucker's three-hundred-pound corpse."

"This has some relevance to Beckert?"

"It dumps the former AG's character into the shitter, which is a plus for Mr. Law-and-Order. Clean new broom to sweep out the nasty crap."

Gurney thought about this for a moment. "You told me the other day that Beckert's first wife died of a drug overdose. You have anything more on that?"

"There was no legal case, so no case records. The fuck would that have to do with anything anyway?"

"No idea. I'm just asking questions."

When Gurney arrived home he found Geraldine Mirkle's yellow Beetle parked by the asparagus patch. He was led by the sound of female laughter to the patio.

Geraldine and Madeleine were doubled over. Finally Madeleine got hold of herself and said, "Welcome home, sweetheart. Gerry was just describing an encounter with a client."

"Sounds like fun."

"Oh, you have no idea!" said Geraldine, her round face a picture of glee. "I've got to be going now. Buford gets a little crazy if he doesn't get his dinner on time." She stood up, surprisingly nimble for a rotund woman, and hurried off to her Beetle. As she was fitting herself into the driver's seat she called back, "Thanks for the tea, my dear." With a burst of giggles she drove off.

Madeleine responded to Gurney's quizzical expression with a dismissive little wave of her hand. "Just a bit of dark clinic humor. Hard to explain. You had to be there." She wiped her face again and cleared her throat. "I thought we'd have dinner out here this evening. The air is pure heaven."

He shrugged. "Fine with me."

She went into the house and came back ten minutes later with place mats, silverware, and two large bowls brimming with her favorite salad of cold shrimp, avocado, diced tomatoes, red-leaf lettuce, and crumbled blue cheese.

They were both hungry and hardly spoke until they were finished. The four chickens were pursuing their own daylong meal, pecking in the grass around the edges of the patio.

"Buford is her cat," said Madeleine, putting down her fork.

"I thought it was her husband."

"Hasn't got a husband. Seems happy enough without one."

After a pause Gurney launched into a summary of all that had transpired that day, including his meeting with Kline in the parking lot.

"The more he tells me how open and honest he's being with me, the less I believe it. So I guess I need to make a decision."

Madeleine said nothing, just cocked her head and eyed him incredulously.

"You think my involvement is a bad idea?" he asked.

"*A bad idea?* Is it a bad idea to let yourself be used in a murder investigation by a man you think is lying to you? To put your life in the hands of a man you don't trust? My God, David, on what planet would that be considered a *good* idea?"

Putting his life in Kline's hands might be an overly dramatic way of looking at it, but she had a point. "I'll sleep on it."

"Really?"

"Really."

In his own mind he was inclined to continue his investigation, at least for a while. What he intended to 'sleep on' was his relationship with Kline.

She gazed at him for a long moment. Then she gathered up their salad bowls and forks and carried them into the house.

He took out his phone and looked up the number Kim Steele had given him. The call went to her voicemail. He left a message saying it would be helpful for him to have her husband's phone with whatever digital information might be stored in it. He avoided using language that sounded peremptory. He knew his best chance of getting her agreement lay in giving her the option of refusing.

Then he sat back in his chair, closed his eyes, and tried to put the jumble of the day behind him. But his mind kept going back to the unusual power dynamic of the White River meeting—Beckert clearly being the man in charge, despite being outranked by the three elected officials at the table—the mayor, the district attorney, and the blind sheriff.

He was still sitting there on the patio half an hour later, trying to relax in the sweetly scented spring breezes, when he heard Madeleine stepping back onto the patio. He opened his eyes and saw that she was fresh from a shower ... hair still damp, barefoot, wearing only panties and a tee shirt.

She smiled. "I thought we should probably get to bed early."

It proved to be a wonderful solution to his focus problem.

The next morning he awoke with a start. He'd been dreaming that he was lying in the bottom of his excavation, shackled by a black-iron chain to the foundation wall. A blind man in dark glasses was standing at the edge of the excavation, brandishing a long white cane. He slashed the cane viciously back and forth, each slash creating a high-pitched scream.

As Gurney came to his senses in the bed next to Madeleine, the screaming became the ringing of the phone on the nightstand. He picked it up, blinking his eyes to clear his vision. He saw on the screen that the caller was Sheridan Kline.

He cleared his throat and pressed Talk.

"Gurney here."

Kline's voice was shrill. "About time you picked up."

Gurney glanced at the clock on the night table. It was 7:34 AM. "Is there a problem?"

"An hour ago Dell Beckert got a call from the pastor of White River's largest Episcopal church. He was concerned about Beckert's statement on RAM News."

"Meaning what?"

"It sounded to him like Beckert was saying that Jordan and Tooker were cop killers."

"The pastor was upset by that?"

"Furious."

"Because?"

"Because Marcel Jordan and Virgil Tooker just happened to have been meeting with him in the parish house at the time Steele was shot. Discussing ways to end the violence. Jesus! That's why they left the demonstration early. Meaning they have what is known as a rock-solid alibi. They didn't do it. Couldn't have done it. Not unless we want to believe the most popular white pastor in White River is in the pocket of the BDA."

"Okay. So they didn't do it. They have an alibi. So what?"

"So what? *So what?* So they were just found. That's so what."

"Found?"

"Found. Dead."

"What?"

"Stripped naked, tied to the jungle gym in the Willard Park playground, apparently beaten to death. In the goddamn playground!"

II

THE THIRD MAN

15

As they waited for Beckert and Turlock, the members of the critical situation management team were in the same seats they'd been in the previous day, but the mood in the room was markedly different. There was no idle talk—in fact, no talk at all.

Gurney's mind was seesawing between his promise to reconsider his involvement with Kline and this tectonic shift in the nature of the situation.

Dwayne Shucker's eyes were closed, but the tiny tics playing at his eyelids belied any sense of restfulness. Goodson Cloutz's mouth was drawn into a tight line. Sheridan Kline's fingers were drumming lightly on the table. Mark Torres was focused on getting his laptop communicating with the screen on the wall above Cloutz's head. Gurney was struck not so much by everyone's discomfort, but by their apparent unwillingness to say a word before Beckert delivered his own view of the situation.

At precisely 2:00 PM Beckert and Turlock strode into the room and took their seats. If the murder of two men Beckert had wrongly implied were cop killers had any effect on his self-confidence, it wasn't obvious. Turlock looked about as concerned as a sledgehammer.

Beckert glanced at Torres's computer. "You have that ready?"

"Yes, sir." Torres tapped a key, and the screen on the wall displayed the words WILLARD PARK CRIME SCENE.

"Just hold it there for a minute. I want to say a few words about perspective. At noon today I was interviewed by RAM News. Just before the camera started recording, the reporter made a comment to me. 'This new development changes everything, doesn't it?' It wasn't really a question. It was an assumption. A dangerous one. And a false one. What happened last night in Willard Park, far from changing everything, simply narrows our focus."

The mayor's eyes were wide open. The sheriff was leaning forward, as if he'd misheard something. Beckert went on. "We know from our source that three individuals may have been involved in the plot to murder Officer Steele. Two of those conspirators, Jordan and Tooker, provided an alibi covering the time of the shooting. All this means is that the third member of the conspiracy was probably the actual shooter. From a messaging perspective, the focus of our search has been *narrowed*. Not *changed*. Even more important, when mentioning Jordan and Tooker, avoid the word 'innocent.' There are many ways to be guilty of murder. Pulling a trigger is only one of them."

The sheriff was moistening his lips. "I do admire your way with words, Dell."

Kline looked uneasy. "Do we know anything more about this third man?"

"Our source is working on that."

"Are they willing to get on the stand, if it comes to that?"

"One step at a time, Sheridan. Right now, the priority is information. And so far the information from this source has been pure gold. If I mentioned testifying publicly, it would evaporate."

Kline didn't seem surprised by the answer.

"One more point regarding the Willard Park incident," said Beckert. "It's important to avoid incendiary phrases. Let's agree right now on the proper wording. These two individuals were *found dead, details to be determined by autopsy*. Do not refer to them as having been *beaten to death*."

Frown lines creased the mayor's fleshy face. "But if that's what happened . . . ?"

Beckert explained patiently. "*Found dead* is neutral. *Beaten to death* is emotionally charged in a way that could exacerbate the situation on the street. We can't prevent the media from using the term, but we should definitely not encourage it."

Some puzzlement lingered in the mayor's expression, and Beckert went on. "It's the *description* of an event that the public actually absorbs, the images and emotions conveyed by the words, not the event itself. Words matter."

"You're talking about spin?"

Beckert frowned. "That term minimizes its importance. Spin isn't the *icing* on the cake. It's the *cake*. Messaging is everything. It's politics, Dwayne. And politics is no small thing."

Shucker nodded with the dawning grin of a man seeing the light.

Beckert turned toward Torres. "Okay, bring us up to date."

"Yes, sir. At seven ten this morning our 911 center received a call from a local citizen walking his dog—reporting the discovery of two bodies in Willard Park. The 911 center contacted White River PD, and mobile patrol officers were dispatched to the location. First officer on the scene conducted a prelim interview with the caller, observed and confirmed the facts, secured the site, and reported to the duty sergeant, who notified Deputy Chief Turlock, who notified me. Upon arrival, I contacted our evidence unit, the ME's office, and the photographer who—"

Kline interrupted. "You checked the bodies for signs of life?"

"Yes, sir, as part of my initial observations. As additional mobile patrol units arrived I enlisted their support in taping the scene perimeter. When the evidence officer arrived, I assigned three patrol officers to assist him in a wide-area cross-grid search. I ordered the remaining patrol units to close off vehicular and pedestrian access to the vicinity."

The mayor looked worried. "How big a vicinity?"

"About fifty acres in the no-go zone, but the evidence search is currently concentrated in two or three acres."

"How about the media vultures?"

"They're subject to the same no-go zone as the general public."

"I hate them bastards."

"They can be difficult, but we're keeping them at bay."

That got Gurney's attention. "They showed up at the site this morning?"

"Yes, sir. First thing. As we were setting up our perimeter tapes."

"Your initial communication regarding the incident—it occurred by phone or radio?"

"By phone, sir."

"Interesting."

Beckert's gaze rested on Gurney for a moment before he turned back to Torres. "Let's move on to your crime-scene assessment."

"Yes, sir. It will be clearer if I begin with the photographs and video I just received from Paul Aziz."

The sheriff raised his head like a hound catching a scent. "*Azeeez?* I thought Scotty Maclinter did our forensic photos."

"That's correct, sir, but he suffered an injury last night at the VFW. He's in the hospital."

"What kinda injury?"

"He fell down the stairs on his way to the men's room."

"Hah. I do believe the boy's done that before. Be advisable in future for him to pee in the parking lot. Meantime, who's this *Aziz*?"

"One of our dispatchers, who also happens to be a professional photographer. He filled in for Officer Maclinter once before. Excellent work."

"Hell kinda name's *Aziz*?"

"I'm not sure, sir. Possibly Jordanian or Syrian?"

"Well, ain't that somethin'? Seems like our country's gettin' more and more of them kind of people."

Gurney was taken aback by Cloutz's obnoxious tone and depressed by the thought that it was probably a key part of what got him elected.

Torres, after an unpleasant glance in Cloutz's direction, returned to his presentation. "Paul provided us with more than we need for the purpose of documenting the crime scene, but his video coverage of possible approach and departure paths from the location of the bodies could be useful. And it shows the visual limitations of the weather conditions."

Kline frowned. "What limitations?"

"Fog. Began around midnight. Didn't clear up till around ten this morning. You can see for yourself in this opening segment of the video." Torres tapped a computer key and pointed to the monitor on the wall.

At first, all that was visible was the fog itself, a formless gray mass that seemed to be moving in slow motion past the camera. As the dark branches of nearby trees began to emerge from the murky background on both sides of the screen, it became evident that the camera operator was proceeding along a heavily wooded trail. Gurney thought he could hear footsteps and the sound of someone breathing. As he leaned forward to listen more carefully, he was startled by a sudden high-pitched shriek.

"Jesus!" said Kline. "What the hell . . ."

"Blackbirds," said Torres. "Paul was recording audio along with the video."

"Damn things," said the sheriff. "On that twisty little trail that touches the south corner of the lake, am I right?"

The mayor frowned. "How'd you know that?"

"I'm blind, I ain't deaf. Fact I hear better'n most. The wife takes me for walks on that trail sometimes, knowin' I hate the screamin' of them damn birds. I been tryin' to get Clifford Merganthaller to exterminate them in pursuit of peace and quiet. For an animal control officer, he's woefully unwillin' to exert any control at all. Boy's 'bout as useless as them damn birds that don't do nothin' but scream and shit."

The mayor leaned forward. "Glory be to God, you can hear them shit?"

"Don't need to *hear* 'em doin' what I *know* they're doin'. Every livin' bein' shits. Some of 'em a hell of a lot more 'n others." The antic observation had a nasty undertone.

Beckert glanced at Torres. "Let's move this along."

"We're coming up to the place where the trail comes out into the clearing."

The shrieks of the birds on the audio track were growing more insistent.

Out of the dark constriction of the trail, the screen now displayed an open area where the fog had thinned enough for Gurney to make out a wide expanse of lakeside reeds and a shedlike building. As the camera moved forward he was able to read a sign on the building listing hourly rates for kayak rentals.

The black form of a bird swooped through the camera's field of view.

As the camera moved on, the ghostlike shapes of playground equipment began to come into view—a tall slide, a pair of seesaws, the angled braces of a swing set, and finally the geometrical structure of a large jungle gym.

Gurney could feel his chest tightening in anticipation of what he was about to see. No matter how many times he'd come upon it in his career, the sight of violent death always jarred him.

This time was no exception.

As the camera panned slowly across the front of the jungle gym, the bodies of the two victims were gradually revealed. They were tied to the structure in standing positions, side by side—secured in place by ropes around their legs, stomachs, and necks. Both men were African American. Both were stripped naked. Both bodies showed obvious signs of having been beaten. Their faces were swollen, their expressions grotesque. Between the feet of one there appeared to be a deposit of feces.

"Christ Almighty," murmured Shucker.

Kline's lips drew back in revulsion.

Turlock was gazing at the screen with icy detachment.

Beckert turned to Torres, who was looking sick. "Who has custody of this material?"

"Sir?"

"This video and whatever still shots were taken of the bodies—who has possession of the original digital files?"

"I do."

"In what form?"

"The memory chips from the cameras Paul used."

"Did he make copies?"

"I don't think so. He warned me not to lose the chips."

"If one frame of that leaks onto the internet, we'll have a race war on our hands."

"I'm aware of the risk, sir."

"We'll come back to that," said Beckert. "Let's move on to the details."

"Right." Torres took a deep breath and continued. "Our initial inspection of the victims revealed livor mortis. We left both bodies in situ, pending the ME's—"

Shucker interrupted him. "That the same as what they call *rigor* mortis?"

"No, sir. Rigor refers to the stiffening of the deceased's muscles, usually two or three hours after death. Livor mortis occurs sooner. It refers to the pooling of the blood in the lowest parts of the body, once the heart stops beating. In this case it was observable in their feet." He tapped a computer key several times, scrolling rapidly through a series of photos and stopping when the screen showed a close-up of the victims' legs from the knees down. The skin tone was brown except on the feet, where it was a dark purple. There were bruises on the shins and abrasions on the ankles.

Shucker's expression suggested he'd been given more information than he'd wanted.

Torres continued. "In a few minutes, we'll come back to some marks on the feet that could be very significant. But first we'll proceed in the normal order of our victim close-ups, starting at the head and working our way down."

Displaying photos of both men in a split-screen format as he spoke, he pointed out numerous contusions on their faces, torsos, and legs. His voice was tight with an apparent effort to control his distress—but the details of his commentary were vivid enough to provoke a response from the blind sheriff.

"It does sound like them boys truly got the shit beat out of them." To say his tone was uncaring would overestimate its warmth.

Torres stared at him. He tapped a key and brought up a final pair of photos on the split screen—closeup shots of the soles of the victims' feet.

Kline leaned forward. "Jesus, what on God's earth . . . ?"

Turlock gazed at the screen with no more reaction than a boulder.

A frown darkened Beckert's face—a cloud passing over Mount Rushmore.

The mayor looked confused and worried.

Burned deeply into the sole of each victim's left foot were three capital letters, a grotesque monogram. It brought to Gurney's mind an image from an old Western—red-hot letters on the end of a branding iron, smoking and hissing into the side of a steer.

KRS

16

The sheriff broke the fraught silence. "The hell y'all gone quiet for?"

Torres described the photo.

"Shit," muttered the sheriff.

Shucker looked around the table. "KRS? What the hell's that, somebody's initials?"

"Could be," said Beckert.

Gurney was pretty sure it was something else. He knew from experience that initials left at murder scenes generally stood for an organization the killer considered himself part of or for a title he'd given himself.

"KRS brings to mind KKK," said the sheriff. "If this damn thing gets pegged as a white-supremacist hate crime, we'll get overrun by the feds, which is unpleasant to contemplate. You got any thoughts on that, Dell?"

"I'm sure we can postpone FBI intrusion for a while. After all, this could be a personal revenge killing rather a racial act—a tricky argument to make, I know, but it could serve our purposes."

"BDA agitators'll be screamin' for federal intervention."

"No doubt. To keep control of the process, we need to—number one—craft the right public message. And—number two—demonstrate rapid progress toward an arrest. Those are both achievable objectives—so long as we adhere to procedures, manage our communications carefully, and avoid stupid mistakes."

Shucker looked miserable. "I just hope to God we don't start hearing on TV that White River's got Ku Kluxers running around killing people in public parks. The tourist-dependent members of the Chamber would go—"

Shucker's worry was cut off by three loud raps at the conference room door. Before anyone could respond, it was thrust open and the lanky medical examiner strode in and hefted his fat briefcase onto the chair next to Kline's.

"Hate being late, gentlemen, but there's been more autopsies in the past three days than in three normal months."

Beckert told him to proceed.

Thrasher removed a sheet of paper from his briefcase, perused it for a few seconds, and put it back. He pushed his horn-rimmed glasses higher on the bridge of his nose and surveyed the group around the table. His gaze hesitated for only a moment at Gurney before he launched into a summary of his findings.

"Both victims suffered death by asphyxiation, consistent with strangulation. Multiple contusions on face, torso, arms, and legs are consistent with a methodical assault, utilizing at least two distinct club-like instruments."

Torres asked, "Like baseball bats?"

"One of them, possibly. There were also contusions caused by something the approximate diameter of a police nightstick."

"So," Kline mused, "at least two assailants."

Thrasher nodded. "A reasonable inference."

Torres looked uncomfortable. "You say one of them used a nightstick?"

"Or something similar. Typical nightsticks have circular grooves at one or both ends to improve the wielder's grip. Welts across the lower back of the victims display patterns consistent with grooves."

The sheriff spoke up. "Anyone can get anything these days on the internet. So I hope we ain't assumin' the presence of a nightstick implies the presence of a police officer."

Beckert nodded. "There are people who'd gladly leap to that conclusion, so we'll stick to the word 'club' rather than 'nightstick' in any press statements."

Thrasher continued. "Interestingly, the injuries show a remarkable similarity in the number and placement of the blows to the two bodies."

Kline looked puzzled. "Similarity?"

"In my experience as an emergency room physician and as a pathologist, I've examined hundreds of victims of assaults. Such injuries tend to be of a more random nature—random in placement and in force."

Torres looked as puzzled as Kline. "What are you getting at?"

"These blows were not delivered in the heat of passion characteristic of assaults in general. Their similar distribution on each body, the similar force with which they were delivered, and their similar number—twenty-one distinct contusions on Tooker, twenty-two on Jordan—are consistent with a methodical approach."

"Designed to achieve what?"

"That's what you gentlemen are paid to figure out. I merely observe and report."

Kline asked if he'd noted any other oddities.

"Well, naturally the burn marks on the feet. They're consistent with the application of a custom-made branding iron—like a hobbyist's wood-burning instrument. An unusual element in itself, even without the additional peculiarity."

"What peculiarity?"

"The burned-in letters have perfectly sharp borders."

"Meaning what?"

"During the application of the red-hot iron the feet remained perfectly motionless."

Torres spoke up. "I saw ligature marks on the ankles, meaning they were tied together. Also, one of the assailants could have been holding them down. Wouldn't that account for it?"

"Not completely. The application of the hot iron to a sensitive area of the foot would have produced a spasm, creating observable blurring at the border of the impression."

"So that means what? That they were unconscious?"

"Almost certainly. Yet none of the cranial injuries appear to be sufficient to cause loss of consciousness."

"So they were drugged?"

"Yes. To the point of zero physical sensation. Something to think about."

Beckert nodded thoughtfully. "When you think about that—the difficulties that would pose, the possible motives—what comes to mind?"

"That question moves beyond medical facts into the area of criminal hypothesizing—your specialty, not mine. I wish you the best of luck." He picked up his briefcase and headed for the door. "My office will forward you the initial autopsy report later this afternoon. The simple opiate screens were negative, by the way. Alcohol screens were above the legal limit for driving, but hardly consistent with anesthesia. Full tox screens will be available in another day or two."

After Thrasher's parting comment the mayor spoke up. "What the hell was he getting at—that business about the beating they got not being normal?"

The sheriff was the first to respond. "He implied it was done with a high degree of plannin' and purpose."

"What kinda purpose?"

"Sounded a little like he didn't know, and a lot like he didn't want to say."

Beckert addressed the table in general. "Our ME has a habit of making dramatic entrances, stirring the pot, and dashing off. We'll stick to his professional observations, evaluate them in the light of all the other evidence, and form our own conclusions." He turned to Torres. "Let's take a look at what you discovered at the crime scene."

Torres tapped a couple of computer keys, resuming his description of the evidence photos as they appeared. "These are the ropes that were used to tie the victims to the crossbars of the jungle gym. We preserved the knots and the rope-end cuts for eventual matching if we can find the source."

"How come you saved the knots?" Shucker asked.

"They would have been handled the most, so they'd be most likely to have retained abraded skin cells." He went on to the next photo. "We found these tire tracks approaching the jungle gym structure and stopping in front of it . . . and we found these similar tracks on one of the trails in the adjacent woods. The forensics team—"

Kline interrupted. "Have you determined the type of vehicle?"

"We believe it was a full-size UTV, something like a Kawasaki Mule. Forensics is looking to match the tread pattern and width to a specific model and year. Actually, we had a piece of luck with those tires. They dropped some compacted soil on the ground near the swing set, soil that had been trapped in the tread grooves. And it doesn't appear to be native to that part of the park."

Gurney smiled. "Nice, Mark. A possible link to the primary crime scene."

The mayor looked bewildered. "What primary crime scene?"

"The location where Jordan and Tooker were drugged, stripped, beaten, and branded," explained Gurney. "Because that earlier site would be where most of the violence took place, it would be the most promising site for recovering physical evidence." He turned to Torres. "If I were you, I'd have that tread soil analyzed. There may be something distinctive about it."

The sheriff cleared his throat. "Assumin' it ain't horseshit."

Torres blinked. "Sir?"

"Folks ride horses on them trails."

Torres continued, "We found several items in the immediate area that may be related to the incident. Human hairs, a lottery ticket, two cigarette butts, a flashlight battery, and an item of special interest—a used condom. It was discovered in a grassy area about a hundred feet from the bodies, partly sheltered by a row of bushes. It didn't look like it had been there very long."

"And you're thinking whoever left it there might be a witness?" asked Kline.

"It's a possibility, sir. We rushed it to Albany. We might get a hit on CODIS and get an ID. It's a long shot, but . . ."

Beckert nodded. "Anything more to show us?"

"Some satellite views of the area to identify possible site entry and exit routes. Judging from the leaves partly off the trees, the photos were probably taken last autumn."

Centered on the jungle gym, the first photo encompassed the immediate area of the crime scene—the kayak rental building, the reedy shore of the lake, some of the surrounding trees. Torres pointed out the locations of the tire tracks.

The next two photos showed more of the park and more of the wooded areas. The final shot showed the entire park, bordered on three sides by city streets and on the fourth by an extensive wilderness area into which some of the park's trails extended.

A couple of miles into that wilderness area another lake was visible. Along its shore were a number of small clearings. Torres explained that the White River Gun Club owned the lake and the land around it, and in the clearings there were cabins owned by club members. "Mostly White River cops, as far as I know," he added. He glanced at Beckert and Turlock as if for confirmation, but neither man responded.

"The dog walker who discovered the bodies," said Kline, "where did he come from?"

Torres got up, went over to the screen, and traced the route as he was describing it. "He came into the park through the entrance on the east side, crossed the main field, passed the statue of Colonel Willard, and headed down toward the lake. Because of the fog this morning, he got within about fifty feet of the bodies before he realized what he was looking at. Was still a nervous wreck when we arrived."

Beckert pointed at the screen. "That large field he crossed, the one taking up the northeast quadrant of the park—that's where the BDA demonstration was held and where our officer was shot. I don't think it's just a coincidence that Jordan and Tooker were executed in that same park. Clearly a symbolic action. Which re-inforces the importance of our maintaining control of the narrative. It's vital that any new piece of evidence, information, rumor—anything at all with any bearing on any of the three killings—be reported at once to Judd or to me directly."

Evidently satisfied that silence meant agreement, Beckert moved on. "Given the pressures of dealing with two explosive crimes—and the need to make rapid progress on both fronts at once—I'm dividing the investigative duties. Detective Torres, your primary responsibility will be the Steele sniper shooting. With our first two suspects out of the picture, your focus will be identifying and locating the third man—the actual shooter."

Gurney was struck by the insinuation in Beckert's choice of words—how the third man being the "actual" shooter subtly maintained, in some non-trigger-pulling capacity, the involvement of Jordan and Tooker.

Beckert went on, "Because of its complex public relations dimensions, I'll assume personal responsibility for the investigation into these playground homicides. The case file, incident report, site sketches, and photos should be turned over to me as soon as we're finished here. Including the memory chips from Paul Aziz's cameras. Understood?"

Torres looked puzzled by the shift in responsibility. "Yes, sir."

"Then that's all for now. Except for one thing." He looked at Gurney. "The phone. Is Steele's wife going to hand it over voluntarily or not?"

"We'll see. I left a message for her."

"She has until tomorrow morning. Either she hands it over by then, or we visit her with a warrant and take it. Questions, anyone? No? Good. We'll meet here tomorrow the same time."

He placed his hands on the table, pushed back his chair, and stood up decisively—the very image of determination. Behind him, the picture window displayed its panorama of stone buildings with spirals of razor wire gleaming in the afternoon sun.

17

When Gurney came out into the police headquarters parking lot and headed for his Outback, he saw Kline standing next to it, taking a deep drag on a cigarette. He exhaled slowly, the hand holding the cigarette moving in a wide arc down to his side.

Déjà vu—a disturbing decades-old image of Gurney's mother. Her bursts of nervous chain-smoking. The desperate pursuit of peace revealing a terrible anxiety.

When Kline saw Gurney approaching, he took a final drag, threw the butt to the ground, and stepped on it as if it were a wasp that had just stung him.

There was a briefcase at his feet. He reached down and pulled a large manila envelope out of it. "Everything you asked for yesterday. Full copy of the Steele case file. Incident and interview reports, crime-scene photos and sketches, ballistics report. Plus Jordan's and Tooker's past arrests and your temporary credentials—special senior investigator, office of the district attorney." He handed the envelope to Gurney.

"Anything on the so-called third man?"

"If there's anything on that, Beckert's keeping it to himself."

"Like the identities of his informants?"

"Right." He took out another cigarette, hurriedly lit it, and took a particularly long drag before continuing. "So . . . what are your observations so far?"

"You look like an extremely worried man."

Kline said nothing.

That in itself said something.

Gurney decided to push further. "The obvious interpretation of the message on Steele's phone is that someone in the department might take advantage of the chaos in the streets to get rid of him. If that someone turned out to be Turlock, or even Beckert—"

"Jesus!" Kline raised his hand. "You have any evidence for what you're saying?"

"None. But I don't have any evidence that points to a third man from the BDA either."

"What about these two new homicides? You have any thoughts?"

"Only that they may not be what they seem to be."

"What makes you think that?"

"Thrasher's comments about the damage to the bodies."

Kline was looking increasingly miserable. "If they aren't what they seem to be, what the hell are they?"

"I need time to think about that."

"While you're thinking about Steele?"

"I guess."

"So which case is your priority?"

"The Steele shooting."

"Why?"

"Because it came first, and something in it may explain the odd aspects of the other."

Kline frowned, evidently trying to digest this. Then he pointed to the manila envelope in Gurney's hand. "Let me know if anything in the case file pops out at you. You have my personal cell number. Call me anytime. Day or night."

Away from the depressing environs of White River, the countryside had a bucolic timelessness, displaying the glories of early May. Black Angus cows dotted the hillsides. Apple trees were in blossom. The black earth of freshly tilled cornfields alternated with fields of emerald grass and buttercups. Only dimly aware of the beauty around him, Gurney spent the drive home pondering the strange facts of both cases. Despite his decision to focus on the sniper attack, he found it difficult to keep Thrasher's comments about the beatings and brandings from intruding into his thoughts.

As he arrived at the narrow road that led to his hilltop property, his attention switched to a more pressing issue. Having told Madeleine that he'd sleep on the question of whether to continue his involvement with Kline, he felt the need to make a decision. On the one hand, there was the growing challenge of the situation itself and the accelerating pressure to avert an escalation of violence. Daunting as that sounded, it was the kind of challenge he was built for. On the other hand, there was his discomfort with the district attorney himself.

He felt as if he were locked in a loop of indecision. Each time he was about to conclude that the importance of the case might outweigh the risk of trusting Kline, the memory of Madeleine's question intervened. *My God, David, on what planet would that be considered a* good *idea?*

As he was parking by the side door of the old farmhouse, still wrestling with his dilemma, his phone rang.

"Gurney here."

"Thanks for picking up. It's Mark Torres. Do you have a minute?"

"What can I do for you?"

"I'm calling about the photos Paul Aziz took at Willard Park. I was wondering if you might want to see them."

"The photos you showed at the meeting today?"

"I just showed the ones I thought were most important. Paul took over two hundred shots. Before I turned the camera chips over to Chief Beckert, I downloaded everything to my laptop."

"And you want me to have all that?"

"As you know, I've been taken off the Jordan-Tooker case to concentrate on the Steele shooting. But I figured you'd still have an interest in both cases and the photos might be helpful to you."

"You don't think Beckert will share them with me?"

Torres hesitated. "I couldn't say."

Gurney wondered if Torres was suffering from the same distrust of the WRPD brass that seemed to have infected Kline. In any event, it wouldn't hurt to take a look at Aziz's photos. "How do you want to get them to me?"

"Through a file-sharing service. As soon as I get it set up, I'll email you."

Viewing this minor involvement with the photos as a separate matter from any decision about his overall commitment, Gurney thanked Torres and said he'd watch for the email. He ended the call, got out of the car, and went into the house.

According to the old regulator clock on the kitchen wall, it was a minute past five. He called Madeleine's name. There was no response. He knew it wasn't one of her workdays at the clinic; and if she'd been called in, she'd have left a note for him on the door.

He went back outside and checked the areas where she enjoyed busying herself—the garden beds, the asparagus patch, and the prefab greenhouse they'd erected earlier that spring to get a head start on the short upstate growing season.

He called her name again. He went around to the rear of the house, looking across the high pasture to the edge of the encircling forest. The only living creatures he saw were the distant vultures riding the updrafts over the ridge.

He decided to go back inside and call her cell phone. But just then he caught sight of her, making her way up through the low pasture from the direction of the pond. He noted something different about the way she was walking, something less spirited than usual in her step. When she came closer he could see that her expression was almost grim. And when she was closer still, he could see in her eyes the signs of recent tears.

"What is it?" he asked.

She looked around uncertainly until her eyes came to rest on the pair of Adirondack chairs facing each other in the middle of the stone patio. "Can we sit out here for a while?"

"Sure. Is something wrong?"

When they were both seated, their knees almost touching, she closed her eyes for a long moment, as though trying to arrange her thoughts.

"Maddie? Did something happen?"

"Kim Steele was here."

"What did she want?"

"She brought her husband's cell phone."

"She left it with you?"

"Yes."

He waited for her to go on, but she didn't. "Her visit was . . . upsetting?"

"Yes."

"Because of what happened to her husband?"

"Because of the kind of person he was." She swallowed. "He was like you."

"And you're thinking . . . what happened to him could have happened to me?"

"Yes." After a few moments she continued. "The way she described him . . . was exactly how I would describe you. Believing that being a cop was a good way of life, a way of being useful. Believing that doing what's right was the most important thing."

They sat there for a long while in silence.

"There's something else," she said, wiping away a tear. "They lost a child."

He felt a chill rising into his chest.

"An infant. A car accident."

"Jesus."

"They're us, David, twenty years ago. The only difference is that you're alive, and her husband isn't."

Looking into her eyes, he could see that the power of her identification with another woman's pain had upended yesterday's reality.

"I didn't want you getting into this thing, getting tangled up with Sheridan Kline. But now, I can't help thinking that if this had happened to you . . ."

"You would have wanted someone to do something about it."

"Yes. Someone good and honest and determined enough to get to the bottom of it." She paused, then added emphatically, "Yes. I would have wanted that."

18

The shift in Madeleine's view had a profound effect on Gurney. Her change of heart felt to him like a kind of liberation. What was clear to her was now clear to him. His job was simply to solve the murder of Kim Steele's husband.

The rest—Kline's shadowy motives for pulling him in, the putative political connections and ambitions of Dell Beckert, White River's potential race war—were important but secondary issues. They would become relevant only if they helped explain the death of John Steele.

After dinner, Gurney retreated to the den with the case file Kline had given him in the parking lot and the cell phone Kim had left with Madeleine. The first thing he did—after checking for the phone's call records and text chains and discovering they'd all been deleted except for the final warning—was to call the district attorney's personal number.

Kline picked up immediately, his voice anxious. "Yes?"

"I have Steele's cell phone."

"His wife gave it to you?"

"Yes."

"Did you . . . find anything in it? Anything relevant?"

"Nothing but the last message."

"How quickly can you get the phone to me?"

Gurney was struck by the wording of Kline's question, the *me* in particular. He wondered if the intention was as exclusive as it sounded. "I could bring it to tomorrow's team meeting. Beckert seemed eager for it."

When Kline responded with silence, he went on. "Or, since time is a critical factor, you might want to send one of your people to my house for it, and they could drive it directly to computer forensics in Albany. And in the meantime you could get a warrant for the service provider's call records."

"Hmm ... so ... you're suggesting that in the interest of saving time we bypass White River PD and go directly to the state lab?"

Gurney almost laughed out loud. Instinctive ass-coverer that he was, Kline was making it clear that this route, which he obviously preferred, was Gurney's suggestion.

"It would be a reasonable way to proceed," said Gurney.

"You're probably right. Considering the importance of the time factor. Okay. I'll have a car at your house tomorrow morning at seven sharp."

The conversation confirmed for Gurney that the man was uneasy enough with Beckert, or someone else in the department, to keep the phone out of their hands until there was an objective record of whatever information could be extracted from it.

He turned his attention to the manila envelope, pulled out the case file, and spread out its contents on the den desk. He saw the standard items—the incident report, witness statements, site photos and sketches, early progress reports, various updates and addenda—none of which at first glance were especially helpful or surprising. There was also a DVD. It was labeled RAM-CAM VIDEO, WILLARD PARK, STEELE HOMICIDE. He pushed aside the other items and inserted it in his laptop's external drive.

The video was as he remembered it from the big-screen TV at the Gelters' party and again at the first CSMT meeting. Presumably excerpted from a longer recording, the segment began about three minutes prior to the shot and continued for about two minutes after it. During this viewing, Gurney timed the appearance of the red laser dot on the back of Steele's head, confirming his initial estimate that it preceded the fatal shot by just over two minutes. The precision with which the dot followed Steele's movements confirmed his impression that the rifle that fired the shot was mounted on a tripod, possibly one with a motion-dampening mechanism of the kind used in filmmaking.

He watched the video three times. On the third viewing he noted an oddity that hadn't struck him before. When Steele was shot he was moving to a new position on the sidewalk. But for nearly twenty seconds leading up to that he'd been standing still. Why had the shooter bypassed that easy opportunity in favor of a riskier moving target?

He continued going through the file until he came to a computer printout labeled "Potential Shooter Sites Defined by Bullet Trajectory Parameters." The printout displayed a narrow, triangular outline overlaid on a map of White River. The tip of the triangle touched the spot at the edge of the park where Steele was shot. The outline extended out from that point approximately a quarter of a mile across the center of the city—enclosing the likely area from which the shot had come, based on the calculated trajectory.

Although there was no indication in the file what was being done with this diagram, it was obvious to Gurney that the next step would be to narrow the possibilities by going to the spot where Steele was standing at the moment of impact and with binoculars survey the area contained within the triangle to find the clear lines of sight to windows, rooftops, and open areas not obscured by other structures. Since the target had to be visible to the sniper, the sniper's location would have to be visible from the target's location. Taking this simple step would dramatically limit the areas that needed to be searched.

He was tempted to call Mark Torres and make sure this was happening. But something told him not to interfere. The sniper's location would soon be identified and turned over to the crime-scene team with their cameras, vacuums, evidence bags, and fingerprint kits. In the interim there was plenty for him to do that didn't involve stepping on other people's toes.

Another face-to-face conversation with Kim Steele, for example, might be a more productive use of his time. During her visit earlier that day Kim had given Madeleine her address, email, and phone number.

He picked up his phone and entered Kim's number.

"Yes?" Her voice was leaden.

"Kim, this is Dave Gurney."

"Yes?"

"I have a meeting in White River tomorrow. I was wondering if I could stop by on my way and talk to you."

"Tomorrow?"

"It would be sometime in the morning. Is that all right?"

"It's all right. I'm here."

He wondered whether her monotone responses were coming from the exhaustion of grief or an emotion-deadening medication. "Thank you, Kim. I'll see you tomorrow morning."

That night, for the first time in more than a year, he had *the dream*—a dreadful, disjointed replaying of the accident, long ago, that killed his four-year-old son.

On their way to the playground on a sunny day.

Danny walking in front of him.

Following a pigeon on the sidewalk.

He himself only partly present.

Pondering a twist in a murder case he was working on.

Distracted by a bright idea, a possible solution.

The pigeon stepping off the curb into the street.

Danny following the pigeon.

The sickening, heart-stopping thump.

Danny's body tossed through the air, hitting the pavement, rolling.

Rolling.

The red BMW racing away.

Screeching around a corner.

Gone.

Gurney awoke in an agony of grief. In the gray light of dawn. Madeleine holding his hand. She knew about the dream. He'd been having it, on and off, for nearly twenty years.

When the lingering images had subsided and the worst of the feeling had passed, he got up, took a shower, and dressed.

At 7:00 AM Kline's man arrived as promised, accepted Steele's cell phone, and departed with hardly a word.

At 7:45 AM Geraldine Mirkle arrived to pick up Madeleine for one of their same-schedule days at the clinic.

At 8:30 AM Gurney left for his meeting with Kim Steele.

His GPS directed him off the interstate at the Larvaton-Badminton exit onto Fishers Road heading north toward Angina. A few miles later it directed him onto Dry Brook Lane, a gravelly road that rose in a series of S curves through an old hardwood forest. At a driveway marked by a brightly painted mailbox, his GPS announced he had reached his destination. The driveway brought him into a clearing, at the center of which stood a small farmhouse surrounded by flower beds and lush spring grass. A red barn with a metal roof stood at the edge of the clearing. Kim Steele's small white car was parked by the house, and he parked next to it.

He knocked on the side door and waited. He knocked again. After a third attempt he went around to the back door, with the same result. While he was puzzling over the situation, he looked out over the back field toward the barn and noticed a riding mower next to the barn door.

As he headed across the field, Kim Steele emerged from the barn toting a large red gas can. She carried it to the mower and was in the process of opening the gas tank when she saw him. She watched him approaching, then returned to her task, hefting the can into position and wrestling its stiff spout into the tank opening. She spoke without looking up.

"Things have to get done."

"Can I help?"

She seemed not to hear him. Appearing marginally more organized than the last time he'd seen her, she was wearing the same shirt, but the buttons were now aligned. Her hair seemed neater, shinier.

"They called him in on his day off," she said, trying to balance the big can over the tank. "He wanted to mow this field. He said it was important to mow it at least once a week. Or the grass would clog the mower. Once it gets clogged . . ."

"Let me help you with that." He reached for the can.

"No! This is my job."

"Okay." He paused. "You were saying they called him in?"

She nodded.

"Because of the demonstration?"

"They were calling everyone in."

"Did he say who in the department called him?"

She shook her head.

"Do you remember if there were any other calls for him that day?"

"The day he was *killed*?" It wasn't a question so much as a burst of anger.

He paused again. "I know it's horrible to think about this—"

She cut him off. "It's all I think about. There's nothing else I *can* think about. So ask whatever you want."

He nodded. "I'm just wondering if John got any other calls that day, other than the message you found on his phone."

"Shit!"

The mower's gas tank was overflowing. She yanked the can away and dropped it on the ground. She appeared close to tears.

The situation touched him in a way that made it difficult for him to speak.

The strong odor of the fuel filled the still air.

"That overflowing-gas thing happens to me all the time," he said awkwardly.

She said nothing.

"Can I mow the field for you?"

"What?"

"I spend a lot of time mowing at home. I enjoy it. It would be one less thing for you to have to do. I'd be happy to do it."

She looked at him, blinking as if to clear her vision. "That's kind of you. But I have to do these things myself."

A silence fell between them.

He asked, "Have John's friends from the department been coming by to see you?"

"Some people came. I told them to go away."

"You didn't want them here?"

"I can't bear to even look at them until I know what happened."

"You don't trust anyone in the department?"

"No. Only Rick Loomis."

"He's different from the others?"

"Rick and John were friends. Allies."

"*Allies* suggests they had enemies."

"Yes. They had enemies."

"Do you know the names of their enemies?"

"I wish to God I did. But John didn't believe in bringing the ugly details of his work home. I'm sure he thought he was making my life easier by keeping things to himself."

"Do you know if Rick Loomis shared your husband's suspicions about things that were going on in the department?"

"I think so."

"Was he helping him look into old cases?"

"They were working on something together. I know I sound hopelessly vague." She sighed, picked up the gas tank cap, and screwed it back on. "If you'd like to come in for a while, I could make some coffee."

"I'd like that. And I'd like to hear more about your husband—anything you want to tell me. I'd like to understand who he was." As soon as he said it, he could see in her eyes the impact of that past tense verb, *was*. He wished he'd found another way of saying it.

She nodded, wiped her hands on her jeans, and led the way across the field to the house.

The back door opened into a narrow hallway that led to an eat-in kitchen. There was a broken dish on the floor by the sink. The khaki jacket she'd worn on her first trip to Gurney's house was lying across the seat of a chair. The table was covered with a disordered pile of papers. She looked around in dismay. "I didn't realize . . . what a mess. Let me just . . ." Her voice trailed off.

She gathered the papers together and took them into the next room. She returned, got the jacket, and took that away. She seemed not to notice the broken dish. She gestured toward one of the chairs at the table, and Gurney sat down. Distractedly, she went through the steps of setting up the coffee machine.

While the coffee was brewing, she stood gazing out the window. When it was ready, she poured a mug and brought it to the table.

She sat down across from him and smiled in a way that he found almost unbearably sad. "What do you want to know about John?" she asked.

"What was important to him. His ambitions. How he ended up in the WRPD. When he started getting uncomfortable with it. Any hints of trouble, prior to the text message, that could relate to what happened."

She gave him a long, thoughtful look. "Interesting questions."

"In what way?"

"They have nothing to do with the WRPD theory that the attack was a political act by black radicals."

He smiled at her perceptiveness. "The WRPD theory is being pursued by WRPD people. There's no point my heading down the same avenue."

"You mean the same dead end?"

"Too soon to say." He sipped his coffee. "Tell me about John."

"He was the nicest, smartest man in the world. We met in college. Ithaca. John was a psych major. Very serious. Very handsome. We got married right after graduation. He'd already taken the state police exam, and a few months later he was inducted. I was pregnant by then. Everything seemed to be going well. He graduated from the academy at the top of his class. Life was perfect. Then, a month after our baby was born, there was an automobile accident. She didn't survive." Kim fell silent, biting her lower lip and looking away toward the window. A few moments later she took a deep breath, sat up straight in her chair, and continued.

"He spent the next three years as a state trooper. He got a master's degree in criminology in his spare time. It was around that time that Dell Beckert was hired to clean up the White River Police Department. He made a big impression—forcing a lot of people out on corruption charges, bringing in fresh faces."

She paused. When she went on, something rueful, maybe even bitter, entered her voice. "The image Beckert projected—sweeping out the dirt, purifying the place—I think that struck a chord with John. So he moved from the NYSP to the supposedly wonderful new WRPD."

"When did he realize it might not be as perfect as he'd imagined?"

"It was a gradual thing. His attitude toward the job changed. I remember it getting darker a year ago with the Laxton Jones shooting. After that . . . there was a kind of tension in him that wasn't there before."

"How about recently?"

"It was getting worse."

Gurney took another sip of his coffee. "You said he'd gotten degrees in psychology and criminology?"

She nodded, almost smiled. "Yes. He loved his work and loved learning anything connected with it. In fact, he just started taking some law courses."

Gurney hesitated. "He was a basic patrol officer, right?"

There was a combative flash in her eyes. "You mean *just* a basic patrol officer? You're asking why he wasn't chasing promotions?"

He shrugged. "Most cops I've known who've pursued advanced degrees—"

She cut him off. "Pursued them because of career ambitions? The truth is, John has . . . *had* . . . enormous ambition. But not for promotions. He wanted to be out on the street. That's what he signed up for. The degrees, all the reading he did, it was to be as good at the job as he could be. His ambition was to lead an honest, useful, positive life. That's all he ever . . ."

She lowered her head slowly and began to sob.

Several minutes later, after that wave of grief had run its course, she sat back in her chair and wiped her eyes. "Do you have any more questions?"

"Do you know if he ever received threats or hints of trouble other than the text message?"

She shook her head.

"If something should come to mind—"

"I'll call you. I promise."

"Okay. One last thing. Do you think Rick Loomis would talk to me?"

"I'm sure he'll talk to you. But if you're asking how open he'll be about what he and John were working on, that I don't know."

"Would you be willing to call him, tell him who I am and that I'd appreciate sitting down with him?"

She cocked her head curiously. "You want me to tell him that he should trust you?"

"Just tell him whatever you're comfortable telling him. It's entirely up to you."

Her eyes met his, and for a moment he had the same feeling he had on the occasions when Madeleine's gaze seemed to be looking into his soul.

"Yes," she said. "I can do that."

19

Toward the end of Gurney's visit with Kim Steele, the vibrating mode on his phone had made him aware of receiving a call, but he'd let it go rather than interrupt the emotional flow of their conversation.

Now, on his way back to the interstate, he pulled over onto the grassy verge of Fishers Road and listened to the message. It was from Sheridan Kline. The man didn't bother to identify himself; his self-important, slightly nasal voice was identification enough.

"I hope you get this message soon. We have a schedule change. Our meeting has just been moved up to twelve noon. Major progress. Noon sharp. Be there!"

Gurney checked the current time—11:04.

He figured that without traffic he could be in White River by eleven thirty. Despite his earlier decision to avoid conflict with the WRPD by avoiding the crime scene, he was tempted now to do at least a drive-by—to get a visceral sense of the location he'd seen only on video.

As expected, there was no traffic. It was just 11:29 when he turned off the interstate. The White River exit ramp led to a local road that descended from a green landscape of woods and meadows into an area of man-made desolation. He drove past the big rusting conveyors of the defunct Handsome Brothers stone quarry and into the city itself, where the stench of smoke and ashes began to infiltrate the car.

Recalling from the White River map how the main streets were laid out, he made his way onto the avenue that skirted the boarded-up buildings of the Grinton section and led directly to Willard Park.

He turned onto the road adjacent to the park, and soon came to a barricade consisting of yellow sawhorses, each of which bore the warning Police Line Do Not Cross.

Leaving his car there and stepping between the sawhorses, he went ahead on foot to a circular area that was more aggressively cordoned off with a double perimeter of yellow police tape. The protected area encompassed the edge of the field where the demonstration had been held, an enormous pine whose lowest branches were a good twenty feet above the ground, and part of the sidewalk. On the sidewalk was a large, irregularly shaped reddish-brown stain.

Gurney was sure that the crime-scene specialists would have been long finished with their evidence gathering and that his presence posed no danger of contamination. When he entered the taped-off area, however, he did step gingerly around that stain as a gesture of respect.

Looking closely at the tree, he could see the remnants of the channel cut by the bullet as it embedded itself in the relatively soft pine trunk. Some of the channel had been chiseled open to extract the bullet.

He took a pen from his shirt pocket and placed it in the channel against the side that appeared intact. The pen, aligned with the path of the bullet, then became a rough pointer to the source of the shot. He could see immediately that it corroborated the trajectory projection on the map in the case file. Gazing out in the indicated direction, he could see that the likely sources were limited to the upper floors of three or four apartment buildings.

He headed back to the barricade where he'd parked, in the hope of finding the binoculars he sometimes kept in the glove compartment. That goal was put aside, however, when he saw a WRPD cruiser pull up at the same barricade. The cop who emerged from the cruiser had an end-of-shift weariness about him. After looking over the Outback, presumably for any signs of official status, he turned his attention to Gurney.

"How're we doing today, sir?" If the question was meant to sound friendly, it failed.

"I'm doing okay. How about you?"

The cop's eyes hardened as if Gurney's reply were a challenge.

"Are you aware that you're in a restricted area?"

"I'm on the job. Investigation department, DA's office."

"That so?"

Gurney said nothing.

"Never saw you before. You want to show me some ID?"

Gurney took out his wallet and handed him the credentials he'd gotten from Kline.

He regarded them with a skeptical frown. "DA's office? You know Jimmy Crandell?"

"Only person I know there is Sheridan Kline."

The cop sucked thoughtfully at his teeth.

"Well, the thing is, this is a restricted area, so I need to ask you to leave."

"The restriction applies to the DA's investigators?"

"PIACA applies to everyone."

"What's PIACA?"

"Primary Investigative Agency Controls Access."

"Nice acronym. Local invention?"

The cop began to redden from the neck up. "We're not having a discussion here. We have a procedure, and the procedure is you leave. Your DA can complain to my chief anytime, if that's what he wants. You want to cross our perimeters, you get permission first. Now move your car before I have it towed."

Red-faced and narrow-eyed, the cop watched as Gurney turned his car around and headed back toward the center of White River.

Five minutes later he arrived at the bleak, colorless police headquarters and parked next to Kline's big black SUV. As he was getting out of the car, his phone rang. There was no caller ID.

"Gurney here."

"This is Rick Loomis. Kim Steele said you wanted to talk. She gave me your number." The voice was young and serious, the accent definitely upstate.

"Did she explain who I am and how I'm involved in the case?"

"She did."

"And you're willing to discuss the . . . events . . . that you and John were looking into?"

"To some extent. But not on the phone."

"I understand. How soon can we get together?"

"I'm off today, but I need to take care of a few things. Getting the garden ready for planting. How about three thirty at the Lucky Larvaton Diner? It's in Angina. On the old Route Ten Bypass."

"I'll find it."

"Okay. See you at three thirty."

"Rick, one more thing. Is there anyone else I should be talking to . . . about the situation?"

He hesitated. "Maybe. But I'll have to check with them first."

"Okay. Thank you."

He slipped the phone back in his pocket and headed into the headquarters building.

In the dreary conference room, he took his customary seat next to the DA at the long table. He noted an intermittent buzz in the room's fluorescent light fixture—a sound so common in his old NYPD precinct house it made him feel for a moment that he was back there.

Kline gave him a nod. Torres entered the room with his laptop a moment later, looking tense but purposeful. At the end of the table, Sheriff Cloutz was moving his fingers in little undulations as though he were conducting a miniature orchestra. The expression in Beckert's hard eyes was difficult to read.

Two seats were empty, Judd Turlock's and Dwayne Shucker's.

The sheriff licked his already moist lips. "Must be about time to begin."

"We're missing the mayor and the deputy chief," said Kline.

"Today's Rotary day for old Shucks," said the sheriff. "Free lunch and a chance to talk up the importance of his reelection. We still expecting Judd?"

"We'll be hearing from him momentarily," said Beckert. He glanced at his phone on the table, moving it a fraction of an inch. "It's a minute past twelve. Let's begin. Detective Torres, tell us where we stand on the Steele shooting—progress made and progress anticipated."

Torres sat up a little straighter in his chair. "Yes, sir. Since our last meeting we've acquired significant physical and video evidence. We located and examined the apartment from which the shot was fired. We found gunpowder residues there, along with a cartridge casing consistent with the bullet extracted from the tree in Willard Park. We have excellent fingerprints on several objects, including the cartridge, plus likely DNA residues on other objects. We even—"

Cloutz broke in. "What kind of residues?"

"Mucus with a trace of blood in a tissue, a Band-Aid with a trace of blood on it, and several hairs with enough follicle material for analysis."

"That all?"

"We even recovered the tripod used to steady the rifle. We found it in the river by the Grinton Bridge, and there are clear fingerprints on it. We also have videos of a vehicle approaching the sniper site, parking behind the building shortly before the shot was fired, and leaving immediately afterward. We have additional video of the same vehicle heading for the bridge and then returning from it. Although the street lighting was poor, we were able to sharpen and read the plate number."

"You sayin' we have an ID on the shooter?"

"We have an ID on the car, a black 2007 Toyota Corolla, and the name and address on the registration—Devalon Jones of Thirty-Four Simone Street in Grinton."

Kline leaned forward. "Related to the Laxton Jones who was killed a year ago?"

"His brother. Devalon was one of the founding members of the BDA—along with Jordan, Tooker, and Blaze Lovely Jackson."

Kline grinned. "That does move the situation in an encouraging direction. Do we have this Devalon person in custody?"

"That's the problem, sir. He's been in custody for over a month now—in Dannemora, starting a three-to-five sentence for aggravated assault. Fractured a security guard's skull at an Indian casino up north."

Kline's grin faded. "So his car was being used by someone else. Maybe another BDA member? I assume you're checking that out?"

"We've started that process."

Beckert turned to the sheriff. "Goodson, if this Devalon Jones passed his car along, one of your more cooperative guests at the jail might know something about that. Meanwhile, I'll call the warden at Dannemora and see if Jones can be persuaded to part with the information himself."

Cloutz licked his lips again before speaking. "Someone could explain to Devalon that the registration bein' in his name makes him the presumptive provider of the vehicle to the shooter and accessory to the murder of a police officer. So he has an opportunity to use the free will with which his creator endowed him and give us the name, or . . . we can fry his ass." He began to move his fingers again, ever so slightly, to some imagined music.

Beckert turned to Torres, who was glaring at Cloutz. "You said we have street videos of the car approaching and leaving the sniper location. Can you show them now?" It was a directive, not a question.

Torres turned his attention back to his laptop, clicked a few icons, and the monitor on the wall showed a grungy, poorly lit street with garbage bags piled along the curbs. A car appeared, passed through the camera's field of view, and turned out of sight at the next intersection.

"This is Girder Street," said Torres. "The footage is from a security camera on the front of a check-cashing place. We've edited it down to a few key moments. Watch this next car."

A small, dark sedan entered the frame. Just before reaching the intersection, it made a turn into what appeared to be a driveway or alley behind an apartment building.

"That's the building where the shot came from. That alley leads to a back entrance. The time code embedded in the video shows that the car arrived twenty-two minutes before the shot was fired. Now we skip ahead twenty-six minutes, exactly four minutes after the shot, and … there … you see the car emerging … turning … proceeding to the intersection … and making a right onto Bridge Street."

The screen showed a wider but equally dismal street with steel-shuttered storefronts on both sides. "This segment comes from a CPSP installation colocated with the intersection traffic light." He glanced over at Gurney. "Crime Prevention Surveillance Program. That's an initiative we—"

He broke off his explanation and pointed at the screen. "Look … there … that's our target vehicle, driving west on Bridge Street. See … right there … it passes the Bridge Closed detour sign and keeps heading toward it."

Kline asked if that road led anywhere except to the bridge.

"No, sir. Just the bridge."

"Is it possible to drive onto it?"

"Yes, simply by moving the cones blocking it off. And they had, in fact, been moved."

"How about the other side? Could the vehicle have driven over the bridge to some other destination?"

"The stage of demolition would have made that impossible. We figured the most likely reason for driving out onto the span at that time of night would be to dump something in the river. And it turned out we were right. That's where we found the tripod used to steady the rifle."

He pointed to the screen. "There … the same vehicle … returning from the bridge."

Kline's smile returned. "Nice work, Detective."

Gurney cocked his head curiously. "Mark, how do you know what the tripod was used for?"

"The proof is in the photos we took at the apartment used by the shooter." He tapped a few keys, and the scene switched to a still photo of an apartment door with a security peephole. The apartment number, 5C, was scratched and faded. The next photo appeared to have been taken from the same position, looking into the apartment with the door open.

"The photos I really want to show you are a little farther on," said Torres, "but I didn't have time to change the sequence."

"Who let you in?" asked Gurney.

"The janitor."

Gurney recalled his own aborted investigation at the Willard Park site and the trajectory indicated by the bullet's penetration of the tree. That trajectory included multiple windows in three different buildings. "How did you zero in on one particular apartment?"

"We got a tip."

"By phone?"

"Text."

"Anonymous or from a known source?"

Beckert intervened. "We have a policy against discussing sources. Let's move along."

The next photo had been taken from inside the apartment door looking through a small foyer into a large unfurnished room. There was an open window on the far side of the room. In the next photo, taken from a position near the center of the room, the open window framed a view of the city. Beyond some low roofs, Gurney could see a grassy area bordered by tall pines. As he looked closer, he could just make out a yellow line—the police tape demarcating the area where he'd just had his confrontation with the local cop. It was clear that the apartment would offer a sniper an ideal perch from which to pick off anyone in the vicinity of the field where the demonstration had been held.

"Okay," said Torres with some excitement, "now we're getting to the key pieces of evidence."

The next photo, taken in the same room at floor level, showed the lower half of a steam radiator and the cramped space under it. In the radiator's shadow, back against the wall, Gurney noted the soft sheen of a brass cartridge casing.

"A thirty-aught-six," said Torres. "Same as the recovered bullet."

"With a clear print on it?" asked Kline.

"Two. Probably thumb and forefinger, the way you'd chamber it in a bolt-action rifle."

"Do we know it was a bolt-action?"

"That's the action in most thirty-aught-sixes manufactured in the past fifty years. We'll know for sure when ballistics takes a closer look at the extractor and ejector marks."

The next photo was of the wooden floor. Torres pointed out three faint marks on the dusty surface, each about the size of a dime, positioned about three feet from each other, the corners of an imaginary triangle.

"See those little impressions?" said Torres. "Their positions correspond exactly to the positions of the feet of the tripod we found in the river. The height of the tripod placed in that spot would have provided a direct line of fire to the impact location."

"You mean the back of John Steele's head?" said Gurney.

"Yes. That's correct."

Torres proceeded to the next photo—a small bathroom containing a shower stall, a dirty washbasin, and a toilet. That was followed by two close-ups—the chrome handle on the toilet tank, then the inside of the toilet bowl. A crumpled ball of colored paper and a discolored Band-Aid were submerged in the water.

"We got lucky here," said Torres. "We got a good thumbprint on the flush handle, and the items in the bowl not only have prints on them but even some DNA material. The paper is a fast-food wrapper with an oily surface that preserved three good prints. The Band-Aid has a trace amount of blood."

Kline was energized. "You've run the prints? Any hits?"

"Nothing at the local or state level. We're waiting on IAFIS. Washington has over a hundred million print records, so we're hopeful. Worst case is that the shooter has never been arrested, never been printed for any reason. But even then, once we zero in on the right guy, we've got overwhelming evidence tying him to the apartment, the casing, the tripod. And there's one more piece I haven't mentioned—a security camera out on Bridge Street recorded a side view of the shooter's vehicle, with a dark image of the driver visible through the side window. It's unreadable in its current condition, but the computer lab in Albany has some powerful enhancement software. So we're hopeful."

His statement was punctuated by the muted *bing* of a text arriving on Beckert's phone.

"A facial ID would be damn near game-over," said Kline.

Torres looked around the table. "Any questions?"

Beckert appeared preoccupied with the message on his phone.

The sheriff was smiling unpleasantly. "If our other inquiries ID the user of Devalon's vehicle, Albany's enhancement abracadabra could nail the boy to the wall. A photo is a beautiful thing. Very convincing to a jury."

"Mr. Kline?" said Torres.

"No questions at the moment."

"Detective Gurney?"

"Just wondering . . . how deep was the water?"

Torres looked puzzled. "In the toilet?"

"In the river."

"Where we found the tripod? Roughly three feet."

"Any prints on the window sash or sill?"

"Some very old and faded ones, nothing new."

"Apartment door?"

"Same."

"Bathroom door and basin faucets?"

"Same."

"Were you able to find anyone in the building who heard the shot?"

"We spoke to a couple of tenants who thought they might have heard something like a shot. They were pretty vague about it. It's not the kind of neighborhood where people talk to the police or want to admit being witnesses to anything." He turned up his palms in a gesture of resignation. "Any other questions?"

"Not from me. Thank you, Mark. Good work."

The young detective allowed himself a small look of satisfaction. He reminded Gurney of Kyle, his twenty-seven-year-old son from his first marriage. Which in turn reminded him that he owed him a call. Kyle had inherited his own tendency toward isolation, so their communications, though enjoyable when they occurred, were sporadic. He promised himself he'd make the call that day. Perhaps after dinner.

Beckert's voice brought him back to the present.

"This would be a good time to transition to our progress on the Jordan and Tooker homicides. We had a breakthrough this morning in that investigation, and we expect another development within the next half hour. So this would be a reasonable time to take a short break." He glanced at his phone. "We'll reconvene at twelve forty-five. In the meantime, please remain in the building. Goodson, do you need any assistance?"

"I do not." He ran the polished nail of his forefinger along the length of the white cane that lay across the table in front of him.

20

The meeting was reconvened at precisely 12:45. It made Gurney wonder if Beckert ever deviated from his strict notions of order and procedure—and what his reaction might be if someone disrupted his plans.

Beckert had brought a laptop with him, which he placed on the conference table. He chose as usual the chair in which he was framed by the room's window and the landscape of prison architecture beyond it.

After syncing his computer with the wall monitor, he indicated that all was ready.

"We'll begin with this morning's discovery—the website of a white-supremacist group that claims to engage in vigilante activities. They maintain that blacks are planning to start a war with whites in America, a war that neither the police nor the military will be capable of stopping, since both have been infiltrated by blacks and their liberal supporters. The group believes it's their God-given duty to eliminate what they call 'the creeping black menace' in order to save white America."

"*Eliminate?*" said Kline.

"*Eliminate,*" repeated Beckert. "They included on the same web page an old photograph of a lynching with the caption, 'The Solution.' But that's not the main reason our discovery of their website is important. Look at the screen. And listen carefully. This is their anthem."

The screen turned bright red. A window opened in the center, and the video began. A four-man heavy-metal band was producing a cacophony of stomping feet, tortured musical notes, and barely intelligible lyrics. A few words, however, came through loud and clear.

"Fire" ... "burning" ... "blade" ... "gun" ... "noose."

The video was grainy and the sound quality dreadful. The faces of the leather-clad, metal-studded band members were too ill-lit to be recognizable.

Kline shook his head. "If those lyrics are supposed to be telling me something, I'll need a translator."

"Fortunately," said Beckert, "the words appear on their site." He clicked on an icon and the rectangle that had framed the video now framed a photo of a type-written page.

"Read the lyrics carefully. They answer an important question. Detective Torres, for the benefit of Sheriff Cloutz, you might want to read them aloud."

Torres did as he was told.

We are the fire, we are the flood.
We are the storm cleansing the land,
the burning light of the rising sun.

We are the wind, the burning rain,
the shining blade, the blazing gun.
We are the flame of the rising sun.

Death to the rats creeping at night,
death to the vermin, one by one,
death by the fire of the rising sun.

We are the whip, we are the noose,
the battering club, the blazing gun.
We are the knights of the rising sun.

We are the storm, the raging flood,
the rain of fire whose time has come.
We are the knights of the rising sun.

"Jesus," Torres muttered as he finished reading. "These people are goddamn off-the-scale crazy!"

"Clearly. But what else do the words tell us?" Beckert was addressing everyone at the table—in the tone of a man who likes asking questions he knows the answers to. A man who likes to feel in charge.

It was a game Gurney didn't enjoy playing. He decided to end it. "They tell us what 'KRS' stands for."

There was a baffled silence around the table. "I see it now," said Torres finally. He turned to Cloutz. "In the lyrics they call themselves the 'knights of the rising sun.' The main initials of that would be 'KRS.'"

"You boys gettin' all excited over a coincidence of three letters?"

Beckert shook his head. "It's not just that. The whole website incriminates them. Anarchist insanity. Terroristic threats. Glorification of vigilantism. Plus the final clincher. On a page titled 'Battle News' there's a description of the situation here in White River. That plus 'KRS' being branded on the feet of Jordan and Tooker has to be more than a coincidence."

Kline looked alarmed. "You think these people are here in White River? Do we have any idea who they are?"

"We have a good idea who two of them may be."

"God Almighty," cried Cloutz, "don't tell me it's the two I'm thinkin' it is!"

Beckert said nothing.

"Am I right?" asked Cloutz. "Are we talkin' about the goddamn twins?"

"Judd is looking into that right now."

"By payin' them a visit?"

"You could put it that way."

"God Almighty!" Cloutz repeated with the unseemly excitement of a man anticipating a spectacular calamity. "I hope Judd realizes them boys are stone-cold crazy."

"He knows who he's dealing with," said Beckert calmly.

Kline looked from Beckert to Cloutz and back again. "Who the hell are *the twins?*"

Cloutz emitted a nasty little laugh. "Fire, brimstone, explosions, every kinda insane shit you can imagine. You got anything you want to add to that, Dell, to flesh out the picture for Sheridan here? I know them boys have a special place in your head."

"The Gort twins look like cartoons of mountain men. But there's nothing funny about them." There was acid in Beckert's voice. "Gorts, Haddocks, and Flemms have been inbreeding and raising havoc in this part of the state for two hundred years. The extended clan is huge. Hundreds of people in this county are connected to it in one way or another. Some are successful, normal people. Some are well-armed survivalists. A few are moonshiners, or meth manufacturers. The worst of them all are the twins. Vicious racists, probable extortionists, possible murderers."

"What am I missing here?" said Kline to Beckert. "I'm the county prosecutor. Why haven't these people been brought to my attention before?"

"Because this is the first time we've been in a position to have a real chance of putting them away."

"*The first time?* After what you and Goodson just said about them?"

This was the closest Gurney had seen Kline come to challenging Beckert about anything.

"Theoretically, we could have arrested them a number of times. The arrests would have been followed by dismissals or weak prosecutions and no convictions."

"*Weak?* What do you mean by—"

"I mean people who make accusations against the Gorts invariably retract them or disappear. At best, you'd have a case that would be dismissed immediately or fall apart halfway through. Maybe you're thinking that we could have put more pressure on them . . . brought them in every week for questioning . . . provoked them into hotheaded, ill-advised reactions. That might be a workable approach with someone other than the Gorts. But there's an aspect to this I haven't mentioned. In the polarized world of White River, the Gorts' racial opinions have made them folk heroes to a large part of the white population. And, of course, there's the religious angle. The twins are joint pastors of the Catskill Mountain White Heritage Church. And one of their devoted parishioners is our ever-popular home-bred white supremacist Garson Pike."

"Jesus," said Kline.

The name Garson Pike rang a bell with Gurney. For a moment he couldn't place it. Then he remembered the RAM-TV debate between Blaze Lovely Jackson and a stiff-looking man with an intermittent stutter—a man whose main point was that blacks were responsible for all the problems in America.

Kline looked troubled. "The decision not to go after them was essentially political?"

Beckert answered without hesitation. "All our decisions are ultimately political. That's the reality of democracy. Government by the will of the people. Attacking popular heroes does no one any good. It just raises everyone's anger level. Especially when evidence evaporates and there's no chance of getting a conviction."

Kline looked less than satisfied, a mark of some intelligence in Gurney's opinion. "What's so different now?" he asked.

"Meaning?"

"You said Turlock was going after the Gort twins. Is that true?"

"Yes."

"With a warrant?"

"Yes."

Kline's frown was deepening. "Issued on what basis?"

"Reasonable certitude that the Gorts are members of a vigilante group called Knights of the Rising Sun, that they may have been directly involved in the Willard Park homicides, and that we expect to find evidence supporting both assertions in the Gorts' private compound."

"What changed the political calculation that kept them off-limits until now?"

"Popular as the Gorts may be in certain quarters, leaving dead bodies in a children's playground is a game changer. It makes their arrest and prosecution acceptable to a majority of our citizens. And achievable—as long as we act quickly."

"And as long as you find some hard evidence linking them to this Knights of the Rising Sun group. And to the murders."

"I'm sure we'll find what we need. But it will still be essential to describe the situation in the right terms. Clear, simple, moral terms that leave no doubt that justice will be done."

"Biblical terms would be the best," said the sheriff. "Folks hereabouts have a fondness for the Bible."

"An interesting point," said Beckert. "And while we're on the subject—"

The soft *bing* of an arriving text stopped him in midsentence. He picked up his phone, and the message on its screen captured his full attention.

Torres, Kline, and Gurney were watching him.

Beckert looked up and announced with an unreadable expression, "Judd Turlock and his team have entered and secured the Gort compound out in Clapp Hollow. They've conducted a preliminary examination of the site, which appears to have been recently vacated. We'll have Judd's initial status report shortly, with on-site photos."

"Gort boys slipped away, did they?" said the sheriff, his tone suggesting this was a predictable event.

"No individuals have been located on the property," said Beckert. "We'll know more soon." He looked at his phone screen. "We'll reconvene at one fifty." He stood up from the table and left the room.

Gurney had a sudden thought about how he could use the free half hour, and he pursued Beckert out into the corridor, calling after him.

Beckert stopped and turned with an impatiently questioning look.

"I thought I'd take a quick run over to that place on the edge of Willard Park where John Steele was shot," said Gurney. "To get a feel for the geography. Any problem with that?"

"No. Why would that be a problem?" Clearly annoyed by the interruption, he turned and strode down the corridor without waiting for an answer.

21

Gurney brought the Outback to a stop at the same barricade of yellow sawhorses where he'd parked earlier. Again he ignored the several Police Line Do Not Cross warnings and proceeded to the sidewalk that ran along the border of the field.

He walked forward slowly, reenacting as best he could the movements of Steele as he remembered them from the RAM-TV videos.

He walked looking to his left—out over the flat, neatly mowed field where the crowd had gathered for the demonstration, their backs to the sidewalk. At the opposite end of the open expanse there was a raised platform, no doubt the one that had been used by the BDA speakers. At the edge of the field loomed the contested statue of Colonel Willard.

He walked on, stopping intermittently, as Steele had, as if to pay closer attention to some part of the crowd. The first four trees he passed as he proceeded along the field's edge were tall but relatively narrow-trunked. The fifth was the massive pine in which the steel-jacketed bullet had lodged itself after passing through the lower part of Steele's skull, brain, and facial bone.

Three more times he walked back and forth, retracing Steele's path to his death, and picturing as he did so the red laser dot of the sniper's scope that had followed the man every step of the way. Gurney found the mental re-creation of this so vivid he had for a moment the disturbing illusion of feeling that dot on the back of his own head. At the end of his third passage, he stopped at the big pine and aligned himself with Steele's position at the moment of impact. In his peripheral vision he was aware of the bloodstain where the man had fallen, his life abruptly over. John Steele. Husband of Kim Steele. Someone's son. Someone's friend. Someone's partner. Reduced in one dreadful moment to memories in the minds of some, to pain in the hearts of others, to a brown stain on a concrete sidewalk.

Gurney was seized by a sudden, powerful sense of grief that took him by surprise. His chest and throat felt constricted. His eyes filled with tears.

He wasn't aware of the cop coming up behind him until he heard a familiar, unpleasant voice. "Okay, buddy, you had a perfectly clear warning this morning about crossing—"

The cop stopped in midsentence when Gurney turned and faced him.

For a few seconds no one said anything.

Gurney wiped his eyes roughly with the back of his hand. "Beckert knows I'm here."

The cop blinked and stared at him, something about the situation finally dawning on him. "Did you . . . uh . . . know Officer Steele?"

"Yes," said Gurney. He didn't feel that the answer was entirely untrue.

Back in the headquarters conference room, Torres and Kline were already in their seats, both checking their phones. The sheriff's seat was empty. The mayor, however, was in his usual seat at the end of the table, engrossed in eating a piece of apple pie out of a Styrofoam box. His rust-colored comb-over was in slight disarray.

Gurney sat next to Kline. "Have we lost the sheriff?"

"He's at the jail. Evidently one of the BDA detainees wants to trade information on our so-called third man for a get-out-of-jail-free card. Goodson likes to handle those interviews personally." It was clear from Kline's tone it was an appetite he didn't share.

Gurney turned to the mayor. "I heard you were tied up at a Rotary lunch."

Shucker swallowed, wiping crumbs from the corners of his mouth with his thumb and forefinger. "Roto-Rooter lunch would've been a better name for it." His tone suggested he considered this comment clever and expected a request to elaborate.

Gurney said nothing.

"Sounds unpleasant," said Kline.

The door opened and Beckert entered. He sat down, opened the laptop, and checked the time.

"It's one fifty," he announced. "Time to reconvene. Our current status is that Judd and his team are continuing their search of the Gorts' compound. They've already found computer evidence that links them to the Knights of the Rising Sun, as well as some physical evidence that may tie them directly to Jordan and Tooker."

Kline sat up a little straighter. "What's the physical evidence?"

"We'll get to that. I want you to see some photos first. They'll give you some insight into the pair of lunatics we're dealing with." He tapped a key on his laptop, and the first photo appeared on the monitor.

It showed a dirt road hemmed in by tangled evergreens, leading to a gate in a high chain-link fence. Affixed to the fence were two square signs. The one to the left of the gate bore two lines of hand-printed words, too far from the camera to be legible. The one to the right, in addition to three lines of printing, had affixed to it what looked like an actual human skull.

The next photo Beckert showed was a close-up of the sign on the left.

> THE LAWS OF MAN ARE TOOLS OF SATAN
> THE GOVERNMENTS OF MAN ARE DENS OF SERPENTS

The next photo was a close-up of the sign with the skull. Gurney could now see that the skull was attached to the sign with a short arrow whose shaft and feathers protruded from the left eye socket. He recognized it as a crossbow bolt, a more powerful and deadly projectile than a normal arrow. The words printed below it were no more inviting.

> CHURCH PROPERTY
> ACCESS RESTRICTED
> TRESPASSERS BEWARE

Shucker was half watching the screen as he pressed the back of his plastic fork into the corners of his pie container to extract the last few crumbs. "You see that skull, makes you wonder whose it is. And how it ended up there, out in the middle of nowhere. You know what I mean?"

No one responded.

Beckert let a few seconds pass before going on to the next shot. "This is a photo of a photo that Judd found in the tray of a computer printer in the Gorts' cabin."

Shucker blinked in confusion. "Say that again?"

Beckert repeated his statement with a slowness someone else might have found insulting, but Shucker just nodded. "Photo of a photo. Got it."

What appeared on the screen was a picture of three strange figures in a room with log walls and a stone fireplace. Two of the figures were gaunt, bearded men in camo hunting clothes. One was much taller than the other—so much so that Gurney concluded that one must be a giant or the other a midget to account for such a difference. Between them stood a large black bear—although "stood" would not be the most accurate word, since the animal's body was being held in an upright position by a rope. One end was fashioned into a sort of noose around the bear's thick neck, and the other end was fastened to a low roof beam. On the mantel above the fireplace were several crossbows fitted with hunting scopes. In a jagged arc above them on the wall were dozens of broadhead hunting bolts.

"The Gorts with their latest trophy," said Beckert.

"The Gorts?" said Gurney. "I thought you said they were twins."

"They are. Ezechias is six foot two, and Ezechiel is four foot ten. Apart from that, they're identical. Same face, same voice, same lunacy."

"There's no spring bear-hunting season, is there?" said Kline.

"Absolutely not."

"So they just do as they please—hunt whenever they feel like it, in or out of season?"

"I'm sure they prefer to do it *out* of season. One more way to tell the law to go to hell."

"They fish with dynamite," said Shucker, pressing his little white fork into another corner of his pie box.

Gurney stared at him. "Dynamite?"

"When the Handsome Brothers stone quarry got shut down after the big explosion, the state auditors discovered someone had made off with a gross of dynamite sticks. Back then, the twins worked there. But every fall folks in the area claim there's a loud thump up to Clapp Hollow Lake and then the Gort boys spend the next week or two salting fish for the winter. Course it's hard to know what's fact or fiction out there in the hollows."

"We're in a position now to say with certainty that the Gorts have the stolen dynamite," said Beckert, "although that's not something we'll be saying publicly. Not at this time."

Kline looked worried. "They have the dynamite? Where is it?"

"Presumably they have it with them. It seems the Gorts were tipped off prior to Judd's raid, and they left with certain items."

"How do you know?"

"We know certain things were there and now they're not. Here's a photo Judd took an hour ago."

A new photo replaced the one of the Gorts with the bear. It was taken in the same room—but without the Gorts, without the bear, without the crossbows on the mantel, without the broadhead bolts on the wall.

"I see what's missing, compared to the other photo," said Kline, "but how do we know those things weren't put somewhere else a long time ago? I mean, there's no proof that the earlier photo of the Gorts with the bear was taken recently. Couldn't the rearrangement of the room have happened weeks or months ago?"

"We have evidence that suggests a very recent time frame." Beckert clicked his way rapidly through a number of photos, stopping at one of a fenced area attached to a large shed. He pointed at it. "That's the kennel. See that material strewn across the ground? That's what's left of the bear meat. Evidently the Gorts dumped the carcass in the kennel and their dogs tore it to shreds. Judd also found a fresh bear pelt in a taxidermy shed next to the cabin. So our timing assumptions are valid regarding the removal of the bear and the crossbows—and the Gorts' dogs as well. They were known to have about a dozen pit bulls that are now missing. But from the condition of the bear meat in the kennel—it's only just beginning to decay—we know the dogs were there until sometime yesterday."

Kline looked uneasy. "And the dynamite?"

"It's likely that the Gorts had in their possession over a hundred sticks. Judd found an empty explosives crate next to a half-empty container of canvas bags. He figures the Gorts transferred the dynamite to the bags to make it easier to carry."

Now it was Shucker's turn to look worried. "You're saying that two of the craziest men in White River have gone underground with a dozen attack dogs, enough arrows to kill off a small village, and enough dynamite to blow up a big one? How come you're not in a panic?"

"I prefer to focus on the progress we've made and the high likelihood of a successful resolution."

"Earlier you mentioned physical evidence linking the Gorts to Jordan and Tooker," said Kline. "Can you tell us what that is?"

"The potentially damning item is a coil of rope found in one of their sheds. Judd's impression is that it's identical to the rope used in the playground. We'll be getting a microscopic confirmation of that. If we get a cut match on the end fibers, that'll clinch it."

"You also mentioned computer evidence linking them to KRS?"

"Yes. On a thumb drive, taped to the bottom of a desk drawer. It contains the text and the graphic elements used to construct the KRS website. Meaning the Gorts either put the site together themselves or provided the elements to someone who did."

Kline's expression brightened. "So we're really getting somewhere."

"We are."

"That thumb drive," said Gurney, puzzled, "how were its contents examined?"

"On site, with Judd's laptop. Minutes after it was discovered."

"The drive wasn't password-protected?"

"Apparently not," said Beckert.

"And none of its individual files were password-protected?"

"Apparently not."

"Did they find the computer that housed the files the thumb drive was backing up?"

"They found a printer, scanner, modem, and router, but not the computer itself."

"Interesting," mused Gurney, speaking to no one in particular. "The Gorts took their dogs, crossbows, arrows, explosives, computer, and God-only-knows what else. But they left an unprotected USB drive and a rope that could incriminate them in a double murder."

Beckert's voice grew noticeably colder. "We can speculate on the reasons for those lapses in judgment later. But right now there's a more urgent priority. We need to encapsulate our progress in an appropriate statement. There are aspects to be emphasized and aspects to be avoided. Remember that we're in the middle of a media minefield. Forgetting it could be fatal."

Fatal to whom or to what? wondered Gurney. Was this about Beckert's own political future? Or was something else involved?

Beckert continued. "Regarding our investigations—"

He was interrupted by a tapping at the door.

Torres stood up and opened it.

It was the sheriff. "I hope my return isn't breakin' the flow of some brilliant crime analysis."

"Come in, Goodson," said Beckert. "We're just summing up a few key points."

"The summin' up is the best part." He made his way toward his seat at the end of the table.

Beckert began as he had before. "Regarding our investigations into the shooting and subsequent Willard Park homicides, there are three points that must guide all statements made outside this room. Number one, we are making rapid progress on both fronts. Arrests in both cases are anticipated within forty-eight hours. Number two, we have obtained evidence that will support airtight prosecutions and convictions. Number three, we are giving these cases equal priority and resources." He looked around the table, then abruptly changed the subject. "Goodson, how did your conversation go with your snitch at the jail? Anything useful?"

"Interesting for sure. You can decide if it's useful."

"He wanted to trade information for a favor?"

"Of course. But it was a *she*, not a *he*. What she said was that Blaze Lovely Jackson, one of the three leaders of the BDA, had a falling out with her two coleaders, Jordan and Tooker."

"How serious a falling out?"

"Serious serious, according to her. Said Blaze don't play well with others. Not big on sharin' power. Way she put it, Blaze is a vicious homicidal bitch, fond of usin' a straight razor to end disputes. Suggested there could be some connection between her homicidal nature and the fate of her coleaders."

"We're now ninety-nine percent certain the Gorts were responsible for the killings. I find it hard to believe that a black female could have had any involvement in what we saw in that playground."

Cloutz moistened his lips. "That would be my feeling too. But my little lady did say with great conviction that Blaze Lovely Jackson was capable of anything. *Absolutely anything.*"

Beckert said nothing. His own thoughts now seemed to be absorbing his full attention.

22

When the meeting broke up, Gurney headed out immediately. He didn't want to be late for his three thirty meeting with Rick Loomis at the Lucky Larvaton Diner. But before he could get in his car, he heard footsteps hurrying toward him.

It was Kline coming across the parking lot, radiating an odd mixture of excitement and anxiety. "Where are you rushing off to?"

"I'm meeting someone for coffee. Did you need me for something?"

"I'd like some explanation of your reactions in there."

"You sound concerned."

"The news we got was all good. Rapid progress on all fronts. Videos of the 'third man' coming and going from the sniper site. The car traced to a BDA member, creating a clear BDA tie-in to Steele's murder. Plus an equally clear vigilante group tie-in to the murder of the BDA leaders. The discovery of solid evidence in both cases. Situation under control. Risk of chaos reduced. A solid victory for law and order." He looked at Gurney expectantly.

"What's your question?"

"Given what I just said, why do you have that doubtful look on your face?"

"I'm a natural skeptic. It's the way my mind works."

"Even when the news is overwhelmingly positive?"

"Is that the way you'd describe it?"

Kline held Gurney's gaze for a few seconds, then reached into his jacket pocket and took out a pack of cigarettes. He lit one up with a vintage Zippo, took a deep drag, and slowly exhaled, watching the smoke dissipate into White River's still-acrid air.

"Those concerns you seemed to have about the depth of the water under the

Grinton Bridge . . . the way you were asking about the USB drive—all that worries me. It worries me not knowing what you're thinking. What you're *suspecting*. If something's wrong, I need to know what it is."

"The truth is, in both of these cases I'm having trouble getting my head around the thought processes of the killers."

Kline took another drag on his cigarette. "I don't find that very enlightening."

"I find it helpful to put myself in the criminal's position. To see the world from his point of view. I do that by studying what he's done. I immerse myself in his preparations, his execution of his plan, his likely actions afterward. This usually gives me a sense of how the perp thinks, how he makes decisions. But this time it's not happening."

"Why not?"

"Half the actions in these cases contradict the other half. The perps are very careful and very careless. Take the sniper. He was careful not to get his fingerprints on the outer door, the window, the bathroom door. But he left a perfect print on the toilet's flush handle. His marksmanship and location planning suggest he's a real pro. But he drives an easily traceable car. He goes to the trouble of ditching the tripod. But he tosses it in water so shallow it's easily visible."

"You're expecting these crazy killers to be totally logical?"

"No. I just think the possible significance of the discrepancies is being ignored. The same sort of peculiar questions arise in the Jordan-Tooker case. The cool and methodical nature of the beatings supposedly administered by crazy, hate-driven, white-supremacist vigilantes. The suspects' prudently removing their computer, but foolishly leaving behind their USB drive with the incriminating website content."

"That USB drive wasn't just left behind. It was hidden under a desk drawer."

"It was hidden in the first place any detective would look for it. Like the tripod, in a way. Hidden where it could easily be found."

Kline sighed in frustration, dropping what was left of his cigarette onto the pavement and staring down at it. "So what's your bottom line? That everybody but you is wrong? That none of our progress is really progress at all?"

"I don't have a bottom line, Sheridan. I just have questions."

Kline sighed again, ground out his cigarette, got into his SUV, and drove away.

The old Route Ten Bypass in Angina ran through a wide green valley dotted with weathered red barns. The sunny slopes of the south-facing hillsides were covered with alternating swaths of clover and buttercups. This idyllic landscape was pockmarked, however, by the detritus of a collapsed economy—abandoned homes, shuttered shops, closed schools.

Half a mile from Gurney's destination, at an unpopulated intersection, an old man was sitting on a low stool by the side of the road. Displayed on a shabby card table next to him were the mounted head of a deer and an old microwave oven. Propped against a leg of the table was a piece of brown cardboard with a scribbled offer: BOTH FOR $20.

Coming to the Lucky Larvaton Diner, Gurney discovered that it shared a weedy parking lot with a small strip mall whose businesses were all defunct—Wally's Wood Stoves, Furry Friends Pet Emporium, The Great Angina Pizzeria, and Tori's Tints & Cuts. The final vacant storefront in the row promised in a curled and faded window poster that Champion Cheese would be "coming soon."

The diner was across the lot from these empty stores. Built in the railroad-car style of traditional diners, it appeared to be in need of a good power-washing. There were two cars parked beside it—a dusty old Honda Civic and a turquoise Chevy Impala from the sixties—and a nondescript pickup truck out in front. Gurney parked next to the truck.

Inside, it looked not so much old-fashioned as just plain old. It had none of that ersatz "country charm" that exists in the minds of people who live in cities. There was a gritty reality to the scuffed brown linoleum, the smell of grease, the poor lighting. On the back wall a MAKE AMERICA GREAT AGAIN poster was curling in at its corners.

A thin, sharp-featured man with an oily black pompadour stood behind one end of the counter, peering down into the pages of a thick ledger. A middle-aged waitress with lifeless blond hair was perched on a stool at the opposite end of the counter examining her fingernails.

Halfway between them a stocky customer in faded farm overalls was hunched forward with his elbows on the worn Formica surface, eyes fixed on an old television that sat behind the counter on a microwave oven. The talking heads on the screen were proclaiming their opinions.

A row of booths ran along the diner's window side. Gurney made his way to the booth farthest from the television. Despite his efforts to gather his thoughts for his meeting with Rick Loomis, snippets of the TV audio kept intruding:

". . . zero respect for the police . . ."

". . . throw away the key . . ."

"... worst elements getting all the sympathy ..."

The blond waitress approached Gurney with a smile that was either sleepy or stoned. Possibly both. "Good afternoon, sir. How are you doing on this beautiful day?"

"Fine. How are *you* doing?"

The vague smile broadened. "I'm doing wonderful. Do you know what you want, or should I give you some time to think about it?"

"Just coffee."

"No problem. Do you have a Lucky Larvaton gas card?"

"No."

"You can earn free gas. Would you like one?"

"Not now, thank you."

"Not a problem. Milk or cream?"

"Cream, on the side."

"Just for one?"

"I'm expecting someone."

"You're the gentleman meeting Detective Rick, is that right?"

"Rick Loomis?"

"Detective Rick is what we call him. A very nice man."

"Yes. I'm meeting him. Did he call?"

"He said he was trying to reach you, but he couldn't get through. There are so many dead cell areas around here. You never know when you're going to get cut off. At the village meetings they keep promising to do something about it. Promises, promises. My granddaddy used to say if promises was poop nobody'd have to buy fertilizer."

"Very wise. Do you recall the message Detective Rick left for me?"

"That he'd be late." She turned to the counter. "Lou, how late did he say he'd be?"

The man scrutinizing the ledger answered without looking up. "Quarter of an hour."

He checked the time on his phone. It was 3:25. So now there was a total of twenty minutes to wait.

"He comes in here a lot, does he?" asked Gurney.

"Not really."

"But you know him?"

"Of course."

"How?"

"Because of the Pumpkin Murders."

"Damn!" Lou spoke without looking up from the ledger. "There you go again!"

"Sorry, say that again?" said Gurney.

"The Pumpkin Murders," repeated the waitress.

"Pumpkin? Is that someone's name?"

Lou looked up. "You can't keep calling them 'murders.' The cops never proved a damn thing. Nobody got incarcerated. You keep saying 'murders' you'll get us sued for defamation."

"Nobody's suing nobody, Lou."

"Whatever you call it," said Gurney, "what did it have to do with Rick Loomis?"

The waitress answered, "He was the one on the case. The Pumpkin Murders."

"There wasn't no murder," insisted Lou, his voice rising.

The waitress's voice took on an edge of its own. "So what did the two of them do, Lou? Just crawl under that pile of pumpkins and lie there till they died of natural causes?"

"I'm not saying the pumpkins didn't get dumped on them. You know I'm not saying that. What I'm saying is, it could've been an accident. Farm accidents happen every day. Worse ones than that. Where's your presumption of innocence?"

The waitress shook her head at Gurney as though they both realized how silly Lou was being. "Here's the real story. Evie Pringle and one of the harvesters out at the Pringle Squash Farm were having an affair." She punctuated "affair" with a flash of knowing approval, as though it were something every woman aspired to.

"Black boy," interjected Lou.

"Lou! You know darn well he was mostly white."

"Black's black. Like being pregnant."

She shook her head and continued her story. "The way Detective Rick figured it, Evie and her boyfriend had gone into the underground entryway to the storm cellar in back of the barn. Earlier in the day Evie's husband, Dick, had been out in the fields with his front loader gathering up all the leftover pumpkins, which folks don't have much interest in after Halloween. He'd loaded all them unsalable pumpkins, three tons of them, in his big dump truck. Then, while Evie and her boyfriend were down in the storm cellar doing what they were doing, with the doors closed over them, Dick went and dumped three tons of pumpkins on top of those doors. And that's the horrible way they met their maker, naked victims of Dick's terrible revenge."

Lou produced another snort. "Dick had a perfectly reasonable explanation."

"A reasonable lie, you mean."

He slammed the ledger shut. "It wasn't no revenge and it wasn't no lie. He was piling them pumpkins there temporary like, until he could move them to the main compost heap."

She shook her head. "You don't know nothing about revenge, Lou."

That seemed to leave him at a loss.

Gurney took the opportunity to ask her a question that had been puzzling him. "Why was Loomis discussing this with you?"

"Because Lou here was in the same school class with Dick Pringle, and I was one year behind with Evie. I suspect he was wanting some character insights."

"What was his conclusion?"

"He agreed with me," said Lou in a loud voice. "There wasn't no murder, because Dick wasn't no idiot. He sold the farm with them bodies still locked in that old storm cellar. If he'd known they was there, he'd a known they'd be found. Stands to reason. Loomis saw that plain as the nose on your face. He figured if Dick had done it on purpose, he'd have done it a lot smarter."

"Like hell he agreed with you," cried the waitress. "All he concluded was that there wasn't enough proof to cook Dick's goose. I believe he knew in his heart that murder had been done."

Gurney was getting restless. "How did Pringle explain the fact that his wife and the hired man weren't around anymore? I assume someone must have noticed."

The waitress answered. "He told everyone they'd run off together. He was getting sympathy for being abandoned. What a shit!"

Lou slapped his hand on the counter. "Your mind is bent! He said they ran off together because that's what he thought they done. It's what any man would think. You suspect your wife's getting it on with the hired help, and then they disappear together, what the hell are you supposed to think? It stands to reason."

"Lou, sometimes I think you wouldn't know reason if it bit you in the ass."

They stared at each other in quiet disdain. Phrases from the television's talking heads intruded into the silence. The thickset man in farm clothes at the end of the counter remained transfixed by the drone of bad news.

". . . murder rate soaring . . ."

". . . criminals empowered . . ."

Gurney's phone rang. The ID told him it was Kline. He headed out into the parking lot, squinting into the bright, broad expanse of the valley, his eyes having just adjusted to the murkiness of the diner.

"Gurney here."

"Where's *here*?" Kline's voice was rushed.

"On the Route Ten Bypass between Angina and White River. Why?"

"We have a situation. Another cop shooting. No details yet."

"Where?"

"Bluestone. The high end of White River. Number Twelve Oak Street. Whatever you're doing, drop it. Put that address in your GPS and go!"

"Will do. But once I get there . . ."

"Once you get there, you observe. No static, no turf wars. WRPD just got there. So you're my eyes on the scene. I can't leave the office right now. Keep me informed."

"You know anything at all about this?"

"Sniper. That's it. Nothing else." As he began to repeat the address, the connection was broken.

It occurred to Gurney that he should call Loomis right away, let him know about the emergency, and reschedule their meeting. As he searched his list of recent incoming calls for Loomis's number, he remembered that it had been blocked, an automatic habit of many cops.

"You never got your coffee."

The voice behind him in the parking lot belonged to the waitress. He turned and saw that she was holding out a Styrofoam cup. "I put cream in it. Sorry about all that in there. Lou can be such a dunce."

Gurney took the cup and reached into his pocket for his wallet.

"Forget it. On the house. Least we can do." She smiled her vague smile.

"Thank you. May I ask for another small favor?"

Her smile showed a spark of interest.

"Detective Rick should be here soon. Could you let him know I had to leave on police business and ask him to call me? He has my number."

"No problem." The spark faded.

He got in his car, entered the address Kline had given him into his GPS, and headed for the interstate at twice the speed limit.

Oak Street turned out to be located at the topographically lower side of the Bluestone section that Kline had described as the "high end" of White River. The street ran along the base of a gentle slope that rose from the grim Grinton section up to a plateau that marked the north edge of the city. As far as Gurney could see, the rest of Bluestone looked like Oak Street—a quiet neighborhood of older, well-maintained homes, neatly mowed lawns, and treelined pavements. The afternoon sun was bathing the area in a warm glow.

When Gurney arrived at number twelve, he counted five WRPD cruisers parked at haphazard angles in front of the house, two with their front doors open, all with their light arrays flashing. A Mercy Hospital ambulance was parked in the driveway. Two uniformed officers were unfurling a roll of yellow crime-scene tape.

Gurney parked next to one of the cruisers and walked up the driveway, holding his DA's office credentials out in front of him.

Several officers and EMTs were gathered on the front lawn around a collapsible rolling stretcher that had been lowered to the ground. A few yards away a woman in a sweatshirt and jeans was sitting on the grass, holding a kitchen spatula, making a sound like a wailing baby. A few feet away on the grass there was a yellow potholder. A female EMT was kneeling next to her, one arm around her. A sergeant was standing over them, his phone to his ear.

The EMTs around the stretcher began to raise it. When it clicked into its upright position the woman on the lawn scrambled to her feet, dropping the spatula. As the EMTs were rolling the stretcher toward the open back doors of the ambulance, Gurney got a passing view of the man lying on it. His face, neck, and one shoulder were covered with blood; a bloody compress was covering the side of his head; the arm nearest Gurney was twitching.

His educated guess, based on the quantity of blood and the position of the compress, was that the temporal artery had been severed. But there was no way of guessing how much damage had been done to the side of the skull and underlying areas of the brain or what the man's chances were of reaching the hospital alive. Many victims of head wounds didn't make it that far.

The woman—auburn-haired, round-faced, and noticeably pregnant—was trying to get to the stretcher. She was being held back by the frowning sergeant and the female EMT.

As the stretcher was being lifted into the ambulance the woman's efforts became wilder. She was screaming repeatedly, "I have to be with my husband!"

The EMT looked distressed and uncertain. The sergeant was grimacing and trying to hold on to her, as she flailed her arms and screamed, "MY HUSBAND!"

Her desperation seized Gurney's heart.

He went over and faced the sergeant. "What the hell's going on here?"

The sergeant was struggling to keep his balance. "Who the fuck are you?"

Gurney held up his credentials. "Why are you holding her here?"

"Deputy chief's orders." His voice was rising.

"She needs to be with her husband!"

"The deputy chief said—"

"I don't give a damn about the deputy chief!"

The ambulance was easing out of the driveway onto Oak Street.

The woman was shrieking, "Let me go . . ."

"That's it," said Gurney. "We're going to the hospital now! I'm taking responsibility. I'm Dave Gurney, DA's office."

Without agreeing to anything, the sergeant loosened his grip enough to let Gurney free the woman and lead her to the Outback. The WRPD officers on the scene appeared agitated by the dispute but unsure what to do.

Gurney helped the woman into the passenger seat. He was heading around to the driver's side when a dark-blue Ford Explorer came to an abrupt stop in front of his car.

The rear door opened, and Judd Turlock stepped out. He looked into Gurney's car.

"What's she doing in there?" He sounded almost disinterested.

"I'm taking her to the hospital. Her husband may be dying."

"You can do that right after I talk with her."

"You've got it backward. Get your car out of my way."

For a split second Turlock looked surprised. Then his expression settled back into a menacing lack of any expression at all. His voice was flat. "You're making a mistake."

"Look around you." Gurney gestured up and down the block, where several residents had come out into the street, holding up their smartphones and other devices. "They're recording everything that's happening. Right now they're recording your car blocking my car. Image is everything, right?" Gurney flashed a humorless smile.

Turlock's reply was a dead stare.

"Some messages have a huge impact," said Gurney, glancing at his car windows to make sure they were closed and the woman inside wouldn't hear him. "So imagine this message on every news site tomorrow morning: 'Deputy Police Chief Stands between Pregnant Wife and Dying Husband.' You think that's the kind of message your boss has in mind? Think fast. Your career is circling the drain."

Turlock's mouth twitched into a hint of an ugly smile. "Okay," he whispered. "We'll do it your way. For now."

He gestured to his driver, who moved the Explorer just far enough to allow Gurney room to turn around and head for Mercy Hospital.

With the help of his GPS, Gurney soon had the hospital in sight at the end of a long avenue, which seemed to calm his passenger just a little. He took the opportunity to ask if she'd actually seen what had happened.

Her voice was shaky. "He'd just gone out the front door. I heard a sound, like a rock hitting the house. I looked out ... I ...." She bit her lip and fell silent.

He assumed that what sounded like a rock was the impact of the bullet that had passed through the side of her husband's head. He asked, "Do you know what a gunshot sounds like?"

"Yes."

"Did you hear anything at all like that?"

"No."

"When you came out, did you see anyone? A car driving away? Any movement at all?"

She shook her head.

When they arrived at the hospital, the EMTs already had the stretcher out of the ambulance and were rolling it toward the open doors of the emergency entrance.

As Gurney brought the Outback to a halt beside the ambulance, his passenger was already stepping out the door. Abruptly she stopped and turned toward him.

"Thank you for what you did back there," she said. "Thank you so much. I don't even know your name."

"Dave Gurney. I hope your husband will be all right."

"Oh my God!" Her hand went to her mouth, her eyes widening.

"What? What is it?"

"You're the person Rick was on his way to meet!"

23

Heather Loomis's frantic need to follow her husband into the hospital prevented any discussion of the unsettling revelation. Gurney decided that sitting there would be a waste of time and would risk another confrontation with Turlock, who'd likely be coming to the hospital to interview Heather. It would make more sense to return to the crime scene, which Kline had asked him to observe.

He retraced his route and was soon back on Oak Street. Clusters of curious neighbors were still in front of their homes. There was no sign of Turlock or his blue Explorer, and only one of the five police cruisers was still there, its lights no longer flashing. On the far side of the cruiser there was a black Ford Crown Victoria—the most common unmarked police vehicle in America. In the driveway there was a gray van with a WRPD logo on its door. Gurney parked next to the cruiser.

Yellow crime-scene tape extended from one corner of the house to a series of metal stakes about twenty feet out on the lawn and back to the far corner of the house. An evidence tech was standing in a flower bed next to the front door. He was probing a hole in the wood trim with a bright metal tool that looked like a surgeon's pliers. He was wearing the latex gloves and Tyvek coveralls common to his occupation.

Gurney got out of his car, credentials in hand, and was heading across the lawn toward the taped-off area when he was stopped by a familiar voice.

"Hey! Dave! Over here!"

He turned around and saw Mark Torres gesturing with his phone through the open window of the Crown Vic. He walked over and waited until Torres concluded his call.

Getting out of the car, the young detective looked concerned. "I was afraid I'd missed you. Was there a problem here . . . after the shooting?"

Gurney shrugged. "Nothing major. Heather Loomis wanted to be with her husband. It could have been her last chance to see him alive. So I took her."

"Ah. That makes sense." Torres looked relieved, but not entirely so.

"Where's Turlock?"

"I don't know. I was at headquarters. He told me to get over here and find the location used by the BDA sniper."

"*The BDA sniper?* Those were his words?"

"Those were his words."

"He was that sure about a BDA connection?"

"Absolutely positive. You have doubts about it?"

"I have doubts about everything connected with this case."

"We'll know more as soon as Garrett pulls the bullet out of the woodwork. It's taking extra time because we're trying to preserve as much of the entry channel as we can."

Gurney looked over at the tech in the flower bed, his coveralls hanging loosely on his tall, gangly frame. He was up to his knees in purple alliums and evening primrose—which Gurney recognized as two of Madeleine's favorites, along with bee balm and foxglove.

Torres went on. "We figure the shot had to have come from up there." He gestured toward a broad area of houses several blocks up the hill. "I have four of our guys up there now doing door-to-doors, trying to find out if anyone heard or saw anything. Somebody up there must have heard the gunshot, even if it was suppressed—which I guess it was, or some of the neighbors down here would have heard it, and nobody did."

Gurney recalled that the police canvassing of the Grinton neighborhood for information at the time of the Steele shooting hadn't produced much cooperation. But Bluestone was a different kind of place, the kind where cops were viewed as allies, not enemies.

"Got it!" With a satisfied smile, the tech in the flower bed was holding up what appeared to be a remarkably intact bullet. Gurney and Torres stepped under the tape and went over for a closer inspection.

"Looks identical to the one you dug out of the tree in Willard Park," said Torres.

"Yep. Same caliber, same full metal jacket, no significant deformation, nice and clean for ballistics." He slipped the bullet into a small evidence envelope, already labeled and dated.

"Great work," said Torres. "Thank you."

"So that's the whole deal here, right? Just the bullet recovery? No combing the site?"

"Nothing here to comb for. We'll be in touch when we find the shooter site."

The tech got into his van and departed.

Gurney, followed by Torres, headed for the hole in the woodwork. After giving it a quick examination, he took out his pen and inserted it as far as it would go, about three inches below the surface. The range of vectors created by the angle of the pen substantially reduced the portion of the hillside that Torres had originally indicated as the area from which the shot had come. Even allowing for the imprecision of the method and the possibility of the bullet channel being skewed one way or the other by contact with the victim or by the grain of the wood, it narrowed the area of interest to a couple of dozen hillside houses.

As Gurney was removing his pen from the channel, Torres's phone rang.

He took the call and mostly listened, eyes widening with excitement.

"Okay, I got it. Thirty-Eight Poulter Street. We'll be right there."

He grinned at Gurney. "We may have lucked out. Uniforms found a couple of homeowners who say they heard something that could have been a shot—coming from a vacant house that sits between them. Let's roll."

They got into the Crown Vic and three minutes later were parked behind two WRPD cruisers at the Poulter Street address. It was a street of two-story Colonials on modest plots of land with driveways leading to detached garages. Most of the front yards consisted of neatly trimmed lawns with a few azaleas or rhododendrons in mulched planting beds.

The exception was number thirty-eight—where overgrown grass, wilted shrubs, and lowered blinds created an impression of abandonment. The open garage door was the only indication of recent use. Two patrol cops with yellow tape were turning the house, garage, driveway, and backyard into a restricted area. A third officer—a heavy-shouldered, thick-necked young man with a shaved head and a stolid expression—was emerging from the neighboring house on the left.

Gurney and Torres met him in front of the driveway. Gurney learned his name was Bobby Bascomb when Torres introduced them. He pointed back to the house he'd come from. "Lady in that house, Gloria Fenwick, says she heard a car pulling into this driveway earlier this afternoon."

"She know the time?" asked Torres.

"Not when it pulled in, but she knows it pulled out at exactly thirty-six minutes after three. And she knows it was a black Corolla sedan and the driver was in a hurry."

"She's that sure about the time and car model?"

"She's sure about the car because she has an old Corolla herself. She's sure about the time because it was unusual for anyone to come to that house, so when she heard a car pulling in she went to her side window, trying to see who it might be. She couldn't see anyone because the car was already in the garage. But she stayed by the window. A few minutes later she heard a loud 'bang'—which she thought was a door slamming. Maybe thirty seconds after that, the car came backing out of the garage onto the street and, as she put it, 'peeled rubber' and was gone. That got her attention. That's when she looked at the clock."

"She get a look at the driver?"

"No. But she said it had to be a man because women don't drive that fast."

"Did you call in a description of the car?"

"Yep. They've put an APB out on it."

Torres called headquarters and told them to add the plate number of the car associated with the Steele shooting to the APB on the black Corolla in Bluestone.

He resumed his debriefing of Bascomb. "Does the lady know anything about the people who own this house?"

"She said they moved to Florida six months ago. They weren't able to sell the house before they left, so they put it up for rent."

"She know anything about the renters?"

"Just that she's never seen them, but a friend in the real estate business told her it was someone from down in Grinton."

"How'd she feel about that?"

Bascomb shrugged. "About like you'd expect. 'Grinton' is not a popular word on this side of town."

"How about the neighbor on the other side?"

"Hollis Vitter. Piece of work. Pissed off at the grass not being mowed, pissed off at 'the Grinton element' moving into Bluestone, pissed off at 'gun-control faggots.' Lot of things piss him off."

"Has he ever seen the people who rented the house?"

"No. But he thinks they must be foreigners."

"Why?"

"Some bullshit about them not cutting the grass. He wasn't making a lot of sense."

"Jesus," muttered Torres. "Did he tell you anything that could be relevant to the case?"

"Actually, yes. And that part's more interesting. Like the lady on the other side, he heard a sharp 'bang,' but he didn't get to the window right away. Says he was locked in the shitter."

"Locked?"

"That's the word he used. The point is, the window was open, and he's sure what he heard leaving wasn't a car. He says it was a motorcycle and that the sound didn't come from the street, it came from the weedy little hill that drops off in back of these houses."

Torres looked uncertain. "Do we trust what he says about the sound?"

Bascomb sucked at his teeth. "I kinda pushed him on that, and he said he used to be a motocross mechanic down at Dortler's Speed Sports."

Torres appeared puzzled by the conflicting vehicle descriptions. "We'll have to get that sorted out. Right now we need Garrett up here. And we need to get into that house. I'll call in a request for a search warrant."

"If you want to, for the record," said Gurney. "But we have justification to go in immediately. We have reason to believe a shot was fired from the premises, and we have to ensure that the evidence techs aren't blindsided when they go in, which they need to do ASAP."

Torres made the warrant call, then a call to Garrett Felder, the head crime-scene tech.

"Okay," he said, putting away his phone. "Let's do it. How many doors does that house have?"

"Three," said Bascomb. "Front, back, and left side."

Torres looked questioningly at Gurney.

"Your show, Mark. Put us where you want us."

"Right. Okay. You take the back. Bobby, you take the side. I'll take the front and give the signal for going in."

One of the two cops taping off the area looked over. "You want us somewhere?"

Torres thought about it for a moment, then pointed. "Go to diagonal corners of the yard, so you can each see two sides of the house, and keep an eye on the windows." They nodded and went to their assigned positions. Bascomb, Gurney, and Torres did the same.

As Gurney was passing the side door, he noted that it was slightly ajar. The back door, he discovered a few seconds later, was wide open. He reached down to his ankle holster, pulled out his Beretta, slipped off the safety, and waited for the entry signal.

A moment later he heard Torres's knocking at the front door, a pause, then more insistent knocking, followed by "Police! Open the door now!" Then several seconds of silence, followed by "Officers going in! Now!" And the sound of glass breaking.

Gurney stepped through the open back doorway into a narrow hall that led past a small bathroom into a stale-smelling kitchen. The layout was similar to that of the Steele house, but everything here was duller, dustier. He passed through the kitchen into a small dining room, separated from the living room by a wide arch.

In the living room there were no rugs, one flimsy-looking floor lamp, and very little furniture—a shabby couch, an armchair, an end table—adding to the uninhabited feeling. In the dim light coming through the partially closed blinds, he could see a stairway to the second floor. A hall behind the stairway led to the side door. He assumed that the door he saw beneath the stairway would lead to the basement.

Torres was at the foot of the stairs to the second floor, his Glock in a two-handed grip close to his chest. Bascomb was in the hall, a similar weapon in a similar position.

Torres called out, "This is the police! Anyone in the house, show yourself now!"

The response was a dead silence. In a low voice he directed Bascomb to check out the basement and asked Gurney to come with him to check out the upstairs.

There was no carpet on the stairs and the creaking of each tread was sufficient to give anyone who might have been lurking up there a step-by-step sense of their approach.

The upstairs turned out to be as bleak and deserted as the downstairs. There were three bedrooms, each containing a double bed. There was a bathroom with a dusty bathtub, a shower stall with no shower curtain, and a towel rack with no towels.

The bedroom that attracted Gurney's attention was facing the rear of the house. The bed and chair had been pushed out of the way against a side wall. The window was open. Enough afternoon sunlight was slanting in to reveal three dime-sized impressions on the dusty floor. From the doorway Gurney could see through the open window, several blocks away and lower on the hill, a row of modest homes. The front yard of one was cordoned off with yellow tape. A few of the local residents were still gathered in the street—like fans lingering at an athletic field after the players have gone home.

Now that the dismal house at 38 Poulter Street had been identified with reasonable certainty as the second sniper site, the collection and protection of trace evidence became a priority. So it was no surprise that Garrett arrived with help. The surprise was the package the help came in—a short, stout woman he introduced as Shelby Towns, whose head was shaved as clean as Bobby Bascomb's. She had silver studs in her lips, nostrils, and ears. She was wearing a black tee shirt with the word GENDER-BENDER emblazoned in white letters across her ample chest.

Perhaps to defend her getup, Torres told Gurney that Shelby was involved in a long-term undercover assignment, but that her dual college degrees in forensic science and chemistry made her an ideal part-time addition to high-priority crime-scene examinations.

Gurney filled her and Garrett in on the layout of the house and what he'd seen in the upstairs bedroom. Bascomb mentioned Gloria Fenwick's report of a car and Hollis Vitter's report of a motorcycle. Torres added that it was strange to find in the bedroom floor dust indications of another rifle-support tripod, apparently like the first. "Why throw the first tripod in the river and keep the rifle?" he mused aloud to no one in particular. "If the shooter was going to get caught with one or the other, it's the rifle that would nail him."

Torres directed Bobby Bascomb and the other two cops at the scene to canvass the neighborhood for witnesses to the arrival or departure of a car or motorcycle, and for any information concerning the renters. Then he called headquarters and asked someone to look into city, county, and law-enforcement records concerning ownership, tenancy, tax payments, liens, complaints, or anything else they could uncover relevant to the use of the property.

Meanwhile, Garrett and Shelby donned disposable coveralls, booties, gloves, and caps. They gathered their special lights, chemicals, and evidence-processing paraphernalia from their van and headed into the house.

Torres suggested that while the techs were going about their business, he and Gurney should reinterview the two immediate neighbors to see if they recalled anything beyond what they'd already reported to Bascomb. Gurney agreed, and Torres volunteered to talk to Gloria Fenwick in the house on the left.

Gurney approached the house on the right. He wanted to hear more about the departure of that motorcycle. He hoped that Hollis Vitter's questionable mental state hadn't skewed his perceptions to the point of uselessness.

The house was of a size and style similar to number thirty-eight. The front lawn was bisected by a neat slate path that led to the front door. Centered in the square of lawn on each side of the path was a small spruce. The driveway had recently been swept clean. The garage door was open, revealing the back end of a military-style Hummer from the early nineties. A Confederate flag decal covered the rear window.

When Gurney was still a good ten yards from the house, the front door opened and a heavyset, balding man in camo fatigues came out, holding a Rottweiler on a short leash. Gurney figured that the vehicle, the flag, the fatigues, and the dog added up to an exaggerated need to project a *don't mess with me* image.

Gurney produced a polite smile. "Mr. Vitter?"

"Who's asking?"

He held up his credentials. "Dave Gurney, office of the district attorney. I need to speak to you about events in the house next door to you."

"You ever hear of the broken-window theory of policing?" he asked in an angry voice.

Gurney was thoroughly familiar with it—a highly confrontational approach to minor incidents in high-crime neighborhoods—from his NYPD days. Every cop in America knew something about it, many departments had tried it, and the results remained a subject of controversy and heated debate.

"I know what it is, sir. Does it have some relevance to the situation next door?"

Vitter pointed to the weedy foot-high grass. "You see that?"

"I see it. What about it?"

Vitter's eyes narrowed. "The broken-window approach says you guys need to address the little signs of big problems. *Infringements.*" He articulated the word slowly, with drawn-out distaste. "The idea is *zero tolerance*. Send a message. What's wrong with the world today is that all the little crap is ignored. Swept under the table. Nobody wants to take on the minority bullcrap, the *sensitivities*, the political correctness that's murdering us."

He waved a finger at Gurney. "You gotta squash the little crap so they understand they can't get away with the big crap. We ought to do what they do other places. Shoot them. Why not? Shoot the scumbags. Shoot the drug dealers. Leave the bodies where they fall. Same with terrorists. Leave them where they fall. Send a message."

Gurney waited to be sure the spiel had run its course.

"Mr. Vitter, I have a question for you."

The man cocked his head to the side. "Yeah?"

"Earlier this afternoon, did you hear a motorcycle leaving the property next door?"

Vitter's demeanor brightened. "Motocross, small displacement, high compression. Something like a Yamaha Dual Sport. That's a guess. But I'm a good guesser."

"You saw it?"

"No need to. I told your fella with the shaved head I was taking a shit, but I have a good ear. Nothing I don't know about bikes, including how they sound."

"When you heard it, did you happen to notice the time?"

"I don't keep a clock in the shitter."

"Any idea who it might have been?"

He looked from side to side and lowered his voice. "Probably one of them."

"Them?"

"Infiltrators. They come into our country illegally and disappear. Disappear into ordinary American life. They stay there, lurking around, waiting until they get the word to launch a terrorist attack. You don't hear about this on regular news. It's all hushed up."

Gurney paused. "Have you ever seen anyone next door?"

"Never," he said, giving the word a fraught significance.

Gurney recognized that familiar quirk of the mind that can transform a lack of evidence into the most convincing evidence of all. In a computer program that logic circuit would be a disabling flaw. In people, however, it was amazingly common.

Gurney thanked the man for his time and headed back to the Crown Vic to wait for Torres and the techs to reappear. He checked the time on his phone and saw that more than an hour had passed since he dropped Heather off at the emergency room. He assumed that Rick Loomis, if he were still alive, would likely be in one of the operating rooms. If he were a very lucky man, he might be having the side of his head reassembled in a way that would make his life livable. Heather would probably be in one of the waiting rooms—sitting, standing, pacing—besieging every passing nurse and doctor for news about what was happening. Gurney had questions he needed to ask her but was hesitant to ask, since none of them could compare in weight to the unknowns facing her at that moment.

Still, on countless occasions in his homicide career, the need for timely information had forced him to interview people in emotional pain. He'd always hesitated before plunging in. But in the end he always came to the same conclusion—that the need for information trumped the potential disturbance his questions might cause.

He got the hospital's number from the internet, called it, explained who he needed to reach, was transferred three times, was put on hold for several minutes, and was about to give up when Heather was finally brought to the phone.

"Hello?" Her voice sounded thin and exhausted.

"This is Dave Gurney. How is Rick?"

"He's in surgery. They can't tell me anything yet."

In the background Gurney could hear a series of little dings, a sound that brought back memories of ICU monitors, injured cops, long vigils in hospital corridors. "I need to ask you a couple of questions. Is that all right?"

"Go ahead."

"When I went to the diner to meet Rick, they told me he'd called to say he'd be late. Do you know why?"

"I think . . . I think he checked with someone. Maybe to ask about meeting with you? Something like that?"

"Do you have any idea who it was?"

"No. But I think whoever Rick was talking to wanted to come with him to your meeting . . . but he had to take care of something first, and then Rick was going to pick him up? I'm sorry, I wasn't paying much attention—" Her voice was stifled by a little sob.

"It's okay, Heather."

"I don't know what else I can tell you about that."

"What you've told me is very helpful. I was just wondering . . . you referred to the person Rick was talking to as 'him.' Are you sure that the person Rick talked to was a man?"

"I don't really know. It never occurred to me that it might not be a man."

"Do you know if the person was a police officer?"

She hesitated. "I don't think so."

"Why not?"

"Rick's voice. There's a certain way he talks to other cops. I think this sounded different."

"That's a good observation, Heather. I know this is a frightening time for you, and I appreciate your willingness to talk to me."

"I want to help you. I appreciate what you did. The risk you took. Getting in Judd Turlock's face like that to bring me here . . . when you didn't even know my name." Her voice was starting to quaver. "Most people . . . wouldn't do that. Something like that . . . takes more than courage. It takes . . . goodness."

A brief silence fell between them. It was broken by Gurney, clearing his throat and trying to speak in a matter-of-fact way. "Turlock and other WRPD people will be questioning you about what happened today. Not just about the shooting itself, but—"

"I know how the process works."

"Are you going to tell them that Rick was on his way to meet me when he was shot?"

"No."

"Or that he and I had spoken on the phone?"

"No."

He paused. "You really don't trust the department, do you?"

"No. I don't."

"Do you know if Rick or John Steele had uncovered any evidence of criminal actions?"

"I think . . . they were getting close."

"Was anyone helping them?"

"Rick didn't like to bring those details home. But I did have the impression that someone was giving them information, telling them which cases they should look into."

"Someone inside the department?"

"Rick never said."

"Do you know if it was information about individuals who'd been framed?"

"I think so."

"Framed by Turlock?"

"Probably. He seems like an awful man."

"And Beckert?"

She hesitated. "Probably not directly. According to Rick, he's the sort of person who makes everything turn out the way he wants it, without leaving his fingerprints on anything."

"I was told he has political ambitions. Do you know anything about that?"

"No, but I'm not surprised. He has that kind of—" She let out a sharp little cry. "Have to go. The doctor's here."

He felt a sudden tightness in his chest, perhaps a contagious germ of her fear.

He hoped with all his heart she'd be able to handle whatever the doctor was about to tell her.

He was just slipping the phone back in his pocket when a call arrived from Sheridan Kline. He was tempted to let it go to voicemail; but he knew that delaying the conversation would accomplish nothing—that procrastination only increased the weight of things that needed to be done.

"Gurney here."

"What on earth is going on?"

"Is there a problem?"

"I was told that you barged into the Loomis crime scene and removed a key witness before she could be interviewed by a senior WRPD officer."

"That's an interesting arrangement of the facts. Let me give you another one. I narrowly averted a public relations disaster that would have had Beckert stumbling all over himself at his next press conference."

"What the hell is that supposed to mean?"

"It means that the desperate wife of a downed police officer was being detained—kept from her possibly dying husband—for the interviewing convenience of a deputy police chief with the sensitivity of a stone. How do you think Beckert's precious media would react to that?"

Kline took so long to reply Gurney began to wonder if they were still connected.

"That's not the way I heard it," he finally said, the energy gone from his voice. "And according to the hospital, Loomis is still alive. I understand the shooter site has been located and Garrett Felder's going over it. Is that right?"

"Yes."

"And the Loomis shooter used the same black Corolla used in the Steele case?"

"Maybe."

"*Maybe?*"

"One neighbor saw the Corolla. Another neighbor claims there was another vehicle present, an off-road motorcycle. Hard to say at this point which one the shooter used."

"What difference does it make? He obviously used one of them. From what you're saying, it appears that he had some kind of BDA backup."

"Maybe."

"I don't see as how there's any *maybe* about it. Two vehicles. One shooter plus one backup."

Gurney remained silent. There were other possibilities, but he didn't feel like discussing them with Kline. At least not until he had a chance to think them through.

"Did you observe the site yourself?" asked Kline.

"I did."

"And?"

"Similar to the first. Some indication that a rifle-support tripod was used. I'm waiting to see what else Garrett and his assistant come up with."

"Good. With that same Corolla involved, any prints they find ought to corroborate the evidence we've gathered on the Steele shooting—which is already a prosecutor's dream."

"As long as you don't think about it too much. Or start wondering *why*."

"What are you talking about?"

"*Why* that laser dot followed the back of Steele's head as long as it did. *Why* he was shot while he was moving, rather than while he was standing still. *Why* the shooter used a full metal jacket, rather than a hollow-point. Things like that keep me awake at night. They ought to keep you awake, too."

"Nonsense. You're overcomplicating everything."

"I thought you wanted my objective view of the case."

"I do. Of course I do. But right now the case is coming together in an ideal way. I don't want your obsession with tiny loose ends derailing your thinking or creating problems with White River PD. Stay with the big picture, is all I'm saying. Avoid unnecessary disputes. Let's move this investigation to a smooth conclusion."

24

When Torres came out of Gloria Fenwick's house he filled Gurney in on the few bits of additional information he'd gotten from her.

The Corolla that backed out of the driveway and sped away was, in her words, "shamefully dirty."

During that year's March and early April snowfalls, the driveway had not been plowed.

In the months since the owners had moved away and consigned the place to its current renters, she'd never seen a window open or a light on.

Apparently all of the owners' mail was being forwarded, and the renters were receiving none, since the postman, a very nice man, never stopped there.

The failure to maintain the property, particularly the failure to mow the grass, was, in her opinion, an insult to the residents of Bluestone and typical of the slovenly ways of "the Grinton element."

"And," Torres concluded, "she's absolutely certain about the presence of that car. How sure was the guy on the other side of the house about the motorcycle?"

"Totally."

"So they're each positive about one vehicle, and neither was aware of the second. Strange."

Gurney thought about that. "Not really. In the sniper house, there's a bathroom by the back door and a living room in the front. The Fenwick and Vitter houses have the same basic design. Vitter says he heard the motorcycle—which was in back of the sniper house—through his bathroom window. Gloria Fenwick was at her living room window. The driveway the car used is on her side of the sniper house. They each noticed what they were closest to."

Torres looked unconvinced. "I get why Vitter might not have heard the car. But motorcycles can be pretty loud. Shouldn't she have heard it?"

"Theoretically. But suppose there was a delay of a minute or two between the car leaving and the motorcycle leaving. I doubt she stayed by her window after the car left. She may even have closed it. If there was another engine sound a couple of minutes later down by that back slope, there's no reason it would have meant anything to her."

"Wouldn't she have at least *heard* it?"

"We hear sounds constantly, but unless they have some significance to us, our brains discard them. Like a spam filter on email. You probably heard hundreds of sounds earlier today—at home, on your way here, down on Oak Street—but I bet you'd have trouble remembering more than a few of them."

"That may be true, but—"

He was interrupted by a contralto voice. "Either of you have a little spare time?"

It was Shelby Towns, the female half of the evidence-collection team, speaking as she emerged from the front door of the sniper house, facial studs shining in the afternoon sun, white coveralls concealing her GENDERBENDER tee shirt.

"Garrett figures he'll be tied up inside for another hour or so," she continued as she approached them, "and I need to lay out a search grid in back. Two people working together can do that four times faster than one. How about it?"

Checking his watch, Torres explained that he was late for a follow-up with the men he'd assigned to canvass the neighborhood.

Gurney offered to give her a hand, motivated less by a spirit of helpfulness than by the curiosity he always felt at crime scenes.

She pointed to the evidence van. "Suit, gloves, booties—right inside the door. You've done this before, right?"

Before Gurney could answer, Torres said, "Jesus, Shel, you're talking to the man who holds the NYPD record for solved homicides. He's probably been at more major crime scenes than everyone in our department put together." He got into the Crown Vic, pulled away from the curb, and was gone.

Shelby Towns gave Gurney a look. "Is that true—the record for solved homicides?"

"They gave me a medal with those words on it. I have no idea whether it's true."

Something about her wide-eyed look made him burst out laughing. Before she could ask what he found so funny, he asked how she wanted to set up the grid.

The backyard was only about twice the width of the house, but it was over a hundred feet deep, extending back behind both the house and the detached garage. The downward slope beyond that added about fifty feet of weeds and briars between the overgrown lawn and the street below.

Working together, they'd managed in half an hour to lay out a string grid composed of nearly two hundred six-foot squares covering the lawn and most of the slope. A careful eyes-to-the-ground walk-through took another half hour.

Their discoveries, photographed by Shelby on her tablet, included tire tracks that indicated a motorcycle with knobby motocross tires had been standing on a patch of grassless soil behind the garage and had subsequently crossed the lawn, descended the slope, and turned onto the lower street—confirming Hollis Vitter's claim. Also behind the garage were boot prints next to the tire marks—and similar prints in the soil at the base of the slope, suggesting that the rider had stopped there, perhaps for passing traffic, before turning onto the street.

At the edge of the lawn by the slope, Gurney spotted a Bic pen. Shelby photographed it in situ before he picked it up, careful not to smudge any prints, and placed it in an evidence bag. As he was filling out the required item-location-date information, his phone was ringing. By the time he got to it, the message was already in voicemail.

On playback it was so broken up it was barely understandable. After listening to it three times, he could be sure only that the caller was Heather Loomis and she wanted him to come to the hospital. The reason was indecipherable, but the urgency was clear.

He called back but just got voicemail. He considered trying to reach her through the hospital number but changed his mind when he recalled the time-consuming runaround involved in his earlier effort. Assuming he'd end up driving there anyway, he decided to just go.

After explaining the situation to Shelby, he jogged the four blocks down the hill to where he'd left his car in front of the Loomis house on Oak Street. The groups of neighbors had dispersed. The yellow police tape and the darkened red stain on the grass were the only signs that something unnatural had occurred.

He got in the Outback and followed the route he'd taken to the hospital with Heather. The traffic was moving more slowly now with people coming home from work. It gave him time to think, a mixed blessing at that time of day, nearing dusk, when his concerns seemed to intensify.

Near the top of his present list was his worrisome position in the investigation of the Loomis shooting. Revealing that Loomis was shot as he set out to discuss his and John Steele's efforts to probe corruption in the department would likely abort any progress in that direction and perhaps even expose other individuals to retaliation. On the other hand, the phone company would have records of Loomis's call to Gurney to set up their meeting and his subsequent call to the diner to change the meeting time. If those records were discovered, and if the waitress identified Gurney, he could be charged with withholding evidence in the investigation of a felony—itself a felony.

Complicating his decision was the larger question of whether the attempt on Loomis's life was a calculated effort to keep that meeting from happening or a mindless shoot-a-cop retaliation for the playground murders. He was pretty sure it was the former.

As Gurney got out of the car at the hospital parking lot he felt, for the first time that day, a chill in the air.

The building's entrance was sheltered under a broad portico. A RAM van was parked next to it, and a small crowd had gathered. A media crew was adjusting TV lights around two central figures. One, in a short red skirt and white blouse, was the news personality he'd seen on *Battleground Tonight*. The other, in a crisply tailored blue uniform with gleaming brass buttons, was Dell Beckert.

A crew member by the open rear doors of the van called out, "Light and sound levels good. Recording and transmitting. You're on!"

The reporter's expression switched from bitchy boredom to the standard RAM-TV expression of concern with the worrisome state of the world. She was holding a wireless microphone. "I'm Stacey Kilbrick at Mercy Hospital in White River, New York, where Detective Rick Loomis is barely hanging on to life after being shot by a sniper in his own front yard—raising the tension in this upstate city to the breaking point. I'm talking to Chief Dell Beckert, who just emerged from the hospital. What can you tell us, Chief?"

Beckert's face was a picture of rock-solid determination. "First, let me assure everyone that we have the tense situation in White River under control. Second, we're making rapid progress toward the identification and apprehension of the coward who tried to kill this fine officer, a servant of our community, a man with a spotless record. Third, you have my personal assurance that law and order will prevail. To the tiny deluded minority who incite violence for their own selfish ends, I say this: you will be brought to justice. Finally, I ask for your prayers for the full recovery of Detective Rick Loomis. Thank you."

Kilbrick stepped forward to ask a question, but Beckert was already striding away toward a dark-blue Ford Explorer idling in the circular drive just beyond the portico. She turned to the camera. "I'm Stacey Kilbrick at Mercy Hospital. I'll be keeping you up to date with developments as they occur. Please, folks, remember to say those prayers."

The video lights went out and the bitch face returned.

Gurney headed into the hospital lobby.

Although the exterior of the building came from the same 1960s manual of bleak design as the police headquarters, the interior had been renovated in accordance with more recent ideas about reducing stress in medical settings through the use of soft lighting, colors, and textures. A gently curved cherrywood welcome desk was staffed by three smiling senior citizens.

Gurney's welcomer was an elegantly dressed woman with a snow-white permanent and light-blue eyes. He told her he'd come to see a patient in the ICU. She regarded him with interest and spoke in a lowered voice. "Are you a police officer?"

"Yes."

"I thought so. They're restricting access, but you probably know that. The media people are just so . . ." Her voice trailed off in disgust, as though media people were sewage that might seep into the building. She told him that the ICU was on the second floor and gave him directions to the elevator bank, adding with a frown, "Such an awful thing."

Stepping out of the elevator on the second floor, he found himself in front of a waist-high partition enclosing an administrative island. On the partition was a sign telling him to turn off his cell phone and other electronic devices before entering the ICU. Behind the island was a nursing station with computer monitors, resuscitation equipment, and rolling IV stands. In a far corner of the station a grinning cop was chatting up an attractive nurse's aide.

At a desk inside the island, a slim young man with short, gelled hair looked up at Gurney. His teal name tag said he was Bailey Laker. "Can I help you?"

"I'm here to see Rick Loomis. Or Mrs. Loomis."

"And you are . . ."

"Dave Gurney. Mrs. Loomis asked me to come."

The cop left the nurse's aide, his grin fading, and came around to Gurney's side of the island. His shiny brass name tag said he was C. J. Mazurk. "Hello, sir," he said with that assessing look common to cops everywhere. "Who did you say you were?"

Gurney presented his ID.

He took it, studied it for a long moment, and handed it back. "DA's office?"

"Right. Mrs. Loomis is expecting me."

"She's down that hall. Visitors area. Turn off your phone."

Gurney complied. Halfway along the corridor there was a room with couches, chairs, and a wall-mounted TV tuned to a weather channel. When he stepped inside he saw at the far end of the room a sideboard with a coffee machine and next to it three women sitting at a small table. Heather Loomis, Kim Steele, and Madeleine.

His surprise at seeing Kim and his wife faded as he recognized a phenomenon he'd witnessed many times—the instinctive support police wives give each other in difficult circumstances. Heather and Kim were already well acquainted, of course, through their husbands. And it had been Madeleine's sense of identification with Kim that had solidified his own involvement in the case.

He greeted them, then sat in the fourth chair at the table.

"There's coffee," said Heather, pointing to the sideboard.

"Maybe later. Is there any news about Rick?"

"They say he's in stable condition."

"Barbiturate-induced coma," said Madeleine evenly. "To relieve the pressure on his brain. So it can heal. Like after my friend Elaine's car accident. She was put in a therapeutic coma for a couple of weeks. And she's perfectly fine today."

Heather blinked and managed a small smile. Kim took her hand and held it.

A cleaning woman with striking almond-shaped eyes, a dust-mask over her mouth and nose, and a name tag identifying her as Chalise Creel came into the room pushing a janitorial cart. She steered it through the obstacle course of couches and chairs to the sideboard, emptied its waste container into one in the base of the cart, and steered her cart back out into the corridor.

Heather turned to Gurney. "You got my message?"

"It was patchy, but I got enough of it to know you wanted to see me."

She reached into her sweatshirt pocket, pulled out an index card, and handed it to him.

Scribbled across the middle of the card were some unevenly spaced letters and numbers:

To L D C 13 111

He examined it for a moment. "What is this?"

"It's a message from Rick. When they brought him in from the ambulance and were attaching the monitor things to him, he was trying to speak. They wanted me to see if I could understand what he was saying, but he couldn't get it out. I asked the nurse to get something for him to write on, and she came back with a pen and that index card. I put the pen in his hand and the card under it on the stretcher. It took him a long time to print those letters, lying on his back, barely conscious. But that's what he wrote."

After studying the sequence of characters, Gurney tried one way of grouping them, reading aloud, "'To LDC thirteen thousand one hundred eleven.'" He looked at Heather. "Do the initials 'LDC' mean anything to you? Or that number? Possibly as an amount of money?"

She shook her head.

"Suppose we grouped the opening letters differently: 'Told C thirteen thousand one hundred eleven.'"

She shook her head again.

"Maybe we should read the number as individual digits, like a zip code."

"It still doesn't mean anything to me."

"It has to mean *something*," said Kim. "Something he wanted you to know."

It occurred to Gurney that the "message" might be nothing more than the product of a delirious brain; but it was clear that Heather and Kim wanted it to be important, and he wasn't going to deflate that hope.

"May I take this with me?" he asked Heather.

She nodded. "I think Rick may have intended it for you."

"I pray to God you get the bastard who shot him," said Kim. Her eyes were welling with angry tears.

Her emotion led to a silence.

Finally Heather spoke up in a controlled voice. "Dell Beckert was here."

"What did he want?" asked Gurney.

"At first? To pretend that he cared about Rick."

"And then?"

"He wanted to know how many phones Rick had."

Gurney had a sinking feeling. "What did you tell him?"

"I told him Rick had a department-issued BlackBerry, an iPhone, and our house phone."

"Did he want to know anything else?"

"He asked if Rick had any contact with individuals from the Black Defense Alliance or from that other one, whatever it's called. White Men for Black Justice? Their spokesman keeps popping up on those programs where everybody yells at each other. Cory Payne? I think that's his name. He hates the police."

"And you said?"

"I said Rick kept his police work to himself. Then Beckert told me the . . . the other shot . . ." She hesitated, glancing at Kim.

"It's all right. Go ahead."

"He told me the shot that hit John Steele came from an apartment linked to a BDA member. And the one that hit Rick may also have come from a house with a BDA link."

Gurney paused, taking this in, before returning to an earlier point. "Those phones you told Beckert about—do you know which of them Rick used for the calls he made to me, or to the diner, or to the person who wanted to come to the meeting we were supposed to have?"

"None of them. Rick has a fourth phone I didn't mention, an anonymous pre-paid one he used for calls about the project he and John were working on."

"Where's that fourth phone now?"

"Rick keeps it hidden. All I know is that it never leaves our house. And that he'd never want Beckert to get hold of it."

Gurney felt a sense of selfish relief. That hidden phone was the only hard evidence of his conversation with Loomis. As long as it remained hidden there was little chance of his being charged with failing to report that conversation. As he was wondering how well hidden it was, a short brown-skinned man in green hospital scrubs entered the room. A white plastic name tag identified him as P. W. Patel, MD.

"Mrs. Loomis?"

She turned toward him, her eyes full of fear.

"I don't bring you any bad news," he said in a softly accented voice. "I came only to tell you that in a few minutes we will take your husband to radiology for another brain-imaging procedure. The neurosurgeon has requested this. It is a normal request, not a cause for worry. If you and your companions wish to see the patient before he is taken to radiology, this must be done now. You understand?"

Heather nodded. "Can you tell if there's been any change in his condition?"

"No change, but this is not bad. With TBI we must wait and see."

"TBI?"

"Traumatic brain injury. We wait and monitor intracranial pressure. Because of damage to the temporal bone structure. Perhaps this will not be a problem, since the bullet did not perforate major brain areas. But we wait and watch."

Heather nodded uncertainly. "Thank you."

"You are welcome, Mrs. Loomis. Perhaps not too far away there can be good news. But now, if you wish to see your husband for a few minutes . . ."

"Yes, I understand."

After he left the room, Madeleine asked Heather, "Do you want us to come with you?"

She blinked in confusion. "Yes. I don't know. Yes, come." She stood up and headed out of the room, seemingly unaware of banging her shin on the corner of a low coffee table.

They followed her—Kim, Madeleine, and Gurney in that order—into the corridor and past the nursing station, where the cop and the nurse's aide had resumed their conversation. Behind the nursing station they came to a row of patient enclosures with sliding glass doors. At the center of each enclosure was a high-tech hospital bed surrounded by monitoring equipment.

Only one enclosure was occupied. The four visitors gathered outside it in the single-file order in which they'd come down the hall. From where Gurney stood, all he could see of the patient in the bed was a massive bandage covering his head, an oxygen mask covering most of his face, and a web of wires and tubes connecting him to the bedside machines. He looked vulnerable and anonymous.

A tall nurse approached Heather. "You know the routine here, but I'll repeat it for your friends. Please do not touch anything beyond those glass doors. Especially do not touch the patient or the devices connected to him. The sensors are sensitive. The alarms go off easily. Are we all okay with this?"

Heather answered for everyone. "Of course. Thank you."

Leaning toward her, the nurse spoke softly. "I've seen folks in worse shape than your husband come through just fine."

Heather opened the sliding glass door and went to her husband's side. Kim followed part of the way, stopping inside the doorway. Madeleine remained outside. Gurney stood behind her.

The intensity of Heather's focus on Rick began to make Gurney feel out of place. It soon appeared to have the same effect on Kim, who backed out of the enclosure. She whispered to Madeleine, "Maybe we should let her be alone with him?"

Madeleine nodded her agreement. Just then they saw Heather bending over the bed, the tip of her forefinger touching the back of Rick's hand.

"I'm here with you," she said gently. "I'm right here beside you."

As Gurney was leaving the ICU, he noted that the cop and the nurse's aide were still very much involved with each other. He stopped by the corner of the nursing station.

"Excuse me, Officer? Over here, please."

The cop stared at him.

"Now. Please."

The nurse's aide raised an eyebrow and stepped away, saying something about making her rounds.

The cop's stare got chillier as he approached Gurney. "What's up?"

"I assume you're here to protect Rick Loomis. Do you have any idea what you're protecting him from?"

"What's that supposed to mean?"

"You think you're here to prevent unauthorized media intrusions, make sure no reporters get in, or try to take pictures, or try to talk to Loomis. That about right?"

His eyes narrowed. "What's your point?"

"My point is that the media idiots are the least of your problems. There's something about the shooting you need to know. The public version is that Loomis was shot by black radicals because he's a cop. But the fact is he may have been shot for another reason. By someone who wanted him dead—not just any cop, but *him* in particular. If that's true, there may be another attempt on his life. It could happen soon, and it could happen here."

"Where the hell are you getting this from?"

"That doesn't matter. What matters is that you understand what's at stake here."

The cop pursed his lips and nodded with obvious skepticism. "What was your name again?"

Gurney repeated his name. "Pass along what I told you to whomever relieves you. They need to understand what they're here for."

The expression on the cop's face gave Gurney the feeling that his comments might or might not get passed along to the next shift, but they'd surely get to Judd Turlock.

Gurney left the ICU and headed for the visitors' lounge. When he got there he found Madeleine waiting for him in the corridor. Kim was inside sitting on one of the couches. Madeleine led him away from the open doorway and spoke in a low voice.

"Is there anything else you need to do here?"

He shrugged. "I've done all I can for the moment. Which isn't much. How about you?"

"Heather wants to stay here overnight. Kim wants to stay with her. I think that's what I should do too."

"Stay here in the ICU?"

"There's a facility here on the grounds. The Mercy Visitors Inn, for family and friends of patients. It just feels right to be with them."

"Do you want me to stay?"

"I'd like that. But I think Heather and Kim would rather you were off somewhere *investigating*—discovering the meaning of Rick's note."

"Isn't tomorrow one of your days at the clinic?"

"I'll call Gerry tonight. If she can't cover for me herself, she'll get someone." She touched his cheek. "Drive safely. I'll call you if anything changes."

He made no move to leave.

She cocked her head and gave him a long sideways look. "There's something you're not saying. What is it?"

"I'd rather you weren't staying here."

"Why?"

"I think there's a possibility of a second attempt on Loomis's life."

"Here?"

"It's possible."

"Is it likely?"

"I don't know. The possibility scares me. It's not a situation I want you to be in."

She uttered a little one-syllable laugh and shook her head. "God knows I've been in worse situations. More than a few times. When we were running the abused women's shelter at the clinic, we were getting horrendous threats all the time. And then there was that other little matter of the firebombing, when someone thought we were resettling refugees. Remember that?"

"Still . . ."

"The *possibility* you're talking about isn't going to convince Heather or Kim to leave. I feel strongly that staying with them is the right thing for me to do."

"Then I really should—"

She cut him off. "Don't even think about staying here for something that iffy.

You've committed yourself to the investigation. Go do your job, and I'll do mine. I'm serious. People are relying on you. We'll be fine here. I'll make sure that Romeo out there keeps his eyes open for strangers and off the nurses."

He reluctantly agreed, wishing he felt better about it.

She kissed him on the cheek.

25

A nearly invisible drizzle began shortly after he pulled out of the hospital parking lot, requiring only a single swipe of the wiper blades every minute or two. The blades needed replacing, having developed a stuttering squeak that kept intruding into his thoughts. On the section of the interstate between White River and Gurney's exit, there was virtually no traffic. On the winding road from there to Walnut Crossing, there was none.

For most of the drive he'd been turning Rick's message over in his mind, with the assumption that it meant something and wasn't just the equivalent of someone talking in his sleep. But whatever that sequence—T O L D C 1 3 1 1 1—might signify, it continued to elude him. It had the appearance of a coded communication, but it seemed a far reach to imagine that a barely conscious man who'd just taken a bullet in the head would have the presence of mind required to encode something. And even if he did, for whom would it be intended? John Steele was dead; and the code meant nothing to Heather.

But if it wasn't a code, what was it? An abbreviation would be one possibility. If he were having a hard time writing, shortening the message as much as he could would make sense. But an abbreviation of what? And which letters were attached to which? Did the message begin, "To LDC"? Or was it "Told C"? Did the following number represent a dollar amount? An address? A quantity of something?

Gurney was getting nowhere as he turned onto the road that led to his property, so he decided to put the issue aside. Perhaps later he'd be able to see whatever he was missing now.

He parked next to the old farmhouse. He went inside, got some carrot soup and salmon out of the refrigerator, and put the soup in a pot to warm it. He went into the bedroom to exchange his sport jacket, button-down shirt, and slacks for a well-worn flannel shirt and faded jeans. Then he donned his old rain slicker and headed out to the chicken coop.

The hens were already up on their perch. He checked the nesting boxes for eggs, checked the levels of chicken feed and water, and redistributed some straw that had gotten pushed into a corner. On his return to the house he stopped at the asparagus patch. Using the miniature jackknife attached to his key ring, he harvested a handful of spears, brought them in, and stood them in a mug with some water in the bottom to keep them fresh. After hanging his slicker to dry, he put his soup in a bowl and his salmon on a plate and brought them both to the table.

As he was eating, his mind returned to the cryptic jottings on the index card. This time, instead of asking which letters and numbers might belong together, he asked himself what sort of information the man might have been trying to convey.

If Loomis believed he was dying, he might have wanted to leave a love note for Heather. Gurney imagined that if he himself were dying, letting Madeleine know he loved her would be the only thing that mattered. But if Loomis's sense of his condition was less than fatal, what might he want the people close to him to know?

Perhaps the identity of the individual who shot him.

Perhaps the identity of the person he was going to bring to his meeting with Gurney.

Perhaps both of the above—especially if they were one and the same.

In that context, "Told C13111" might be a shortened version of "I told C13111 about my planned meeting with Dave Gurney."

But how could those characters be read as someone's name?

The thought occurred to him that they might be an ID number, perhaps belonging to a White River police officer. But then he recalled that Mark Torres's badge number had three digits followed by three letters. So, if it was an ID number, what organization did it belong to? Gurney had no answer. In fact, he had the feeling it was the wrong question.

As for the possibility that the initial *C* might refer to the individual and 13111 be his zip code . . . that seemed such an unlikely way to describe a person he would have dismissed it without another thought, except that the number did fall within the range of zips for upstate New York. He recalled that he was about to check its location when he was at the ICU but couldn't because of the cell phone prohibition.

He realized his phone had been turned off ever since. He picked it up and turned it on.

It told him he'd received three voice messages in the past twenty-eight minutes. The first was from Sheridan Kline, the second from Madeleine, and the third from Dr. Walter Thrasher. He decided to listen to Madeleine's first.

"Hi, hon. Kim and I just checked in to the Visitors Inn. Heather is still over at the ICU waiting for them to bring Rick back from radiology. We're going to pick her up in a little while and get something to eat. There's not much to report. A new cop replaced the other one. This one is a bit more alert than Romeo. I guess that's it for now. Get some sleep. You were looking exhausted. Talk to you in the morning. Love you."

He listened to Kline's message next.

"Where are you? I expected to hear from you by now. When I finally got in touch with someone at the crime scene, I was told you left before the evidence search was completed. Because you got a call from Heather Loomis? Is that right? Christ, David, you're working for me, not Heather Loomis. The point of your involvement was to give me your real-time perspective. Things are moving fast. We have data from the scene, from Beckert's informants, from the traffic and security cameras, from the computer lab in Albany. It's pouring in. And you decide to run off to the hospital and not answer your phone? Jesus!"

He paused and let out an audible sigh before going on in a less agitated tone. "There's a team meeting tomorrow morning at nine sharp to review everything we've got—which may include a clear photo of the Corolla driver. And there's new evidence implicating the Gort brothers in the Willard Park homicides. Please be at the meeting." His tone became more confidential. "The elements of both cases are coming together beautifully. I'd like your concurrence that it all makes sense. I want our ducks lined up. Get back to me as soon as you can."

People who talked about wanting their ducks lined up made Gurney uneasy. The phrase suggested a greater desire for order than for truth.

He postponed listening to the message from Thrasher. He assumed it would be related to the artifacts the man had borrowed for closer examination, and he had no appetite at that moment for discussing the archaeology of Colonial America.

He brought his empty bowl and plate to the sink, washed them, and put them in the dish drainer. By the time he was finished, the pasture, the coop, the barn, and the pond were disappearing into darkness.

He didn't know if it was the suggestive power of Madeleine's commenting on how tired he looked, but he did feel like closing his eyes for a while. He went into the den first to see if there were any messages on the landline answering machine.

There were three. The first was from a strident female voice offering big savings on his electric bill. The second was from a folksy male voice offering a preapproved loan for his nonexistent poultry company. The third was from the Walnut Crossing library informing Madeleine that a book she'd reserved was now available: *Beetles of North America.*

He went from the den to their downstairs bedroom, thinking a quick nap might take the edge off his drowsiness. He removed his shoes and lay down on the soft quilt they used as a bedspread. He could hear the faint yipping of coyotes above the high pasture. Then he fell into a deep dreamless sleep.

He was awakened at 6:40 the next morning by the ringing of the den phone.

He got to it just as Madeleine was starting to leave a message.

"I'm here," he said, picking up the receiver.

"Oh, good! I'm glad I got you."

"Is something wrong?"

"Rick has apparently suffered some kind of respiratory failure. He's on full life support. Heather is falling apart."

"Oh, Christ. Did anything specific happen?"

"I don't really know anything. Just what the doctor told Heather. They're doing some tests. They're trying to figure it out. Maybe there was more brain damage than they realized at first? I don't know."

"I'm just trying get a sense of whether there was any outside interference."

"David, nobody knows anything more than what I've just told you."

"Okay. All right. Are you staying there with Heather?"

"With Heather and Kim, yes."

"Okay. I have a meeting at police headquarters at nine o'clock. I'll stop by the hospital on my way."

After a shower and a change of clothes, he set out for White River. It was a heavily overcast morning, with patches of thick fog adding twenty minutes to his normal driving time. He pulled into the Mercy Hospital parking lot at 8:30 AM.

On his way into the building he noted a pair of WRPD patrol cars by the portico.

Madeleine was waiting for him just inside the main door. They hugged, holding each other longer and more tightly than usual. When they let go and stepped back she smiled, which somehow underscored the sadness in her eyes.

"Any news?" he asked.

"Nothing substantial. More tests, more scans. Another specialist on his way from somewhere. They've temporarily closed the ICU to visitors."

"How's Heather?"

"A complete wreck. Understandably."

"Did they let her stay upstairs?"

"No. She's down in the cafeteria with Kim. She won't eat, but . . ." Her voice trailed off. "Oh God, this is so awful."

A huge man with a neck brace and a bulging bandage covering one eye was making his way past them on a walker. Madeleine watched as he lumbered on, limping and grunting. Then she turned to Gurney. "You better get to your meeting. There's nothing you can do here. If anything changes, I'm sure word will get to Beckert as soon as it gets to us."

Maybe sooner, he thought.

Sheridan Kline, Mark Torres, Dwayne Shucker, and Goodson Cloutz were in their seats at the conference table when Gurney arrived. He sat, as usual, next to Kline, who gave him an icy nod—which reminded him that he hadn't returned the man's phone call.

With the back of his hand Shucker was wiping what appeared to be powdered sugar from the corners of his mouth. There was a container of coffee and an open paper bag in front of him. The printing on the bag said DELILAH'S DONUTS.

Cloutz, in his blind man's glasses, was running the tips of his fingers slowly along the length of his white cane, which was lying crosswise on the table, as though he were stroking a pet snake. His well-tended nails had a higher-than-usual gloss.

Torres was absorbed in some work on his laptop.

At precisely nine o'clock Beckert entered the room and took his central seat opposite Kline, his back to the broad window. The jail was a dim presence in the fog. He laid a file folder down, casually aligning its edge to the edge of the table.

He cleared his throat. "Good morning, gentlemen."

There was a general murmuring of similar greetings around the table.

"I'm pleased to report," Beckert began in an emotionless tone, "that our investigations into the shootings of our officers and the murder of the BDA members are on the verge of completion. Detective Torres will review where we stand on the Steele and Loomis cases, but first I want to pass along some good news from Deputy Chief Turlock. Lab analysis has confirmed an exact match between the rope we recovered from the Gort twins' compound and the ropes used to tie up Jordan and Tooker. A warrant has been issued for their arrest. We have reason to believe they may be hiding up in one of the old quarries above the reservoir. A K9 tracking dog and handler, plus an assault team, have been dispatched to that area."

"The reason being what?" said Gurney.

"Excuse me?"

"The reason you think they're hiding in the quarries—what is it?"

Beckert's expression showed nothing. "Reliable informants."

"Whose identities you can't share with us?"

"Correct." He held Gurney's gaze for a moment before continuing. "The K9 team has an impressive record of success. We hope to bring the Gorts in quickly and have Sheridan launch an aggressive prosecution—to minimize the racial leverage available to the riot inciters."

Shucker pointed an enthusiastic forefinger at Beckert. "To what you just said about bringing them lunatics in, I would personally add *dead or alive*. In fact, *dead*, in my humble opinion, would be a damn sight preferable."

Again Beckert showed no reaction. He simply moved on to the Steele-Loomis shootings. "Mark, your turn now. My impression is that the evidence you've amassed against the BDA 'third man' is pretty conclusive. Take us through it."

Torres reopened his computer.

Gurney cast a glance at Kline, whose anxious frown might reflect some concern with the political impact on himself of an 'aggressive' prosecution of the popular Gorts.

Torres began in his typically earnest manner. "These are the key discoveries we've made since our last meeting. First of all, the rush ballistics report on the bullet used in the Loomis shooting indicates that it was fired from the same rifle used in the Steele shooting. In addition, prints on the cartridge casing recovered at the site used for the Loomis shooting match prints on the one recovered at the Steele site. And the extractor marks indicate both cartridges came from the same rifle."

"Were there any other fingerprints at the Poulter Street house matching the ones on the casing?" asked Gurney.

"There was a matching print on the knob of the side door."

"Not on the back door? The door to the room? The window sash?"

"No, sir. Just on the cartridge casing and the side door."

"Were there any other fresh fingerprints anywhere in the house?"

"None that Garrett found. There was a partial print on a pen, which I believe you discovered in the backyard. And there were footprints. Boot prints, actually. Several in the backyard, some by the side door of the house, partials on the stairs, and a couple in the room where the shot was fired."

Torres then summarized the accounts given by Gloria Fenwick and Hollis Vitter, the neighbors on opposite sides of the Poulter Street house.

"This would be a good time to show the mapping graphic you described to me earlier," said Beckert.

"Yes, sir." A few mouse clicks later the monitor over the sheriff's head came to life, displaying a street map of White River and the adjacent section of Willard Park. Two colored lines, a blue one and a red one, beginning at the same point on Poulter Street, diverged into separate routes through the city streets. Torres explained that the blue line represented the route taken by the Corolla from the sniper house after the shooting and the red line the route taken by the motorcycle.

The blue line proceeded directly along one of White River's main avenues to a point where the city's business section abutted the fire-damaged Grinton neighborhood. The red line, however, zigzagged here and there through the side streets of Bluestone and Grinton to the edge of Willard Park, where it ended.

Shucker removed a powdery doughnut from the bag in front of him and took a thoughtful bite, which turned his lips white. "Looks to me like the Corolla driver knew where he was going, and the motorcycle rider didn't have a clue."

"There's a termination point shown for each route," said Kline. "Were the vehicles found at those locations?"

"Correct, sir, in the case of the Corolla. It was discovered at the corner of Sliwak Avenue and North Street by WRPD patrol officers at approximately six ten this morning. Garrett Felder and Shelby Towns are going over it now for latents and trace evidence."

"You said 'in the case of the Corolla'—meaning the motorcycle wasn't found?"

"Correct, sir. I should explain that the two lines we're showing on the map were constructed differently. Once it left Poulter Street, the Corolla followed a thoroughfare that's covered by traffic department cameras—which gave us a video record of the car's route. But the motorcycle's route had to be reconstructed with the help of witnesses along the way. Starting with Hollis Vitter, we found a sequence of individuals who heard or saw a motocross bike at the time in question. Lucky for us, it was a nice afternoon and a lot of people were outside."

"You got a description of the bike?"

"Red motocross with a loud engine."

"Plate number?"

"Nobody noticed."

"Any description of the rider?"

"Full leather riding suit, full-coverage helmet and visor, no identifying elements."

"And you say the bike wasn't found at the end of the route?"

"The end point shown on the map is just the last place where we have witness observation. It may have cut into the park at that point and taken one of the wilderness trails to just about anywhere."

"Okay," said Kline, with prosecutor-like intensity. "If I've got this right, we have a load of video on the Corolla and no video at all on the motorcycle, even though its roundabout route covered a lot more ground?"

"That's correct, sir."

Shucker took another huge bite out of his doughnut. As he spoke, specks of sugar flew onto the table. "Any of them Corolla videos give us a picture of the driver?"

"I was coming to that, sir. We have partials that were captured under different angle, shadow, and glare conditions. No single video frame provides a usable likeness, but the Albany lab has a composite process that may give us what we need. They can combine the best parts of multiple shots and resolve them into one high-definition image. At least that's the theory."

"When?" asked Kline.

"We emailed them the digital files last night, and I spoke to them this morning. If we're lucky, we may get something back by the end of this meeting."

Kline looked skeptical. "That's amazingly fast for Albany."

The sheriff uttered an unpleasant little laugh. "Upside of an impending race war is we get attention."

Beckert glanced at his watch. "Let's keep this moving along, Mark. Where do we stand on tracking down the rental information?"

"Interesting news there, sir. This morning we finally got hold of the records for the locations used as the sniper sites. Both leases are in the name of Marcel Jordan."

Beckert exhibited a rare fleeting smile. "That eliminates all doubt about BDA involvement."

Something in Gurney's expression caught his eye. "You don't agree?"

"I agree that it provides support for a certain view of the case. As for eliminating all doubt, that's a leap I wouldn't make."

Beckert held his gaze for a moment, then turned mildly to Torres. "Do you have anything else for us?"

"That's it for now, sir, until we get the enhanced photo from Albany and the report on the Corolla from Garrett."

"Speaking of Albany," said Beckert, looking at Kline, "have the computer people gotten back to you regarding Steele's phone?"

"Not with a full report, which is why I haven't mentioned it. But I spoke to a tech yesterday, and he told me their initial analysis uncovered nothing of immediate interest. He emailed me a printout of numbers called and received during the past three months. Steele used that phone to call his wife, his sister in Hawaii, local movie theaters, his dentist, an electrician, restaurants around the area, a takeout pizza joint in Angina, a gym in Larvaton, Home Depot, a few other places like that. Apart from his sister, nothing really personal. And apart from that one strange text the night he was killed, no calls or texts from anonymous prepaids or even from blocked numbers. Really not much to follow up on. They'll be sending us their final report in a day or two."

Beckert's fleeting smile made a second appearance. "So. Much ado about nothing."

"Strange," said Gurney.

Kline gave him a sharply inquisitive look.

"What's strange about it?" asked Beckert.

"No mention of calls to or from Rick Loomis."

"Why is that strange?"

"I got the impression they were in frequent contact."

"Maybe they preferred email."

"That must be the answer," said Gurney, sure that it wasn't the answer at all.

"Right," said Beckert with the finality of a slammed door. "If no one else has anything to contribute at this time—"

"I do," said the sheriff. "Having let certain guests at my facility know I was curious what arrangements Devalon Jones had made for his Corolla during his rehabilitation in Dannemora, I was told he had entrusted said vehicle to Blaze Lovely Jackson. Which makes her the keeper of the shooter's car, which is a hell of a thing to consider."

Kline cast an amazed look down the table. "Christ, Goodson, in our last meeting you suggested she might be responsible for the murders of Jordan and Tooker. Now you're adding Steele and Loomis?"

"Ain't addin' nobody on my own wisdom, counselor. Just sayin' what was said to me by a man with some knowledge of the street."

Cloutz had gone back to lightly stroking his white cane, a gesture Gurney was finding increasingly repellent. He tried to keep his reaction out of his voice.

"What did he get in return for telling you this?"

"Not a damn thing. I told him we'd assess the value of his information to the investigation, and his reward would be contingent. I always say that with a smile—*contingent*—like it is a particularly good kind of reward. Works like a charm with the less educated. Worked so good this time, the man wanted to keep tellin' me things. For instance, he volunteered that Ms. Jackson was fuckin' someone in secret—which I thought was of considerable interest."

Kline looked puzzled. "The relevance of her sexual activity is . . ."

"The relevance of her fuckin' has got no relevance at all. What's of interest is that she's tryin' to keep it a secret. Makes you wonder why."

Beckert pondered this for a few seconds, then shook his head. "The point that matters here is the expanding evidence of BDA involvement. Making threatening antipolice speeches. Renting the sites from which the shots were fired. Providing the vehicle used by the shooter. Beyond that let's not complicate things with extraneous details. Complication makes the public dizzy. Are we clear on this?"

"Simpler the better," said Shucker.

"I prefer my simplicity with a twist," said Cloutz, making his preference sound lascivious. "But I get your point," he added. "A simple tale of the law versus the lawless."

Beckert's gaze moved on to Gurney.

Gurney said nothing.

In the silence there was a sense of imminent confrontation.

Whatever might have occurred was aborted by the surprisingly loud *bing* of an email arriving on Torres's computer.

His eyes widened with excitement. "It's from the Albany computer lab. There's an attachment. I think it's the enhanced Corolla shot we've been waiting for." Two clicks later the screen of the wall monitor was filled by a medium close-up of a young man in the driver's seat. The photo had been taken through the windshield, but whatever glare may have compromised the raw footage had been removed. The sharpness of the image was impressive. The facial details were clear.

The young man's reddish-blond hair was pulled back from his forehead into a loose ponytail, emphasizing his deep-set eyes and angular features.

Shucker's hand stopped halfway to his mouth with the last bit of his doughnut. "That boy looks mighty familiar."

Kline nodded. "Yes. I'm sure I've seen him somewhere before."

Gurney had also seen the face before—on the giant screen at Marv and Trish Gelter's house—but the name was eluding him. He remembered it just as Beckert announced it—in a voice as icy as the look in his eyes. "Cory Payne."

"*Cory Payne.*" The sheriff articulated the name as though it had a foul taste. "Ain't he the one behind White Morons Spoutin' Black Bullshit?"

"White Men for Black Justice," offered Torres mildly.

The sheriff let out a harsh one-syllable laugh.

"Cory Payne," repeated Kline slowly. "I've seen him on those RAM debate shows."

"Nazi storm troopers," said Shucker.

Kline blinked. "How's that, Dwayne?"

"That's what he calls the police," said Shucker. "Boy's got a hair up his ass about law enforcement."

"That strident tone of his always sounded to me like grandstanding," said Kline. "Adolescent nonsense. That's all I thought it was. Talk."

"Have to admit I thought that myself," said the sheriff. "That boy's voice on the TV sounded like a little dog barkin' at big dogs. I never would've thought he had the balls to be a shooter."

"Goes to show you never know before you know," said Shucker, eyeing the piece of doughnut in his hand. "Sometimes the evilest ones are the last ones you'd ever think to look at. Like that sweet little Doris at the Zippy-Mart that chopped up her husband and kept him in the freezer for ten years."

"Twelve," said the sheriff. "Goin' by the dates of the newspapers the pieces was wrapped in."

Beckert stood up abruptly, his voice like a tight fist. "Enough, gentlemen. The fact is we were all deceived by Payne's sophomoric gibberish. The situation is critical and the time element is crucial. Detective Torres, put out an immediate APB on Cory Payne."

"Suspicion of murder?"

"Yes, in the case of John Steele. Attempted murder in the Loomis case. I'll have Baylor Puckett issue the warrant. Judd Turlock maintains a file of local agitators. He can give you Payne's address. Get there ASAP, backed up by an assault team in the event that Payne resists. Seal off the apartment. Seize everything. Get Payne's prints from his personal items and match them to whatever Garrett and Shelby were able to get from the car and the sniper sites. Any questions from the media, refer them to my office. Keep me informed on an hourly basis. Or immediately with any significant development. Questions?"

"No, sir. "

"Then go!" Beckert had the look of a man whose mind was racing to assess an array of unpleasant possibilities.

Torres picked up his laptop and hurried out of the conference room.

"There some reason you don't want to arrest the bitch that gave him the car?" asked the sheriff. There was something vaguely insinuating in his tone.

"I'd rather have her watched. We'll learn more from her movements than from anything she'd be willing to tell us."

Kline's eyes lit up. "You don't suppose that Cory Payne—"

Beckert cut him off. "That Payne might be her secret lover? The rumor that Goodson's snitch told him about? I think it's one of the possibilities we need to look into."

"If it were true, it would give us a damn good motive."

"We already have a damn good motive," interjected the sheriff. "Boy hates cops. Boy shoots cops. Simple."

"This one's better," said Kline. "Love-sick white boy shoots cops to impress black-activist girlfriend. Juries love romantic motives. The more depraved the better."

Beckert was radiating tension. "Gentlemen, we need to get a grip on where we are. I don't want people whose support could be helpful blindsided by sensational news reports." He looked at his watch. "Let's get back together at two o'clock to discuss next steps. I'm sorry if the four-hour gap is inconvenient, but this situation takes priority. Sheridan, you're the farthest from your regular office. If you wish, you can use the one at the end of the hall."

Kline thanked him, and, without another word, Beckert left the room.

26

Gurney was eager to get out of the building, which he was finding increasingly oppressive. He walked out into the parking lot. The sky was still overcast. The air's acrid, smoky edge was as noticeable as ever, but he found it preferable to the atmosphere in the conference room. He couldn't quite sort out the primary source of his discomfort—the repugnant people, the bleak fluorescent-lit room, the surreal view from the window, or his persistent feeling that the official approach to the intertwined attacks on the police and the BDA leaders was profoundly wrong.

As Gurney was thinking about how to utilize the long meeting break, Kline came out into the parking lot after him, looking more anxious than usual.

"Come," he said, gesturing peremptorily toward his SUV.

They got into the front seats. The man seemed to be looking for a place to put his hands, beginning with his lap and ending finally on the steering wheel.

"So," he said after a fraught silence. "What's your problem?"

Gurney found the aggressive tone oddly relaxing. "Be more specific."

Kline's hands opened and closed on the wheel. He was staring straight ahead. "I listen to what you say in these meetings. The kind of questions you ask. How you ask them. The disbelief, the disrespect. If I'm wrong, tell me." There was a tic at the corner of his mouth.

"I'm trying to recall a disrespectful question. Give me an example."

"It's not any one thing. It's the pattern of nitpicking negativity. How come the red laser dot followed Steele as long as it did? How come he was shot moving instead of standing still? When we find fingerprints, you want to know why we didn't find *more* fingerprints. You make a big deal out of there being an odd message on Steele's phone, then you make a big deal out of there not being *more* odd messages. You focus on every minuscule detail that isn't instantly explainable. You totally ignore the big picture."

"The big picture?"

"Perfectly credible narratives for the Steele-Loomis shootings and the Jordan-Tooker beating and strangling deaths. Overwhelming evidence against Cory Payne for the first. Overwhelming evidence against the Gort twins for the second. Slam-dunk cases. But for some reason you can't accept that we've won. I don't get it."

"You're overestimating the slam-dunk potential. I've been pointing out some troubling facts that could undermine—"

Kline interrupted. "The flyspecks you're pointing out won't undermine anything, except your own credibility. I mean it, David. The big picture is what matters, and you're refusing to accept it."

"I'm sorry you see it that way."

Kline finally turned to face him. "This is all about Beckert, isn't it?"

"Beckert?"

"I've seen the expression on your face whenever he has anything to say. Is that what this is all about? A personality conflict? You just want him to be wrong? It's the only explanation."

Gurney quietly considered what he was about to say.

"If that's what you think, Sheridan, there's no way I can be of any further use to you."

Kline went back to staring straight ahead, hands on the wheel. "Unfortunately, I have to agree."

Gurney realized that the sense of relaxation he had felt at Kline's initial aggressiveness came from his anticipation of this moment. What he felt now was pure, unmistakable relief. Relief from a strange burden, never clearly defined, always more or less disquieting. It wasn't that he had any intention of abandoning the case or the responsibility he felt toward Kim and Heather or those who were killed. He would simply be abandoning his murky relationship with Kline.

"Would you like me to withdraw now?" he asked. "Or shall I stay on board until after the two o'clock meeting?"

"It might be better for you to come to the meeting. Smoother. And the investigation will be that much closer to being concluded. Just a matter of making the final arrests. That's the way your exit should be positioned. Not an abrupt decision. A natural event at the end of a process. Better for everyone, don't you think?"

"Sounds very sensible, Sheridan. I'll see you at two o'clock."

Neither offered to shake hands.

Gurney got out of the big black Navigator and headed for his modest Outback.

27

The Willard Park playground was deserted. There was a faint smell of lake water in the still air. The blackbirds in the bulrushes were silent. Under the steel skeleton of the jungle gym the sandy soil was dark and wet from the recent drizzle. Water had beaded on the pipelike crossbars and hung there, ready to drip.

Gurney was using the time available before the afternoon meeting to gain a more visceral sense of the place. He was intrigued by the fact that Willard Park was the location not only where the two BDA victims were found but also where the motorcycle from Poulter Street was last seen. It was the sort of odd little resonance or coincidence that Kline would dismiss as meaningless. But Kline's opinion had become irrelevant.

Standing with his back to the jungle gym, he looked over toward the field where the demonstration and the Steele shooting had taken place. The intervening space was dominated by Colonel Willard on his martial horse. In Gurney's mind the statue's presence—a concrete link to the dark legacy of the Willard slave catchers and the prison itself—cast a pall over the park.

He walked from the playground down to the edge of the lake and gazed out over the glassy gray surface. A trail on his right led into the woods that bordered the lake. He assumed it was the main one shown in the satellite photo Torres had presented—part of a web of trails connecting the park to the wilderness beyond it and to the private preserve of the White River Gun Club, where most of the hunting cabins were owned by White River cops.

It was surely the most tenuous of links ... but it was possible that the motorcycle fleeing from Poulter Street after the shooting of Rick Loomis may have used the same trails as the UTV that brought Jordan and Tooker to the playground. Gurney wasn't sure what that might mean, but the possibility that it was more than a coincidence produced a definite frisson.

A moment later the forlorn cry of a bird deep in the woods gave him goose bumps of a different sort. The eerie, keening sound was one he sometimes heard at dusk coming from the pine thicket on the far side of his pond. Although he knew his reaction was irrational, the strangely wavering note never failed to put him in an uneasy frame of mind.

He walked back from the lake to the jungle gym. He pictured Marcel Jordan and Virgil Tooker bound tightly to the tubular bars.

He peered at the bars to which the ropes had been tied. He had no idea what he was looking for, but he looked anyway, examining the structure as best he could.

The only minor peculiarities that caught his eye were two shiny spots, each about a half inch in diameter, about four feet apart on the bottom of a horizontal bar that according to the photos at the CSMT meeting would have been somewhere just above or behind the victims' heads. He had no idea what those spots might mean, if anything at all; but he remembered that among his saved emails was one Torres had sent with a link to all the photos Paul Aziz had taken. He made a mental note to access and review them as soon as he got home.

He still had some time before the two o'clock meeting at police headquarters, so he decided to take a closer look at the statue.

As he crossed the field, he noticed he wasn't the only one taking an interest in the statue. An African American woman in camo fatigues was approaching it on the opposite side. She appeared to be photographing it with her phone.

She ignored Gurney until they came within speaking distance of each other, and he asked with a smile if she knew anything about the man on the horse.

She stopped and gave him an assessing look. "They send you out here to make sure we don't tear that evil thing down?"

Gurney shook his head. "Nobody sent me."

"Honey, I know a cop when I see one, and the cops I know go where they are sent."

He suddenly recognized her—the voice first, then the face—from her appearance with the white supremacist on RAM-TV. "You may know Dell Beckert's cops, Ms. Jackson, but you don't know me."

Her dark eyes were fixed on his. There was something formidable in her calmness and in the evenness of her tone. "Why are you talking to me?"

Gurney shrugged. "As I said, I was wondering if you could tell me anything about the man on the horse."

She looked up at the mounted colonel, as if evaluating his pose for the first time. "He's the Devil," she said matter-of-factly.

"The Devil?"

"You want me to say it again?"

"Why do you call him that?"

"Man who does the Devil's work is the Devil in the flesh."

"Hmm. What about Dell Beckert? What can you tell me about him?"

There was a sharpness now in the gaze she fixed on Gurney—an almost glittery intelligence. "Isn't that a fascinating fact of life—how people always know the truth without knowing they know it."

"Meaning?"

"Think about it. Here we are, talking about the Devil. And look whose name came into your mind."

Gurney smiled. "Interesting observation."

She started to leave, then stopped. "You want to live, be careful. However well you think you know that law-and-order man, you don't know him any more than you know Ezra Willard."

She turned and walked quickly away toward the park exit.

After Gurney had returned to his car and spent some time contemplating the words of Blaze Lovely Jackson, it occurred to him that he should let Madeleine know his meeting at police headquarters had been extended into the afternoon. He'd be heading home later than expected.

As he was about to place the call, his phone rang.

Seeing Madeleine's name on the screen, he began to explain his situation, but she cut in immediately.

"They took Rick off life support."

"Oh, Jesus. Is Heather . . . okay?"

"Not really. They took her down to the emergency room. They're afraid she may be starting premature contractions." After a pause during which he could hear his wife breathing shakily, she sniffled and cleared her throat. "The doctor said Rick had lost all brain function. There was no chance . . . no chance of any . . . anything."

"Yes." He could think of nothing more to say. Nothing that would be both comforting and honest.

"Rick's brother is flying in from somewhere. And Heather's sister, too. I'll let you know what I'm doing when things are clearer."

As soon as he ended the call, his phone rang again.

When he saw Kline's name on the screen, he assumed the man was calling with the same bad news and decided to let the call go to voicemail. He hardly noticed that the temperature was dropping and it had begun again to drizzle.

He sat in the Outback for a while, losing track of time. He took out the index card and studied the cryptic message. Again, he got nowhere. He put it back in his pocket.

Feeling the need to do something—*anything*—he took out his phone and called Jack Hardwick. He got the man's terse recording: "Leave a message. Be brief."

"We need to talk. The White River mess is getting stranger and uglier. The second cop who was shot—a young detective by the name of Loomis—just died. Kline wants me out of it. He insists that everything's coming together, conclusive evidence, done deal. I don't agree. If you can, meet me tomorrow morning at eight at Abelard's. Call me if you can't. Otherwise, I'll see you there."

Before putting his phone away, he checked his list of messages. There were only two he hadn't listened to—the one from Kline and the older one from Thrasher. He had no interest in listening to either.

The phone was halfway into his pocket when it rang. Kline again. His stubborn streak urged him to ignore it again, but something else—perhaps simple logic—told him to talk to the man and get it over with.

"Gurney here."

"I just wanted to let you know the two o'clock meeting's been canceled."

"Problems?"

"Just the opposite. A major coup. Dell's been invited to appear tonight on *A Matter of Concern with Carlton Flynn*."

"The pompous blowhard on RAM-TV?"

"He happens to be the most widely recognized news personality in the world, with one of the highest rated interview shows in America. He is a *very* big deal."

"I'm impressed."

"You should be. It's the perfect opportunity for Dell to set things straight—the demonstrations, the riots, the shootings—put it all in the right perspective, emphasizing the restoration of law and order. That's what people need to hear."

Gurney said nothing.

"You there?"

"I thought you might have been calling to let me know that Rick Loomis died."

"I assumed you'd have heard that from someone else."

Again Gurney said nothing.

"Not unexpected, given his condition. But now we know who did it, and the arrest is just a matter of time. You might be interested to know that the prints inside the Corolla and at the sniper sites match the prints in Cory Payne's apartment. Torres's guys even found a box of thirty-aught-six cartridges hidden in the back of one of his closets."

"I'm impressed."

"There's more good news. Our information on the Gort twins was right. The K9 team and an assault team are closing in on them up by the quarry ridge. Backup is on the way, and it should all be over within the hour."

"Good to know."

Gurney's tone seemed to finally get through.

"Look," said Kline, "I know we've had some unfortunate events. No one's denying that. Those things can't be undone. But the right steps have been taken. The right results are being achieved. That's the message. And Dell's the perfect messenger."

Gurney paused. "Do you plan to call Rick Loomis's wife?"

"Of course. At the appropriate time. Oh, one more thing. Housekeeping issue. We need you to turn in your credentials—along with an hourly tally of your time on the case."

"I'll do that."

They ended the call. They had ended their earlier conversation in the parking lot without shaking hands. They ended this one without saying good-bye.

Before putting his phone away, Gurney called Hardwick and left an additional message on his voicemail, suggesting that he watch Carlton Flynn's show that evening. Then he deleted the earlier message from Kline on his own phone. He had no appetite for listening to the man twice.

His own plan was to drive home, review Paul Aziz's photos, eat dinner, and then settle down for what promised to be a Dell Beckert master class in message control.

Getting Aziz's photos from the file-sharing service Torres had used to transmit them was easy enough. Sitting at the desk in his den, he began opening them, one after another, on his laptop.

Once he was past the harrowing views of the bodies, there was little that caught Gurney's attention until he was surprised to find closeups of the same two shiny spots he'd noted on the jungle gym crossbar.

Even more interesting were the next photos—close-ups of two separate sections of rope, showing a small, round depression in each. The sequence of the photos suggested a connection between the shiny spots and the depressions in the ropes.

He put an immediate call in to Torres and left a message describing the photos and asking for Aziz's contact information—hoping that word hadn't already gotten from Kline to Torres that he was off the official roster.

He was surprised to get a response less than ten minutes later—and equally surprised that the call came from Aziz himself.

"Mark gave me your number. He told me you had questions about some of the crime-scene shots." The voice on the phone was young and earnest, not unlike Torres's, and with no trace of the Middle East.

"Thanks for getting back to me so quickly. I'm curious about the two shiny spots on the jungle gym crossbar and the flat spots on the ropes—obviously photographed after the bodies were taken down. Do you recall how they were originally positioned in relation to each other?"

"The flat spots on the ropes were located where they went over top of the crossbar. The shiny spots were aligned below them, on the bottom of the bar. If Mark just showed you closeup photos of the bodies in situ, you wouldn't have noticed what I'm talking about, because those ropes were behind the victims' heads, tying their necks to the structure."

"Did any scenario occur to you that would explain the apparent connection between the shiny spots and the flat spots?"

"Not at the time. I just automatically photograph anything that seems odd." He hesitated. "But . . . maybe some kind of clamp?"

Gurney tried to picture it. "You mean . . . as if someone had pulled a rope over the bar to hoist each victim into a standing position . . . then clamped the rope against the bar to hold him in place while they tied ropes around his stomach and legs?"

"I guess it could have been done that way. The way you describe it would be consistent with the markings."

"Very interesting. Thank you, Paul. Thank you for your time. And thank you for your close observation of details."

"I hope it helps."

After ending the call, Gurney sat back in his chair and gazed thoughtfully out the den window, trying to reconstruct the scene in his mind—to imagine circumstances that would *necessitate* the use of clamps. When he soon found himself thinking in circles, and even beginning to wonder if clamps were really the cause of the marks, he decided to take a shower—in the hope that it might clear his mind and help him relax.

In a way, it ended up doing both—although the "clearing" seemed to bring about more emptying than clarifying. Still, a clean mental slate was not a bad thing. And a reduction in tension was always good.

As he was finishing dressing in clean jeans and a comfortable polo shirt, his sense of peace was interrupted by the sound of a door opening and closing. Curious, he went out to the kitchen and met Madeleine coming in from the mudroom.

She said nothing, just walked to the far end of the long open area that served as their kitchen, dining room, and sitting room. She sat down on the couch by the fireplace. He followed and sat in an armchair facing her.

Not since the death of their four-year-old son more than twenty years ago had he seen her look so drained, so hopeless. She closed her eyes.

"Are you okay?" he asked, the question immediately striking him as absurd.

She opened her eyes. "Remember Carrie Lopez?"

"Of course."

It was the kind of situation a cop never wants to think about, but can never forget. Carrie was the wife, then widow, of Henry Lopez, an idealistic young narcotics detective who was pushed off the roof of a Harlem crack house one winter night shortly after Gurney had been assigned to the same precinct. The next night three local gang members were killed in a shootout with two members of the narcotics squad and subsequently blamed for the Lopez homicide. But Carrie never believed the story. She was sure her husband's murder was an inside job, that the guys in narcotics were on the take and Henry's honesty was becoming a problem for them. But she got nowhere with her requests for an internal affairs investigation. She gradually fell apart. A year to the day after Henry's death she committed suicide—by jumping from the roof of the same building.

Gurney moved next to Madeleine. "Do you think that's the state of mind Heather is in?"

"I think it could go that way."

"What about Kim?"

"Right now her anger is holding her together. But . . . I don't know." She shook her head.

28

At eight o'clock that evening, as they both sat in front of his desk in the den, Gurney went to the "Live Stream" section of the RAM-TV website and clicked on the icon for *A Matter of Concern with Carlton Flynn.*

In a modest departure from the flashing colors and exploding graphics that introduced most RAM-TV programs, the Carlton Flynn show began with a staccato drumbeat under a barrage of black-and-white photos of Flynn. In rapid sequence they showed the man in various moods, all of them intense: Pensive. Amused. Outraged. Appraising. Alarmed. Tough. Skeptical. Disgusted. Delighted.

With a final sharp drumbeat, the scene transitioned to the live face of the man himself looking directly into the camera.

"Good evening. I'm Carlton Flynn. With a matter of concern." He showed his teeth in a way that was not quite a smile.

The camera pulled back to reveal him sitting beside a small round table. Dell Beckert was on the other side of the table. Beckert was wearing a dark suit with an American flag lapel pin. Flynn was wearing a white shirt, open at the collar, sleeves rolled up to the elbow.

"My friends," said Flynn, "tonight's show will be one for the history books. Earlier today I was given some news that absolutely amazed me. It made me do something I've never done before. I canceled my scheduled guest—to make room for the man sitting here with me. His name is Dell Beckert. He's chief of police in White River, New York—a city where two white police officers have been murdered in just the past few days. With his city on the verge of a race war—with lawlessness in the streets—this man's toughness is turning back the tide of chaos. His pursuit of justice and order is prevailing. He is doing this at a staggering personal cost—a fact we'll return to in a moment. But first, Chief Beckert, can you bring us up to date on your investigation of those fatal police shootings?"

Beckert nodded grimly. "Since the cowardly sniper attacks on our brave officers, our department has made rapid progress. The sniper has been identified as Cory Payne, a twenty-two-year-old white supporter of radical black causes. Late this morning I received conclusive evidence linking him to both shootings. At one fifteen this afternoon I issued a formal order for his arrest. At one thirty I submitted my resignation."

Flynn leaned toward him. "You submitted your resignation?"

"Yes." Beckert's voice was hard and clear.

"Why did you do that?"

"To ensure the integrity of the system and the impartial application of the law."

Madeleine looked at Gurney. "What's he talking about?"

"I think I know, but let's wait and see."

Flynn, who obviously knew all about it—it was why Beckert was there—affected a puzzled look. "Why would that require your resignation?"

"Cory Payne is my son." The bombshell was dropped with jarring calmness.

"Cory Payne . . . is your son?" Flynn's question seemed designed to extend the dramatic impact of the revelation.

"Yes."

Madeleine stared at the screen in disbelief. "Cory Payne killed John Steele and Rick Loomis? And Cory Payne is the police chief's son? Can that be true?"

"Maybe half true."

Flynn placed his hands flat on the table. "Let me ask you the obvious question."

Before he could ask it, Beckert put it in his own words. "How could I have been so deceived? How could a trained police officer have missed the signs that must have been there? Is that what you want to know?"

"I think that's what we all want to know."

"I'll give you the best answer I can. Cory Payne is my son, but we've been estranged for many years. When he was barely a teenager, he began acting out. He broke the law more than once. As an alternative to the juvenile detention system, I arranged for him to be sent to a strict boarding school. When he graduated at eighteen I had hopes for him. When he changed his name to Payne, his mother's maiden name, I hoped it was just another example of the rebellion he'd eventually grow out of. When he came to live in White River last year, I thought we might be able to forge a relationship after all. In retrospect, that hope was foolish. The desperate delusion of a parent. It temporarily blinded me to the depth of his hostility to anything connected with law, order, discipline."

Flynn nodded understandingly. "Did anyone in White River know that Cory Payne's real name was Beckert?"

"He told me he didn't want anyone to know we were related, and I respected that. If he revealed it to anyone for reasons of his own, I was never aware of it."

"How much contact did you have with him?"

"I left that up to him. He'd visit me from time to time. We had an occasional lunch together, usually someplace where neither of us would be recognized."

"What did you think of his racial politics, his criticisms of the police?"

"I told myself it was just a lot of words. Adolescent playacting. A warped search for attention. The feeling of power that comes from criticizing powerful people. I imagined he'd eventually come to his senses. Obviously, he went in the opposite direction."

Flynn sat back in his chair and gave Beckert a long, sympathetic look.

"This must be incredibly painful for you."

Beckert produced a brief, thin-lipped smile. "Pain is part of life. The main thing is not to run from it. Or let it motivate you to do the wrong thing."

"The wrong thing?" Flynn produced his pensive expression. "In this case, what would that be?"

"Bury evidence. Call in favors. Twist arms. Influence the outcome. Conceal the fact that we're father and son. All those actions would be wrong. They'd undermine the law—the ideal of justice that I've devoted my life to preserving."

"Is that why you're resigning—why you're voluntarily ending one of the most distinguished law-enforcement careers in America?"

"Respect for the law is built on public trust. The case against Cory Payne must be pursued vigorously and transparently without the slightest suspicion of interference. If giving up my position supports that goal, it's well worth whatever sacrifice it entails."

"Wow." Flynn nodded appreciatively. "Well said. Now that you've submitted your resignation, what's the path forward?"

"With the approval of the White River city council, Mayor Dwayne Shucker will appoint a new chief of police. Life will go on."

"Any final words of wisdom?"

"May justice be served. May the families of the victims find peace. And may the sanctity of the law always rise above every other consideration—however powerful, however personal, however painful. God bless White River. God bless America."

The camera slowly moved in on Flynn, looking tough-but-touched. "Well, my friends, didn't I tell you this would be one for the history books? In my not-so-humble opinion, we just witnessed one of the most principled and heartfelt resignation speeches ever made. Godspeed, Dell Beckert!"

Concluding with a combination wave and salute in Beckert's direction, Flynn turned back to the camera and addressed with his trademark intensity his millions of loyal fans. "I'm Carlton Flynn, and that's how I see it. I'll be back after these important messages."

Gurney left the RAM-TV website and closed his laptop.

Madeleine shook her head in bewilderment. "What did you mean when you said it might only be half true that Payne was Beckert's son and that he was the sniper?"

"I have no doubt about the son part. But I think the sniper part is less certain."

"The slimy Mr. Flynn sure did love that resignation speech."

"Did seem that way. Of course, it wasn't really a resignation speech."

"You don't think he's resigning?"

"Oh, he's resigning all right. He's resigning from the White River Police Department to run for New York State Attorney General. If I'm not mistaken, what we just witnessed was his kickoff campaign speech."

"Are you serious? On the same day that Rick—"

The ringing of Gurney's phone interrupted her.

He glanced at the screen. "It's Hardwick. I suggested he listen to the Flynn show."

He pressed Talk. "So, Jack, what do you think?"

"The fucking manipulative bastard is doing it again."

He figured he knew what Hardwick meant, but he asked anyway. "Doing what again?"

"Riding a disaster to victory. First it was his son's juvenile delinquency. Then his wife's drug OD. Now a goddamn double murder by the same crazy son. Somehow in Dell's magic hands all this crap ends up illustrating what a prince he is. Selfless defender of high ideals. This guy manages to turn every new family horror into a platform for promoting his high-minded horseshit. Give me a fucking break!"

After ending the call Gurney sat for a long moment in troubled silence. Dusk had turned to darkness beyond the den window.

"Well, what did Hardwick have to say?" Madeleine asked.

"About Beckert? That he's a self-serving, manipulative, deceptive bastard."

"Do you agree?"

"Oh, he's at least all of that."

"At least?"

Gurney nodded slowly. "I have a sick feeling that under those fairly common vices, there may be something much worse."

III

TRUST NO ONE

29

Gurney arrived at Abelard's a few minutes before 8:00 AM. He sat at one of the rickety little hand-painted cafe tables. Marika, looking hungover and sleepy, brought him a double espresso without asking. Her ever-changing hair color was a mix of deep violet and metallic green.

As he was savoring his first sip, his phone rang. Expecting it to be Hardwick giving some reason he couldn't be there, he was surprised to see Mark Torres's name on the screen.

"Gurney here."

"I hope I'm not calling too early."

"Not at all."

"I heard that you were off the case."

"Officially, yes."

"But not completely?"

"That's one way of putting it. What can I do for you?"

"The thing is, I got the impression you have some doubts about the way things are going."

"And?"

"And . . . I guess I do, too. I mean, I get it that there's a ton of evidence—videos, fingerprints, statements from informants—linking Cory Payne to the shootings and to the Corolla and to people in the Black Defense Alliance. So I have no real doubt he's the shooter. Probably acting on behalf of the BDA."

"But?"

"What I don't get is the choice of victims."

"What do you mean?"

"John Steele and Rick Loomis were both loners. As far as I could see, they hung out only with each other. And unlike most guys in the department, they didn't regard the BDA as the enemy. I got the impression they wanted to establish some kind of dialogue, to look into the accusations of brutality and evidence-planting. You see what I'm getting at?"

"Spell it out."

"Of all the cops in the White River department—and there are more than a hundred, some of them obviously racist—it seems odd that the BDA would target Steele and Loomis. Why kill the two people who were the most sympathetic to their cause?"

"Maybe the shootings were random—and it's just a coincidence that the victims felt that way about the BDA."

"If just one of them was shot, I could buy that. But both?"

"Why are you telling me this?"

"Because I remember something you said in your investigation seminar in Albany a couple of years ago—that it's important to examine the little discrepancies. You made the point that when something doesn't seem to fit, it's often the key to the case. So I'm thinking maybe the odd choice of victims could be the key here."

"It's an interesting idea. You have a next step in mind?"

"Not really. For now, maybe I could just sort of keep you in the loop? Let you know what's happening?"

"No problem. Actually, you'd be doing me a favor. The more I know, the better."

"Great. Thank you. I'll be in touch."

As Gurney ended the call, the old wooden floor creaked behind him.

A raspy voice said, "The boy gets his ass kicked out of the DA's office and stays on the job. Nose to the grindstone. Hand on the phone. Goddamn impressive."

"Good morning, Jack."

Hardwick came around to the other side of the table and sat down on a chair that squeaked ominously under him. "Good fucking morning yourself."

He called to Marika, "Coffee, strong and black."

He fixed his pale malamute eyes on Gurney. "All right, tell Uncle Jack what's troubling your sleep."

"The Carlton Flynn thing last night . . ."

"Flynn the Fuckwit meets Beckert the Bullshitter. You have a question about that?"

It was part of Hardwick's nature to believe nothing, ridicule everything, and be generally snarly. But Gurney was willing to put up with it because underneath the cynical needling there was a good intellect and a decent soul.

"According to some articles," said Gurney, "Flynn built his success on being the hard-nosed questioner—the no-nonsense tough guy who pulls no punches. That about right?"

"Yep. Just a regular fella who happens to get paid thirty million a year. Hugely popular with angry white guys."

"But last night he was a fawning promoter of Dell Beckert, lobbing him softball questions, looking awestruck. How do you figure that?"

Hardwick shrugged. "Follow the money. Follow the power."

"You think there's enough of both behind Beckert to turn Flynn into a pussycat?"

"Flynn's a survivor. Like Beckert. Or like a giant rat. Always has an eye out for the next advantage. Onward and upward, no matter how much wreckage piles up behind him—dead wife, crazy son, whatever."

He stopped speaking as Marika placed his coffee in front of him. He picked it up and consumed about a third of it. "So Kline gave you the boot after, what, like two days?"

"Three."

"How the fuck did you manage that?"

"I had questions about the case he didn't want to hear."

"Sniper case or playground case?"

"I have a feeling it may be one case."

Hardwick showed a flash of real curiosity. "How so?"

"It seems to me that the playground murders were too smoothly executed to have been a spontaneous retaliation for the Steele shooting."

"Meaning what?"

"Meaning they must have been in the planning stage before Steele was shot."

"You're suggesting there's no connection?"

"I think there's a connection, just not the one Beckert's promoting."

"You're not imagining the same people are behind the shootings and the beating deaths, are you?"

"It's not impossible."

"For what? To start a fucking race war?"

"It's not impossible."

"It's goddamn doubtful."

"Okay. Then maybe for some other purpose." He paused. "I was on the phone with Mark Torres, CIO on the shootings. He's bothered by the fact that two supposedly BDA-executed attacks targeted the two White River cops who were the most sympathetic to the BDA. Which presumably would have put them at odds with their chief."

Hardwick blinked, the curiosity back in full force.

Gurney went on. "Combine that with the text message on John Steele's phone . . . telling him to watch his back."

"Wait a fucking minute. You're not suggesting that Beckert, patron saint of law enforcement, put a hit on two of his own men just because he didn't like their politics?"

"Nothing quite that ridiculous. But there are definite signs that the link between the attacks on Steele and Loomis and the attacks on Jordan and Tooker is more complicated than the way it's officially being described."

"What signs?"

Gurney ran through his litany of strange combinations of care and carelessness in the behavior of the killers. His last example was the perplexing difference in the routes of the two vehicles leaving the Poulter Street house. "The driver of the Corolla, Cory Payne, took a direct route through the city on a main avenue full of obvious security and traffic cameras. But the motorcycle rider took a jagged route, turning at least a dozen times and managing to avoid being caught on a single camera. Taking precautions to avoid cameras is understandable. The puzzling question is why Payne didn't bother to do the same thing."

Hardwick made his acid-reflux face. "These oddities don't trouble Sheridan?"

"He claims they're insignificant in the big picture."

"What big picture?"

"The one in which the sniper attacks are blamed on black radicals and a demented white boy; and the playground murders are blamed on a pair of backwoods white supremacists; and all the evildoers are captured or killed, order is restored, and Beckert ascends into the political stratosphere—bringing with him his key supporters."

"If the plan is that clear, why the hell did Kline want you involved in the first place?"

"I think the text message Kim Steele showed him shook him up—with its suggestion of police involvement in her husband's death. He wanted to get on board the Beckert rocket ship, but he wanted to make sure it wasn't going to blow up on the launch pad. I was supposed to observe discreetly and warn him of any imminent disasters. But apparently the so-called progress being made on the case has settled his nerves to the point where he's more concerned about me weakening his relationship with Beckert than about any weakness in the case."

Hardwick flashed his chilly grin. "Kline the Slime. So what now?"

"Something's screwy, and I intend to find out what it is."

"Even though you've been fired?"

"Right."

"One last question. What the fuck am I doing here at the crack of dawn?"

"I was hoping you might be willing to do me a favor."

"Doing favors for you is the icing on the cake of my perfect life. What is it this time?"

"I thought maybe you could use your old NYSP contacts to dig a little deeper into Beckert's past."

"Digging for what?"

"Anything we don't already know about his relationship with Turlock, his first wife, his son. If a cop's son starts killing cops, it doesn't take a genius to suspect there's something ugly in their past. I'd like to know what it is."

Hardwick produced another grin.

"What's funny?"

"Your obvious effort to concoct a theory that blames Beckert for everything."

"I'm not trying to concoct anything. I just want to know more about these people."

"Horseshit. You don't like the tight-ass son of a bitch any more than I do, and you're searching for a way to slam him."

The fact that Hardwick was saying essentially what Kline had said gave the notion some extra weight, but he still wasn't about to agree with it.

Hardwick took a thoughtful sip of his coffee before going on. "What if Beckert is right?"

"About what?"

"About Steele and Loomis. About Jordan and Tooker. About rotten-apple Cory and the crazy Gorts. What if the prick is right about everything?"

"What Beckert's right about seems to have a way of shifting in the wind. Three days ago he was blaming the Steele shooting on Jordan and Tooker. When it turned out they were with a prominent pastor, he did a little rhetorical dance and said that while they might not have pulled the trigger, they certainly aided and abetted."

"Which may be true. And by the way, how much do you know about that pastor?"

"What do you mean?"

"You're assuming he's telling the truth. Maybe you just want to believe him because those alibis he provided embarrassed Dell Beckert."

Gurney didn't want to believe his thinking was that twisted, but the suggestion made him uneasy. Up to that point the pastor hadn't been very high on his mental list of people to interview. Now he was at the top.

30

The Reverend Whittaker Coolidge, rector of Saint Thomas the Apostle Episcopal Church, agreed to a meeting that morning as long as it could be concluded prior to a scheduled ten thirty baptism. By breaking the speed limit all the way to White River, Gurney arrived at the church at nine forty-five.

It was located on a broad avenue that separated Bluestone from Grinton. An old redbrick building with a steeply angled slate roof, stained-glass windows, and a square bell tower, it was set back from the avenue—surrounded on three sides by an ancient churchyard with moss-covered mausoleums, statues of angels, and weathered gravestones, and on the fourth side by a parking lot.

Gurney parked at the back of the empty lot. From there a path led through the churchyard to a rear door, which Reverend Coolidge had told him to use to get to the office.

A little way along the path, he stopped to pay closer attention to the inscriptions on the gravestones. A few of the birth dates went back as far as the late eighteenth century. Most of the death dates were in the eighteen thirties and forties. Typical of old cemeteries, a number of the stones recorded sadly short lifespans.

"Dave?"

A large sandy-haired man in a short-sleeved shirt, Bermuda shorts, and Birkenstock sandals was standing under the outstretched wing of a stone angel that adorned one of the more elaborate graves. Taking a final drag on a cigarette, he extinguished it on the tip of the angel's wing and dropped it in a graveside watering can. Then he strode toward Gurney with a toothy smile. "I'm Whit Coolidge. I see you're intrigued by our slice of history. Some of the folks buried here were contemporaries of the controversial Colonel Ezra Willard. Are you familiar with him?"

"I'm familiar with his statue in the park."

"A statue some of our citizens would like to see removed. Not without reason."

Gurney said nothing.

"Well," said Coolidge after an awkward silence, "why don't we go into my office, where we can have some privacy."

Gurney wondered how much more private than a yard full of dead people the office could be, but he nodded and followed the man through the church's back door into a hallway that smelled of dust and dry wood. Light was spilling from a doorway on the right, and that's where Coolidge led him.

The room was about twice the size of Gurney's den. There was a desk at one end with a leather desk chair. At the other end was a small fireplace with a low fire in its final stages. There were two leather armchairs on either side of the hearth. On one wall a window looked out on the part of the churchyard that wrapped around that side of the building. On the opposite wall were two enormous photographic prints—one of Mother Teresa and one of Martin Luther King.

Seeing Gurney looking at them, Coolidge offered an explanation. "I prefer contemporary incarnations of goodness to the bizarre and dogmatic characters of the Middle Ages." He gestured toward one of the armchairs. When Gurney was seated he took the one facing it. "You said on the phone you were involved in the investigation of this awful violence. May I ask in what capacity?"

Something in his tone suggested that he'd checked and discovered the severing of Gurney's official ties to the case.

"The wives of the murdered officers have asked me to look into the circumstances of their deaths. They want to be sure they're getting the truth, whatever it turns out to be."

Coolidge cocked his head curiously. "I was under the impression that our police department had already arrived at the truth. Am I mistaken?"

"I'm not sure the confidence the police seem to have in their hypothesis is justified by the facts."

Gurney's answer appeared to have a positive effect. The tense creases at the corners of Coolidge's eyes began to relax. His smile became more natural.

"Always a pleasure to meet a man with an open mind. What can I do for you?"

"I'm searching for information. With a wide net. Because I don't know yet what will be important. Perhaps you could start by telling me what you know about Jordan and Tooker?"

"Marcel and Virgil." He made the emendation sound like a mild reprimand. "They were slandered. Even now they continue to be slandered with the implication that they were somehow involved in Officer Steele's murder. There is, to my knowledge, no evidence of that whatsoever."

"I understand they were with you the night Officer Steele was shot."

Coolidge paused for a moment before going on. "They were here in this very room. Marcel in the chair you now occupy. Virgil in the one next to it. I sat where I am now. It was our third meeting."

"Third? Was there an agenda for these meetings?"

"Peace, progress, legal process."

"Meaning?"

"The idea was to channel negative energy toward positive goals. They were angry young men, understandably so, but not bomb throwers. Certainly not killers. They were justice seekers. Truth seekers. Perhaps like you in that way."

"What truth were they seeking?"

"They wanted to expose the numerous criminal actions and cover-ups in our police department. The pattern of abuse."

"They knew of specific instances? With evidence to back up their charges?"

"They knew of instances in which African Americans had been framed, illegally detained, even killed. They were pursuing the necessary corroboration, case files, et cetera."

"How?"

"They were being helped."

"Helped?"

"Correct."

"That doesn't tell me much."

Coolidge turned his gaze to the small blue flames flickering up from the coals in the fireplace. "I'll just say that their desire for justice was shared, and they were optimistic."

"Perhaps you could be just a bit more specific?"

Coolidge looked pained. "There's nothing more I can say without discussing the implications with . . . those who might be affected."

"I can understand that. In the meantime, can you tell me how Marcel and Virgil happened to come to you?"

Coolidge hesitated. "They were brought to me by an interested party."

"Whose name you can't reveal without further consultation?"

"That's right."

"Were you aware that John Steele and Rick Loomis wanted to establish some level of dialogue with the Black Defense Alliance?"

"I'd rather not get on the slippery slope of saying what I was or wasn't aware of. We live in a dangerous world. Confidences must be respected."

"True." In Gurney's experience, agreeing with someone he was interviewing often produced more information than questioning him. He sat back in his chair. "Very true."

Coolidge sighed. "I'm a student of history. I realize that political divisions are nothing new in America. We've had angry disagreements over all sorts of things. But the current state of polarization is worse than anything I've seen in my lifetime. It's stunningly ironic that the explosion of available information on the internet has led to the irrelevance of actual facts. More communication has led to more isolation. Political discourse has become nothing but shouts and lies and threats. Political loyalties are about who you hate, not who you love. And all this ignorant bile is justified by making up nonsensical 'facts.' The crazier the belief, the more strongly it's held. The political center, the rational center, has been driven to extinction. And the justice system . . ."

He shook his head, his hands opening and closing into fists. "The *justice* system! Sweet Jesus, what a misnomer!"

"In White River in particular?"

Coolidge was silent for a long moment, staring into the remnants of the fire. When he spoke again his voice was calmer, but a bitterness remained. "There used to be a car wash out in Larvaton. In cold weather, when there was salt on the roads and cars needed washing, the mechanism was either not operating at all or doing crazy things. Soaping when it should be rinsing. Rinsing when it should be soaping. Squirting wax on the tires. Freezing shut with the sprayers on full blast, turning the car into a block of ice. With the driver trapped inside. The blowers were so powerful they'd sometimes rip the trim off a car."

He looked away from the fire and met Gurney's puzzled gaze. "That's our court system. Our *justice* system. An unpredictable farce in the best of times. A disaster in times of crisis. Seeing what happens to vulnerable people pushed into the maw of that insane machine can make you cry."

"So . . . where does all this take you?"

Before Coolidge could respond, Gurney's phone rang. He took it out, saw that it was Torres, silenced it, and put it back in his pocket. "Sorry about that."

"Where does all this take me? It takes me in the direction of Maynard Biggs—in the upcoming election for state attorney general."

"Why Biggs?"

Coolidge leaned forward in his chair, his hands on his knees. "He's a reasonable man. A principled man. He listens. He begins with what *is*. He believes in the common good." He sank back in his chair, turning up his palms in a gesture of frustration. "I realize, of course, that these qualities are severe disabilities in today's political climate, but we must stand up for sanity and decency. Move from darkness toward the light. Maynard Biggs is a step in the right direction, and Dell Beckert is not!"

Gurney was surprised at the sudden venom in the rector's voice.

"You don't regard Beckert's resignation speech as his withdrawal from public life?"

"Hah! The world should be so fortunate! Obviously you didn't catch the latest news."

"What news?"

"A flash-polling outfit connected to RAM-TV asked registered voters who they would be likely to vote for in a hypothetical election matchup between Beckert and Biggs. It was a statistical tie—a frightening fact, given that Beckert hasn't officially entered the race."

"You sound like you've had unpleasant encounters with him."

"Not personally. But I've heard horror stories."

"What kind?"

Coolidge appeared to be choosing his words carefully. "He has a double standard for judging criminal behavior. Crimes that arise from passion, weakness, addiction, deprivation, injustice—all those are dealt with severely, often violently. But crimes committed by the police in the name of maintaining order are ignored, even encouraged."

"For instance?"

"It wouldn't be unusual for a minority resident who dared to talk back to a cop to be arrested for harassment and jailed for weeks if he wasn't able to make bail—or beaten within an inch of his life if he offered the slightest resistance. But a cop who gets into a confrontation and ends up killing some homeless drug addict suffers zero consequences. I mean *zero*. Exhibit a human failing Beckert doesn't like and you're crushed. But wear a badge and shoot someone at a traffic stop, and you're barely questioned. That's the vile—dare I say *fascist*—culture Beckert has installed in our police department, which he seems to consider his private army."

Gurney nodded thoughtfully. Under other circumstances, he might have probed Coolidge's generalizations, but right now he had other priorities.

"Do you know Cory Payne?"

Coolidge hesitated. "Yes. I do."

"Did you know that he was Beckert's son?"

"How could I?"

"You tell me."

Coolidge's expression hardened. "That sounds like an accusation."

"Sorry. Just trying to find out as much as I can. What's your opinion of Payne?"

"People in my line of work hear thousands of confessions. Confessions of every crime imaginable. People bare their souls. Their thoughts. Their motives. Over the years, all those revelations make one a good judge of character. And I'll tell you this—the notion that Cory Payne murdered two police officers is nonsense. Cory is all talk. Angry, overheated, accusatory—I'll grant you that—but it's just talk."

"The thing is," said Gurney, "there's extensive video and fingerprint evidence that he was in the right place at the right time for each shooting. And he fled the scene after each one."

"If that's true, there must be an explanation other than the one you're assuming. The idea that Cory Payne killed anyone in cold blood is ridiculous."

"You know him well enough to say that?"

"White political progressives in this part of the state are a rare breed. We get to know each other." Coolidge looked at his watch, frowned, and stood up abruptly. "We're out of time. I need to get ready for that baptism. Come."

Gesturing for Gurney to follow him, he led the way out through the church-yard to the parking lot. "Pray for courage and caution," he said as they reached the Outback.

"An unusual combination."

"It's an unusual situation."

Gurney nodded but made no move to get into his car.

Coolidge looked again at his watch. "Is there something else?"

"I'd like to meet Payne. Is that something you could arrange?"

"So you could arrest him?"

"I have no authority to arrest anyone. I'm a free agent."

Coolidge gave him a long look. "With no agenda other than gathering information for the wives of the dead officers?"

"That's right."

"And you think Cory should trust you?"

"He doesn't have to trust me. We can talk on the phone. I just have one question for him. What was he doing at those sniper locations if he wasn't involved?"

"That's it?"

"That's it." Gurney could easily think of a dozen other questions, but this was no time for complications.

Coolidge nodded uncertainly. "I'll think about it."

They shook hands. The man's large, soft palm felt sweaty.

Gurney looked up at the redbrick edifice. "Saint Thomas the Apostle—wasn't he the so-called *doubting* one?"

"He was. But in my humble opinion, he should have been called the *sane* one."

31

If doubt was an indication of sanity, Gurney mused as he drove out of the church parking lot, he had an abundance of sanity, and it was a very uncomfortable attribute.

He was filled with questions. Were Coolidge's statements fact-based conclusions or the reflex expression of his political views? Had Jordan and Tooker been well-meaning solution seekers or had they been running a con job on the rector to gain his approval and an aura of respectability? Was Beckert an evil control freak or a champion of law and order in a pitched battle with criminals and chaos? And then there was Judd Turlock. Was he the tough cop advertised by the set of his jaw, or was he the hit man dwelling behind emotionless eyes? And what about Mark Torres? Were the young detective's efforts to stay in communication to be taken at face value? Or were they signs of something more manipulative—possibly even an assignment he'd been given?

Thinking of Torres reminded Gurney that he'd received a call from him during his meeting with the rector. He pulled over to the curb on a burned-out street at the edge of Grinton and listened to the message.

"This is Mark. Just wanted to let you know there's been a setback up in the quarries. I'll tell you more when we talk."

Curious to discover if the setback would be throwing yet another aspect of the case into doubt, Gurney returned the call.

Torres sounded apologetic. "The situation is kind of sensitive. I didn't want to spell it out in a message."

"What's the problem?"

"The K9 dog was killed."

"The one tracking the Gorts?"

"Right. Just below the abandoned quarries."

"Killed how?"

"A crossbow arrow through the head. Pretty weird. Kind of reminds me of their gate sign."

Gurney remembered it vividly—the human skull hanging there from a crossbow arrow through an eye socket. As a Keep Out message, it was hard to beat.

"Anything happen to the dog's handler?"

"No. Just the dog. Arrow came out of nowhere. Another dog is on the way. And a state helicopter with infrared spotting equipment. And a backup assault team."

"Any official statement to the media?"

"Not a word. They want to keep the lid on—make sure it doesn't look like things are getting out of control."

"So the Gorts are still out there with their crossbows and pit bulls and dynamite?"

"Looks that way."

Torres fell silent, but Gurney had the impression their conversation wasn't over. "Anything else you want to talk about?"

Torres cleared his throat. "I'm not comfortable suggesting things I have no evidence for."

"But . . ."

"Well, I guess it's no secret that Chief Beckert hates the Gorts."

"And . . ."

"This thing with the dog seems to have tripled it."

"So?"

"If the Gorts are captured, I have a feeling something will happen. Judd Turlock is going out to the quarries to direct the operation personally."

"You think the Gorts will be killed? Because of the way Beckert feels about them?"

"I could be wrong."

"I thought Beckert left the department."

"He did, technically. Turlock will be acting chief until there's an official appointment. But the thing is, Turlock always does what Beckert wants. Nobody here believes that's going to change."

"That worries you?"

"It always worries me when the face of a situation is different from the truth. A resignation should mean that you're actually gone. Not just pretending to be gone. You understand what I'm saying?"

"Perfectly." Not only was an appearance-reality gap a worrisome thing, it was the basic challenge in every investigation—breaking through the shell of a situation to discover what was really there. "Anything else you want to tell me?"

"That's it for now."

As Gurney ended the call he noted that he still had one message he hadn't listened to yet—from Dr. Walter Thrasher. Now, while he was still parked, was as good a time as any.

"David, this is Walt Thrasher. Based on what you've found so far, that excavation of yours may turn out to be of considerable historical interest. I'd like your permission to probe the area further. Please get back to me as soon as you can."

Whatever it was that might be of interest to Thrasher was at that moment of little interest to Gurney. But a phone conversation with the ME could provide an opportunity to address other subjects.

He placed the call.

The man answered on the first ring. "Thrasher."

"I got your message. About the dig."

"Ah, yes. The dig. I'd like to scrape around a bit, see what's there."

"Are you looking for something in particular?"

"Yes. But I'd rather not say what—not yet, anyway."

"Something of value?"

"Not in the normal sense. No buried treasure."

"Why all the secrecy?"

"I hate speculation. I have a fondness for hard evidence."

That was, Gurney thought, as good an opening as he was likely to get. "Speaking of evidence, when do you expect to get your tox screens on Jordan and Tooker back from the lab?"

"I emailed the report to Turlock yesterday afternoon."

"To Turlock?"

"He's still the CIO on that case, is he not?"

"Yes, he is," said Gurney confidently, trying not to expose any out-of-the-loop uncertainty. "He'll probably forward your report to the DA's office, and I'll get a copy from Sheridan. Is there anything I should pay special attention to?"

"I report facts. Prioritizing them is up to you."

"And the facts in this instance are . . ."

"Alcohol, midazolam, propofol."

"Propofol . . . as in the Michael Jackson OD?"

"Correct."

"Propofol's administered intravenously, right?"

"Right."

"I didn't think it was commonly available on the street."

"It's not. It would be a tricky substance for the average addict to deal with."

"How so?"

"It's a powerful sedative with a narrow therapeutic window."

"Meaning?"

"The recommended dosage level is relatively close to the level of toxicity."

"So it's easy to OD on it?"

"Easier than with most street drugs. And there's no antidote—no equivalent to Narcan for opiates—no way to bring you back once you go over the edge."

"Could a propofol OD have been the cause of death?"

"Direct cause of death for both individuals was strangulation, leading to heart and respiratory failure. I'd say the propofol was administered earlier for its sedative rather than toxic effects."

"To eliminate the pain of the branding? To keep the victims quiet and manageable?"

"The sedative effect would be consistent with those outcomes."

"This case gets more interesting every day, doesn't it?"

"Indeed. In fact, your call caught me on my way from the autopsy table back to my office."

"Autopsy on who?"

"Officer Loomis."

"I assume his death was the result of the complications you'd expect from a bullet to the temporal lobe?"

"The temporal lobe was creased but not perforated. He almost certainly would have recovered from that, possibly with some ongoing deficits. Of course, one can never be sure with brain injuries. His death was actually caused by complications arising from tissue destruction, sepsis, and hemorrhaging in critical brain-stem structures, primarily within the medulla oblongata."

Gurney was puzzled. "What's the connection between that area and the part of his head where he was shot?"

"No connection relevant to the outcome."

"I'm confused. Are you saying that his death was not caused by the delayed effects of the gunshot to his temple?"

"His death was caused by the delayed effects of an ice pick driven into his brain stem."

32

Gurney didn't have time to ask Thrasher all the questions that came to mind. He settled for three big ones.

First question: How long before Loomis's deteriorating condition was noted could the stabbing have occurred?

The answer was that it could have occurred anywhere from one to twenty-four hours prior to the onset of symptoms. There was no way of being more specific without a more extensive analysis of the affected area of the brain—which would be undertaken if requested by the WRPD or the office of the district attorney.

Second question: Why hadn't one of the monitor alarms sounded at the moment of the stabbing itself?

The answer was that the deep sedation brought about by Loomis's barbiturate coma would have substantially blunted any immediate physiological reaction. The monitors would register the ensuing symptoms of heart and respiratory failure only as they developed during the course of the gradual brain-stem hemorrhaging, deterioration, and sepsis.

Third question: Wouldn't a crude instrument like an ice pick have produced a bleeding wound that the nursing staff would have noticed?

The answer was that bleeding could be avoided by angling the entry pathway to avoid the principal neck arteries and veins, which is exactly what the autopsy revealed had been done. With some medical knowledge and a good anatomical diagram, it would not be all that difficult. In addition, a small Band-Aid had been applied to the puncture site.

Gurney couldn't help but be impressed by the simplicity of that last touch.

Thrasher went on to explain that his medical intern would soon be transcribing the audio recording of the detailed comments he'd made during the autopsy procedure. He would review the report, mark it "Preliminary, Subject to Revision," and send an electronic copy to Mark Torres, the official CIO on the Loomis case.

Gurney knew that Torres would then share it up the chain of command to Turlock, who would in turn share it with Beckert. At some point in that process it would occur to someone to go to the hospital and request a list of all personnel and ICU visitors who could have had access to Loomis during the broad time period in which the stabbing could have occurred.

Gurney's own goal was to get to the hospital, secure the same list, and get out of there before anyone knew he'd been deprived of his official standing.

The elegant lady with the white permanent and bright-blue eyes was again at the welcome desk, and she remembered him. She smiled, with a touch of sadness. "So sorry about your associate."

"Thank you."

She sighed. "I wish more people appreciated the sacrifices made by you people in law enforcement."

He nodded.

She smiled. "What can we do for you today?"

He spoke in a confidential tone. "We're going to need a list of hospital personnel and visitors who may have had contact with Rick Loomis."

She looked alarmed. "My goodness, why . . ."

"Routine. In the event that he may have regained consciousness temporarily and said something in someone's presence that could be helpful."

"Oh. Yes. Of course." She looked relieved. "You'll need to see Abby Marsh. Let me call to make sure she's in. Do you have something with your exact title on it?"

He handed her his DA credentials.

She laid them in front of her as she entered an extension number on her desk phone.

"Hello, Marge? Is Abby in? I have a special senior investigator here from the district attorney's office . . . That's right . . . Yes, he's one of the officers who was here before . . . A personnel list . . . He can explain it better than I can . . . All right . . . I'll send him in."

She handed back his credentials and gave him directions to the office of Mercy Hospital's director of human resources.

He was greeted by Abby Marsh at her office door. Her handshake was firm and brief. She was as tall as Gurney, probably in her late forties, thin with brown hair cropped so short it suggested recent chemotherapy. Her harried expression suggested that the days were long gone when a personnel job was a stress-free sinecure. An expanding minefield of regulations, entitlements, resentments, and lawsuits had turned the position into a bureaucratic nightmare.

He explained what he needed. She asked to see his credentials and studied them in a distracted way. She told him she could provide a list of names with addresses, phone numbers, job titles, and dates of employment, but no other file information. As for indicating specific staff members with ICU access, that was impossible since staff access to that area was neither restricted nor monitored.

She looked hurriedly at her watch. Did he prefer a paper printout or a digital file? Digital.

Did he want it emailed to the DA's office, or did he want it now on a USB drive?

Now on a USB.

It was as simple as that.

He hoped his lack of candor in getting what he needed wouldn't create problems for her. There could be repercussions arising from his having presented credentials that were arguably no longer valid, but he figured that any blowback from that would be directed at him, not her.

His plan was to head home and review the list she'd given him. Not that he thought it would produce any sudden insights, but it couldn't hurt to gain a familiarity with the names in the event that one popped up later in a related context. And there was a fair chance that someone on that list had been sufficiently afraid of Loomis's possible recovery, afraid of what he might reveal, to make sure it wouldn't happen.

The sequence of letters and numbers on the index card flashed through Gurney's mind. If those obscure characters did in fact represent the information that Loomis had been shot and then fatally stabbed with an ice pick to prevent him from divulging, it was now more vital than ever to decipher their meaning.

As he was passing the Larvaton exit on the interstate on his way back to Walnut Crossing, wondering if the digits in the message, 13111, might be a postal box number, his phone rang.

It was Whittaker Coolidge.

His voice was tight. Gurney couldn't tell whether from excitement or fear.

"I was able to get in touch with the individual you were asking about. I think some communication can be arranged."

"Good. Is there a next step?"

"Are you still here in town?"

"I can be back there in twenty minutes."

"Come to my office. I'll know then how to proceed."

Gurney exited at the next cloverleaf and headed back to White River. He parked in the same space by the graveyard, and went into the church building by the back door.

Coolidge was in his office, seated at his desk. He was in his clerical uniform—black suit, dark-gray shirt, white collar. His sandy hair was combed and parted.

"Have a seat." He pointed to a wooden chair by his desk.

Gurney remained standing. The room felt chillier than it had earlier. Perhaps because the fire in the grate had gone out. Coolidge interlaced his fingers. The gesture looked half prayerful, half anxious.

"I spoke to Cory Payne."

"And . . ."

"I think he wants to talk to you as much as you want to talk to him."

"Why?"

"Because of the murder charge. He sounds furious and frightened."

"When do we meet?"

"There's an intermediate step. I'm supposed to call a number he gave me and put the phone on speaker. He wants to ask some questions before you get together. Is that okay?"

Gurney nodded.

Coolidge picked up his landline handset, tapped in a number, and held it to his ear. A few seconds later he said, "Yes . . . all set . . . I'm putting you on speaker." He pressed a button and returned the handset to its base. "Go ahead."

A sharp, edgy voice from the speaker said, "This is Cory Payne. David Gurney? Are you there?"

"I'm here."

"I have questions for you."

"Go ahead."

"Do you agree with what Dell Beckert has been saying about the shootings and the Black Defense Alliance?"

"I don't have enough facts to agree or disagree."

"Do you agree with his accusation against me?"

"Same answer."

"Have you ever shot anyone?"

"Yes. A couple of psychotic murderers who were pointing guns at me."

"How about shootings that weren't so easily justifiable?"

"There were no others. And 'justifiable' has never meant much to me."

"You don't care if a killing is justifiable?"

"To kill or not to kill is a question of necessity, not justification."

"Really? When is killing another human being *necessary*?"

"When it will save a life that there's no other way of saving."

"Including your own?"

"Including my own."

"And you're the sole judge of that necessity?"

"In most cases there's no opportunity for a broader discussion."

"Have you ever framed an innocent person?"

"No."

"Have you ever framed a guilty person—someone you were sure was guilty but you didn't have enough legitimate evidence to prove it in court?"

"No."

"Have you ever wanted to?"

"Many times."

"Why didn't you?"

"Because I hate liars, and I don't want to hate myself."

There was a silence, lasting long enough that Gurney thought the connection might have been broken.

Eventually Coolidge intervened. "Cory? You still there?"

"I'm thinking about Mr. Gurney's answers."

There was another silence, not quite so long.

"Okay," said the voice on the speaker. "We can go ahead with this."

"As planned?" asked Coolidge.

"As planned."

Coolidge pressed a button on the handset to end the call. He looked relieved if not quite relaxed. "That went well."

"Now what?"

"Now we talk." The sharp, edgy voice came from behind Gurney.

33

Cory Payne's lean body in the doorway appeared poised to spring—but whether toward or away from Gurney was unclear. There were traces of Dell Beckert in his athletic physique, chiseled face, and unblinking stare. But there was something else in his eyes as well, an acid in place of his father's arrogance.

Payne and Gurney were facing each other. Coolidge was sitting behind his desk. He pushed his chair back, but remained seated—as if by some peculiar calculation he had decided that the available standing room was already occupied.

Gurney spoke first. "I appreciate your willingness to talk to me."

"It's not a favor. I need to know what the hell is going on."

Coolidge eased his chair back a few more inches and gestured toward the armchairs by the fireplace. "Would you gentlemen like to sit down?"

Without taking his eyes off Gurney, Payne moved cautiously to the brown leather chair on the far side of the hearth. Gurney took the matching one facing it.

Gurney studied Payne's face. "You resemble your father."

His mouth twitched. "The man who's calling me a murderer."

Gurney paused, struck by the young man's voice. The timbre was the same as his father's, but the tone was tighter, angrier.

"When did you change your name from Beckert to Payne?"

"As soon as I could."

"Why?"

"*Why?* Because that patriarchal thing is bullshit. I had a mother as well as a father. Her name was Payne. I preferred it. What difference does it make? I thought we were going to talk about these murders I'm being accused of."

"We are."

"Well?"

"Did you commit them?"

"No! That's ridiculous! A stupid, disgusting idea."

"Why is it ridiculous?"

"It just is. Steele and Loomis were good people. Not like the rest of that stinking department. What's happening now scares the shit out of me."

"Why?"

"Look at who's dead. Look at who's being blamed. Who do you think will be next?"

"I'm not following you."

Payne counted the names off on his fingers with increasing agitation. "Steele . . . Loomis . . . Jordan . . . Tooker. All dead. And who's being blamed? The Gort brothers. And me. You see the pattern?"

"I'm not sure I do."

"Seven people with one thing in common! We've all created problems for the sainted police chief. He'd be much happier if none of us existed. And now he's got four of us out of the way."

"Are you claiming that your father—?"

"Not with his own hands. That's what he has Judd Turlock for. It's amazing how many people have been killed or put in the hospital for 'resisting arrest' since Turlock and the great Dell Beckert came to White River. That's all I can think about. The minute I heard my name on that Flynn thing last night, that was my thought—*I'm next*. It's like living in some gangster dictatorship. Whatever the big man wants, somebody makes it happen. Whoever gets in his way ends up dead."

"If you're afraid of being tracked down and shot in a manufactured confrontation, why not get yourself a good lawyer and turn yourself in?"

Payne burst out in a harsh laugh. "Turn myself in and sit for God knows how long in Goodson Cloutz's jail? That would just make it easier for them. In case you haven't noticed, Cloutz is a slimy piece of shit. And there are people in that fucking jail who'd actually pay him for the chance to kill a police chief's son!"

Gurney nodded thoughtfully. He sat back in his chair and let his gaze drift out the far window into the churchyard. In addition to giving himself a moment to consider the implications of what Payne was saying, he wanted to create an emotional break to let the young man's level of agitation subside before moving on to another subject.

Coolidge's voice interrupted the silence, asking if they'd like some coffee. Gurney accepted. Payne declined.

Coolidge went to prepare it, and Gurney resumed his inquiry.

"We need to address some evidence issues. There's video footage of you driving a black Corolla to and from both sniper locations."

"The apartment building in Grinton and the private house up in Bluestone?"

"Yes."

"When they showed those places on the news this morning, I almost threw up."

"Why?"

"Because I recognized the buildings. I'd been there. To both of them."

"Why?"

"To meet someone."

"Who?"

He shook his head, looking both angry and scared. "I don't know."

"You don't know who you were meeting?"

"I have no idea. People contact me. It's no secret where I stand politically. I founded White Men for Black Justice. I've been on TV. I ask for information. I publicize my phone number. Sometimes I get anonymous tips from people who want to help me."

"Help you do what?"

"Expose the rot in our fascist police establishment."

"That's why you went to those places? To meet someone who promised to help you?"

"He said he had a video—the actual dashboard video from the police car at the Laxton Jones shooting. A video that would expose what really happened—and expose the police story as total bullshit."

"It was a man's voice?"

"It was a text. I guess I just assumed it was from a guy. There was no name on it."

"So you got this anonymous text offering you the video?"

"Yes."

"Telling you to go to that apartment building on Bridge Street to get it?"

"Yes."

"This was the evening of the BDA demonstration in the park?"

"Yes. I was supposed to drive into the alley behind the building and wait."

"And you did that."

"I followed the directions. I'm there in the alley at the right time, waiting. I'm there maybe twenty minutes. Then I get a text changing the plan, telling me I should drive to the far side of the Grinton Bridge. So I do. And I wait. After a couple of minutes, I get a third text. This one expresses some concern about surveillance, says we need to postpone the meeting until it's safer. I drive home to my apartment. I'm thinking, that's the end of that. Until I get a new text a couple of days later. This time it's a big rush. I have to drive immediately to a house up on Poulter Street in Bluestone. I'm supposed to drive straight into the garage and wait. I manage to get there on time; and I'm waiting, waiting, waiting. After a while I'm thinking maybe I misunderstood. Maybe whoever's got the video is waiting in the house. I get out of the car and go to the side door. It's unlocked. I open it. Then I hear a sound that could be a gunshot. From somewhere in the house. So I get the hell out. I jump in my car. Tear out of there. Drive home. End of story."

"You drove directly to your own apartment?"

"To a parking spot near it. About a block away."

"Any further messages from your supposed tipster?"

"Nothing."

"Did you save the texts?"

"No. I wrote down the number they came from, but I deleted the actual texts."

"Why?"

"A precaution. I'm always afraid of phone hackers or someone getting hold of private information. And this was a supersensitive thing, the dashboard video. If the wrong people found out I was going to be getting it . . ." His voice trailed off.

"Did you ever call the number the texts came from?"

"I tried maybe five, six times. No answer, just anonymous voicemail. I remember thinking maybe they had been in that house after all, and maybe *they* got shot. Then this morning RAM-TV runs this story on the places where the sniper shots were fired from. Up till then, all they'd talked about was where the cops were when they got shot, not where the bullets came from. But now they showed the apartment building on Bridge Street and the private house on Poulter Street, with some asshole reporter standing in the street pointing at it. I'm thinking, shit, that's where I was, I was in both of those places. I'm thinking, what the fuck's going on? I mean it was obvious that something weird was going on. Put that on top of the Flynn bullshit—with the great police chief pointing his goddamn finger at me—and I'm thinking, What the fuck? What the bloody fuck?"

Payne was sitting on the edge of his seat, rubbing his thighs with the palms of his hands as if he were trying to warm them, shaking his head and staring a little wildly at the floor.

"There are fingerprints," Gurney said mildly, "in both locations."

"My fingerprints?"

"That's what I've heard."

"That has to be a mistake."

"Could be." Gurney shrugged. "If it's not, do you have any idea how they could have gotten there?"

"The only place my fingerprints could be would be in the car, which I never left, except to open the side door of the house. But I never went inside. And at the apartment building I stayed down in the alley. In the car. I never got out of it."

"Do you own a gun?"

Payne shook his head, almost violently. "I hate guns."

"Do you keep any kind of ammunition in your apartment?"

"Bullets? No. Of course not. What would I do with them?" He paused, looking suddenly dumbfounded. "Fuck! Are you saying someone found *bullets* in my apartment?"

Gurney said nothing.

"Because if someone's saying they found bullets in my apartment, that's total bullshit! What the fuck is going on?"

"What do *you* think is going on?"

Payne closed his eyes and took a long, slow breath. He opened them and met Gurney's inquisitive gaze with an unblinking Beckert stare. "It would appear that someone is trying to frame me, someone who's covering up for whoever was actually involved in the shootings."

"Do you believe your father is trying to frame you?"

He continued staring at Gurney, as if he hadn't heard the question. Then the hard expression began to break down. There were little tremors around his eyes and mouth. He stood up abruptly, turned away, and walked to the window that looked out on the old graveyard.

Gurney waited.

A long minute passed.

Payne spoke, still facing the window. "I think so, I don't think so. I'm sure, not sure. I think, sure, of course he'd frame me, why not, he has no feelings other than ambition. Ambition is sacred to him. Success. Sacred to him and his horrible second wife. Haley Beauville Beckert. You know where her money comes from? Tobacco.

Her great-great-grandfather Maxwell Beauville owned a huge slave plantation in Virginia. One of the biggest tobacco growers in the state. Jesus. You know how many people tobacco kills every day? Fucking greedy murdering scumbags. And then I think, no. My father? Frame me for murder? That's impossible, right? Yes, no, yes, no." He let out a small gasping sound that might have been a stifled sob. "So," he said finally, taking a deep breath, "I don't know a single fucking thing."

Gurney decided to change the subject. "How close are you to Blaze Jackson?"

Payne turned from the window, calmer now. "Blaze *Lovely* Jackson. She insists on the whole name. We had an affair. On and off. Why?"

"Is she the one who gave you Devalon Jones's Corolla?"

"She lets me use it whenever I need it."

"Are you staying with her now?"

"I'm moving around."

"Probably not a bad idea."

There was a silence.

Coolidge came back into the room with Gurney's coffee. He laid the mug on a side table by the arm of Gurney's chair, then, with a concerned glance in the direction of Payne, retreated behind his desk.

Payne looked at Gurney. "Can I hire you?"

"Hire me?"

"As a private investigator. To find out what the hell is going on."

"I'm already trying to do that."

"For the cops' wives?"

"Yes."

"Are they paying you?"

"Why do you ask?"

"Because you're bound to have expenses. Investigations can be expensive."

"What's your point?"

"I'd like to make sure you have the resources to do whatever you have to do."

"You're in a position to supply those resources?"

"My grandparents left their money to me, not to my mother. They locked it up in a trust fund that only I could access, and only after I turned twenty-one. Which was last year."

"Why did they do that?"

Payne paused, gazing at the ashes in the fireplace. "My mom had a serious drug problem. Giving someone with a drug problem a pile of money is like a death sentence." He paused again. "Besides, they hated my father and wanted to make sure he wouldn't get his hands on it."

"They hated him? Why?"

"Because he's a horrible, heartless, controlling bastard."

34

The meeting ended with Gurney declining to be "hired" but leaving open the possibility of billing Payne for any extraordinary expenses—if they happened to result in the discovery of facts that exonerated him. With Payne leery of providing Gurney with his cell number—a new one, anonymous and prepaid—for fear of the police getting hold of the number and tracking his location, Coolidge had nervously agreed to act as a middleman.

Now, thirty-five minutes later, Gurney was finishing a quick lunch in an empty coffee shop on one of White River's main commercial avenues, playing back in his mind everything he remembered Payne saying, how he said it, his expressions, gestures, apparent emotions. The more he thought about it, the more inclined he was to accept the feasibility of Payne's narrative. He wondered how Jack Hardwick, ultimate skeptic, would react to it. He was sure of one thing. If it was all just a performance by a clever murderer, it was one of the best—maybe *the* best—he'd ever witnessed.

He took a final bite of his ham-and-cheese sandwich and went to the cash register to pay. The apparent owner, a middle-aged man with a sad Slavic face, stood up from a nearby booth and came over to take his money.

"Nuts, huh?"

"Excuse me?"

The man gestured toward the street. "Lunatics. Wild. Smash. Burn."

"Even in this part of town?"

"Every part. Maybe not burning yet. But could be. Just as bad, almost. How can you sleep, thinking how crazy? Burning, shooting, crazy shit." He shook his head. "No waitresses today. Afraid, you know. Okay. I understand. No matter, maybe. No customers. They afraid, too, so everybody stay home. Hide in closet maybe. What good is this shit? They burn down their fucking house, right? For what? For what? What we supposed to do now? Buy guns, all of us, we shoot each other? Stupid. Stupid."

Gurney nodded, took his change, and headed for his car on the nearly deserted street.

By the time he got to it his phone was ringing.

"Gurney here."

"This is Whit Coolidge. After you left, Cory was thinking about something you said—about video footage of him driving to and from the places where the shots were fired?"

"Yes?"

"He says—and I agree—the traffic cameras along those routes are pretty obvious. Anyone who'd ever driven around White River would know they were there."

"So?"

"If the killer knew they were there, wouldn't he avoid them?"

"It's a reasonable question."

"So what we're thinking is, maybe it would make more sense to be looking for someone who *doesn't* appear on those videos."

"That did occur to me."

"Oh. Well. You said so little at the meeting it was hard to know what you were thinking."

"I learn more from listening than from talking."

"Absolutely true. A principle we should all live by. And one we so easily forget. Anyway, we just wanted to share that thought with you on the video issue."

"I appreciate it."

After he ended the call, Gurney sat for a while in his parked car, picturing the map Mark Torres had displayed, the one showing the route taken by the red motorcycle and its anonymous leather-clad rider—the route painstakingly reconstructed by interviewing people who'd glimpsed or heard the loud bike zipping by—a route that went all the way from Poulter Street to Willard Park, managing to avoid every traffic camera in the city, while Cory Payne in the black Corolla was being recorded by one after another.

Gurney was tempted to drive over to the park yet again—to the last reported location of the motorcycle, before it presumably disappeared into one of several wilderness trails. But he'd been there three times already, and there were two locations critical to the case that he hadn't yet visited. It was time he did.

Keys would be required. He placed a call to Mark Torres.

While Gurney's exiled status had not diminished Torres's willingness to cooperate with him, it had made it inadvisable to do so openly.

They arrived at a plan that would allow Gurney to examine Cory Payne's apartment and the apartment used for the Steele shooting without necessitating any direct contact. Torres would see to it that the doors of both apartments would be unlocked for one hour that afternoon—from two thirty to three thirty. It would be up to Gurney to conduct his examinations within that time frame, attracting as little attention as possible.

He arrived at the Steele sniper site at 2:31. The five-story building, like many in White River, had seen better days. He recalled from the video shown in one of the CSMT meetings that the apartment number was 5C. Apartment buildings of less than six stories were not legally required to have elevators, and this one didn't. By the time he reached the fifth floor he was breathing a bit more heavily than he would have liked. It reminded him to add some aerobic exercise to his regimen of push-ups and chin-ups. He'd recently turned fifty, and staying in shape required more effort than it used to.

The apartment door looked as if it hadn't been cleaned in years. The reinforced steel peephole was as clear a statement of urban decline as the stink of urine in the stairwell. As planned, the door was unlocked. If there had been crime-scene tape across it, it had been removed.

The interior layout—a small foyer leading into a large room with a kitchenette and bathroom on the right—was as he remembered it from the video, except that the large window was now closed. The faint tripod marks were still visible on the dusty floor.

Standing in the center of the triangle formed by the three marks and gazing out through the streaky windowpanes, he could see in the distance the spot at the edge of Willard Park where John Steele had been struck down. Looking around the empty room, his gaze fell on the ancient steam radiator under which the brass casing had been found. The bottom of the radiator was at least four inches from the floor, leaving the space beneath it easily visible.

He went into the small kitchen and saw nothing out of the ordinary beyond the residue of fingerprint powder left by the evidence tech on various handles, cabinets, and drawers.

Next he went into the bathroom, the room that most interested him—especially the toilet, and the flushing lever in particular. He inspected it carefully, then opened the water tank and examined the inner workings. His eyes widened. What he was looking at suggested an explanation for Payne's prints being found on the flushing mechanism, on a greasy food wrapper in the toilet bowl, on the brass casing in the living room, and nowhere else in the apartment.

It had bothered him from the beginning that no fresh prints had been found on any of the doors or on the open window sash. Now he thought he knew why, but he wanted an additional piece of evidence to corroborate the explanation before he shared it with Torres.

He took several photos of the toilet tank with his phone, then took a quick look around the apartment to be sure he was leaving everything as he found it. He hurried down the four flights of stairs, breathing in as little as possible of the sour smell, went out through the lobby onto Bridge Street, and drove to the address Torres had given him for Payne's apartment.

It was located on the far side of Willard Park. The neighborhood was run down but had not yet been visited by the sporadic fires and looting that had pockmarked the rest of the Grinton section. The air, however, had the ashy odor that seemed to have penetrated every corner of the city.

The building was a narrow three-story brick structure with a weedy vacant lot on either side. There were two apartment floors above a storefront. Steel security shades were pulled down over the store windows. A hand-printed sign on the door said Closed. A more professional sign over the barricaded window said Computer Repairs. The building had two front entrances, one to the store, the other to a stairwell providing access to the apartments.

Payne's was on the second floor. The door, unlocked as promised, opened into a dark foyer that led to a living room with a partial view of the forested area of the park. There was a faint sewer-like smell in the room. The furniture was disarranged. The rug had been rolled back to one side of the room, the couch and chair pillows heaped on the floor. Chairs had been turned over, desk drawers removed, bookcase shelves emptied. A power strip and a tangle of wires on the floor indicated the former presence of a computer. Light fixtures had been opened, blinds taken down from the windows. The place had evidently been subjected to a thorough police search.

A doorway on the left side of the living room led to a bedroom, with what appeared to be the apartment's only closet. The bureau drawers had been removed and emptied. The mattress had been removed from the box spring and the clothes from the closet. In the corners of the room there were random piles of underwear, socks, shirts, pants.

If Gurney had more time he would have gone through all of it, but he had a more urgent interest. He left the bedroom and crossed the living room to a pair of open doorways. One led to the kitchen, where he found fingerprint dust everywhere, ransacked cabinets and drawers, an open refrigerator. The sewer-like odor was stronger here than in the living room.

The doorway next to the kitchen led to a hallway at the end of which he could see the bathroom, the room he was most interested in—and the source of the foul odor. The drainage trap under the sink had been removed, opening the room to the effluvia of the building's sewer lines. The medicine cabinet was empty. There were no towels. The toilet seat had been removed.

Gurney lifted the top off the toilet tank and peered down at the flushing mechanism and at the flushing lever on the outside of the tank. With a feeling of satisfaction, he took out his phone and photographed both.

He checked the time. There were still fifteen minutes remaining of the hour Torres had given him. His initial thought was to use every minute of it sifting through whatever the police had left behind. His second thought was to be satisfied with what he'd discovered and get the hell out of there.

That was the thought he acted on. He was out of the building, in his car, and heading for Walnut Crossing with thirteen minutes to spare. He didn't stop until he reached the interstate rest area where he'd had his initial conversation with Torres. It seemed an appropriate place to pull over, thank him for his assistance, and fill him in on the progress it had made possible.

As he placed the call, he wrestled with the question of how much to reveal—not only about his new view of the fingerprint issue but about his shifting sense of the whole case.

He opted to be fairly open, omitting only his direct contact with Payne.

Torres answered on the first ring. "How'd it go?"

"Smoothly," said Gurney. "I hope you didn't run into any problems on your end."

"None. I just finished relocking the apartment doors. Did you discover anything useful?"

"I think so. If I'm right, it raises some major questions."

"Like what?"

"Like how sure are you that Payne is the shooter?"

"As sure as I could be without a confession."

"Sell it to me."

"Okay. *Number one*, we know he was in the right places at the right times. We have time-coded videos to prove it. *Number two*, we have his fingerprints on the side door at Poulter Street and on the toilet and a fast-food wrapper in the Bridge Street apartment. *Number three*, we have his fingerprints on the cartridge casings found at both shooting sites. We know the prints are his because they match almost all the prints found in his apartment. *Number four*, a box of thirty-aught-six cartridges—with two missing—was found hidden under some shirts in his bedroom closet. *Number five*, we just got a DNA report showing a match between the Band-Aid recovered from the toilet at the Bridge Street apartment and hair follicles recovered from the sink drain in Payne's apartment. *Number six*, we have a confidential tip from a BDA informant naming him as the shooter. *Number seven*, his own public statements reveal an obsessive hatred for the police. So there it is. A hate-filled kid, aided and abetted by an organization with some hate-filled members. It's a convincing case with a ton of incriminating evidence—a lot more than we usually have."

"That's part of the problem."

The confident tone of Torres's summation dissolved. "What do you mean?"

"There does seem to be a ton of evidence. Almost too much of it. But no single piece of it is solid."

"What about the videos?"

"The videos tell us where he was at certain times. They don't tell us why."

"Wouldn't it be a pretty extreme coincidence if he just happened to be in both those places for some other reason when those shots were fired?"

"Not if someone sent him there."

"To set him up?"

"It's possible. It would explain why he made no effort to avoid traffic cameras or to obscure his plate number."

Gurney could imagine Torres's earnest frown as he considered the implications. "But how do you explain the fingerprints?"

"There's an interesting fact about those prints. They're all on portable objects, with one exception, the outside doorknob of the house on Poulter Street."

"What do you mean by portable objects? Toilets aren't that portable."

"Right. But the print wasn't on the toilet itself. It was on the flushing lever."

"Okay, on the lever . . . so . . . where does that take you?"

"An hour ago it took me from the apartment on Bridge Street to Payne's own apartment. I checked both toilets and took some photos that I'll send you."

"Photos that show what?"

"That the flushing levers may have been switched."

"*What?*"

"It's possible that the flushing lever on the Bridge Street toilet—the one with Payne's prints on it—may have come from his own bathroom."

"God, if that were true . . . that would turn everything upside down. Are you suggesting all the evidence was planted? The Band-Aid with Payne's DNA? The cartridge casings with his prints on them? That everything implicating him is part of a giant frame job?" Torres's tone was stunned and questioning rather than challenging.

"The facts are not inconsistent with that scenario."

Torres paused. "It sounds like I need to get forensics involved again . . . to take a look at this switched-flusher business . . . but suppose . . . Jesus . . ."

Gurney finished the thought. "But suppose the switch was done by someone in the department?"

Torres said nothing.

"It's a possibility. So if I were you, I'd keep the flusher issue to myself until we dig a little deeper and you can be sure you're not discussing it with the wrong person. This case could be a lot nastier than anyone realizes."

As he ended the call, the text message sent to John Steele the night he was killed came vividly to mind: *Watch ur back. EZ nite for mfs to ice ur ass n blame the BDA.*

For the next couple of minutes he sat there looking out over the field by the little brick building that housed the restrooms. The local vultures were circling idly on the updrafts from the sun-soaked ground.

He decided to call Hardwick and fill him in on the day's events.

The man's first words when he picked up were, for him, not unusual.

"The fuck do you want now?"

"Charm, warmth, and a welcoming voice."

"You got the wrong number, bro."

It was always best with Jack to cut to the chase, so Gurney did so. "The ME claims Loomis didn't die from the aftereffects of the gunshot. Somebody got to him in the hospital with an ice pick."

"No shit! Bit of a security fuckup. Any leads?"

"Not that I know of."

"Inside job? Somebody on the hospital staff?"

"Could be. But before we get into that, the ground is shifting under the whole case. It looks like Payne is being . . ." Gurney stopped speaking at the sight in his rearview mirror of a blue Ford Explorer pulling into the rest stop. "Hold on a second, Jack. I may be about to have a little trouble with Judd Turlock."

"Where are you?"

"Deserted rest stop near the Larvaton exit on the interstate. He just drove in behind me. I didn't see him following me, so either he planted a tracker on my car or he's been having my phone pinged for location. Do me a favor. I'm going to leave my phone on. Keep listening in case I need a witness later."

"You have your weapon?"

"I do." As he spoke he removed the Beretta from his ankle holster and tucked it under his right leg, flicking off the safety.

"If you feel your life is in danger, just shoot the fucker."

"That's what I rely on you for—nuanced advice."

As Turlock came to the side of the car, Gurney slipped the live phone in his shirt pocket and rolled down his window.

Turlock's voice was as expressionless as his eyes. "Busy day?"

"Busy enough."

"You get too busy, you start making stupid mistakes."

Gurney met his gaze and waited.

"Like with that lady back at the hospital. The credentials you showed her said you were from the DA's office. But you're not. Not anymore. I could arrest you for impersonating an officer. Maybe let you spend a little time in Sheriff Cloutz's hotel. What do you think of that?"

"I think it could create a problem. Actually, two problems. First problem, there's no expiration date on my credentials, and I have a contract that requires written notice of termination, which I never received. Which means the impersonation charge is groundless. So right off the bat you'd be facing a false arrest charge. Second problem, I heard a rumor that somebody got to Rick Loomis in the ICU." Turlock's eyes seemed to widen just a little.

Gurney went on. "The security you provided was inadequate, and I told your skirt-chasing officer in front of witnesses that Loomis was in serious danger. That warning was ignored. Now here's the thing, Judd. I have no desire to publicize your major screw-up, but when people get threatened with arrest they often do destructive things."

"Who the hell told you somebody got to Loomis?"

"I have informants. Just like you and Chief Beckert. Except my informants actually know what they're talking about."

Something new entered Turlock's eyes, something like the strange calm before a violent storm. Then his gaze fell on the phone in Gurney's shirt pocket and the strange look was replaced by something more controlled if no less hostile.

"You fuck up this murder investigation, Gurney, there's going to be a price to pay. In White River we consider obstruction of justice a serious crime. *Very* serious."

"I couldn't agree with you more."

"I'm glad we understand each other," said Turlock, staring at him for a long moment with an expression full of stone-cold hatred. He slowly raised his right hand in the shape of a gun, the forefinger pointing at Gurney's face. He dropped the thumb like a hammer. Without another word, he returned to his big blue SUV and drove out of the rest area.

Gurney took his phone out of his pocket. "You hear all that, Jack?"

"Jesus, was that your idea of nuance? You're lucky the crazy fucker didn't kill you."

"He'd love to. Maybe someday he'll try to. But right now there are other things I need to talk to you about." Gurney proceeded to bring Hardwick up to date on the events of the day, beginning with his conversations with Whittaker Coolidge and Cory Payne and ending with his discovery of the possible switching of the flush handles.

Hardwick grunted. "That toilet thing sounds like a stretch."

"I agree."

"But if it's true, we're dealing with a goddamn elaborate setup."

"I agree."

"Shitload of planning."

"Yep."

"Big risk would suggest a big payoff."

"Right."

"So the questions would be whodunit, and why."

"There's another interesting question. If Payne was framed, was that a tactic to divert blame, or was it the goal?"

"The hell does that mean?"

"Did the killer pick Payne as a convenient framing victim to misdirect the investigation into the cop killings, or were the cops killed for the explicit purpose of framing him?"

"Jesus, don't you think that's a little twisted? Why the hell would framing him be important enough to kill two cops?"

"I admit it's pushing the possibilities a bit."

"More than a fucking *bit*."

"I'd still like to know for sure which end is the dog and which end is the tail. In the meantime, how's your poking around in Beckert's past going?"

"Couple of guys are supposed to be getting back to me. I should be able to tell you something later tonight. Or maybe not. Who knows how eager these cocksuckers are to return favors."

35

At 5:00 PM Gurney was heading up the hillside road to his property, weary from his obsessive analysis of scenarios involving the framing of Cory Payne. From the moment he'd noticed the plier marks where the outside flush handle joined the flushing mechanism inside the tank, he'd been able to think of little else.

When he reached the end of the road, however, and came abreast of his barn, that subject was nudged aside by the presence of Walter Thrasher's sleek black Audi.

Gurney remembered the phone call in which he'd agreed to let the man search for artifacts that might support whatever notion he'd gotten about the history of the place. He was tempted to go up to the excavation site to see if he'd found what he was looking for. But the prospect of trudging up the hill was discouraging, and he continued on to the house.

Madeleine, in her straw gardening hat, was kneeling at the edge of the asparagus bed, prying out weeds with a trowel. She looked up at him, tilting the brim of her hat to shield her eyes from the afternoon sun.

"Are you all right?" she asked. "You look worn out."

"I feel worn out."

"Any progress?"

"Mostly uncovering new questions. We'll see where they lead."

She shrugged and went back to her weeding. "I assume you know about that man down by the pond?"

"Dr. Walter Thrasher. He asked me if he could poke around in our excavation."

"You mean *your* excavation."

"Apparently he's an expert on the Colonial history of this area." He paused. "He's also the county medical examiner."

"Is that so?" She stabbed her trowel down around a dandelion root.

He watched for a while in silence before asking, "How's Heather doing?"

"Last I heard, the contractions stopped—or what they thought were contractions. They're keeping her in the hospital for at least another twenty-four hours for evaluation." She yanked a long root out of the ground and tossed it on a pile beside her. She gazed at the trowel for a moment, laid it on top of the weeds, and looked up at him again. "You really do look like you had a difficult day."

"I did. But I have a recovery plan. A hot shower. I'll see you in a little while."

As usual, the shower worked at least some of its hoped-for magic. It struck him as an odd irony of the human animal that the most complex mental tangles could be relieved by the application of warm water.

By the time they sat down to dinner, he felt calm and refreshed. He was even able to appreciate the scent of apple blossoms in the soft spring air coming in through the French doors. They were well into their asparagus soup before Madeleine broke the silence. "Do you want to tell me about your day?"

"It's a long story."

"I'm not going anywhere."

He began with his morning visit to Saint Thomas the Apostle. He told her about the Reverend Coolidge's sympathy for the BDA and for Marcel Jordan's and Virgil Tooker's supposed efforts to expose police wrongdoing, about the man's almost violent aversion to Dell Beckert, and about his insistence on the innocence of Cory Payne.

He told her about his subsequent meeting with Payne himself—about Payne's explanation for his presence at the shooting sites, about his open contempt for his father, about his fear of being next in line for assassination.

He also told her about his phone conversation with Thrasher, about the appearance of propofol in Jordan's and Tooker's tox screens, and about the chilling discovery made during the Rick Loomis autopsy.

At Gurney's mention of the ice pick Madeleine uttered a guttural cry of revulsion. "Are you saying that someone . . . just walked into the ICU . . . *and did that?*"

"It could have happened in the ICU. Or when he was being brought back from radiology."

"My God! How? I don't understand how someone could just . . ."

"It could have been a hospital employee, someone familiar to the nurses. Or someone in uniform. Maybe a security person. Or someone pretending to be a doctor."

"Or a cop?"

"Or a cop. Someone who wanted to make sure Rick would never come out of that coma."

"When will Heather be told?"

"Not right away, I'm sure."

"Won't she automatically be given a copy of that autopsy report?"

"She'll have to request it, and the official version probably won't be available for another thirty days. What Thrasher gave me on the phone was an oral heads-up on the preliminary report, which doesn't go to anyone except to the police—as an aid to the investigation."

She started to take a spoonful of her soup, then laid the spoon down as though she'd lost her appetite and pushed the bowl toward the center of the table.

After a while Gurney went on with the story of his day. He talked about his visits to the two apartments, his discovery of the suspicious tool marks on the toilet handles, his growing sense that everything Dell Beckert was saying about the case was either a mistake or a lie, and the unnerving possibility of police involvement in the shootings.

"That isn't exactly news," said Madeleine.

"What do you mean?"

"Isn't that what the text on John Steele's phone said from the beginning?"

"The text didn't provide any real information. It could have been an intentional misdirection. It still could be. This case is like a buried city. We're only seeing pieces of it. I need more facts."

"You need to *do* something. Two women lost their husbands. An unborn baby lost her father. Something has to be done!"

"What do you think I should be doing that I'm not doing already?"

"I don't know. You're good at assembling bits of information and seeing a pattern in them. But I think sometimes you enjoy the intellectual process so much you don't like to rush it."

He said nothing. His normal impulse to defend himself seemed to have gone missing.

The list of hospital employees he'd gotten from Abby Marsh was divided into six functional categories: Administration and Technical Support; Physicians and Surgeons; Nursing and Therapy; Laboratory and Pharmacy; Security, Maintenance, and Housekeeping; Kitchen, Cafeteria, and Gift Shop. A seventh cross-functional category was labeled Current Year Resignations and Terminations. It was apparently updated monthly, covering January through the end of April, making it useless for identifying staff members who might have been terminated during the current month.

Going through the six functional lists produced no instant revelations. He came upon several names familiar from his visits. He noted a predictable relationship between job description and home address. Most of the housekeeping staff lived in Grinton. The nursing, lab, and technical support people were more likely to live in Bluestone. Physicians and surgeons preferred Aston Lake and Killburnie Heights.

Although he was aware that the largest part of detective work involved slogging along unproductive paths, Madeleine's comment had left him with a feeling of restlessness, an itch to accelerate the process. After considering some actionable next steps, he decided to pursue an answer to a question that intrigued him.

If there was a reasonable doubt about the involvement of Cory Payne, then any possible aid provided to him by the Black Defense Alliance was equally questionable. But if the BDA was not involved in the planning or execution of the shootings, why had Marcel Jordan leased the two shooting sites? Or had he, in fact, even done so? The fact that his name appeared on the leases fell short of proving his involvement. The leasing brokers might be able to shed some light on the matter. Gurney placed a call to Torres to get the brokers' names.

Torres responded without hesitation. "Laura Conway at Acme Realty."

"She's the broker for both locations?"

"For most of the rental properties in White River. There are other brokers in town, but Acme manages almost all the rentals. We have a good relationship. Is there some way I can help?"

"I want to find out about the lease agreements on the Bridge Street apartment and the Poulter Street house—specifically, whether anyone at the realty company had direct contact with Marcel Jordan."

"If you want, I can ask about that for you. Or if you'd rather, I can have Laura Conway call you directly."

"The second option would be best. Depending on what she says about Jordan, I may have follow-up questions."

"I'll see if I can reach her now. Sometimes she works late. Let me get back to you."

Five minutes later Torres called back.

"Conway is on vacation up in the Maine woods, no cell phone, no internet, no email, but she should be back in the office in three or four days."

"Do you know if anyone else in the office was involved with those contracts?"

"I asked. The answer was no. Laura handled both of them personally."

"Okay, I appreciate the effort. You'll try again when she's due back?"

"Absolutely." He hesitated. "You think there's something wrong with the contracts?"

"I'd like to know whether Jordan himself personally leased those places. By the way, you mentioned the department has a good relationship with Acme. What sort of good relationship?"

"Just . . . good."

"Mark, you're not a particularly good liar."

Torres hesitated. "I have to testify at a trial in Albany tomorrow morning. I need to be there by ten. I could stop off in Walnut Crossing around eight. Could we meet someplace and talk?"

"There's a place for coffee in Dillweed. It's called Abelard's. On the county road in the center of the village. I can be there at eight."

"I'll see you then."

Gurney knew if he gave in to the inclination to speculate, he'd waste a lot of time trying to arrive at an answer that would likely be handed to him the following morning. Instead he placed a call to Jack Hardwick.

It went to voicemail, and he left a message.

"Gurney here. I'm getting some ugly ideas about this case, and I need you to tell me what's wrong with them. I'm going to be at Abelard's tomorrow morning to meet with a young detective. He has to get to Albany for a trial, and he'll need to be on his way by eight thirty. If you can come then, that would be ideal."

36

When Gurney pulled into the tiny parking area in front of Abelard's at 7:55 AM, the Crown Vic was already there.

He found Torres at one of the rickety antique tables in the back. Every time he saw the young detective, he looked a little younger and a little more lost. His shoulders were hunched, and he was holding his coffee mug in both hands as if he were trying to give them something to do.

Gurney sat opposite him.

"I remember this place when I was a little kid," said Torres. His voice conveyed the special tension produced by trying to sound relaxed. "Back then it was a dusty old general store. Used to sell live bait. For fishing. Before it got all fixed up."

"You grew up in Dillweed?"

"No. Out in Binghamton. But I had an aunt and uncle here. They immigrated from Puerto Rico about ten years before my parents and I came up. They had a small dairy farm. Compared to Binghamton, this was real country. The area hasn't changed much. Mostly got poorer, more run-down. But this place sure got fixed up." He paused, lowering his voice. "Have you heard about the latest problem in the search for the Gorts?"

"What now?"

"That second K9 dog they brought in—it got a crossbow arrow through its head, just like the first. And the state police helicopter had to make an emergency landing in one of the old quarries—some kind of mechanical problem. Just the kind of a mess the media loves—and Beckert hates."

Gurney said nothing. He was waiting for Torres to get to the real point of their meeting. He ordered a double espresso from Marika, whose spiked hair that morning was only one color, a relatively conservative silver blond.

Torres took a deep breath. "Sorry about dragging you out here like this. We probably could have talked on the phone, but . . ." He shook his head. "I guess I'm getting kind of paranoid."

"I know the feeling."

Torres's eyes widened. "You? You seem . . . unshakable."

"Sometimes I am, sometimes I'm not."

Torres bit his lower lip. He seemed to be steeling himself for a dive off the high board. "You asked about Acme Realty."

"About Acme's relationship with the department."

"The way I understand it, it's kind of a reciprocal arrangement."

"Meaning what?'

"Rental management can be a tough business in some neighborhoods. Not just trying to collect rent from deadbeats, but nastier stuff. Dealers turning the property into a crack house. Illegal activity that can void the owner's insurance. Tenants threatening to kill landlords. Gangbangers scaring decent tenants away. Apartments getting trashed. You're a landlord in a tough area like Grinton, you're going to be dealing with some dangerously crazy tenants."

"So what's the reciprocal arrangement?"

"Acme gets the support it needs from the department. Gangbangers, drug dealers, and crazies are persuaded to move on. People who don't pay their rent are persuaded to do so."

"What does the department get in return?"

"Access."

"Access to what?"

"To any rental unit Acme manages."

"The Poulter Street house?"

"Yes."

"The Bridge Street apartment?"

"Yes."

"Cory Payne's apartment?"

"Yes."

Marika arrived with his espresso. "God," she said. "You boys look super serious. Whatever you do for a living, I'm glad I don't do it. You want sugar with that?"

Gurney shook his head. When she was gone he said, "So, we're talking about warrantless searches?"

Torres said nothing, just nodded.

"So let's say you have a vague suspicion there might be some illegal activity in a particular apartment, but nothing concrete. And you know that no one is home during the day. So what then? You call up that Conway woman and ask her for a key?"

Torres looked around nervously. "No, you go to Turlock."

"And he calls Conway?"

"I don't know. I just know he's the one you'd go to, and he'd supply the key."

"So you take the key, you check out the premises, you see the evidence you guessed might be there. Then what?"

"You leave everything like it was. You get a warrant from Judge Puckett, specifying what you expect to find, claiming it was based on reliable tips from two sources. Then you go back and find it. All neat and legal."

"You've done this?"

"No. I'm not comfortable with it. But I know some guys have."

"And they have no problem with it?"

"They don't seem to. It's blessed from the top. That means a lot."

Gurney couldn't disagree with that. "So the bad guys get put away or run out of town. Acme has fewer problems, and their business is more profitable. Meanwhile, Beckert gets credit for reducing the population of undesirables and cleaning up White River. He becomes a champion of law and order. Everybody wins."

Torres nodded. "That's pretty much the way it works."

"Okay. Big question. Do you know of situations where evidence was planted by the same officer who later found it?"

Torres was staring down into the coffee mug he was still grasping with both hands. "I couldn't say for sure. All I know is what I'm telling you."

"But you're uncomfortable with all that illegal access?"

"I guess so. Maybe I'm in the wrong line of work."

"Law enforcement?"

"The *reality* of it. The version you learn in the academy is fine. But it's a whole other thing out on the street. It's like you have to break the law to uphold it."

He was gripping his mug so tightly now his knuckles were white. "I mean, what's 'due process' anyway? Is that supposed to be a real thing? Or do we just pretend it's a real thing? Are we supposed to respect it even when it's inconvenient, or only when it doesn't get in the way of what we want to achieve?"

"Where do you think Dell Beckert stands on that question?"

"Beckert is all about the result. The final product. Period."

"And how he gets there doesn't matter?"

"It sure doesn't seem to. It's like there's no standard other than what that man wants." He sighed and met Gurney's gaze. "You think maybe I should be in another profession?"

"Why do you ask?"

"Because I hate the conflicts that are part of the job."

"Part of the job? Part of this peculiar case? Part of working in a racially divided city? Or just part of working for Beckert?"

"Maybe all of those. Plus . . . being a Latino in a very Anglo department can get a little tense. Sometimes more than a little."

"Let me ask you something. Why did you become a cop to begin with?"

"To be helpful. Make a difference. Do the right thing."

"And you don't think that's what you're doing?"

"I'm trying. But I feel like I'm in a minefield. Take this situation with the toilet handle. I mean, if Payne is being set up by someone in the department . . ." His voice trailed off. He looked down at his watch. "Christ, I better get going."

Gurney walked out with him to the parking area.

Torres opened his car door, but didn't immediately get in. He uttered a small humorless laugh. "I just said in there that I wanted to be helpful. But I don't have a clue how to do that. It seems that the longer this case goes on, the less I know."

"That's not the worst thing in the world. Realizing you have no idea what's going on is a hell of a lot better than being totally sure about everything—and totally wrong."

37

Three minutes later, as Torres's Crown Victoria was pulling out onto the county road, Hardwick's growling red GTO was pulling in.

Hardwick got out and swung the heavy door shut with the crashing thump that only vintage Detroit cars make. He cast a sideways glance at the departing sedan. "Who's the dick in the Vic?"

"Mark Torres," said Gurney. "CIO on the Steele and Loomis cases."

"Just the shootings? Who caught the playground murders?"

"He did, for about ten minutes. Then Beckert took over and handed them off to Turlock."

Hardwick shrugged. "Like it's always been. Dell calls the shots, the Turd does the work."

Gurney led the way back inside to the table he'd occupied with Torres. Marika came over and Gurney ordered another double espresso. Hardwick ordered a large mug of Abelard's special dark roast.

"What did you learn about Beckert?" Gurney asked.

"Here's what I was told—mostly secondhand stuff, rumors, bullshit. Some of it might be partly true. No telling which part."

"You inspire confidence."

"Confidence is my middle name. So here's the story. 'Dell' is a shortened form of 'Cordell.' Specifically, Cordell Beckert the Second. Known to some of his associates as CB-Two. Meaning there was another Cordell Beckert somewhere in the family tree. Cory Payne was actually christened Cordell Beckert the Third.

"Dell was born in Utica forty-six years ago. His father was a cop, disabled in a shootout with a drug dealer. Quadriplegic. Died when Dell was ten. After grammar school—I already told you some of this—Dell got a scholarship to a military prep school in the redneck end of Virginia. Bayard-Whitson Academy. Where he met Judd Turlock. And where Judd had his juvie legal problem. I'll come back to that in a minute. After Bayard-Whitson, he went to—"

Gurney interrupted. "It's interesting that Beckert never used what happened to his father as a credential for his war on drugs, like he did with his wife's death."

Hardwick shrugged. "Maybe he didn't give a shit about the old man."

"Or the opposite. Some people never mention the things that affect them the most."

Marika arrived at the table with Hardwick's coffee, then left.

When she was out of earshot, he continued. "After Bayard-Whitson, Dell went to Choake Christian College, where he met and married his first wife, Melissa Payne. Cory was born right after he graduated from Choake's ROTC program. He joined the Marines as a lieutenant, completed a four-year tour, came out as a captain, then joined the NYSP. With his Marine officer background he moved up quickly during the next seven or eight years. The job was first, family a distant second. Along the way Melissa fell in love with painkillers and Cory became a festering thorn in his side, which I told you about."

"Culminating in the attempted torching of the recruiting office?"

"Right. But there's something else I was just told by someone who knew the family back then. But it might be total bullshit. See, to do you a fucking favor, I've been making a giant pain in the ass of myself, calling people I haven't spoken to in years, annoying them with one goddamn question after another. They may be making up crap to get rid of me."

"You love making a giant pain in the ass of yourself. What did you find out?"

"Two, three months before Dad finally sent the little bastard away to the boot-camp boarding-school prison—whatever the fuck you want to call it—Cory supposedly had a druggie girlfriend. He was a large, aggressive twelve. She was maybe fourteen and dealing a little pot here and there. Dell had her picked up and tossed into juvie detention for possession and intent—to make a point to Cory about what happens when you hang out with people Dad doesn't approve of. Problem is, she was raped in the detention center, supposedly by a couple of COs, and hanged herself. Or so the story goes. Anyway, it was after that that Cory went totally batshit and got sent away to the discipline farm."

"No blowback on Beckert from the kid's death?"

"Not even a breeze."

Gurney nodded thoughtfully, sipping his espresso. "So he puts his son's girl-friend in a place where she gets raped and ends up dead, and when the kid reacts, he sticks him in some behavior-mod hellhole. His desperate addict wife either accidentally or not-so-accidentally ODs on heroin, and he uses that to sanctify his image as a determined drug fighter. Fast-forward to the present. Two White River cops get killed, he's handed some shaky evidence that his son may have been involved, and he appears on one of the most popular interview shows in the country to announce not only that he's ordered his son's arrest for murder but that he's sacrificing his outstanding police career in the interest of *justice*. You know something, Jack? This guy makes me want to throw up."

The challenging look that was never completely absent from Hardwick's eyes sharpened. "You don't like him because you think he's accepting shaky evidence against his own son as gospel? Or is it the other way around—you're seeing the evidence as shaky because you don't like him?"

"I don't think I'm being delusional. It's a simple fact that all the so-called evidence is portable. None of it was found on the interior doors, walls, windows, or any other structural parts of those premises. Doesn't that strike you as peculiar?"

"Peculiar shit happens all the time. The world is a factory for peculiar shit."

"One more point. Torres just told me that Turlock has a deal with the rental agent that would have given him easy access to the locations where the so-called evidence was found."

"Wait a minute. If you're suggesting that Turlock planted that evidence, you're really suggesting it was Beckert, since the Turd does nothing without a nod from God."

"The toilet-handle switch indicates that *somebody* planted it with the intention of incriminating Cory Payne. There's no other reasonable interpretation of that. All I'm saying about Turlock and Beckert is that their involvement is possible."

Hardwick made his acid-reflux face. "I'll admit Beckert is a prick. But to frame his own son for murder? What kind of person does that?"

Gurney shrugged. "A blindly ambitious psychopath?"

"But why? Even psychopaths need motives. It makes no fucking sense. And it's a hell of a shakier premise than Cory being the shooter. Take that weird flush-handle thing out of the equation, and your whole 'framing' theory collapses. Couldn't you be mistaken about the significance of those tool scratches?"

"It's too big a coincidence for both those handles to have been removed and replaced—with one of them providing a key fingerprint in a murder investigation."

Hardwick shook his head. "Look at it from the motive angle. Look at what we know about Cory Payne. Radical, unstable, full of rage. Hates his father, hates cops. Has a long history of public rants against law enforcement. One of his favorite lines is the BDA motto: 'The problem isn't cop killers, it's killer cops.' I was listening to one of his speeches on YouTube. He was talking about the moral duty of the oppressed to take an eye for an eye—which is essentially invoking the Bible to advocate the murder of police officers. And that business about his girlfriend being raped by a couple of COs—can't you see that festering in his mind? Shit, Gurney, he sounds to me like a prime suspect for exactly what he's being accused of."

"There's just one problem with it. He might have all the motivation in the world, but he's not an idiot. He wouldn't leave brass casings with his prints on them at the shooting sites. He wouldn't leave a Band-Aid floating in the toilet with his DNA on it. He wouldn't drive an easily traceable car with visible plates past a series of traffic cameras and park it next to each shooting location, unless he were doing it for some other reason. It's not like he wanted to be caught or to claim responsibility for the shootings—he's adamantly denying any involvement. And there's the problem of victim selection. Why would he pick the two cops in the department who were the least like the cops he supposedly hates? Logically and emotionally, none of it makes sense."

Hardwick turned up his palms in exasperation. "You think Beckert framing his own son makes logical and emotional sense? Why the hell would he do that? And by the way, do *what*, exactly? I mean, are you suggesting Beckert framed his own son for two murders someone else committed? Or are you saying that Beckert also arranged the murders of two of his own cops? Plus the BDA murders? You seriously believe all that?"

"What I believe is that the people he's blaming for it had nothing to do with it."

"The Gorts? Why not?"

"The Gorts are violent, uneducated, redneck racists—men whose approach to life involves skulls, crossbows, pit bulls, and chopping up dead bears for dog food."

"So what?"

"The playground murders were carefully planned and executed. They required knowledge of the victims' movements, a flawless double kidnapping, and the sophisticated administration of propofol. And Thrasher told me the tox screens on the victims included not only propofol but alcohol and benzodiazepines. That suggests a scenario that began with a friendly meeting over a few drinks—something I can't imagine occurring between the BDA leaders and the Gorts."

"What about the evidence they keep talking about on TV—the rope they found in the Gorts' compound, and the computer drive with the KRS website elements on it?"

"Both could have been as easily planted as the items they're trying to hang Cory with."

"Christ, if we had to exclude every piece of evidence that *could* have been planted, no one would ever be convicted of anything!"

Gurney said nothing.

Hardwick stared at him. "This fixation you have on Beckert—what's that really based on, besides his crazy son blaming him for everything?"

"Just a feeling at this point. Which is why I want to find out everything I can about the man's history. A few minutes ago you alluded to Turlock's juvie legal problem when he was in school with Beckert. Were you able to find out anything more about that?"

Hardwick paused. When he finally spoke, his tone had become less argumentative. "Maybe something, maybe nothing. I called the Bayard-Whitson Academy and got the headmaster's assistant. I told her I was interested in speaking with any staff members who'd been at the school thirty years ago. She wanted to know why. I said that one of their eminent graduates, Dell Beckert, who was a student at that time, could be the next New York State attorney general—and that I was writing an article about him for a journalism course I was taking, and I'd love to be able to include the perspective of any of his teachers who might be willing to share an anecdote or two."

"She bought this?"

"She did. In fact, after a little more back-and-forth, she told me that she had been there herself, as assistant to the previous headmaster, when Beckert was a student."

"She say anything about him?"

"Yep. Cold, calculating, clever, ambitious. Was awarded 'Top Cadet' distinction in every one of his four years there."

"He must have made a big impression on her for it to last thirty years."

"Judd Turlock apparently made a bigger one. When I mentioned his name, there was total silence. I thought the call was cut off. She finally said she had no desire to talk about Turlock, because in all her time at Bayard he was the only student who'd made her feel uneasy. I asked if she knew of any trouble he'd gotten into, and there was another dead silence. Then she told me to hang on a minute.

When she came back to the phone she gave me an address in Pennsylvania. She said it belonged to a detective by the name of Merle Tabor. Said if anyone could tell me anything about the incident involving Turlock, it would be Merle."

"The *incident*? She didn't say anything specific about that?"

"No. My mention of Turlock pretty much shut her down. Seemed like after she gave me that address, she just wanted to get off the phone."

"Quite a reaction after thirty years."

Hardwick picked up his coffee mug and took a long swallow. "There's something unnerving about the Turd. He tends to stick in the mind."

"Interesting. You plan to follow up with Merle Tabor?"

"Hell, no. According to the school lady, Merle's an off-the-grid kind of guy. No phone, no email, no computer, no electricity. You can pay him a visit and find out for yourself, if the spirit moves you. Probably no more than a four-hour trip, assuming you don't get lost in the woods."

Hardwick pulled a scrap of notepaper out of his pocket and slid it across the table. There was an address of sorts scrawled on it in his nearly indecipherable handwriting—BLACK MOUNTAIN HOLLOW, PARKSTON, PA. "Who knows? Couple of old retired farts like you might hit it off. Merle could end up handing you the key to the whole goddamn mess."

It was clear from his tone that he considered such an outcome unlikely. Gurney saw no reason to disagree.

38

After Hardwick roared off in his eco-hostile muscle car, Gurney stayed at Abelard's for a little while to finish his coffee and organize the rest of his day.

Merle Tabor had suddenly become the elephant in the room, and despite Gurney's mixed feelings about the usefulness of a visit to Black Mountain Hollow, he found it impossible to dismiss. He took out his phone and went to a Google satellite view of Parkston, Pennsylvania. There wasn't much to see. The place appeared to be a crossroads in the middle of nowhere. He typed in "Black Mountain Hollow" and discovered that it was a narrow dirt road proceeding from a county route three miles up into the hills. There was one house on it, at the very end.

He clicked on Directions, entered his Walnut Crossing address as the starting point, and found that the distance to Parkston was 142 miles. The estimated drive time was just under three hours, not Hardwick's four. Even so, he was reluctant to make the trip without some indication that Merle Tabor would be there. He looked up the number for the Parkston Police Department.

His call was automatically transferred to the county sheriff's office. He assumed he must have misheard the name given by the man who answered—*Sergeant Gerbil*—but he didn't question it. He explained that he was a retired NYPD homicide detective, had been hired to look into an old case down in Butris County, Virginia, and had reason to believe that a Parkston resident by the name of Merle Tabor might be able to give him some useful information. But he didn't know how to get in touch with the man. He was starting to explain that Tabor lived on Black Mountain Hollow and had no phone when the sergeant interrupted him with a nasal Appalachian accent.

"You plannin' on payin' him a visit?"

"Yes, but I'd like to know that he's there before I drive for three—"

"He's there."

"Excuse me?"

"He's always there in the spring of the year. Most other times, too."

"You know him?"

"Somewhat. But it don't sound like *you* do."

"I don't. His name was given to me as someone familiar with the case I'm looking into. Is there any way of getting in touch with him?"

"You want to see him, you just have to go see him."

"His house at the end of the Hollow road?"

"Only house up there."

"Okay. Thank you."

"Your name again?"

"Dave Gurney."

"NYPD?"

"Homicide. Retired."

"Good luck. By the way, make sure it's daylight."

"Daylight?"

"Merle don't like people on his property after dark."

After ending the call, Gurney checked the time. It was just five after nine. If he left immediately, allowing six hours for the total round-trip drive time, plus forty-five minutes with Merle Tabor, he could be home before four.

He had some phone calls to make, but he could make them en route. He paid Marika for the coffees, left a generous tip, and set out for Parkston.

As he was heading southwest through the long river valley toward Pennsylvania, he made the first call—to Madeleine. It went to her voicemail. He left a detailed message explaining where he was going and why. Then he checked his own voicemail and discovered that she'd left a message for him since he'd had his phone shut off all morning. He played it back.

"Hi. I just arrived at the clinic. I don't know if that Thrasher person was there when you were leaving for Abelard's this morning, but when I was leaving at eight forty I saw his fancy car down by our barn. I don't like the idea of him coming up on our property whenever he feels like it. In fact, I don't like him being there at all. We need to talk. Soon. See you later."

Aside from feeling the automatic negative reaction he felt whenever Madeleine raised a problem, he had to admit he wasn't especially pleased with Thrasher's presence either. And he certainly wasn't pleased with the man's secretiveness about what he was looking for.

His next call was to Torres—to raise a point he'd meant to bring up at Abelard's, before he was distracted by the young detective's slide into self-doubt.

He got his voicemail.

"Mark, it's Dave Gurney. I want to suggest something. If Cory Payne wasn't the shooter at the Bridge Street apartment building, obviously someone else was. You need to take another look at the traffic and security videos. The shooter may have used that red motocross bike. Or another vehicle. Even a police car. If the pattern from Poulter Street is repeated, he may have tried to stick to side streets to avoid being caught on camera. He may even have walked most or all of the way. But there are a hell of a lot more cameras in that part of town than around Poulter Street, and I'd be willing to bet he ended up within range of at least one of them. Unless you actually recognize a vehicle you know, you'll have to go by the timing—looking for vehicles that enter and then leave the area at times consistent with the shooting. It'll be a time-consuming job, but it could break the case."

His next call, as he crossed a modest bridge over the headwaters of the Delaware River into Pennsylvania, was to the Episcopal rector in White River.

The man's greeting was so smoothly delivered that Gurney thought for a second he'd reached another voicemail recording. "Good morning! This is Whittaker Coolidge at Saint Thomas the Apostle. How can I help you?"

"This is Dave Gurney."

"Dave. I was just thinking about you. Any encouraging news?"

"Some progress, but I'm calling with a question."

"Fire away."

"It's for Cory, actually, unless you happen to know the answer. I need to know if he's ever owned any thirty-aught-six rifle cartridges."

"Didn't you raise that point when you were here?"

"I said that the police found a box of cartridges in his closet and—"

Coolidge cut him off. "And he denied it. Vehemently."

"I know. This is a different question. I want to know if he's *ever* owned any— or maybe just had a few in his possession, maybe holding them for someone else. Maybe just for a day."

"I seriously doubt it. He hates guns."

"I understand, but I still need to know if he's ever had any sort of contact with any thirty-aught-six cartridges. And if so, what the circumstances were. Would you pass the question along to him?"

"I will." There was an edge of annoyance in Coolidge's cultured voice. "I'm just giving you a preview of the likely answer."

Gurney forced himself to smile. He'd read somewhere that speaking through a smiling mouth made one sound friendlier, and he wanted to maintain the rector's goodwill. "I really appreciate your help with this, Whit. Cory's answer could make a big difference in the case." He was tempted to add that the time factor was crucial, but he didn't want to push his luck.

In fact, adding that note of urgency turned out to be unnecessary. Less than five minutes later, he received a call from Payne.

His tone was brusque. "I'm not sure I understand your question. I thought I explained that I don't have a gun. You're still asking if I have bullets?"

"Or if you ever did. Thirty-aught-sixes."

"I've never owned a gun. I've never owned bullets of any kind."

"Have you ever had any in your possession? Perhaps storing them for someone else. Or buying them and passing them along. Possibly as a favor for someone?"

"I've never done anything like that. Why?"

"Two cartridge casings were found with your fingerprints on them."

"That's impossible."

"I've been told the prints are of good quality."

"I said it's impossible! I don't own a gun. I don't own bullets. I've never bought bullets, kept bullets in my apartment, or held bullets for anyone else. Period! End of story!" The words came racing out, his voice brittle with anger.

"Then there must be another explanation."

"Obviously!"

"Okay, Cory. You think about it, I'll think about it, maybe we'll figure it out."

Payne said nothing.

Gurney ended the call.

A minute later his phone rang. It was Payne. "I thought of something—something that happened two, three months ago." He was still speaking rapidly, but the anger was gone. "My father was having one of his brief human periods. We were—"

"Human periods?"

"Every once in a while he'd act like a normal person, actually talk to me. It would only last a day, if even that, then he'd go back to being God."

"Okay. Sorry, I interrupted what you were starting to say."

"So the time I'm talking about, we had lunch. We managed to get through our burgers without him telling me what a waste I was. Then we drove out to his cabin. You know what reloading is?"

"You're referring to custom-making ammunition?"

"Exactly. He's a gun fanatic. Him and Turlock. In fact, they share that cabin. For hunting."

"Why did he take you there?"

"His idea of a father-son thing? He said he wanted me to help him do some re-loading. Like it was a privilege. Allowing me into the world of guns and hunting—murdering animals. So he's got this contraption that funnels gunpowder into the brass part, and a thing that pushes the bullet part in. He's got this intense look, like he loves doing this. How crazy is that?"

"He wanted you to help him?"

"He had some little boxes to put the reloaded ones in. He had me doing that."

"So you were handling those cartridges?"

"Putting them in boxes. I didn't think of it at first, when you were asking about having bullets *in my possession*. I didn't think of it that way."

"Do you know if they were thirty-aught-sixes?"

"I have no idea."

"You say this happened two or three months ago?"

"Something like that. And you know what? Now that I think of it, that was the last time I saw him—until I saw him calling me a murderer on TV."

"Where were you living at the time?"

"The apartment I still have. I heard the asshole cops tore it apart."

"How long have you lived there?"

"A little over three years."

"How did you find it?"

"When I first came to White River, I stayed at my father's house for a couple of months. I started taking computer science courses at the community college in Larvaton, and I got a job at that computer repair shop in town. There was an apartment for rent upstairs in that same building. Living with my father and his sickening bitch of a wife wasn't working. So I took the apartment. How does any of this matter?"

Gurney ignored the question. "You've been there ever since?"

"Yes."

"Ever try going back to your father's house?"

"No. I stayed over a few times. I could never stay more than one night. I'd rather sleep in the street."

As Payne was speaking, Gurney slowed down and pulled into a gas station. He parked by the seedy-looking convenience store in back of the pumps.

"I have another question for you. How did you meet Blaze?"

Payne hesitated. "I met her through her half brother. Darwin. He owns the computer business where I work. Why are we talking about Blaze?"

"She's prominent in the Black Defense Alliance. The case against you involves your connection to that. And she lent you the car you drove to the shooting sites."

"I told you the case against me is bullshit! And I explained why I went to those places!"

"What kind of a relationship do you have with her?"

"Sex. Fun. Kind of an on-and-off thing. Nothing serious. No commitments."

He found it hard to imagine this tense, sharp-edged, angry young man having *fun*.

"How did she feel about Marcel Jordan and Virgil Tooker?"

"She didn't talk about them."

Gurney made a mental note to probe that further, then changed the subject.

"Do you know anything about the legal difficulty Judd Turlock got into when he and your father were teenagers in school together?"

There was a moment of silence. "What difficulty?"

"You have no idea what I'm talking about?"

Another moment of silence. "I'm not sure. I think there was something . . . something that happened. But I don't know what it was. I haven't thought about this for years."

"Haven't thought about what?"

"When I was a kid . . . when they were both still with the state police . . . they were talking one night in the den about some judge down in Virginia . . . some judge who'd taken care of something for Judd years earlier . . . something that could have been a huge problem. When they saw me at the door they stopped talking. I remember it felt weird, like I wasn't supposed to have heard them. I guess whatever it was must have happened when they were in school, because I know the school was in Virginia. But I don't know if that's the same thing you're talking about."

"Neither do I. By the way, where did you have lunch?"

"Lunch?"

"With your father, the day he took you to his cabin."

"A place by the strip mall. I think it's a McDonald's. Or a Burger King. Why?"

"The more facts I have, the better."

After Gurney ended the call he went into the convenience store. The place had a sour smell of old pizza and burned coffee. The register clerk was a tall, gaunt, vacant-eyed twentysomething male covered with a lacework of arcane tattoos. He had the rotten teeth that came with the use of methamphetamine, rural drug of choice prior to the tidal wave of heroin.

Gurney bought a bottle of water, took it out to the car, and sat there for a while pondering what Payne had told him. It was actually quite a lot. But perhaps most important was the possible explanation of how his fingerprints might have gotten on the brass casings found at both shooting sites as well as on the fast-food wrapper in the Bridge Street apartment. And if the casings and wrapper did in fact come from Payne's day with his father, then Dell Beckert must have been involved in the framing scheme. It was a scenario that seemed to increase in ugliness the more likely it became.

39

As Gurney drove southwest through a progression of black-cherry copses and open pastures, he was haunted by the empty stare of the convenience store clerk and what it suggested about the rotting underside of rural life in America.

The problems, of course, weren't just rural. Urban areas were often dirtier and more dangerous to live in. But here the contrast between the verdant beauty of the landscape and the gray hopelessness of so many of the inhabitants was jarring. Worst of all, in an age of vicious polarization, there seemed to be no acceptable way of addressing the problem. Add a few layers of racial animosity, cultural resentment, and political grandstanding, and solutions seemed far out of reach.

As he was sinking into the edgy depression these thoughts generated, his phone rang. "Private Caller" was all the ID screen revealed.

"Gurney here."

"Dave! So glad I got you. This is Trish Gelter."

"Trish. Hello." The first image of her that came to mind was the last glimpse he had caught of her—a memorable rear view of her progress across the room in her slinky dress at the fund-raising party for the animal shelter. "This is a surprise. How are you?"

"That depends."

"Depends on what?"

"On how soon I can see you."

"See me?"

"I heard a rumor you were working on that terrible shooting case."

"Who did you hear that from?"

"I was afraid you'd ask that. I'm terrible with names. Is it true?"

"More or less. Why?"

"I thought the police had it all wrapped up."

Gurney said nothing.

"But you don't think so?"

"I'm not sure yet what to think." He paused. "Is there something you wanted to tell me?"

"Yes. But not on the phone."

But not on the phone. He wondered for a moment who else had used that phrase, then remembered it was Rick Loomis, when he suggested they meet at the Larvaton Diner—the meeting he was heading to when he was shot.

"How, then?"

"Face-to-face." She made it sound like her favorite sex position.

He hesitated. "It's not something you can tell me now?"

"It's too complicated." She sounded pouty. "And I'd really like to see you."

Again he hesitated. "Where would you like to meet?"

"It would have to be here. I'm marooned. My Porsche is in the shop. And Marv took the Ferrari out to the Hamptons for a couple of days."

When he didn't answer immediately, she added, "I know Lockenberry is out of your way, but I really feel it's urgent."

The combination of her missing husband and *urgent* was . . . distracting.

"How soon can you come?" she asked.

He thought about it—from multiple angles, some more distracting than others, which made him wonder if he was making the right decision for the right reason. "I'm down in Pennsylvania right now for a meeting. Maybe late this afternoon? Or early evening?"

"Either way is good. I'll be here. It'll be really nice to see you again."

The call from Trish Gelter pushed aside Gurney's musing over the social and economic desolation of the rural northeast and replaced it with a specific, vivid recollection from the Gelter fund-raiser: Trish coming over to Marv to let him know that Dell Beckert was on the phone, and Marv leaving the party immediately to take the call.

He had wondered then what sort of relationship might exist between Gelter and Beckert, and that same question returned now with additional force. As he considered the possibilities, his GPS guided him into an even remoter area in which the houses were increasingly far apart. Eventually it announced that he had arrived at his destination—the foot of the road that led to Merle Tabor's house.

Black Mountain Hollow Road was, for all practical purposes, unmarked. Its identifying sign had been used for target practice. The letters that were partly legible among the rust-edged bullet holes could make sense only if you already knew the words they were part of.

The road was narrow, twisty, rutted, and full of rocks and deep puddles. Once it began climbing to higher ground there were no more puddles, but the rocks, ruts, and sharp turns persisted. At three miles in, according to Gurney's odometer, this rough dirt track emerged from the scrubby forest that had hemmed it in most of the way and entered a grassy clearing, where it ended. On the right side there was a mud-spattered Toyota pickup truck and an old Suzuki motorcycle. Straight ahead there was a larger-than-average log cabin with a green metal roof, a long covered porch, and small windows. The clearing itself was bordered by raspberry brambles.

Gurney parked behind the motorcycle. When he got out of the car he heard a sound that was familiar from a gym he used to work out in—the rhythmic thumping of blows on a boxer's heavy bag. The persistence and power of the impacts got his attention. He started walking toward the sound, which seemed to be coming from the left side of the house.

"Mr. Tabor?" he called out.

The thumping continued.

"Mr. Tabor?"

"Over here."

He was startled by the closeness of the voice.

The man was standing on the far side of the pickup truck, eyeing Gurney with calm curiosity. A weathered, hardscrabble seventysomething, he was still in good shape, judging from the sinewy arms resting on the truck bed. A thatch of gray hair showed traces of once having been red.

Gurney smiled. "Glad to meet you, sir. My name is Dave Gurney."

"I know who you are."

"Oh?"

"News travels fast."

"From the sheriff's deputy I spoke to on the phone?"

Tabor said nothing.

"I thought you were unreachable up here."

Tabor shrugged. "Man's got a car, I've got an address."

"I didn't realize my visit would stir up that kind of interest."

"Harlan looked you up on the internet. You being a big star from the big city.

What he didn't tell me is what the hell interest you have in the ancient history of Butris County."

"You may be aware of a case up in White River, New York, where two police officers—"

Tabor cut him off. "Heard all about it."

"Then you know that the case is being investigated by—"

"Dell Beckert. Man gets a lot of attention for a small-city chief."

"Are you aware that he resigned?"

"I hear he made a show of it, made it sound like a grand gesture. Course he really had no choice, his son being the perp."

"And are you aware that the acting chief is Judd Turlock?"

Tabor stared at Gurney for a long moment with the unreadable expression of a longtime cop. "I was not aware of that."

Gurney stepped over to the near side of the pickup, directly across from him. "I've been told they go back a long way."

"That what brings you down here?"

"I've been told you might be able to give me some information regarding an incident Turlock was involved in at Bayard-Whitson Academy."

"Am I missing something here?"

"Sir?"

"Why are you investigating the background of the acting police chief? Is this an official or private matter?"

"I'm acting on behalf of the wives of the slain officers."

"They have a problem with Turlock?"

"It may be a bigger issue than that. The evidence against Beckert's son has more holes in it than your road sign."

Tabor raised a hard-looking hand to his chin and massaged it thoughtfully. "Anybody but you think that?"

"The detective reporting to Turlock is on the fence."

"You think somebody's putting the kid in the frame?"

"I do."

He gave Gurney another expressionless stare. "What's any of this got to do with what happened in Butris County nearly thirty years ago?"

"I don't know. I have a bad feeling about Turlock. Maybe I'm looking for something to justify it. Maybe some insight into who he really is." He paused. "There's another aspect to this. Beckert is probably going to run for state attorney general.

If he wins, Turlock is virtually certain to be deputy AG. Powerful position. Makes me uncomfortable."

Tabor's jaw muscles tightened. After a long silence, he seemed to reach a decision. "Let me see your phone."

Gurney took it out of his pocket and held it up.

"Turn it off."

He did.

"Lay it down where I can see it."

Gurney placed it in the truck bed.

"This is not something I want recorded," said Tabor. He paused, staring down at his hands. "I haven't talked about this in years. Of course, it still comes to mind. Even came to me in a nightmare once."

He paused again, longer this time, then met Gurney's gaze. "Judd Turlock talked a retarded black man into hanging himself."

"*What?*"

"There was a creek with a swimming hole off the back of the Bayard-Whitson campus. There was a high bank with a big elm tree. Branch went out over the swimming hole. Boys used to tie a rope to it, swing out over the water, let go. One day Turlock and Beckert were there. There was a third boy sitting a little ways down the bank. And there was George Montgomery, sitting in his underwear in a shallow part of the creek. George was twenty years old, mentally maybe five or six, son of one of the kitchen help. There's two stories of what happened next. One story, told by the boy sitting on the bank, is that Turlock called to George to come up and join them. George came up, shy like, and Turlock showed him how he could take the rope and swing out over the water. Except he went on to show him it would be safer if he tied the loose end of the rope around his neck, so it wouldn't get in the way. George did like he was told. Then he swung out over the creek." Tabor paused before adding in a strained voice. "That was that. George hung there, out over the middle of the swimming hole, kicking, strangling. Until he was dead."

"What was Turlock's version?"

"That he never said a word to George, that George came up on the bank, wanting to use the rope like he'd seen other people do. He somehow got all tangled up in it, and once he swung himself out there, they had no way of reaching him."

"And Beckert told the same story?"

"Of course."

"Then what?"

"The kid on the bank took a lie detector test and passed. We considered him a highly credible witness. The prosecutor agreed we should charge Turlock with manslaughter and petition to have him tried as an adult."

"So at trial it was Turlock's and Beckert's word against the word of the kid on the bank?"

"Never got that far. The kid changed his story. Said he didn't actually hear what was being said. Maybe Turlock was saying to George *not* to put the rope around his neck. Or maybe he wasn't saying anything at all."

"Someone got to him?"

"The Turlock family. Lots of money. Long history of corrupt construction deals with the county board. Judge dismissed our case and sealed the file. And Judd Turlock walked away from a sadistic murder without a goddamn scratch. There were times . . . times I must admit I came damn close to ending his life the way he ended George's. Used to think about him strangling on the end of a goddamn rope. Thinking about it right now makes me wish I'd done it."

"Sounds like Beckert was as much a part of it as Turlock."

"That's a fact. While we were thinking we had a case, we went back and forth on how to deal with him, but it all fell apart before we decided anything."

"Did it occur to you at the time that it might have been Beckert's idea?"

"Lot of things occurred to us."

A silence fell between them, broken by Gurney. "If you don't mind my asking, why did you move up here?"

"Wasn't so much about moving here as leaving there. The Montgomery case changed everything. I approached it pretty aggressively. I didn't leave any doubt with the Turlocks how I felt about their piece-of-shit son. They got the local racists riled up, claiming I was favoring a retarded black man over a nice white boy. Meanwhile my daughter was seeing a black man, who she ended up marrying, and the local reaction was ugly. I was counting the days till I could get my pension. I knew I had to get out of there before I killed someone."

In the ensuing silence the thumping of the heavy bag seemed to grow louder.

"My granddaughter," said Tabor.

"It sounds like she knows what she's doing."

Tabor nodded, came around from behind the pickup bed and gestured for Gurney to follow him to the corner of the big cabin.

There, in a level shaded area scuffed free of any grass, a wiry young girl in gym shorts and a tee shirt was delivering a series of hard right and left hooks to a leather heavy bag suspended from the branch of an oak tree.

"Used to be where her swing was hung."

Gurney watched the flurry of punches. "You teach her how to do that?"

There was pride in Tabor's eyes. "I pointed out a few things."

The girl, apparently in her early teens, clearly had a mixed racial background. Her natural Afro had in it a hint of Tabor's red-hair gene. Her skin was a deep caramel, and her eyes were green. Except for a brief assessing glance at Gurney, her attention was centered on the bag.

"She has power," said Gurney. "She get that from you?"

"She's better now than I ever was. Straight-A student, too, which I never was." He paused. "So maybe she'll survive this world. What do you think her chances are?"

"With that kind of concentration and determination, better than most."

"You mean better than most black girls?" There was a sudden combativeness in his voice.

"I mean better than most black, white, tan . . . girls, boys, you name it."

Tabor shook his head. "Might be that way in the right kind of world. But we're not there. Real world is still the kind of world that killed George Montgomery."

40

Gurney's conversation with Merle Tabor gave him a lot to think about during the long drive to the Gelter house in well-tended Lockenberry.

The hanged black man in Judd Turlock's past set up a disturbing echo with the two men strangled by the ropes tying them to the jungle gym in the Willard Park playground. Gurney couldn't help thinking that a man who thirty years earlier had been responsible for one such horror might well be capable of two more. This hypothetical link received some support from one fact—the web of trails that made the Willard Park site easily reachable from the hunting cabin Turlock shared with Beckert. If one or both of them had seized Jordan and Tooker, or tricked them into meeting on some pretext, the cabin would have been an ideal location for the administration of the benzos and propofol, the beatings, the branding.

His mind leapfrogged to the shootings—specifically to the fact that the red motocross bike racing away from Poulter Street was last seen at the edge of Willard Park, within a short distance of those same trails leading to the Beckert-Turlock cabin.

Might Turlock have been the second man at Poulter Street, the one who actually shot Loomis? Wasn't it at least conceivable that Turlock had engineered and carried out, for reasons yet to be determined, both the police and the BDA murders? It had seemed to Gurney all along that the Jordan-Tooker executions were too smoothly organized to have been a spur-of-the-moment response to the first shooting. The planning required for the acquisition of the propofol alone would preclude that.

Thinking about the propofol angle gave Gurney a little jolt. He pulled over onto the shoulder of the road and used his phone to access the internet. He wanted to check on the shelf life of propofol. The first pharmaceutical database he came upon provided the answer: two years in an unopened vial, one year in a preloaded hypodermic.

He felt like a fool, realizing he'd been overlooking something obvious. He'd been focusing on Mercy Hospital for its connection to the ice-pick murder of Rick Loomis and ignoring its possible connection to the murders of Jordan and Tooker. And because of his focus on the ice-pick wielder as a possible member of the current staff, he hadn't bothered looking through the personnel list section containing employees who'd resigned or been terminated prior to Loomis's hospitalization. But given the likelihood that the Jordan-Tooker murders were planned well in advance of their execution—and given the long shelf life of propofol—the list of former employees could be as relevant as the current list.

In his eagerness to rectify his oversight, he was tempted to postpone his meeting with Trish Gelter. But his desire to find out what she wanted to tell him, and to learn something about her husband's connection to Dell Beckert, won out. The list research would have to wait. He decided to call Madeleine and let her know about his detour to Lockenberry and that he'd be home later than planned.

As he was about to place the call to her, he discovered that a message from her had arrived while his phone was turned off at Merle Tabor's request.

"Hi, hon. I may not see you this evening. I'm going to Mercy after work to be with Heather. Apparently Rick's brother and Heather's sister both got delayed somewhere by weather conditions, canceled flights, general confusion. Kim Steele plans to come to the hospital too. Comfort in numbers. If it gets late I might stay at that visitors' inn overnight. I'll call when I have a better idea what I'm doing. Hope your trip to Pennsylvania was useful. Love you."

For the rest of his trip to Lockenberry, Gurney entertained his growing suspicions that the shootings and BDA murders were directly linked but not in the way anyone had assumed; that Turlock and Beckert may have been central to both; and that the hospital that hosted the murder of Loomis may also have been the source of the drugs that facilitated the killing of Jordan and Tooker.

If those conjectures were facts, however, what did they add up to? What payoff was big enough to justify all that planning, effort, risk, and grisly violence? What goal required the deaths of those specific victims? Might there be other links to Mercy Hospital?

When his GPS announced that he had arrived at his destination—the iron gateway in the stone wall fronting the Gelter property—he'd made little progress on those questions.

Driving up through the wildflower meadow and on through the astonishing field of daffodils, he refocused himself on the nature of his visit and what he hoped to get from it. He parked in front of the looming cube of a house.

As he approached the huge front door, it slid open without a sound, just as it had on the first occasion. As then, Trish was standing in the doorway. As then, she was smiling, displaying the little Lauren Hutton gap between her front teeth. On that first occasion, however, she was dressed. This time she was wearing only a silky pink robe, and a rather short one at that. Her long shapely legs appeared to be the platonic ideal of female legs, although there was nothing platonic about the impact they made. Nor about the look in her eyes.

"You came quicker than I imagined. I just got out of the shower. Come in. I'll get us something to drink. What would you like?"

Where she was standing forced him to pass very close to her. The cavernous room was bright, the afternoon sunlight slanting through the glass roof.

"Nothing for me," he said.

"You don't drink?"

"Not often."

She moistened the corners of her mouth with the tip of her tongue. "Maybe I shouldn't say this, you being a detective and all, but I might be able to find a couple joints. If you're interested."

"Not right now."

"Pure of body, pure of mind?"

"Never thought of it that way."

"Maybe there's hope for you yet." She smiled. "Come. Let's sit by the fire." She touched his arm and led him through the room's cubical furniture to the edge of a brown fur rug in front of the wide modernistic hearth. Green flames were rising from an arrangement of realistic-looking logs. The sight brought to mind what she'd said at the party. *I love a green fire. I'm like a witch with magic powers. A witch who always gets what she wants.*

To one side of the hearth there was a sort of couch made of low cubes and giant pillows. She picked up a small remote device from one of the pillows and pressed a button. The light level in the room dropped to something resembling dusk. Gurney looked up and saw that the glass roof had become less transparent. The color of the sky had changed from blue to deep purple.

"Marv explained it to me," she said. "How it works. Some kind of electronic something or other. He seemed to find it fascinating. I told him he was putting me to sleep. But I like making it dark. It makes the fire greener. You like the rug?"

"It's some kind of fur?"

"Beaver. It's very soft."

"I never heard of a beaver rug."

"It was Marv's idea. So typical of him. There were a bunch of beavers damning up his trout stream. He hired a local trapper to kill the beavers and skin them. Then he had someone make a rug out of them. So he could stand on it, drinking his six-hundred-dollar cognac. On *them*, really—the beavers who had inconvenienced him. I think the idea is kinda sick, but I love the rug. You sure I can't get you a drink?"

"Not now."

"Can I see your hand?"

He turned up his right palm.

She took it in one of her hands, studied it, and slowly ran her forefinger along its longest line. "Have you ever killed anyone?"

"Yes."

"With this hand?"

"With a gun."

Her eyes widened. She turned his hand over and touched each of his fingers.

"You wear your wedding ring all the time?"

"Yes."

"I don't."

He said nothing.

"Not that we have a bad marriage or anything. It just feels too *wifey*. You know, like being someone's wife is the main thing. I think that's very . . . limiting."

He said nothing.

She smiled. "I'm glad you could come."

"You said you wanted to tell me something. About the case."

"Maybe we should sit down." She looked toward the rug.

He stepped back in the direction of the couch.

She slowly let go of his hand and shrugged.

He waited for her to sit at one end, then sat a few feet away from her.

"What did you want to tell me?"

"You should get to know Dell better. He's going far. Very far."

"How do you know?"

"Marv has a knack for picking winners."

"Why are you telling me this?"

"It would be nice if you were part of the team."

Gurney said nothing.

"You just need to get to know Dell a little better."

"What makes you think I don't know him well enough already?"

"I hear things."

"From who?"

"I have a terrible memory for names. I heard you don't like him. Is that true?"

"True enough."

"But you and Dell are so much alike."

"How?"

"You're both strong . . . determined . . . attractive."

Gurney cleared his throat. "What do you think of his son?"

"Cory the Monster? Too bad he didn't shoot himself instead of those cops."

"What if he didn't shoot those cops?"

"What are you talking about? Of course he did."

"Why?"

"*Why?* To attack Dell any way he could? To show him how much he hated him? To act out his little power fantasies? Why does any maniac kill anyone?"

Gurney remained silent for a while before asking, "Is that what you wanted to tell me?"

She turned halfway toward him on the couch, letting her robe ride up higher on her legs. "I wanted to tell you that you could be on the winning side of this. The farther Dell goes, the farther we all go." She smiled slowly, holding his gaze. "It could be a fun ride."

He stood up from the couch. "I'm not really a fun guy."

"Oh, I'm sure you could be. I can tell a lot from a man's hands. You just need the right encouragement."

Halfway between Lockenberry and Walnut Crossing, Gurney stopped at Snook's Green World Nursery. He knew Madeleine liked the place for its unusual selection of plants and the horticultural tips she got from Tandy Snook. He was thinking he'd pick up something special for one of her flower beds. He was also hoping that the task would dislodge the remarkably vivid thoughts he was having about Trish Gelter.

Those thoughts, of course, were divorced from reality in more ways than one. There was the simple fact that he would never want to destroy the closeness of his relationship with Madeleine with the secrets and lies required by any affair, however brief. And then there was the matter of Trish herself. Although the woman was quite open about her availability, her motives might not be. It would be no surprise to discover that everything in that peculiar house was being recorded. And a video of certain activities could be employed later to influence one's actions, even the course of an investigation. Despite Trish's pointed mention on the phone that her husband was away in the Hamptons, he may have been aware of her intentions—may even have encouraged them. Or he may not have been away at all.

They did not seem to be, in any normal sense of the word, nice people.

As Gurney stepped out of his car in front of the nursery's greenhouses, he spotted Rob Snook striding in his direction, sporting that golly-gee smile of a particularly annoying sort of churchgoer. He was a short, well-fed man whose eyes sparkled with shallowness.

"Dan Gurney, if I recall, husband of Marlene! A pleasure to see you on this beautiful day the Lord has given us! How can I serve you today? Florals or edibles?"

"Flowers."

"Annuals or perennials?"

"Perennials."

"Small, medium, or large?"

"Large."

Snook squinted thoughtfully for a moment, then thrust a victorious forefinger in the air. "Giant delphiniums! Purple and blue! Absolutely glorious! The perfect thing!"

Once the delphiniums were stowed securely in the back seat of the Outback, Gurney decided to call Mark Torres for an update before resuming his drive home.

The young detective picked up immediately. He sounded agitated.

"Dave? I was just going to call you. I've been doing what you suggested, going through the street videos from the night Steele was killed."

"You found something."

"I did. I'm about a third of the way through the digital files, and Judd Turlock's Explorer has popped up twice. Fairly close to the apartment location, and the timing factor is right."

"What do you mean by 'fairly close'?"

"The video the Explorer appears on comes from a security camera mounted over the door of a jewelry store two blocks away."

A beep alerted Gurney that another call was coming in, but he let it go to his voicemail.

"Tell me about the timing."

"The Explorer passes the camera going in the direction of Bridge Street about forty minutes before the shooting. Then passes in the opposite direction eight minutes after it."

"Did the camera get a shot of the driver?"

"No. Wrong angle."

"If I remember correctly, there's no video available of the apartment building front entrance, just the street shot showing the way into the back alley. Is that right?"

"Right. But if the timing of the Explorer's coming and going isn't related to the shooting, that would be a pretty big coincidence."

"I agree."

"I'll go through the rest of the video material we have, and I'll let you know what I find."

"Thanks, Mark. You're doing a great job."

"One other thing, in case you weren't aware of it—Carlton Flynn is going to be interviewing Maynard Biggs tonight."

Gurney almost asked who Maynard Biggs was, then recalled Whittaker Coolidge mentioning him as the man Dell Beckert would be contending with for the state AG position.

That, he realized, could make it a very interesting interview.

41

As Gurney resumed his trip home to Walnut Crossing, it seemed to him there was no end to the odd twists in the entangled White River cases—all reinforcing Cory Payne's stated suspicion that it was really one case with multiple victims.

Torres's video discovery of Turlock's SUV in the vicinity of Bridge Street provided some support for the framing theory, although it fell far short of proving that Turlock was the actual shooter. The lack of video evidence that Turlock himself was in the vehicle that night didn't help. It could have been Beckert. But Gurney was in no position to demand alibis from the people running the investigation.

Still, there were steps that could be taken. The relationship between Turlock and Beckert suggested their shared hunting cabin might be a place worth visiting.

He had a general idea where the gun club preserve was located. He decided to get in touch with Torres for directions to the cabin. He parked in his usual spot by the mudroom door. The call went to voicemail, and he left a message explaining what he needed.

He got out of the car and was stopped for a moment by the sweetness of the spring air. He took a few slow, deep breaths, stretched his back, and looked around at all the shades of green in the high pasture. The scene seemed to drain the tension out of his muscles. It also reminded him of the delphiniums in the Outback. He got them out of the back seat and placed them, still in their plastic pots, alongside Madeleine's main flower bed.

He went into the house, took a quick shower, fixed himself a plate of scrambled eggs and ham, and washed it down with a large glass of orange juice.

By the time he'd washed his dishes it was a quarter past seven, the sun was just setting behind the western ridge, and the air coming in through the open French doors had become noticeably cooler.

He retrieved his laptop from the den, along with the USB drive containing the Mercy Hospital personnel list, and settled into an armchair by the fireplace.

Before getting into the list he decided to check his email. The server had been troublesome lately, and the items were downloading with painful slowness. He put his head back, closed his eyes, and waited.

He opened them with a start nearly an hour later. His phone was ringing. The time was 8:03 PM. The caller was Cory Payne.

"Maynard Biggs is on RAM-TV. Being interviewed by that scumbag Flynn. You have to watch."

"Where are you calling from?"

"From a safe place in White River. Look, you need to listen to him *now*. He's on. I'll talk to you later."

Gurney went to the "Live Stream" page of the RAM website, found *A Matter of Concern with Carlton Flynn*, and selected it.

A moment later the video box on the website page came to life. Flynn, in his signature white shirt with rolled-up sleeves, sat opposite an athletic-looking brown-skinned man with gray eyes wearing a tan crewneck sweater. In contrast with Flynn's projection of aggressive energy, he radiated stillness.

Flynn was in the middle of a sentence. ". . . feel about the uphill battle you'll be waging against a man who's come to symbolize law and order in a time of chaos, a man whose poll numbers have now passed yours and keep going up."

"I believe that waging this battle, if you wish to call it that, is the right thing to do." The man's voice was as calm as his demeanor.

"Right thing to do? To try to defeat one of today's greatest champions of law and order? A man who puts the law above all other considerations?"

"Lawfulness and orderly public behavior are desirable characteristics of a civilized society. They are natural signs of health. But making orderliness our top priority makes its achievement impossible. Like many good things in life, good order is the byproduct of something else."

Flynn raised a skeptical eyebrow. "You're a professor, am I right?" He made the title sound like an indictment.

"That's correct."

"Of psychology?"

"Yes."

"Neuroses. Complexes. Theories. I'm sure there's a place for all that. But we're in the middle of a crisis. Let me read you something. This is a statement by Dell Beckert that lays out in simple terms the nature of the crisis we're in right now." Flynn took a pair of reading glasses out of his shirt pocket and put them on. He picked up a sheet of paper from the table and read:

"'Our nation is afflicted with a cancer. This cancer has infiltrated our society in many ways over many years. The burning of a flag. The abandonment of dress codes in our schools. Hollywood's vilification of our military, our government, our corporations. The popularization of casual obscenity. The demeaning of religious leaders. The glorification of crime in rap music. The war on Christmas. The terrible erosion of authority. The infantile mindset of entitlement. These trends are the termites devouring the foundation of America. Our civilization is at a tipping point. Shall we encourage our society's fatal descent into the jungle of violence? Or shall we opt for order, sanity, and survival?'"

Flynn waved the paper at Biggs. "That's what your likely opponent in the race for attorney general has to say about the state of our nation. What's your response?"

Biggs sighed. "Lack of order isn't the problem, it's a symptom. Suppressing a symptom doesn't cure the disease. You don't cure an infection by suppressing the fever."

Flynn responded with a dismissive little snort. "In your public statements, you sound like a messiah. A savior. Is that how you see yourself?"

"I see myself as the most fortunate of men. All my life I have been surrounded by the fires of racism and hatred, crime and addiction, rage and despair. Yet by the grace of God I remain standing. I believe that those of us who know the fire, yet have not been consumed by it, owe a life of service to those the fire has crippled."

Flynn grinned unpleasantly. "So your real goal as attorney general would be to serve the crippled black ghettos, rather than the broad population of our state and our nation?"

"No. That's not my goal at all. When I say I owe service to those the fire has crippled, I mean all those crippled by racism. Black and white alike. Racism is a razor with no handle. It cuts the wielder as deeply as the victim. We must heal both or we are doomed to endless violence."

"You want to talk about violence? Let's talk about your supporters in the Black Defense Alliance, the violence they've stirred up, the fires, the looting—and this Blaze *Lovely* Jackson person who spews out hatred for the police every time she speaks! How can you justify accepting support from people like that?"

Biggs smiled sadly. "Should we reject someone because of their rage at injustice? Should we reject them for the damage that has been done to their heart, for their feelings of fear, for their marginalization, their frustration? Should we reject them because their rage frightens us? Do you tell your angry white listeners to stop listening to you? Do you tell every white man who condemns black men to go away and never turn on your program again? Of course you don't."

"So what's your answer? To embrace the hate-spewing Blaze *Lovely* Jacksons of the world? To overlook the fact that she thinks killing police officers is no big deal?"

Biggs turned his sad eyes on Flynn. "Rodney King asked, 'Why can't we all just get along?' It sounded like a naïve question. But if you take that question—"

Flynn interrupted, rolling his eyes. "Here we go with the Saint Rodney baloney!"

"If you take King's question literally, it leads us into a morass of historical reasons why white America and black America do not get along as well as we might like. But I prefer to interpret his question in a different way—as a plaintive cry for a solution. The question I hear is this: *What would it take for us to come together?* And the answer to that can be summed up in one word. *Respect.*"

"Fine! No problem!" cried Flynn. "I'll happily show *my* respect for anyone who shows *their* respect for our country, our values, our police!"

Biggs shook his head. "I'm talking about *unconditional* respect. The *gift* of respect. To withhold respect until we feel that it has been earned is the formula for an endless downward spiral—the spiral that has brought us to where we are today. Respect is not a bargaining chip. It's the gift a good man gives to every other man. If it is given only after certain conditions have been met, it will achieve nothing. Respect is not a negotiating tactic. It is a form of goodness. May God grant us the humility to embrace what is good, simply because it is good. May God grant us the sanity to realize that respect is its own reward, that respect—"

Flynn, who'd been nodding condescendingly as Biggs was speaking, cut him off. "That's a lovely speech, Maynard. A nice sermon. But the reality we're facing won't—"

Gurney's attention was diverted abruptly by a sound he associated with a small-displacement motorcycle. As he listened, it seemed to grow louder. It brought to mind the elusive red motocross bike.

He put his computer down on the hassock in front of his chair and went quickly to the side of the house that provided a view of the high pasture where the sound seemed to be coming from. By the time he got to the den window it had stopped.

In the less-than-ideal dusk light he saw nothing unusual. He opened the window quietly and listened.

He heard only the distant cawing of crows. Then nothing at all.

Even though he suspected he was overreacting, he went to the bedroom where he'd left his Beretta in its ankle holster. When he sat on the bed to strap it on, he saw something he'd missed earlier—a note under the alarm clock on the bedside table. It was from Madeleine.

"Hi, sweetheart. I decided to stay over at the hospital inn tonight. So I came home to get a few overnight things and fresh clothes for tomorrow. In the morning I'll go straight from White River to work. Love you."

He made a mental note to call her later that evening. Then he left the bedroom and made a circuit of the ground-floor windows, peering out into the adjacent fields and woods. He repeated the circuit. Seeing nothing out of the ordinary, he returned to his chair by the hearth, and picked up his computer.

Carlton Flynn was in the midst of giving his wrap-up statement directly to the camera and his millions of faithful viewers.

". . . up to each of you to consider the sentiments expressed here tonight by Dr. Maynard Biggs and to compare them with the positions laid out by Dell Beckert. In my opinion, it boils down to one question: Do we keep extending, again and again, the respect that Biggs claims will solve all our problems, or do we draw the line and say, loud and clear, *enough is enough!* How many times are we supposed to turn the other cheek before we admit it isn't working? My personal belief—and this is just me, folks—my belief is that *peace is a two-way street.* I'm Carlton Flynn, and that's how I see it. I'll be back after these important messages."

As Gurney was closing the RAM-TV website, his phone was ringing. It was Torres.

"Gurney here."

"You asked how to get to the gun club? And how to identify Beckert's cabin?"

"Right."

"The most direct access is from Clapp Hollow, which you get to off County Route Twenty, also called Tillis Road. About three miles into Clapp Hollow there's a bridge over a stream, and right after that there are two trailheads across from each other. The one on the right leads up to the old quarries. The one on the left leads to the gun club preserve. I just emailed you a marked-up satellite map showing the route to the preserve, along with the GPS coordinates of the cabin."

"You think my Outback can get through those trails?"

"It would depend on how much mud there is. And whether any trees are down."

"You said one of the trails leads up to the old quarries—is that the area where the Gorts are holed up?"

"Yes. But it's not just old stone quarries up there. There are interconnecting caves and abandoned mining tunnels that don't appear on any maps. It's a wild area. Dense forest and thorn bushes and no roads. The Gorts were born and raised in those hills. They could hide up there forever."

"An interesting situation."

As he was ending the call, Gurney heard the *bing* of an email arriving on his computer. It was the satellite trail map Torres had mentioned. As he adjusted the laptop screen for a closer look, his phone rang again.

It was Cory Payne, his voice sharp with excitement.

"Did you watch it?"

"I did."

"What did you think?"

"Biggs seems to be a decent man. More decent than most politicians."

"He understands the problem. He's the only one who does."

"The problem of disrespect?"

"Disrespect is another word for belittling. The literal *belittling* of the black man by the white man. The belittling of the powerless by the powerful. The belittling of the weak by the control freaks who want everything their own way. They beat their victims into the ground, into the dirt. Every so often those beatings—that endless *belittling* provokes rage. The control freaks call that rage the breakdown of civilization. You know what it really is?

"Tell me."

"It's the natural human reaction to unbearable disrespect. The assault on the heart, on the soul. Disrespect that makes me less than you. Before the Nazis killed the Jews, they made them *less than* equal, *less than* citizens, *less than* human. You see the horror in those words? The horror of making one man *less than* another?"

"Is that what your father does?"

Payne's voice was pure acid. "You've been in the same room with him? You've watched him? You've listened to him? You've seen him on TV in a lovefest with that thug Flynn? You've heard him call his own son a murderer? What kind of man do you think he is?"

"That's too big a question for me to answer."

"I'll make it simple. Do you think he's a good man or a bad man?"

"That's not a simple question at all. But I have a simple one for you—about that cabin where you helped him with those cartridges."

"What about it?"

"Is it locked?"

"Yes. But you can get in if you know where the spare key is." Curiosity seemed to be diluting the acid. "You think something there will tell you what you want to know?"

"Possibly. Where's that key?"

"You'll need to use the compass app on your phone. Stand at the northeast corner of his cabin. Walk due east, maybe thirty or forty feet, until you come to a small square piece of bluestone in the grass. The key is under it. Or at least it was the day he took me out there."

"Do you know if any other club members use the property this time of year?"

"It's only used in the hunting season. Do you know what you're looking for?"

"I'll know it when I see it."

"Watch your back. If he thinks you're a danger to him, he'll have Turlock kill you. Then he'll frame someone for it. Probably me."

42

After ending the call, Gurney remained in his chair by the fireplace, musing over Payne's comments and the intensity with which he'd embraced Maynard Biggs's analysis of the problem.

As for the actual interview, Gurney couldn't help feeling a visceral revulsion to Carlton Flynn—as it occurred to him once again that a sure sign of a man's dishonesty was his characterization of himself as a truth teller. Self-described "straight talk" usually amounted to nothing but mean-spirited self-righteousness.

Gurney turned his attention back to his computer and the satellite map Torres had emailed him showing the trail route from Clapp Hollow to the gun club. The two-mile route he'd highlighted passed through a succession of three forks, taking right turns at the first and second and a left at the third before arriving at a series of linked clearings next to a long, narrow lake. The image of the cabin in the first of those clearings had been labeled with GPS coordinates.

Gurney memorized the coordinates as well as the approximate distances from Clapp Hollow to each of the trail forks. It seemed simple enough, assuming the trails were passable.

His thoughts were interrupted by the shrill beep of the house smoke alarms, indicating a power outage. The only light he'd turned on in the room, the lamp next to his armchair, went out.

At first he did nothing. Momentary electrical interruptions had become common as the local utility company cut back on routine maintenance operations. After several minutes had passed with no restoration of power, however, he called the company's emergency number. The automated answering system informed him that there was no known outage in his area but his report would be forwarded to the service division and that a representative would be responding shortly. Rather than wait in the dark for the power to come back on, or to discover what "shortly" might mean, he decided to get his generator going—a gas-powered unit that sat out on the tiny back porch and was wired into the circuit panel in the basement.

He went out the side door and around to the back of the house. It was a couple of minutes past nine. Dusk had become night, but a full moon made a flashlight unnecessary.

The generator had a pull-cord starter. He grasped the handle and gave it a few energetic yanks. When the engine didn't start, he bent over to be sure that the choke and gas-line levers were in their proper positions. Then he took hold again of the cord handle.

As he was adjusting his stance for the best leverage, he caught just at the edge of his vision a moving speck of light. He glanced up and spotted it on the corner post of the porch, just above his head. It was tiny, round, and bright red. He dived off the porch step into a patch of unmowed grass. He heard, almost simultaneously, the thwack of the bullet hitting the post and the sharper crack of the gunshot from somewhere at the top of the high pasture.

As he scrambled through the thick, damp grass toward the nearest corner of the house, he heard an engine suddenly rev up. He rolled over and pulled the Beretta from his ankle holster. But the high-pitched engine sound seemed to be receding. He realized the shooter wasn't coming down the hill toward him. He was heading in the opposite direction—up through the pines toward the north ridge.

As he listened, the whine of the motorcycle faded away completely into the night.

Torres arrived at the Gurney farmhouse an hour after the attack. He was followed a few minutes later by Garrett Felder and Shelby Towns in the crime-scene van. Gurney could have dug the bullet out of the post himself, but doing it by the book with an official chain of custody from crime scene to ballistics was always best.

He was already doing a minor end run around local law enforcement and didn't want to add to the irregularities. He'd reported the incident to Torres, not to Walnut Crossing PD, and left it up to Torres to deal later with the turf issues. It would have been a waste of time to involve the locals in the initial response to an incident that could only make sense in the context of an investigation centered in White River.

While the evidence techs were doing their jobs outside, Torres was sitting inside by the fireplace with Gurney, asking questions and taking notes the old-fashioned way with a notepad and pen. The generator, which Gurney had gotten started once the shooter was gone, was humming along reassuringly.

After Torres had recorded the basic facts he closed his notepad and gave Gurney a worried look. "Any idea why you'd be a target?"

"Maybe somebody thinks I know more than I do."

"You think it could have been Cory Payne?"

"I have no reason to think so."

Torres paused. "Are you going to make use of that map information I sent you?"

Before he could answer there was a knock at the French doors. Gurney went over and opened them. Felder came in, obviously excited. "Two discoveries. First, the bullet is a thirty-aught-six, full metal jacket, just like the other two. Second, the power failure was caused by the electrical supply line to the house being severed."

"Severed how?" asked Gurney.

"My guess would be some sort of heavily insulated cable cutter."

"Where was the cut made?"

"Down by your barn. At the base of the utility company's last pole on the town road, at the point where the line to your house goes underground."

Shortly after Torres, Felder, and Towns departed, the utility repair crew arrived. Gurney pointed them to the damage, which he opined was the product of vandalism. This was met with some skepticism, but he saw no point in attempting a more truthful explanation.

Then he called Jack Hardwick, got in his Outback, and headed for the man's rented farmhouse. He wanted to expose his ideas about the case once again to the man's skepticism. In addition, he couldn't imagine getting any sleep that night in his own far-from-secure house.

Hardwick's place, a nineteenth-century white clapboard structure of no recognizable style, was at the end of a long dirt road high in the hills above the village of Dillweed. When Gurney arrived just before midnight, Hardwick was standing in his open front doorway, a nine-millimeter Sig Sauer in a shoulder holster strapped over his black tee shirt.

"Expecting trouble, Jack?"

"I figure whoever took a shot at you might want to follow you, take a few more. Full moon tonight. Makes crazy people do crazy shit."

He moved out of the doorway, and Gurney stepped into the small entry foyer. A few jackets were hanging on hooks. Boots were lined up on the floor under them. The sitting room beyond the foyer had a bright, clean look about it, accented by a vase of spring wildflowers, suggesting that Esti Moreno, Hardwick's state trooper girlfriend, was back in his life.

"You want a beer?"

Gurney shook his head. He sat at a spotless pine table in the corner of the room nearest the kitchen, while Hardwick fetched himself a Grolsch.

After settling himself across the table and taking his first sip from the bottle, he flashed the supercilious grin that always got under Gurney's skin. "So how come he missed?"

"Possibly because of my fast reaction."

"To what?"

"The laser dot projected by his scope."

"Causing you to do what?"

"Hit the ground."

"So how come he didn't shoot you on the ground?"

"I don't know. Maybe the miss was intentional?"

"Kind of a high-risk play just to scare you off, don't you think?"

Gurney shrugged. "It doesn't make a lot of sense either way. If he wanted me dead, why only one shot? And if he didn't, what was the point? Did he really think I was going to drop the case because he put a bullet hole in my back porch?"

"Fucked if I know. So what's the plan?"

"Did you know Beckert and Turlock share a hunting cabin?"

"I'm not surprised."

"I want to have a look at it."

"You trying to prove something?"

"Just gathering information."

"Open mind, eh?"

"Right."

"Bullshit." Hardwick took another sip of his Grolsch.

Gurney paused. "I tracked down Merle Tabor."

"So?"

"He told me a story."

"About Turlock's juvie problem?"

"That's a mild way of describing it." Gurney recounted in grim detail what Tabor had told him about the death of George Montgomery.

Hardwick was quiet for a long moment. "You believe Tabor?"

"I do. The event and how it was resolved with no real closure seem to have had a devastating effect on him."

"So you've concluded that Beckert and Turlock are sociopaths?"

"Yes."

"Sociopaths capable of shooting their own cops, beating and strangling a pair of black activists, and framing innocent people for all four murders?"

"Anyone who did what they did to that retarded man is capable of just about anything."

"And because they're *capable* of committing the White River murders, you think they actually *did* commit them?"

"I think it's possible enough that I should take a closer look."

"A look that involves breaking and entering?"

"There's a key. At the most, that makes it trespassing."

"No concerns about security cameras?"

"If they have a camera, they'll get a picture of a guy in a ski mask."

"Sounds like your decision's been made."

"Unless you can talk me out of it."

"I said it all at Abelard's. There's a hole in your hypothesis the size of an elephant's anus. It's called 'motive.' You're claiming that a major law-enforcement figure and his deputy are running around killing people for no goddamn reason. The thing is, they'd need one giant motherfucker of a reason to justify that murder spree. And that vague crap about all the victims being potential threats to Beckert's political ambitions doesn't cut it."

"You're forgetting the little bit of static that got us involved to begin with."

"The fuck are you talking about?"

"The text on Steele's phone. The warning that someone on his side of the fence might want to get rid of him and then blame the BDA. And that's exactly what Beckert did—the blaming part, anyway."

Hardwick uttered a derisive little laugh. "You think Beckert took that shot at you?"

"I'd like to find out."

"You figure he left a signed confession in his cabin?"

Gurney ignored the comment. "You know, the motive may not be as big a mystery as you think. Maybe there's more at stake in the upcoming election than we know about. Maybe the victims posed bigger threats than we've imagined."

"Christ, Gurney, if every politician with hopes for a big future started exterminating everyone who might get in the way, Washington would be dick-deep in dead bodies." Hardwick lifted his Grolsch bottle and took a long, thoughtful swallow. "You by any chance catch the Carlton Flynn show before you got shot at?"

"I did."

"What'd you think of Biggs?"

"Decent. Caring. Authentic."

"All the qualities that guarantee defeat. He wants to take an honest, nuanced approach to interracial problems. Beckert just wants to lock the troublemaking bastards up and throw away the key. No fucking contest. Beckert wins by a landslide."

"Unless—"

"Unless you manage to come up with a video of him deep-frying live kittens."

Gurney had set the alarm on his phone for 3:45 AM, but he was awake before that. He used the tiny upstairs bathroom next to the spartan bedroom where Hardwick put him up for the night. He dressed by the light of the bedside lamp, strapped on his ankle-holstered Beretta, and quietly descended the stairs.

The light in the kitchen was on. Hardwick was sitting at a small breakfast table, loading a Sig Sauer's fifteen-round magazine. A box of cartridges was open next to his cup of coffee.

Gurney stopped in the doorway, his questioning gaze on the Sig.

Hardwick flashed one of his glittery grins as he inserted a final round in the magazine. "Figured I'd ride shotgun on your trip to the cabin."

"I thought you considered it a bad idea."

"Bad? It's one of the worst fucking ideas I've ever heard. Could easily produce a hostile confrontation with an armed adversary."

"So?"

"I haven't shot anybody in a long time, and the opportunity appeals to me." The glittery grin came and went. "You want some coffee?"

43

With the full moon lower in the sky now and a thin fog creating a reflective headlight glare, the trip from Dillweed to the Clapp Hollow trailheads took nearly an hour. Gurney drove the Outback. Hardwick followed in the GTO so they'd have a backup vehicle, just in case. In case of what, exactly, hadn't been discussed.

When they arrived at the trailheads, Hardwick backed his GTO into the one that led to the quarries, far enough to be out of sight from the road, then joined Gurney in the Outback.

Gurney checked his odometer, dropped the transmission into low, and drove slowly into the gun club trail.

It was half an hour before dawn. There was no hint of moonlight in the thick pine forest. The tree trunks cast eerily shifting shadows in the foggy headlight beams as the car crept along the rutted surface. Gurney lowered the front windows, listening, but heard nothing beyond the sounds made by his own vehicle and the occasional scrape of a low-hanging bough against the roof. The air flowing in was cool and damp. He was glad he'd accepted the offer of one of Hardwick's light windbreakers.

They arrived at the first two forks at the odometer readings predicted by Torres's map. At the third fork, he purposely turned onto the wrong branch of the trail and kept going until he was sure the car could no longer be seen from the branch leading to the gun club.

"We'll leave it here and walk in," said Gurney, donning a ski mask and gloves. Hardwick pulled a wool hat down over his head, added sunglasses, and wrapped a scarf around the exposed portion of his face. Activating the flashlights on their phones, they got out the car, walked back to the trail intersection, and proceeded along the correct side of the fork. They soon came to a large printed sign nailed to the trunk of a trailside tree.

STOP!

WHITE RIVER GUN CLUB

TRESPASSERS PROSECUTED

A quarter mile farther the trail ended at a broad, grassy clearing. Here, in the misty overcast, Gurney could see the first hint of dawn. On the far side of the clearing he could just make out the flat gray surface of a lake.

To the left of the clearing's edge, his flashlight revealed the dark bulk of a log cabin. He knew from Torres's map that this was the one Beckert and Turlock shared. He remembered that there were a dozen similar clearings and cabins along the edge of the lake, connected by a trail which, going in the opposite direction, led eventually to the playground at Willard Park.

"I'll check out the inside," said Gurney. "You take a look around the outside."

Hardwick nodded, unsnapped the safety strap on his holster, and headed for the far side of the cabin. Gurney moved the Beretta from his ankle holster to the pocket of his windbreaker and approached the log structure. The moist air here carried the distinctive scents of pine and lake water. As he got closer he noted that the cabin was resting on a traditional concrete-block foundation, suggesting the existence of at least a crawl space beneath it.

He switched his phone from its flashlight to its compass app and proceeded per Payne's instructions to the northeast corner of the building and from there due east to a foot-square piece of bluestone. Lifting it, he found a small plastic bag. Switching back to his flashlight, he saw that the bag contained two keys rather than just the one Payne had referred to.

He returned to the cabin. The first key he tried unlocked the door. As he was about to push it open Hardwick reappeared from the opposite side of the building.

"Find anything?" asked Gurney.

"Outhouse with a composting toilet. Small generator. Big shed with a big padlock."

Gurney handed him the second key. "Try this."

"Better not be full of spiders," said Hardwick, taking the key and heading back the way he came. "I fucking hate spiders."

Gurney pushed the cabin door open. Sweeping his flashlight back and forth, he entered cautiously and advanced slowly toward the center of a good-sized, pine-paneled room. At one end there was a stove, a sink, and a small refrigerator, no doubt run by the generator when the cabin was in use. At the other end there was a propane heater, a spartan couch, and two hard-looking armchairs set at right angles to the couch. Directly in front of him, there was a rectangular table on a rectangular rug with a rectangular pattern. Behind the table a ladder ascended to a loft.

Curious about the possibility of a crawl space, he began looking for access. He worked his way around the room, examining the floorboards. Coming back to where he started, he moved the table, folded back the rug, and ran his light over the area.

Had it not been for the gleaming brass finger hole, he might have missed it, so precisely aligned was the trapdoor with the surrounding boards. Bending over and placing his finger in the hole, he found that the door pivoted up easily on silent hinges. Shining his light down into the dark space below, he was surprised to see it was nearly as deep as a regular cellar.

He descended the plain wooden stairs. When his feet reached the concrete floor he discovered that his head just cleared the exposed floor joists above him. Everything in the beam of his flashlight appeared remarkably clean—no dust, no cobwebs, no mold. The air was dry and odorless. Against one wall there was a long worktable, and on a pegboard above it were rows of tools—saws, screwdrivers, wrenches, hammers, chisels, drill bits, rulers, clamps—each group arranged in size order from left to right.

It reminded him of the way the nuns at his grammar school used to line up the kids in the schoolyard after recess, in size order, from the shortest to the tallest, before marching them back into the building. He found the thought, like most of his childhood memories, unpleasant.

He turned his attention back to the matter at hand, noting that the only empty space on the pegboard occurred near the larger end of the row of clamps. The missing clamp triggered the memory of his conversation with Paul Aziz and the photos of the crime-scene ropes showing flattened spots consistent with the use of a clamp.

Against the opposite wall he saw a stack of two-by-four framing studs. He walked slowly around the cellar, making sure he wasn't missing anything signifi-cant. He checked the floor, the concrete-block walls, the spaces between the joists above his head. He found nothing unusual, other than the remarkable orderliness of the place and the absence of dust.

When he came to one end of the stack of studs he noted that it was twelve studs high by twelve deep. The ends on that side were aligned perfectly with each other, no stud even a millimeter out of place. It occurred to him that such an obsessive concern for symmetry could be the basis of a clinical diagnosis.

As he was moving past the perfect eight-foot-long stack, however, his eye was caught by an irregular shadow at its opposite end. He stopped, aimed his beam of light across that end of the stack, and saw that one stud was sticking out about a quarter of an inch, noticeable only because of the faultless alignment of the others.

It seemed unlikely that a factory-cut stud could have emerged from the process a quarter inch longer than others in the same batch. He laid his phone-flashlight on a stair tread, the beam aimed at the stack. He began to disassemble the stack, one row at a time.

When he reached the level of the protruding stud, he felt, for the second time since he'd become involved in the case, an unmistakable frisson.

The center sections of four studs in the middle of the stack had been cut away, leaving only about two feet at each end. The result was a concealed compartment two studs wide, two studs deep, and four feet long. The ends of the cut studs had been lined up with the ends of the intact studs—with the exception of that one stud end that stuck out.

He saw the reason for it. The end was kept from being aligned with its neighbors by the contents of the hidden compartment: a classic Winchester Model 70 bolt-action rifle, emitting the distinctive odor of a recently fired weapon; a red-dot laser scope; a muzzle-blast suppressor; and a box of 30-06 full-metal-jacket cartridges.

Gurney gingerly made his way back up the stairs. As he stepped up through the open trapdoor into the main room of the cabin, Hardwick came in the front door. In the pale light Gurney could see that he'd removed the sunglasses, hat, and scarf that were supposed to be hiding his identity from possible security cameras.

"No need for that ski mask," he said to Gurney. "We've got what we need to go public."

"You found something?"

"A used branding iron." He inserted a small dramatic pause. "How do I know it was used? Because there appears to be burned skin stuck to the letters on the end of it. The letters, by the way, are KRS."

"Jesus."

"That's not all. There's also a red motocross bike. Like the one that was seen zipping away from Poulter Street. You find anything in here?"

"A rifle. Probably *the* rifle. Hidden in a pile of lumber in the cellar."

"Is it possible we've got these evil bastards by the balls?" Hardwick's innate skepticism appeared to be battling with the satisfaction of a successful hunt. He looked around suspiciously, his flashlight beam stopping at the loft. "What's up there?"

"Let's find out." Gurney led the way up the ladder and stepped into an open-ended room above the kitchen. The underside of the steeply pitched roof was paneled with pine boards, and their distinctive scent was strong. There were two beds, one on each side of the space, made up in crisp military style. There was a low bench at the foot of each and a rectangular rug on the floor between them. The loft reflected the obsessive orderliness apparent everywhere in the cabin—all straight lines, right angles, and not a speck of dirt.

Gurney began checking one of the beds and Hardwick the other. Feeling under the mattress, he soon came upon something cold, smooth, and metallic. He lifted the mattress out of the way, revealing a slim notebook-style computer. Almost simultaneously Hardwick pointed to a cell phone taped to the bottom of the footboard of the other bed.

"Leave everything where it is," said Gurney. "We need to call this in, get an evidence team out here."

"Who are you going to call it in to?"

"The DA. Kline can get Torres reassigned to him on a temporary basis, along with the evidence techs, but that'll be his call. The key going forward will be for the investigation and the personnel working on it to be controlled by an agency outside the WRPD."

"Another option would be the sheriff's department."

The thought of Goodson Cloutz gave Gurney a touch of nausea. "I'd vote for Kline."

Hardwick's icy grin appeared. "Sheridan will have a hard time with this—having been such a huge fan of Beckert. Going to be tough for him to see the big shit getting sucked down the drain. How you think he's going to deal with that?"

"We'll find out."

Hardwick's eyes narrowed. "You think the little creep'll try to pull off an end run around the branding iron and rifle to keep from admitting he was wrong?"

"We'll find out." Gurney switched his phone from Flashlight to Call mode.

In the middle of entering Kline's number, he was stopped cold by a burst of canine howling and snarling. It sounded like a crazed pack of—of what? Wolves? Coyotes? Whatever they were, there were a lot of them, they were in full attack mode, and they were coming closer.

In a matter of seconds the chilling sound had reached a wild intensity—and it seemed to be concentrated directly in front of the cabin.

The frenzy of the sound was raising gooseflesh on Gurney's arms.

He and Hardwick reached for their weapons in unison, flicked off the safeties, and moved to the open edge of the loft where they had clear lines of sight down to the windows and door.

A high-pitched whistling sound pierced the din, and as suddenly as the savage uproar began, it stopped.

Cautiously they descended the ladder, Gurney first. He moved quietly to the front of the cabin and peered out through one of the windows. At first he saw nothing but the dark, drooping shapes of the hemlocks surrounding the clearing. The grass, which in the beam of his phone light had been a deep green, was in the dawn mist a featureless gray.

But not entirely featureless. He noted a patch of darker gray, perhaps thirty feet out from the window. He switched his phone back to Flashlight mode, but its beam only created a glare in the fog.

He gradually eased the front door open.

All he could hear was the slow dripping of water from the roof.

"The fuck are you doing?" whispered Hardwick.

"Cover me. And hold the door open in case I need to come back in a hurry."

He stepped quietly out of the cabin, Beretta in a ready-to-fire two-handed grip, and advanced toward the dark shape on the ground.

As he drew nearer, he realized he was looking at a body . . . a body that was somehow contorted, twisted into an odd position, as if it had been thrown there by a violent gust of wind. After moving a few steps closer, he stopped, amazed by the amount of blood glistening in the wet grass. Still closer, he could see that much of the clothing on the body was shredded, exposing ripped and gouged flesh. The left hand was mangled, the fingers crushed together. The right hand was missing, the wrist a grisly red stump with splintered bones sticking out of it. The victim's throat had been lacerated, the carotid arteries and windpipe literally torn to pieces. Less than half of the face was intact, giving it a hideous expression.

But there was something familiar about that face. And the muscular bulk of the body. Gurney realized with a start that he was looking at what was left of Judd Turlock.

IV

THE HORROR SHOW

44

Twenty-four hours after the discovery of the gruesome homicide at the cabin, Gurney was heading into the County Office Building for an early-morning meeting with Sheridan Kline.

The ponderous redbrick exterior, coated with a century of soot and grime, dated back to the structure's original use as a mental facility—the Bumblebee Lunatic Asylum—named after its eccentric founder, George Bumblebee. In the midsixties the interior of the structure had been gutted, redesigned, and repurposed to house the local bureaucracy. Cynics enjoyed pointing out that the building's history made it an ideal home for its current inhabitants.

The lobby security system had been upgraded since Gurney's last visit during the harrowing case of the bride who'd been decapitated at her wedding reception. It now involved two separate electronic screenings and the presentation of multiple forms of identification. He was eventually directed to follow a series of signs that brought him to a frosted-glass door bearing the words DISTRICT ATTORNEY.

He wondered which version of Kline he'd be meeting with.

Would it be the baffled, disbelieving, nearly speechless man he'd encountered on the phone the previous morning when he'd called to tell him about the discovery of the rifle, the branding iron, the red motorcycle, and Turlock's mauled body? Or would it be the man who showed up an hour later at the scene with Mark Torres, Bobby Bascomb, Garrett Felder, Shelby Towns, and Paul Aziz—hell-bent to demonstrate his decisiveness by issuing nonstop orders to people who knew far more about processing crime scenes than he did?

Gurney opened the door and walked into the reception room. Kline's alluring assistant, who had clearly maintained her fondness for formfitting cashmere sweaters, eyed him with a subtle smile.

"I'll let him know you're here," she said in her memorably soft voice.

As she was about to pick up her phone, a door in the back wall of the reception room opened and Sheridan Kline came striding over to Gurney, hand outstretched with that same semblance of warmth Gurney remembered from their first meeting years earlier.

"David. Right on time. I'm always impressed by punctuality." He led the way into his office. "Coffee or tea?"

"Coffee."

He clicked his tongue approvingly. "You a dog man or a cat man?"

"Dog."

"I thought so. Dog people prefer coffee. Cat people like tea. Herbal tea. Ever notice that?" It wasn't a question. He turned to the door and called out, "Two coffees, Ellen."

He pointed Gurney toward the familiar leather sofa, while he sat in the leather armchair across from it, a glass coffee table between them.

Gurney was for the moment absorbed in the déjà vu experience not only of the seating arrangement but of Kline's comments on punctuality and the dog-coffee cat-tea associations. The man had made exactly the same observations when they'd met during the Mellery case. Perhaps he was trying to reset their relationship to an earlier, more positive status. Or maybe these were things he said so often he had no idea to whom he'd said them before.

He leaned forward with what could be mistaken for companionable intensity. "That was really something yesterday."

Gurney nodded.

"God-awful homicide."

"Yes."

"Plus evidence connected to all the murders. What a shock!"

"Yes."

"Hope you didn't mind my asking you to leave the scene after you got us oriented."

Gurney had seen it as a sign of Kline's annoyance at the fact that the people reporting to him were addressing their questions to Gurney and Hardwick.

"The thing was," explained Kline awkwardly, "with Hardwick not having official LEO status, there could have been issues down the road about crime-scene protocol."

"No problem."

"Good. We've received some more information, amplifying what you'd already found. An overnight ballistics comparison connected the rifle in Beckert's cellar to the Steele and Loomis shootings as well as to the incident in your backyard." Kline paused. "You don't seem surprised."

"I'm not."

"Well, there's more. Thrasher did a prelim autopsy on Turlock's remains. Guess what he found."

"A steel arrow buried in his back?"

"Thrasher told you?"

"No."

"Then how—?"

"When I was still inside the cabin, I heard the dogs coming. Probably from a point in the woods near the edge of the clearing, about a hundred yards away. Turlock would have heard them, too. But he never fired a shot. In fact, his Glock was still holstered. That makes no sense, unless he was already incapacitated when the dogs started coming. And the Gort brothers seem to be awfully good with those crossbows."

Kline stared at him. "There's no doubt in your mind it was them?"

"I don't know of any other homicidal crossbow experts around here with a large pack of attack dogs and a major murder motive."

"The motive being revenge for Turlock's raid on their compound?"

"That, and for publicly blaming them for the BDA murders." Gurney paused. "That gives us means and motive. Opportunity isn't quite so obvious. It would depend on the Gorts knowing that Turlock was going to show up at the cabin when he did. That's a big issue. So you're not quite to home base."

"I'm aware of that."

"You have Beckert in custody yet?"

"We're working on it. Currently he's nowhere to be found. Which brings me to the main point of this conversation." Kline paused, sat back in his chair, and steepled his fingers in front of his chin. "Your discoveries, for which you deserve tremendous credit, have turned the case around a hundred eighty degrees from the way we all saw it."

Gurney calmly pointed out that from the beginning he'd been uneasy with the way everyone saw it, that he'd raised objections, and that Kline had essentially fired him for not embracing the official version.

Kline looked pained. "That seems a little oversimplified. But the last thing I want to do now is debate what's behind us—especially considering the challenge in front of us. We've had more upheaval in the past twenty-four hours than I've ever seen in any case, anytime. So far we've managed to keep a lid on what's going to be an explosive story, but that won't last. The facts will come out. We'll have to do our best to present them in a positive way. Keep control of the narrative. Maintain public trust in law enforcement. I assume you agree?"

"More or less."

Kline blinked at Gurney's less-than-enthusiastic response but continued along his path. "Handled correctly, this huge mess can be positioned as a law enforcement triumph. The message we have to convey is that nobody is above the law, that we follow without fear or favor wherever the truth leads us."

"That was Beckert's message, before he ended up on the wrong end of it."

"That doesn't mean it was the wrong message."

Gurney smiled. "Just the wrong messenger?"

"In hindsight, obviously. But that's not my point. The problem now is that everything's upside down. Could be viewed by the media as chaos. We need to convey the opposite. We need to convey stability. The message is that law enforcement is still operating on an even keel. The public needs to see stability, continuity, competence."

"I agree."

"Stability, continuity, and competence are the three keys to keeping external conditions from sinking the ship. But here's the thing. These qualities by themselves are just words. They need life. And you're a big part of that life."

Kline was leaning forward now. He seemed to be drawing energy and conviction from his own statements. "David, you've been pursuing the truth from the start like a heat-seeking missile. And, because of you, we're practically there. I don't think I exaggerate when I say that this could be the single greatest triumph of your law-enforcement career. Best of all, it would be a triumph for law enforcement itself. For the rule of law. And that's what it's all about, right?"

The moment he fell silent, his attractive assistant entered the room carrying a black-lacquered tray with a silver coffeepot, two cups, and a china creamer and sugar bowl, and set it all down on the glass coffee table.

When she left, Gurney refocused. "What do you want from me, Sheridan?"

"I just want to know I can count on your continuing insights and advice to . . . to help bring this ship into port."

Gurney pondered his apparent transformation from heat-seeking missile to harbor pilot, as well as Kline's endless capacity for duplicity.

"You want me to stay involved in the investigation?"

"In wrapping up the loose ends. Pulling it all together. Continuity." When Gurney didn't respond, Kline added, "On your own terms."

"Freedom to follow the loose ends wherever they lead, without interference?"

Kline bridled for a moment at that last word, but then emitted a sigh of resignation. "We need some clarity regarding the motivation for each of the four homicides. Plus Turlock's. We need to know specifically who did what. And we need to find the Gorts. You can follow any of those trails however you want."

"I'll have full access to Torres, Felder, Thrasher, lab personnel, ballistics, et cetera?"

"No problem." Kline eyed him anxiously. "So . . . you'll do it?"

Gurney didn't reply right away. He asked himself yet again why he was doing what he was doing. The virtuous answers, of course, were simple. He was seeing the case through to its conclusion because of his commitment to the wives of the murdered officers. And because the deaths of Jordan and Tooker deserved every bit as much of his attention as those of Steele and Loomis. And because the solution of these murders, along with Turlock's, might lead to the exposure of underlying patterns of corruption. And because bringing closure to so many open wounds might bring a modicum of peace to White River.

These motives were real and they were powerful. But he knew there was also something driving him forward that was less altruistic, something in the wiring of his brain—a relentless desire to *know*, to figure things out. It had been his driving force throughout his career, perhaps throughout his life. He really had no choice.

"Have Mark Torres call me."

Gurney wasn't even a third of the way back to Walnut Crossing when he got Torres's call.

"The DA asked me to provide you with any information you want, especially the stuff that came to light after you left the site yesterday. Is this a good time?"

Gurney saw that he was approaching Snook's Nursery and figured it would be a convenient place to stop. "Yes, this is a good time." He pulled into the long narrow parking lot in front of the greenhouses. "How late were you there?"

"All day, all night. Garrett and Shelby set up their halogens and worked until dawn."

"Tell me about it."

"Well, first Paul Aziz photographed the whole site, then Turlock's body, then each piece of evidence before it was bagged and labeled. Most of the items were found in and around the shed where your guy Hardwick found the branding iron. There were two sets of clothes, buried behind the shed, with bloodstains that match the positions of abrasions on Jordan's and Tooker's bodies. Inside the shed there was a coil of rope that matches the rope segment recovered from the Gorts' compound—which seems to link Beckert and Turlock to the playground murders as well as an attempt to frame the Gorts for it. There were bloodstains on the back seat of the UTV. Thrasher did a quick field test on the blood types, and they match those of Jordan and Tooker."

"Any fingerprints on the UTV steering wheel?"

"Old, smudged, not useful."

"How about on the handgrips of the Yamaha bike?"

"Same. But Beckert's prints appear in various other places on the UTV, and Turlock's appear on the bike's gas cap, which you'd expect, with the UTV being registered to Beckert and the bike to Turlock. And speaking of prints, this morning we finally got a reply from AFIS on that pen you found in the yard behind the Poulter Street house. The print on it is definitely Turlock's."

"That's quite a pile of evidence."

"There's more. In a fire pit in the woods in back of the shed we found burned pieces of a baseball bat and nightstick—the likely weapons used on Jordan and Tooker—plus two hypodermic needles of the preloaded type."

"Used?"

"Used and tossed in the fire with the bat and nightstick. But the labeling on one needle didn't burn completely. Enough was left for Thrasher to tell it was propofol."

"So the evidence pile keeps growing."

"And there's more. Remember at your house the other night Garrett said your power line had been severed by some sort of cable cutter? We found one under loose floorboards in the shed."

"Quite a productive evening."

"And I haven't even mentioned the most interesting find—a pair of pliers that prove you were right." Torres inserted a dramatic pause.

Gurney hated dramatic pauses. "What are you talking about?"

"There was a small tool kit under the sink in the cabin. Garrett thinks the pliers in the kit made the marks on the switched toilet handles. He's having the lab do a comparison to be sure, but he tends to be right about stuff like that."

Gurney felt the satisfaction of being on the right track. "Anything else?"

"Maybe, maybe not. That notebook computer and the phone you found in the cabin loft—they were password-protected, but we sent them to the forensic computer lab in Albany, and we hope to hear something back from them later this week."

"This all sounds like a prosecutor's dream. Do we know yet why Turlock showed up at the cabin when he did?"

"We think so. There were two battery-operated silent alarm systems— motion-activated—one in the cabin, one in the shed. They were programmed to contact certain phone numbers, presumably Turlock's being one of them, which would explain why he showed up. Garrett was having trouble with a privacy code protecting the numbers, so we sent the devices to Albany along with the phone and computer."

"Any leads on locating Beckert?"

"Not yet. His cell phone's apparently been turned off. His wife claims she has no idea where he is. The DA's getting a search warrant for their house in case she refuses access. Beckert doesn't seem to have any personal friends, so that's not a useful avenue. We've put a watch on his credit cards. So far no activity. He was seen leaving headquarters around five thirty the night before last. But we haven't found anyone who saw him after that. His wife was at some three-day spa getaway with a couple of friends and claims she has no idea what time he got home that night or whether he came home at all."

"He took his car?"

"Probably. All we know for sure is that it's gone from the headquarters parking lot."

A silence ensued as Gurney pondered the timing of the man's disappearance the night before the incident at the gun club.

Torres spoke first. "It's really pretty amazing."

"What is?"

"How you've been right about everything. I remember in the very first meeting you came to—your uneasiness with the assumptions everyone was making about the case. It was like you knew instantly there was something wrong with the basic hypothesis. I could see how disturbed Beckert and Turlock were by the issues you were raising. Now we know why."

"We still have a long way to go. A lot of open questions."

"That reminds me of something you commented on in the video of the Steele shooting—the red laser dot on the back of Steele's head as he was patrolling the edge of the crowd. You wondered why the dot followed him as long as it did. I think you said it was like two minutes?"

"That's right."

"Have you figured it out?"

"Not yet."

"You still feel it's significant?"

"Yes."

"It seems like such a small thing."

Gurney said nothing. But he was thinking it was the small things that often mattered the most, especially the ones that didn't seem to make sense.

45

Gurney remained parked in front of the nursery greenhouses after ending his call with Torres. Hoping he wouldn't be spotted by Rob Snook, he leaned back in his seat and tried to clear his mind and sort out his priorities for the rest of the day.

Clearing his mind, it turned out, wasn't so easy. Something was bothering him, though he wasn't sure what. Perhaps Madeleine's prolonged absence? He always felt odd when she was away from home, and phone conversations didn't really solve the problem.

He'd filled her in the previous evening on the gun club discoveries and the Turlock homicide, minus its more grotesque details. He'd cautioned her against saying anything yet to Kim or Heather, adding that he'd be meeting with the DA to review the situation. She'd told him she'd be staying at the inn on the Mercy medical campus for at least another twenty-four hours, at which point various Steele and Loomis relatives were expected to arrive. She'd reminded him to refill the feeders and let the chickens into their fenced run. He'd told her he loved her and missed her, and she'd said the same.

What he hadn't mentioned was that someone had taken a shot at him. He told himself at first it was because he didn't want to alarm her with the specter of a possibly ongoing danger. A day later—with the rifle recovered, Turlock dead, and Beckert apparently on the run—he told himself it was because there was no longer any danger, and therefore no urgency in discussing the matter. But he had to admit now, sitting there in front of Snook's greenhouses, that he always found it suspicious when someone offered shifting reasons for the same conclusion. A wise friend once commented that the more reasons someone gave you for their behavior, the less likely any of them was the *real* reason.

Perhaps that was what was bothering him—not so much Madeleine's absence as his own evasiveness. He resolved to be more open with her in their next conversation. That simple resolution, as resolutions often do, lightened his mood. He pulled out of the parking lot—focused now on getting home, reviewing the case files, and trying to make sense of the inconsistent details.

Twenty-five minutes later, as he was driving up through the low pasture to the house, deciding which file to tackle first, he was surprised to catch a glimpse of Madeleine in her straw gardening hat by one of the flower beds.

When he got out of the car, he found her kneeling by the bed next to the asparagus patch. She was planting the delphiniums he'd brought home two days earlier. She looked pale and exhausted.

"Did something happen?" he asked. "I thought you were staying over at the hospital."

"The relatives arrived sooner than expected. And I was more worn out than I realized." She laid her trowel down by the flowers, shaking her head. "It's awful. Kim is full of such a terrible anger. At first it was all inside. Now it's coming out. Heather is worse. Completely shut down. Like she's not there at all." Madeleine paused. "Is there anything we can tell them about the progress you're making? What you told me on the phone last night sounded huge. It might offer them some kind of relief. . . or distraction."

"Not yet."

"Why not?"

"The current status of an investigation is not something that can be—"

She cut him off. "Yes, yes, I know all that. It's just . . . there's so much misery, not knowing anything. I was just hoping . . ." She picked up her trowel, then put it down again and got to her feet. "Did you have your meeting with Kline?"

"That's where I'm coming from."

"Did anything get resolved?"

"Not really."

"What did he want?"

"On the surface, my help in wrapping things up. In reality, my silence. The last thing he wants is for the media to find out he fired me three days ago for suggesting he had the case all wrong."

"What did you tell him?"

"That I'd see the case through to the end."

She looked confused. "Isn't it essentially over?"

"Yes and no. There's a lot of evidence implicating Beckert and Turlock—the things I told you about on the phone, plus a lot more that was discovered overnight and this morning, including the fact that Beckert seems to have disappeared."

"*Disappeared?* Does that make him a fugitive?"

"I don't know what language Kline will be using publicly, but it sounds like a reasonable label to me. The new evidence doesn't leave much doubt about his involvement in the playground murders as well as the shootings. So everything's turned around, with Cory for all practical purposes exonerated."

She laid her trowel down and regarded him closely. "Do I hear a reservation in your voice?"

"Just a feeling that I'm still missing something. I'm having trouble matching the risk and brutality of the murders with the supposed reward."

"Doesn't that happen? What about the people who get shot for a pair of sneakers?"

"That *happens*. But not as part of a well-thought-out plan. Cory is convinced that it's all about Beckert's political future—eliminating people who might create problems for him."

"You think the man is capable of that?"

"He's cold enough. But it still seems out of proportion. There's something in the payoff that I'm not seeing clearly. Maybe I'm asking the wrong questions."

"What do you mean?"

"Years ago in the academy I attended a class on investigatory techniques. One morning the instructor asked us, 'Why do those deer always run out in front of cars at night?' He got a bunch of answers. Panic, disorientation caused by the headlights, evolutionary dysfunction. Then he pointed out that there was a flawed assumption in the wording of the question itself. How did we know deer *always* did that at night? Maybe most of them *didn't* run out in the road, but we didn't realize it, because we could only see the ones that did. And he pointed out that there was a subtle misdirection lurking in the phrase *run out in front of cars*—making it sound as though the activity were something clearly dysfunctional. Suppose the question were reworded this way: 'Why do some deer attempt to cross the road when a car is approaching?' That way of asking points toward a different set of possible explanations. Since deer are very territorial, perhaps their first instinct in a moment of danger is to head for the part of their territory in which they feel most secure. Perhaps they're just moving instinctively toward a place of safety. Other deer in the immediate area may be running in the opposite direction—away from the road—to get to *their* places of safety, but those deer are less likely to be seen, especially at night. Anyway, his point was simple. Ask the wrong question, and you never get to the truth."

Madeleine's impatience was showing. "So what question about the case do you think you're getting wrong?"

"I wish I knew."

She stared up at him for a long moment. "What's your next step?"

"Review the files, look for things that should be done, and do them."

"And report back to Kline?"

"Eventually. He'd be quite content to have me do nothing—so long as I don't rock the boat or make him look bad."

"Because he has political ambitions of his own?"

"Probably. Until yesterday that meant hitching a ride with Beckert. I assume now he's seeing his future more as a solo act."

Rising to her feet and brushing the soil off her hands, she produced a less-than-happy smile. "I'm going inside. Do you want some lunch?"

A short while later, as they were silently finishing their meal, it occurred to Gurney that if he didn't tell her now about the severing of the power line and the subsequent gunshot, he probably never would. So he did, describing the event as unthreateningly as he could—as Beckert or Turlock simply taking a shot at the back of the house when he went out to get the generator started.

She gave him a look. "You don't think he was aiming at you?"

"If he wanted to hit me, he would have kept shooting."

"How do you know it was Beckert or Turlock?"

"I found the rifle that fired the shot in their cabin the next morning."

"And now Turlock is dead."

"Yes."

"And Beckert is on the run?"

"So it seems."

She nodded, frowning. "This shooting incident was . . . the night before last?"

"Yes."

"What took you so long to tell me?"

He hesitated. "I think I was afraid of bringing up memories of the Jillian Perry case."

Her expression darkened at the mention of the invasion of their home during that particularly disturbing series of murders.

"I'm sorry," he said. "I should have told you right away."

She gave him one of those long looks that made him feel transparent. Then she picked up their plates and carried them to the sink.

He suppressed an urge to make more excuses for himself. He went into the den and took out the case materials. With the branding iron and propofol needles now linking Beckert and Turlock directly to the BDA deaths, he opened the consolidated file on Jordan and Tooker.

It contained surprisingly little beyond the incident report, notes on the interview with the dog walker who found the bodies, printouts of some of Paul Aziz's photos, the two autopsy reports, an investigatory progress form with little progress recorded beyond a description of Turlock's raid on the Gort brothers' compound and the evidence he supposedly "found" there. There was also some bare-bones data on the victims. Tooker, according to the file, was a loner with no known family connections nor any personal associations outside the BDA. Jordan was married, but there was no record of any interview being conducted with his wife, beyond a note indicating that she had been informed of his death.

It was clear to Gurney that the decision to target the Gorts for the murders of Jordan and Tooker had dramatically narrowed the scope of the investigation, eliminating virtually all activities not directly supportive of that view of the case. The decision had created a yawning information gap that he felt an itch to rectify.

Remembering that the Reverend Coolidge had provided an alibi for Jordan and Tooker after the Steele shooting and had later spoken highly of them, Gurney thought the pastor might have a phone number for Jordan's wife.

He placed a call to Coolidge. As he was leaving a message, the man picked up, his tone professionally warm. "Good to hear from you, David. How's your investigation going?"

"We've made some interesting discoveries. Which is why I'm calling you. I want to get in touch with Marcel Jordan's wife. I was hoping you might have a number for her."

"Ah. Well." Coolidge hesitated. "I don't believe Tania is willing to speak to anyone in law enforcement—which is how she'd view you, regardless of how independent your relationship with officialdom might be."

"Not even if she could be helpful in solving her husband's murder—and possibly revealing the complicity of people in law enforcement?"

There was a pregnant silence. "Are you serious? That's . . . a possibility?"

"Yes."

"Let me get back to you."

It didn't take long.

Coolidge called back in less than ten minutes to inform Gurney that Tania declined to speak to him on the phone but that she'd be willing to meet with him at the church.

Forty-five minutes later Gurney was pulling into the lot at Saint Thomas the Apostle. He parked and took the path through the old churchyard.

He was almost to the building's back door when he saw her, standing very still among the moss-stained gravestones. A tall, brown-skinned thirtysomething woman in a plain gray tee shirt and sweatpants, she had the lean body and wiry arms of a long-distance runner. Her dark, suspicious eyes were fixed on him.

"Tania?"

She didn't answer.

"I'm Dave Gurney."

Again she remained silent.

"Would you prefer to talk out here or inside?"

"Maybe I've decided not to speak to you at all."

"Is that true?"

"Suppose it is."

"Then I'll get back in my car and go home."

She cocked her head, first one way then the other, with no discernible meaning. "We'll talk right here. What did it mean, what you said to the pastor?"

"I told him we've made some discoveries concerning your husband's murder."

"You told him police might have been involved."

"I said it looked that way."

"What facts do you have?"

"I can't reveal specific evidence. But I suspect that your husband and Virgil Tooker, as well as the two police officers, may all have been killed by the same person."

"Not by the Payne boy or them Gort lunatics?"

"I don't believe so." He studied her impassive face for some reaction but saw none. Behind her loomed the marble angel on whose wing Coolidge a few days earlier had extinguished his cigarette.

"The man you're calling my husband," she said after a pause, "was really more my ex, though we never got divorced. We were living in the same house, for the economies of it, but we were separated in our minds. Man was a fool." Another pause. "What do you want from me?"

"Your help in getting to the truth of what happened."

"How am I supposed to do that?"

"You could start with why you say Marcel was a fool."

"He had a weakness. Women loved him . . . and he loved them back."

"That's what ended your marriage?"

"It created situations that were a pain to my heart. But I tried to live with the weakness because there was so much strength in him otherwise. Strength and a true desire for justice—justice for people who have no power. He wanted to stand up for those people—to do what he could to take some of the strife and fear out of their lives. That was his vision for the BDA."

"How did he get along with the other two BDA leaders?"

"Virgil Tooker and Blaze Jackson?"

Gurney nodded.

"Well . . . I'd have to say that Virgil wasn't really what you'd call a leader. He was just a good man and happened to be close to Marcel, and Marcel pretty much pulled him into that position because he trusted him. The man had no huge talent, no huge fault. He just wanted to do the right thing. That's all Virgil wanted. To be helpful."

Gurney was struck by the echo of Mark Torres's goal as a police officer.

"And Blaze Jackson?"

The first sign of emotion appeared on Tania's face, something hard and bitter. When she spoke, her voice was almost frighteningly calm. "Blaze Lovely Jackson is the Devil incarnate. Ain't nothing that bitch wouldn't do to get what she wants. Blaze is all about Blaze. Fiery talker, loves to be onstage, loves the attention, people looking up at her. Loves to lay it down hard on the corrupt police and stir up the crowd. But all the time she's got her evil eye on what's in it for her—what she can take from someone else."

"Was she the reason for your separation from your husband?"

"My husband was a fool. That was the reason for our separation."

A brief silence fell between them.

Gurney asked if she'd seen Marcel or Virgil at any time in the forty-eight hours before they were killed. She shook her head. He asked if she'd seen or heard any-thing before or after their murders that might relate to them in any way.

"Nothing. Only the fact that Blaze is now the sole leader of the Black Defense Alliance, a position which the bitch surely loves."

"She likes being in charge?"

"Power is what she likes. Likes it way too much."

Gurney sensed the beginning of restlessness in Tania's body language. He wanted to keep the door open for possible future conversations, so he decided to end this one now. "I appreciate your taking the time to meet with me, Tania. You've been very open. And what you've told me is quite helpful. Thank you."

"Don't misunderstand me. I'm not here to do you a favor. You said police could be involved in the shit that went down, and I'd love to see that get proven and them get put in the penitentiary with the brothers waiting for them. That would be a sweetness to my heart. So don't go thinking the wrong way. I live in a divided world, and not on your side of the line."

"I understand."

"Do you? Do you know why this spot right here is my favorite place in all of White River?"

He glanced around the old graveyard. "Tell me."

"It's full of dead white people."

46

Gurney's route from Saint Thomas the Apostle back toward the interstate put him on the road that bordered Willard Park. As he approached the main entrance, Paul Aziz's photos came to mind, and he decided to take another look at the playground area.

The parking lot was nearly full, unsurprising on a balmy spring afternoon. He found a spot, then took the pedestrian path along the edge of the mowed field where the BDA demonstration had taken place. The statue of the colonel had been cordoned off with Police Line Do Not Cross yellow tape, an apparent effort to keep it from being toppled or defaced before an official decision could be made regarding its fate. Although the rest of the park appeared well populated with sunbathers, Frisbee tossers, dog walkers, and young mothers with toddlers, the playground was deserted. Gurney wondered how long it would take for its forbidding aura to fade. A hand-printed sign on the kayak rental shed said CLOSED UNTIL FURTHER NOTICE.

The blackbirds, however, continued to occupy the dense reeds along the edge of the lake. As Gurney approached the swing set, they rose up and began shrieking and swooping over his head. But when he stopped there they soon lost interest and settled back into the reeds.

The UTV tire tracks documented in Aziz's photos were no longer visible, but Gurney remembered where they'd been. He looked once more at the jungle gym crossbar with the two shiny spots that his conversation with Aziz had persuaded him were indeed clamp marks.

He began running scenarios through his head, picturing the likely steps that would have been taken in bringing the two victims to that point and binding them to the bars.

He imagined Jordan and Tooker being persuaded to attend a meeting at some site where they were rendered controllable with a combination of alcohol and midazolam. They were then brought to the cabin, or more likely to the shed behind it. There they would have been heavily sedated with propofol, preparatory to being beaten, stripped, and branded—creating the illusion of a violent racist attack. They would then have been strapped into Beckert's UTV and transported from the cabin via the connecting trail system to the playground.

He pictured the UTV emerging from the woods in the predawn darkness, proceeding toward the jungle gym, stopping in front of it—a chill mist drifting through the headlight beams. Beckert and Turlock were in the front seat. Jordan and Tooker—naked, anesthetized, close to death—were in the back seat. Behind them in the utility box were coils of rope and a sturdy clamp.

He pictured Beckert and Turlock getting out with flashlights, quickly deciding which man would be bound up first . . . and then what?

One option would be for Beckert and Turlock together to lift one of the victims out of the UTV and stand him upright with his back against the bars. While one of them held the man in place the other could get the clamp and one of the ropes, tie an end of the rope around the man's neck, loop the rest of it over the bar in back of his head, and hold it in place with the clamp until it could be knotted securely. They could then tie the man's torso and legs to the lower bars to ensure that he remained in a standing position. Meanwhile a slow, fatal strangulation would likely be occurring.

As Gurney thought about it, the process seemed revolting but feasible. Then it dawned on him that there was an easier way—a way that would have required virtually no physical effort. Each victim in turn could have been pulled out of the back of the UTV and dumped on the ground in front of the jungle gym. After one of the ropes had been tied around the victim's chest, the free end could be passed over a bar and tied to the back of the UTV. The UTV could then be driven forward, causing the rope to lift the victim up toward the bar. The clamp could then be employed to hold the rope in place while the end was detached from the UTV, wrapped around the bar, and knotted. Finally, the victim could be secured in his grotesque standing position by pulling the rest of the rope tightly around his legs, torso, and, with fatal effect, his neck.

That way would definitely be easier. In fact, it would be so easy it obviated the need for two men—meaning that the double murder could have been carried out by *either* Beckert *or* Turlock. It was even possible one had acted without the other's knowledge. If so, Gurney wondered if that might have had something to do with Turlock's murder.

After a final look around the playground, as he turned to head back to the parking lot, he noticed he was being watched by one of the dog walkers—a short, muscular man with a gray buzz cut and two large Dobermans. He was standing in the middle of the path about fifty yards away. As Gurney got closer he could see anger in the man's eyes. With little appetite for confrontation, Gurney stayed toward the edge of the path. "Good-looking dogs," he said pleasantly as he was passing.

The man ignored the compliment and gestured toward the playground. "You one of the cops looking into this thing?"

Gurney stopped. "That's right. Do you have any information about it?"

"Couple of the *brothahs* got what they deserved."

"How do you figure that?"

"White River used to be a nice place to live. Great place to bring up kids. Safe little town. Look at it now. Street I live on used to be beautiful. You should see it today. Section Eight housing. Free rent for freeloaders. Next door I got a crazy son of a bitch in a dashiki. Like he's actually from Africa. Lives with his two *baby mamas*. You and I pay for that! And here's the thing. He's got this black rooster. And white hens. That's a hostile message. Every year he slaughters the white hens. In his backyard. Where I can see it. Chops their heads off. But never the black rooster. What do you call that?"

"What do *you* call it?"

"What it is. A terroristic threat. That's what you should be worried about."

"Do you want to make a complaint?"

"That's what I'm doing. Right here. Right now."

"To make a formal complaint, you need to visit police headquarters and fill out—"

The man interrupted with a disgusted wave of his hand. "Waste of time. Everybody knows that." He turned away abruptly, gave a tug on the dogs' leashes, and strode out into the field, muttering obscenities.

Gurney proceeded along the path to his car, reminded once more of the fear and loathing in the melting pot of America.

Once he was sitting in the Outback, it occurred to him that he should pass along to Mark Torres the fact that the murders of Jordan and Tooker could have been managed by one person. He placed the call. As usual, Torres picked up quickly and sounded eager to hear whatever Gurney had to say.

He explained his one-man theory.

Torres was quiet for a moment. "Do you think this should change our focus?"

"For now we just need to keep the possibility in mind and see how it fits with whatever else we learn. Speaking of which, have we found out if Beckert and Turlock have alibis for the night of the Jordan-Tooker murders or the night of the sniper shootings?"

"So far, no one we've spoken to recalls being with them on those occasions. But that's not surprising. They didn't exactly hang out with the troops. Turlock reported only to Beckert, and Beckert reports only to the mayor. You met Dwayne Shucker, so you can imagine there wasn't much actual reporting going on there. Beckert's wife's been no help. Apparently has a busy social life, isn't home much, and doesn't keep tabs on her husband. As for Turlock, he lives alone. Nearest neighbor is a mile away and claims to know nothing about him."

The Outback was getting hot in the afternoon sun in the unshaded parking area, and Gurney opened the windows. "The Jordan-Tooker file shows no real interviews after the murders, other than a couple of cryptic notations about tips from unnamed informants and a brief statement from the guy who found the bodies. Am I missing something?"

"Not as far as I know. Remember, I had the case for less than a day. Once Turlock took it over, it was all about the Gorts."

"None of Jordan's or Tooker's associates were interviewed?"

"The only associates either of them seemed to have were the BDA members who were arrested in the raid on their headquarters. With charges pending, they were advised by counsel not to make any statements at all to the police."

"What about Jordan's wife?"

"She refused to talk to Turlock." Torres paused. "Some people here see us as an occupying army."

"Actually, I spoke to her today."

"How'd you manage that?"

"I told her I thought that someone in law enforcement might go down for the killing. She liked that idea."

"I bet. Did she say anything useful?"

"She made it pretty clear that Marcel had gotten sexually involved with Blaze Jackson. And that Blaze is a nasty piece of work."

"Wait, hold on a second."

Gurney could hear an indistinct conversation in the background. When Torres got back on the line he sounded upbeat. "That was Shelby Towns. She said that a pair of boots found in the cabin are a perfect tread match for the boot prints found on the stairs in the Poulter Street house."

"Are they Turlock's or Beckert's? Or could she tell?"

"Turlock's. She could tell by the size. Looks like he was the Loomis shooter. So this is coming together in a way that—sorry, hold on again."

After another background conversation, Torres returned. "Shelby says that Cory Payne's fingerprints are on all those cartridges you found with the rifle."

"That's consistent with Cory's story of helping his father with the reloading process. Any other news?"

"Just that the DA will be appearing this evening on *NewsBreakers*."

"What's that?"

"It's the lead-in program to RAM's *Battleground Tonight*. Should be interesting to watch Kline explaining how his godlike hero turned into a devil overnight."

Gurney agreed. Since Kline couldn't keep the media at bay forever, he'd evidently decided to jump in with both feet in a desperate effort to shape the narrative.

47

Just before 6:00 PM Gurney opened his laptop and went to the RAM website. As it was loading, something caught his eye through the window next to his desk—a spot of fuchsia moving along the top of the high pasture. He realized it was Madeleine in her bright windbreaker mowing the grass swath that separated the pasture from the woods. He watched as she turned the riding mower onto a path that led down to the house. Then he went to the "Live Stream" page and clicked on View Now. A moment later the screen was filled with bright-blue words flashing against a black background:

RAM *NEWSBREAKERS*

SPECIAL EARLY EDITION

WHAT YOU NEED TO KNOW NOW

The words exploded into pieces, then the pieces flew back together to form new words:

THE HUNTER BECOMES

THE HUNTED

IN STUNNING REVERSAL

Those words in turn exploded, only to be immediately reconstituted in another headline:

TOP COP

NOW PRIME SUSPECT

IN SENSATIONAL WHITE RIVER MURDERS

On a final drumbeat the scene switched to a shot of a male and female news team, making a show of jotting down last-minute notes at their RAM-TV news desk. The female member was the first to put down her pen and look directly into the camera.

"Good evening. I'm Stacey Kilbrick."

Gurney noted that her default expression of serious professional concern had been ratcheted up into a grim intensity. He was momentarily distracted by the ringing of his phone. He saw that it was Thrasher and he let it go to voicemail.

The male on the screen put down his pen. Neat and petulant, he looked like a flight attendant with a grievance. "Good evening. I'm Rory Kronck. We have a big story for you tonight—a *NewsBreakers* exclusive report on the mind-boggling developments in White River, New York. Lay out the facts for our viewers, Stacey."

"As you were saying, Rory, those facts are nothing short of amazing. The hunter has become the hunted. Disturbing new evidence is linking Dell Beckert, former White River police chief and nationally known law-and-order advocate, to four shocking murders that his own department was investigating. And now it appears that he's taken off for parts unknown, under a heavy cloud of suspicion." She turned toward Kronck. "We've covered our share of wild stories over the years, Rory, but I've never seen the likes of this. Have you?"

"Never, Stacey. And the vanishing chief is just part of it. The deputy chief, we've just learned, has turned up dead. And we're talking about the kind of grisly murder that's usually reserved for horror movies."

Kilbrick produced a theatrical look of revulsion. "Apart from the gory details, the real shocker to me is the way the whole case has been flipped upside down. Don't you agree?"

"Totally."

"I understand a lot of the credit goes to the district attorney and to a very special homicide detective attached to his department."

"That's absolutely true. In fact, just before this program I had a revealing conversation with DA Kline."

"Great, Rory. Let's run that tape right now."

Gurney heard the side door out by the mudroom open and close. A minute later Madeleine came into the den.

She peered at his laptop screen. "What are you watching?"

"Live interview with Kline."

She pulled a chair over and sat down.

The scene on the screen had shifted to a bare-bones interview setting. Kline and Kronck were sitting in chairs facing each other with a bookcase in the background. Kline appeared to have just gotten a haircut.

Kronck was leaning forward, in the middle of a sentence. ". . . a word that's on everyone's mind: 'shocker'! Top cop becomes top suspect. And his son, who *was* your top suspect, has essentially been declared innocent. Our heads are spinning. Let me ask you the obvious question. If your view of the case today is right, how could you have been so wrong yesterday?"

Kline's reaction was a pained smile. "That sounds like a simple question, Rory, but the reality isn't simple at all. You have to remember that the earlier case hypothesis that zeroed in on Cory Payne for the sniper shootings and the Gort twins for the playground murders was a willful deception created by our current suspect. From the very beginning there was a concerted effort by WRPD leadership to mislead my office. This is not a matter of our misreading the case. What we're dealing with is a vicious and devious betrayal of the public trust by a man whose sworn duty it was to treat that trust as sacred."

"You make it sound like an act of real treachery."

"I see it as a form of moral decay."

"How deep in the department might that decay go?"

"That's something we're actively looking into."

"Your resources must be stretched pretty thin. With so many unanswered questions about these terrible crimes, and who's trustworthy and who's not, not to mention the ongoing racial unrest in parts of White River, where's the necessary manpower coming from?"

Kline moved uncomfortably in his chair. "The situation is actually well in hand."

"Are there any plans to bring in the state police? Or the FBI, considering the possible hate-crime angle?"

"Not at this time."

"So you're saying you have all the resources you need?"

"I'm not just *saying* it, Rory, I know it for a fact."

"You sound amazingly confident, considering what you're facing. Four sensational murders—five now, counting the deputy chief. Wouldn't it make sense to bring in the kind of expertise that the state police could offer? With all due respect, sir, yours is a rural county in which the typical crimes are drunk driving, minor drug offenses, and disturbing the peace. What you're facing now is infinitely more complicated. Doesn't that worry you?"

Kline took a deep breath. "Normally we don't reveal staffing details, Rory, but for the sake of public confidence I want to put this expertise issue to rest. The fact is, our level of investigatory sophistication right now is unsurpassed. A key member of my current team happens to be Dave Gurney, the highly decorated detective who holds the record for the largest number of cleared homicide cases in the history of the New York City Police Department. I'm talking about close to a hundred homicides solved personally by this man—including famous serial murder cases. It's through his relentless questioning and his insights that we've arrived at our current understanding of the situation in White River. You asked why I wasn't bringing in state police investigators. The fact is, Dave Gurney has given advanced seminars on homicide investigation at the state police academy. So in the matter of expertise, we take a back seat to no one. We have the best there is."

"That's fascinating news. I'm impressed."

Kline said nothing.

"I appreciate that your time is limited, sir, and I know you have a final message you want to leave with our viewers."

"Yes, I do." He gazed sternly into the camera. "Our top priority right now is locating Dell Beckert."

A phone number appeared at the bottom of the screen.

Kline continued, "If you know anything about his whereabouts, or if you know anyone who does, please call this number. He may be driving a black Dodge Durango, New York plate number CBIIWRPD."

The screen displayed the plate number, a photograph of Beckert in his police uniform, and the phone number.

Kline concluded, "If you have any information that might help us find this man, please call this number now. You don't need to identify yourself unless you wish to. We just want whatever information you can provide. Thank you."

The screen was filled briefly with just the phone number, which was then replaced by a live shot of Stacey Kilbrick and Rory Kronck at their news desk.

"Wow," said Kilbrick. "The DA has some big-city talent in his little upstate department."

"So it seems," said Kronck.

"Hmm. How much do we know about this Dave Gurney?"

"We know that *New York* magazine ran a front-page profile on him a few years ago. The article title was 'Supercop'—which I guess says it all."

"So there's no end to the surprises in this story. Great job, Rory."

He produced a self-satisfied smirk.

"I'm Stacey Kilbrick for *NewsBreakers*. After these important messages I'll be back with the latest battle over transgender troops serving in the U.S. Marine Corps."

Gurney closed the "Live Stream" page and left the RAM website.

Madeleine was watching him. "Are you concerned about Kline going public with your involvement?"

He turned up his palms in a gesture of resignation. "I'd rather he hadn't. But I don't think he's any happier about it than I am."

"What do you mean?"

"Kline is not a credit sharer. He did it because he was trapped. Kronck was poking at the weakness of his resources and implying that he ought to bring in an outside agency, which Kline absolutely doesn't want to do. He's afraid it would be portrayed as a surrender on his part, and he wants to come out of this with a personal victory. Bragging about my background was a way to beat back Kronck's suggestion that his department couldn't handle the challenge."

"I bet that Kilbrick woman tries to get you on her program."

"It'll be a snowy day in hell when I say yes to that." He glanced at the time in the corner of the screen. "It's twenty past six. You have any ideas about dinner?"

She frowned. "Tonight is my dinner meeting with the town political action group. You remember I told you about this, right?"

"I forgot it was tonight."

"I may be late. Our discussions have a way of going on and on. There's all sorts of stuff in the fridge. And pasta in the yellow cabinet."

An hour later—as he was finishing the plate of spaghetti, diced tomatoes, zucchini, and Parmesan cheese he'd prepared for himself—he got a call from Cory Payne. There was a level of excitement in the young man's voice that Gurney hadn't heard before.

"Dave! Are you seeing the news stories on the internet?"

"About what?"

"The case! It started with RAM News announcing that you guys are focused on my father—who's disappeared. The DA gave an interview about it, and all the other news sites are picking it up. Wild headlines are popping up. 'Son Innocent, Father Guilty'—stuff like that. It's all turned around. I'm not the target anymore. You must know all this, right?"

"I know some significant discoveries have been made."

"That's a mild way of putting it. I feel like I owe you my life!"

"It's not over yet."

"But it sounds like everything's finally going in the right direction. Jesus, God, what a relief!" He paused. "Is this because of stuff you found at his cabin?"

"I can't talk about that. Evidence disclosures would need to come from the DA. But that reminds me—why didn't you tell me about the second key?"

"What?"

"You told me about the key for the cabin, but not the other one for the shed."

"You just lost me."

"The shed behind the cabin."

"I don't know anything about a shed. I've only been to his cabin." Payne sounded mystified.

"Did he show you the cabin basement?"

"No. I didn't realize it had one."

"Where did he set up his reloading equipment?"

"On a dinner table in the middle of the room."

"What was he wearing?"

"Maybe a flannel shirt. I don't know about his pants. Maybe chinos? He never wore jeans. Oh, and some kind of disposable gloves, like doctors wear. I think to keep the gunpowder off his hands."

"Since you came to live in White River, how much contact have you had with Judd Turlock?"

"I've seen him with my father. He wasn't the sort of person you'd want to get to know. Even making eye contact with him was scary. One of the news stories said that he was found murdered at the gun club. Are you the one who found him?"

"I was there."

"How was he killed?"

"Sorry, that's another one for the DA to answer."

"I understand." He paused. "Well, the main reason I called was to thank you. Thank you for giving me back my life."

Now Gurney paused. "I have another question. When you were a kid, before you got sent to that boarding school, did your father try to interest you in guns or hunting or anything like that?"

There was a long silence. When Payne finally replied, the excitement had drained from his voice.

"My father never tried to interest me in anything. The only concern he had was that I never do anything that might embarrass him."

Gurney felt an unpleasant tremor of recognition. There was a time when he had a similar resentment toward his own father.

48

He wasn't sure what to do next. He had the feeling that things were coming to a head and he needed to press forward. While the next step was eluding him, he decided to check his phone to make sure he was up to date with his messages.

There was just one, the call from Thrasher that had come in while he was watching *Battleground Tonight*. He pressed the Play icon.

"Detective Gurney, Walter Thrasher here. No doubt the nonstop horrors of White River are absorbing your attention. But I feel the need to fill you in on the even more gruesome history of your own idyllic hillside. Call when you can. In the meantime, I'd strongly advise you not to do any more excavating—not until I prepare you for what you're likely to find."

Gurney felt a surge of curiosity and alarm.

He called Thrasher back immediately, got his voicemail, and left a message.

Then he forced his attention back to the White River affair and what unresolved aspect he should address first. The ice-pick murder of Rick Loomis came to mind, which in turn reminded him of the hospital personnel list and the fact that he still hadn't examined the section covering employees who had resigned or been terminated.

He went to his desk, got out the USB drive containing the list, and inserted it in his laptop. A few moments later he was opening the Res-Term section of the Mercy Hospital Consolidated Personnel File. As he went through the columns of names and addresses, he recognized only one name. But it definitely got his attention:

JACKSON, BLAZE L., 115 BORDEN STREET, WHITE RIVER, NY

Her resignation or termination—the file didn't indicate which—had occurred on February 12, just three months earlier. The remaining data was limited to her landline and cell phone numbers.

As he was entering this information in his address book, the Borden Street location was ringing a faint bell. He was sure he'd seen that address before, but he couldn't place where. He opened Google Street View and entered the address, but what he saw wasn't familiar. He returned to the personnel list and looked again at the address. That's when it occurred to him that it wasn't the physical location that was ringing a bell, it was the typed address on the file page. He'd seen that address somewhere else in the same document.

He went to the main part of the list that was devoted to active employees and began scrolling slowly through the names and addresses. Finally, there it was—in the section covering security, maintenance, and housekeeping:

CREEL, CHALISE J., 115 BORDEN STREET, WHITE RIVER, NY

The landline number given for her was the same as the one listed for Blaze Jackson, but she had a different cell number. So, thought Gurney, they were roommates at least. And possibly more than that.

Just as interesting was the fact that Chalise Creel was a name he'd seen before, and not just in the personnel list. It had appeared on the name tag of the cleaning woman on the ICU floor at the hospital—the woman with the almond-shaped eyes who'd emptied the trash basket in the visitors' lounge the day he was there with Kim, Heather, and Madeleine. A woman who would have had easy access to Rick Loomis. A woman whose routine presence the nursing staff would have had no reason to question.

The insertion of the ice pick, however, into Loomis's brain stem would have required specific medical knowledge. Which raised questions about Creel's background, as well as Jackson's. Gurney needed to find out what Jackson's job at the hospital had been, and the reason she was no longer there. Could the Jackson-Creel relationship be connected directly to the murder of Rick Loomis? Might one of them have been the source of the drugs used on Jordan and Tooker? And perhaps the biggest question of all—were Jackson and Creel entangled with Judd Turlock and Dell Beckert?

The hospital seemed the logical place to start searching for answers. Gurney's call was answered by an automated branching system that connected him eventually to Abby Marsh in the HR department. She was still in her office at a quarter past eight. She sounded as harried as she was the day Gurney had gotten the file from her.

"Yes?"

"Abby, this is Dave Gurney. I was wondering if—"

She broke in. "The man of the hour."

"Sorry?"

"We have a TV in our cafeteria. I was grabbing a quick dinner, and saw the interview with the district attorney. What can I do for you?"

"I need some information on two of your employees—one past, one present. Blaze Jackson and Chalise Creel. Are you familiar with them?"

"Jackson, definitely. Creel, slightly. Is there a problem?"

"That's what I'm trying to find out. Is Creel working now?"

"Hold on. I'll check . . . Okay, here it is. According to the schedule, she's on the four-to-twelve shift. So, yes, she'd be working now."

"Sorry, what I meant was, do you know for a fact that she's actually there?"

"That wouldn't be in our computer system."

"But someone must know whether she's there or not."

"Her shift supervisor. Do you want me to call him?"

"Please."

"I'm going to put you on hold."

"Thank you, Abby."

Five minutes passed. When she finally reconnected with Gurney she sounded worried. "Chalise Creel didn't show up for her shift this afternoon, she didn't show up yesterday, and she didn't call in either day. Her supervisor tried to reach her yesterday. When he tried again today he got an automated message saying her voice-mail was full."

"She's been reliable until now?"

"Apparently. No red flags in her file. But the fact that you're asking about her— is that something we should be concerned about?"

"Too soon to tell. Did you know that she has the same address as Blaze Jackson?"

"The same address?" The worry in Abby Marsh's voice went up a notch.

"Yes. And the same landline number."

Marsh said nothing.

Rather than ask whether Jackson had resigned or been terminated—a question that Marsh might not be able to answer for privacy reasons—Gurney employed the presumptive approach detectives often used in dealing with similar situations. "When Jackson was terminated, were there any repercussions?"

"What kind of repercussions?"

"Did she deny what she was being accused of?"

"Of course. Until we showed her our pharmacy security video."

Gurney decided to continue his presumptive approach. "She had the propofol in her possession? And the midazolam?"

"The propofol was right there on the video. The midazolam would have been harder to prove. Bottom line, she agreed to resign, and we agreed not to press charges. There would have been no point. Propofol is not technically a controlled substance like midazolam, so legally the charges wouldn't have amounted to much. But who gave you all this information?"

Gurney was tempted to tell her that she just did. But revealing that he'd tricked her would do no one any good. And he wasn't particularly proud of it. He said instead, not untruthfully, "The truth has a way of leaking out."

She paused. "Can you tell me why you're looking for Chalise Creel?"

He worded his answer conservatively. "She may have been in the vicinity of the ICU at the time Rick Loomis was attacked."

Abby Marsh's dead silence indicated that she got the point.

The first thing Gurney did after thanking her for her help and ending the call was to check Creel's landline and cell numbers and place calls to them both. Both calls went to voicemail, and both mailboxes were full. He placed a call to Jackson's cell number. That call also went to voicemail, and that mailbox was also full. He sat back in his chair and gazed out the rear window at the hillside, now almost entirely enveloped in darkness.

Somewhere in the high pine forest a coyote pack began to howl.

He thought about the link between Blaze Jackson and Chalise Creel. He thought about their unwillingness or inability to accept phone calls, about Jackson's drug-related exit from Mercy Hospital, about Creel's access to the ICU.

After a quarter of an hour of indecision he called Torres.

"Mark, there's a situation we need to look into." He related his conversation with Abby Marsh and asked Torres to get over to the Jackson-Creel apartment as soon as possible. "If either one of them is present, hold on to them. I'll meet you there."

He drove well above the speed limit all the way to the White River exit on the interstate, then relied on his GPS to lead him through the city's maze of one-way streets. His destination turned out to be in the middle of a ragged block in the Grinton neighborhood.

In the light of the sole functioning street lamp, the side of Borden Street on which number 115 was located appeared intact. On the opposite side only burned-out shells remained. Torres's Crown Victoria was already there. Gurney pulled in behind it.

Getting out of his car he was struck by the sharp odor of wet ashes and underlying decay. Like the adjoining structures to its left and right, number 115 was a grimy four-story tenement with a steel door. A man and a woman were sitting in plastic lawn chairs in the semidarkness in front of the building. The man was small, wiry, and brown-skinned, with an unkempt gray Afro. The woman was blond and remarkably rotund—creating an impression of having been inflated. Her face was illuminated by the cold glow of her phone screen.

The man watched Gurney approaching. "Apartment you want's on the fourth floor," he announced in a loud voice. "Man who came before you has been up there awhile."

Gurney stopped. "Do you happen to know the women who live there—Blaze Jackson and Chalise Creel?"

The man grinned. "Everybody knows Miss Lovely. She's famous."

"What about Chalise?"

"Chalise don't talk to nobody."

"Have you seen either of them in the past few days?"

"Don't believe so."

Gurney looked at the woman. "How about you. Do you know either of the ladies on the fourth floor?"

She showed no sign of hearing the question.

The man leaned forward in his lawn chair. "Brenda only knows what's on her phone."

Gurney nodded. "Do you know if the ladies had any recent visitors?"

"Brothers comin' and goin' all the time."

"Anyone else?"

"Man in the big car, couple days back."

Gurney pointed to the Crown Vic. "Big car like that?"

"Taller. More shine. Cowboy kind of name."

"Durango?"

"Yeah. Pretty sure. Durango."

"You saw the driver?"

"White man. Saw him from my window." He pointed toward the second floor.

"Can you describe him?"

"I just did."

"Tall? Short? Thin? Fat?"

"Regular size."

"Type of clothing?"

"Dark."

"Hair color, length?

"Dark hat, didn't see no hair."

"And this was when?"

"Had to be night before last."

"Do you know what time he arrived?"

"Nighttime. Maybe ten, eleven."

"Do you know how long he was here?"

"The man came in the night, is all I know. Car was gone in the morning."

Gurney was considering his next question when he heard his name being called. He looked up and saw Torres at an open window on the top floor.

"Dave, you need to come up here!" The strain in his voice gave Gurney a hint of what to expect when he reached the apartment.

Gurney entered the building and bounded up through the stairwell two steps at a time. The fourth-floor apartment door was open, held that way by Torres, who stepped back to let Gurney into a narrow foyer lighted by a single ceiling fixture. He handed Gurney a pair of latex gloves and Tyvek shoe covers.

Gurney put them on without asking any questions. He knew he'd have the answers soon enough.

"They're in the living room," said Torres.

The sickening smell that intensified as Gurney passed through the foyer was one he knew well but had never gotten used to.

Two African American women in short skirts and satin tops were sitting on the living room couch. They were leaning against each other—as though, instead of going out for the evening, they'd fallen asleep in the middle of an intimate conversation. Looking closer, Gurney could see on their skin the characteristic sheen of autolysis. In addition, there were signs that the first gases of decomposition were beginning to bloat their bodies. But the faces were still recognizable. He was sure the one on the left belonged to the fiery woman he'd seen on RAM-TV's *Battleground*

Tonight. And he had a feeling that the face on the right belonged to the almond-eyed cleaning woman he'd seen in the ICU visitors' lounge.

As was usually the case with corpses at this stage, flies were everywhere—most thickly concentrated on the mouths, eyes, and ears. The apartment's two front windows were wide open, likely an effort by Torres to mitigate the stench.

There were two empty glasses, open bottles of vodka and raspberry liqueur, and two glittery purses on the coffee table in front of the couch—along with a number of hypodermic needles. Gurney counted eight, all used and empty. Their labels indicated they were of the preloaded type containing propofol.

"Blaze Lovely Jackson and Chalise Jackson Creel," said Torres. "At least that's what it says on the driver's licenses in those purses. Sounds like they might be sisters."

Gurney nodded. "Have you called the ME's office?"

"Thrasher said he could be here in twenty-five minutes, and that was twenty minutes ago. I called Garrett Felder, too. He's on his way."

"Good. You've been through the apartment?"

"A general look-around."

"Anything get your attention?"

"One thing, actually." Torres pointed to a small desk against the wall opposite the couch. He opened the top drawer all the way. In the back behind a ream of paper there was a plastic zip-top bag containing what appeared to be a stack of twenty-dollar bills. Gurney guesstimated the total, if they were all twenties, to be at least three thousand dollars.

He frowned. "Interesting."

"The money?"

"The plastic bag."

"The bag? Why—?"

Torres's question was truncated by the sound of a car door closing in the street below.

49

Shortly after Thrasher's arrival, Garrett Felder came trudging up the stairs with his evidence-collection equipment, followed by Paul Aziz with his camera. While the three donned their Tyvek suits, Torres acquainted them with the basic facts of the situation, after which he and Gurney took a low-profile position, mostly observing the technical work in progress and being careful not to get in the way.

From time to time Felder and Aziz expressed their dismay at the odor that had permeated the apartment. Thrasher acted as if it didn't exist.

After watching them for a while, Torres took Gurney aside and informed him that he'd been contacted earlier that day by the lead singer of an obscure old rock band. "He told me he'd heard a news report a few days ago that members of a white-supremacist group called Knights of the Rising Sun were wanted by the police in White River. That would have been when Turlock and Beckert were publicly linking the KRS website to the Jordan-Tooker murders and to the Gorts. Anyway, the news reporter included the website address in the story. The rock-band guy got curious and went to the site—because he remembered the phrase 'knights of the rising sun' was in one of his old songs."

Gurney chimed in. "And on the website he found the video of him and his band performing that song. But he didn't know anything about any white-supremacist group and his band had never given anyone the rights to the video."

Torres looked baffled. "How on earth do you know that?"

"It's the only way it would make sense, considering the fact that the whole KRS business was a fabrication. I figure the website creator found the old video somewhere—maybe on YouTube—copied it, and used it. I'd also bet that the band's actual name has the phrase 'white supremacist' or words to that effect in it."

Torres stared at Gurney. "He told me his band, as sort of a joke, was named 'The Texas Skinhead *White Supremacy* Heavy Metal Rockers.' But how could you possibly know that?"

"Once it was apparent that the KRS thing was a form of misdirection, I asked myself how I'd go about creating a phony website like that. Rather than trying to invent the content from scratch, I'd do an internet search of terms like 'white supremacist' to see what was out there—what I could adapt or just plain steal. The next step—"

Thrasher interrupted their conversation. "Cadaver van'll be here momentarily. Time of death I'd put in a window of forty-eight to seventy-two hours ago. I may be able to be a bit more precise when I get them open—day after tomorrow if nothing unforeseen occurs. Meanwhile it looks similar in both cases to the chemical pre-amble to the Jordan and Tooker homicides. I would expect our lab tests to reveal alcohol, metabolites of midazolam, and signs of propofol toxicity."

"Why midazolam?" asked Gurney. "Aren't the other benzodiazepines more readily available?"

"Generally, yes."

"Then why—"

"Anterograde amnesia."

"What's that?"

"One of the special effects of midazolam is to impair the creation of memories. That might be advantageous to a perpetrator in a criminal situation—in case the victim survived. There could, of course, be other reasons for its selection. Up to you to sort that out." He pointed at one of the bottles on the coffee table. "While you're at it, I suggest you get an analysis of that raspberry liqueur."

"Any reason in particular?" asked Gurney, his annoyance rising at Thrasher's habit of doling out information in pieces rather than laying it all out at once.

"Midazolam is available as a syrup. Has a bitter taste. A strong, sweet liqueur might be an ideal delivery vehicle."

"I take it there's no chance of this being a double suicide?"

"I wouldn't say *no* chance. But damn little chance." Thrasher stepped out of the living room into the little foyer and began removing his Tyvek suit.

Gurney followed him. "By the way, I got your phone message."

Thrasher nodded, peeling off his latex gloves.

"I'd like to know what this excavation mystery is all about," said Gurney. "When can we sit down and talk about it?"

"How about right now?"

Thrasher produced an unpleasant smile. "The subject is a sensitive one. This is neither the time nor the place."

"Then pick a time and place."

Thrasher's smile hardened. "Your house. Tomorrow evening. I'm speaking at the annual dinner of the Forensic Pathology Association in Syracuse. I should be passing through Walnut Crossing on my way there around five."

"I'll see you then."

Thrasher rolled up his Tyvek coveralls, removed his shoe covers, stuffed everything in an expensive-looking leather bag, and left without another word.

Gurney returned to Torres in the living room, intending to resume his explanation of the likely KRS website creation process, when Garrett Felder came over, smartphone in hand, obviously excited.

"Look at this!" He held up his phone so Torres and Gurney could both see the screen. It displayed side-by-side photos of two thumbprints. They appeared to be identical.

"Clean, shiny, nonporous surfaces are a godsend. Look at these prints! Like they get on TV. Perfect!"

Gurney and Torres peered at them.

"There's no doubt these two came from the same thumb," continued Felder. "Different time, different place. But the same thumb. Print on the left I just lifted from the plastic bag of twenties in the desk drawer. Print on the right I lifted yesterday from an alarm clock in the loft of Dell Beckert's cabin. It also matches a bunch of prints on his furniture, his faucets, his UTV."

"Do we know for a fact those prints in the cabin are Beckert's?" asked Gurney.

Felder nodded. "Confirmation yesterday from AFIS—from their file of active LEO prints."

Torres seemed taken aback. "Jackson and Creel got that money directly from Beckert?"

"We know Jackson did," said Felder. "Her prints and Beckert's are both on the bag."

"You took prints from Jackson's body?" asked Gurney.

"Quick ones. Thrasher'll do the official set at autopsy. Anyway, I've got more work to do now. Just wanted to clue you in." Felder slipped his phone through a slit in his Tyvek coverall into his pocket and headed for a hallway off the side of the living room. On the wall next to the hallway there was a poster-sized print of a famous sixties radical thrusting an iconic black power fist into the air.

A moment later Paul Aziz came out of the same hallway. He announced that he'd finished. Patting his camera affectionately, he asked if Gurney or Torres had any special requests beyond the standard crime-scene collection. Torres looked questioningly at Gurney, who said no. Aziz promised to email them photo sets the following morning and was gone.

Torres turned to Gurney with a puzzled look. "This financial connection between Dell Beckert and Blaze Jackson . . . it doesn't seem to surprise you."

"I'm only surprised that we found such clear evidence of it. When the hospital HR director admitted that Jackson was fired for stealing propofol hypodermics, and propofol hypodermics had been found on Beckert's property, it was natural to suspect a connection."

"You think the money was Beckert's payment to her for the drugs?"

Gurney shrugged. "It would seem to be payment for something. We need to know more about what went on between them. Obviously the chief of police wouldn't ask a leader of the BDA to steal propofol for him unless they had an established relationship."

Torres looked baffled. "Like what?"

"There are some interesting possibilities. Remember that revelation a few years back that one of the biggest mobsters in Boston was a major FBI informant?"

Torres's eyes widened. "You think Jackson was fingering people for Beckert?"

"We've heard she was ambitious and ruthless. She could have been selectively informing on people she wanted out of her way. It could have been a useful association that got deeper as time passed. It's not inconceivable that they collaborated on the elimination of Jordan and Tooker—an outcome we've been told they may both have wanted for their own reasons."

"Are you suggesting Beckert did *this*?" Torres gestured toward the couch.

"The guy downstairs in the lawn chair claims that a white man in a black Durango was here two nights ago—just within Thrasher's time-of-death window."

"Jesus," said Torres softly.

Gurney looked over at the bottles and glasses on the table and Jackson and Creel in their party clothes. "Maybe Beckert suggested a little toast to their success."

Torres picked up the hypothetical narrative. "The midazolam in the drinks relaxes them to the point of not knowing what's going on. Then he injects them with fatal overdoses of propofol. And just leaves everything there, so it'll look like a drug party gone bad." He hesitated, frowning. "But why kill them?"

Gurney smiled. "The demon of negative projection."

"The what?"

"Let's assume that Beckert relied on their help to get rid of people who could cause problems for him. At least Jordan and Tooker, and probably Loomis in the hospital. But that put them in a position where they could cause even bigger problems, because of what they knew. Once he started envisioning situations in which they might roll over on him, or even try to blackmail him, that would have done it. His political future and personal safety would have been far more important to him than the lives of two potential troublemakers."

Torres nodded slowly. "You think he might have set Turlock up? By sending him out to the gun club and letting the Gorts know he'd be there? I mean, Turlock probably knew more damaging stuff about him than anyone else on earth, and if he'd outlived his usefulness . . ."

"That would depend on Beckert being in contact with the Gorts, which—"

Torres's phone rang. He frowned at the screen. "It's the DA's office." He listened intently for a minute or two. The only sound in the apartment was the hum of Felder's evidence vac as he ran it slowly over the rug in front of the couch.

Torres finally spoke. "Okay . . . Yes, I know the area . . . Right, it looks that way . . . I agree . . . Thank you." He ended the call and turned to Gurney. "That was the woman in Kline's office who's taking calls in response to his TV request for information on Beckert's whereabouts."

"Anything useful?"

"A caller said he saw a man earlier tonight in a gas station over near Bass River. The man was filling a couple of five-gallon gas cans in the back of a black Durango. The Durango plate number ended with the letters WRPD."

"Did the caller identify himself?"

"No. He asked if there was a reward. She told him there wasn't, and he hung up. Phone company says the call came from a prepaid."

"Does Kline's office have a recording of it?"

"No. The line they're using bypasses their automatic system."

"Too bad." Gurney paused. "Bass River's out by the reservoir, right?"

"Right. Other side of the mountain from the gun club. Heavily forested land.

Not many roads." Torres eyed Gurney's expression. "Something about that bothering you?"

"I'm just thinking that if Beckert's on the run, it's surprising he's still in the area."

"Maybe he's got a second cabin nobody knows about. In the woods somewhere, off the grid. Maybe that's what the gas cans were for—a generator. What do you think?"

"I guess it's possible."

"You sound doubtful."

"Driving his own vehicle with a distinctive plate number close to home seems like a stupid thing to do."

"People make mistakes under pressure, right?"

"True," said Gurney.

In fact, he thought with a twinge of anxiety, he might be doing that himself.

50

It was after midnight when Gurney got home from White River. He parked by the side door. The thought occurred to him, as it had done on many previous occasions, that it would make sense to add a garage to the house. It was something Madeleine had mentioned from time to time, and it was the sort of thing they could work on together. After the case was wrapped up he'd have to give the project some serious thought.

Before going into the house he stood for a while next to the Outback in the moonlight, inhaling the sweet, earthy spring air—an antidote to the odor of death he had experienced earlier. However, the nights were a lot chillier up in the hills around Walnut Crossing than down in White River, and it wasn't long before a shiver persuaded him to go inside.

Despite feeling wired from the intense evening, he decided to lie down, close his eyes, and try to get some rest. Madeleine was asleep, but when he got into bed she woke up enough to murmur, "You're home."

"Yes."

"Everything all right?"

"More or less."

It took a moment for that to register.

"What's the 'less' part?"

"The White River thing keeps getting crazier. How was your political action meeting?"

"Stupid. Tell you about it in the morning."

"Okay. G'night."

"G'night."

"Love you."

"Love you too."

A minute later the soft rhythm of her breathing told him she was asleep.

As he lay staring out the open window at the shapes of the trees, just visible in the silvery moonlight, his thoughts centered on the relationship between Dell Beckert and Blaze Jackson. He wondered if she might have been the unnamed informant referred to more than once in the critical-situation-management team meetings. Did Beckert have something on her that forced her cooperation, or had the initiative been hers? Was the bag of money in the drawer a onetime transaction, or was it part of an ongoing arrangement? Was it a payment for value received, or money extorted in return for silence? Given Jackson's physical attractiveness and reputed sexual appetite, might her connection to Beckert have included that element? Or was it purely a business relationship?

And what about the Rick Loomis connection? If Beckert and Turlock were behind the Poulter Street attempt on Loomis's life, then presumably they were also behind the fatal attack in the hospital. Did Beckert and Jackson enlist Chalise Creel and show her how to drive that ice pick into the man's brain stem?

The thought of Poulter Street reminded Gurney of a question he'd asked Torres to pursue: Had the real estate agent who'd arranged for the leases on the two sniper sites actually met with Jordan, whose name was on the leases, or had the transaction been handled by an intermediary?

Torres had told Gurney the information would be available as soon as the agent returned from vacation. Gurney's eagerness to pursue the matter, along with the impossibility of doing so at two o'clock in the morning, kept him spinning what-if scenarios until he finally drifted into an uneasy sleep.

When he awoke at nine the next morning the sky was blue, and through the open windows he could hear Madeleine out mowing. His first thought was to get in touch with Acme Realty.

He called Mark Torres for the agent's name, which had slipped his mind.

"Laura Conway," said Torres. "I have a reminder on my phone to check with her this morning. I'm on my way into Kline's office to brief him on the Jackson-Creel homicides. By the way, we've confirmed that Blaze and Chalise are sisters. And it seems that Chalise has a pretty extensive mental health history, which we're trying to get access to. As for Laura Conway, if you want to talk to her yourself—"

"I do. Can you give me the number?"

Three minutes later, Laura Conway was telling him what he'd half expected to hear.

"It was all handled by Blaze Jackson. I believe she was Mr. Jordan's business manager, or something like that. She chose the apartment on Bridge Street and the house over on Poulter."

"But both of those leases were signed by Marcel Jordan?"

"That's correct. As I remember, Ms. Jackson took the physical documents to him and brought them back to our office."

"Were you aware of her prominent role in the Black Defense Alliance?"

"I have no interest in politics. I avoid watching the news. It's too upsetting."

"So you never met Marcel Jordan?"

"No."

"Or spoke to him?"

"No."

"Did he provide you with any financial references?"

"No."

"You didn't require assurances that he could afford those rentals?"

"We didn't consider it necessary."

"Isn't that unusual?"

"It's not the normal thing. But neither was the arrangement."

"Meaning?"

"Both rentals were paid for in advance. For the entire year. In cash."

"Did that concern you?"

"Some people like cash transactions. I don't question things like that."

"Did it cross your mind that Mr. Jordan might not know that his name was on that lease?"

"I don't understand. Why wouldn't he know?"

Gurney was sure the answer was that Jordan was being set up in a complex Beckert-Turlock conspiracy to frame him and his BDA associates, along with Cory Payne, for the murders of John Steele and Rick Loomis. So he wasn't surprised to learn of the man's potential ignorance of the lease. What got his attention was the presence of Blaze Jackson—with its suggestion of her involvement in the affair from the beginning.

He ended the call and stood for a minute at the window, gazing out at the row of blooming chokecherry trees along the side of the high pasture. He was wondering how extensively involved Blaze Jackson had been in the White River deaths and whether she had been the brains or the tool. As he was turning this over in his mind, his eye caught a movement in the sky above the trees. A red-tailed hawk was circling the edge of the field, searching no doubt for some smaller bird or furry creature to pierce with its talons, tear apart, and devour. Nature, he concluded for the hundredth time, for all its sweetness and blossoms and birdsong, was essentially a horror show.

His phone rang on the nightstand behind him. He turned away from the window and took the call. "Gurney here."

"Hello, Dave. It's Marv Gelter."

"Marv. Good morning."

"Good and busy is what it is. You're quite the disrupter, my friend. Whole new political landscape out there."

Gurney remained silent.

"No time to waste. Let me get to the point. You free for lunch?"

"That would depend on the agenda."

"Of course it would! The agenda concerns your future. You just turned the world upside down, my friend. Time to take advantage of that. Time to take a look at the rest of your life."

Gurney's visceral dislike of Gelter was outweighed by his curiosity.

"Where do you want to meet?"

"The Blue Swan. Lockenberry. Twelve noon."

By the time he was ready to leave, Madeleine's mowing had taken her up around the high pasture into one of the grassy trails through the pines. He left her a note with a brief explanation hoping he'd be back by three that afternoon. Then he got the address of the restaurant from the internet, put it into his GPS, and set out.

The immaculate village of Lockenberry, just a mile or so past the Gelters' strange cubical house, was nestled in its own small valley where spring was further advanced than in the neighboring hills. Daffodils, jonquils, and apple blossoms were already giving way to a profusion of lilacs. The Blue Swan was located on a tranquil, shaded lane off the main street. An elegantly understated sign beside a bluestone path leading to the front door was all that distinguished it from the picture-book Colonial homes on either side of it.

Gurney was met in the cherrywood entry hall by a statuesque blonde with a faint Scandinavian accent.

"Welcome, Mr. Gurney. Mr. Gelter will be here shortly. May I show you to your table?"

He followed her along a carpeted hallway to a high-ceilinged room with a chandelier. The walls consisted of alternating panels of impressionist-style floral murals and gleaming mirrors. There was a single table in the center of the room—round, with a white linen tablecloth, two French provincial dining chairs, and two elaborate place settings. The statuesque blonde pulled out one of the chairs for him.

"May I get you something to drink, Mr. Gurney?"

"Plain water."

Moments later, Marv Gelter strode into the room—concentrated energy and darting gaze belying the laid-back look of his country-squire tweeds. It was as though a Ralph Lauren weekend ensemble was being modeled by a large caffeinated rat.

"Dave! Glad you made it! Sorry to be late." He sat across the table from Gurney, glancing back toward the hallway. "Lova, darling, where the hell are you?"

The Nordic beauty entered the room, bringing them two glasses on a silver tray—plain water for Gurney and a rosy-hued drink that looked like a Campari and soda for Gelter. She placed them on the table, stood back, and waited. Gelter took a quick swallow of his. Gurney wondered if he did anything slowly.

"No menu here, David. They do the classics. Fantastic cassoulet. Coq au vin. Confit de canard. Boeuf bourguignon. Whatever you like."

Gurney looked up at the Nordic beauty, who seemed faintly amused.

"The beef," he said.

She smiled and left the room.

He looked at Gelter. "You're not eating?"

"They know what I like." He took another swig of his drink and grinned with more adrenaline than warmth. "So. You triggered an earthquake. How's it feel?"

"Unfinished."

"Hah! *Unfinished.* I like that. A man who's never satisfied. Always moving forward. Good! Very good!" He eyed Gurney with a glittery intensity. "So here we are. Dell Beckert, God rest his soul, is a dead issue. Even if he's alive, he's dead. You saw to that. Fine. The question is, what's next?"

"Next for who?"

"You, David. You're the one I'm having lunch with. What's next for you?"

Gurney shrugged. "Mow my fields, feed my chickens, build a bigger woodshed."

Gelter pursed his lips unpleasantly. "Kline'll probably make you an offer. Maybe to run his investigation department. That something you'd like?"

"No."

"I don't blame you. Waste of your talents. Which are more substantial than you know." The adrenaline grin returned. "You've got a shitload of modesty. Shitload of integrity. Big balls. You walked into that White River cesspool where nobody knew what the fuck was going on, you figured it out, showed the district attorney which end was up. That's impressive." He paused. "You know what else it is? It's a *story*. A story with a hero. A cool, smart, straight-shooter hero. *Supercop.* That's what that magazine called you, am I right?"

Gurney nodded uncomfortably.

"Damn, David, you are the man! You even have those old blue-eyed cowboy good looks. A goddamn real-life hero. You know how deep a hunger there is out there for a real hero?"

Gurney stared at him. "What are you talking about?"

"The hell you think I'm talking about? Beckert's out, Gurney's in!"

"In what?"

"The office of the attorney general."

The Nordic beauty appeared with two delicate china plates. The one with an artfully arranged antipasto she placed in front of Gurney. The one with a dozen or so mandarin orange segments arranged in a circle around a small finger bowl she placed in front of Gelter. She left the room as quietly as she'd entered it.

Gurney's tone matched his incredulous expression. "You're suggesting I compete in the special election?"

"I can see you winning it by a bigger margin than Beckert would have."

Gurney was silent for a long moment. "You don't seem upset by what's happened."

"I was extremely upset. For ten minutes. More than that's a self-indulgent waste of time. Then I asked myself the only sane question. *What now?* It doesn't matter what life puts in front of us. Could be a gold mine. Could be a pile of crap. The question's the same. *What now?*"

"Does it bother you that you were so wrong about Beckert?"

Gelter picked up a little wedge of orange and examined it before popping it in his mouth. "Life goes on. If people disappoint you, fuck 'em. Problems can become solutions. Like this situation right here. You're better than Beckert, which I might not have realized if he was still around. That worthless lump of socialist shit, Maynard Biggs, won't have a chance against you."

"You hate him that much?"

He examined another orange wedge before devouring it. "I don't hate him. Don't give a flying fuck about him. What I hate is what he stands for. The philosophy. The belief system. The *entitlement*."

"The entitlement?"

"With a capital fucking *E*. These useless fuckers have rights! Rights to whatever they want. No need to work, save, support their own children. No need to do a damn thing—because they had a great-great-great-great-fucking-grandfather who three hundred fucking years ago got sold by some African scumbag to a slave trader. This ancient history, you see, *entitles* them to the fruits of my current labor." He turned his head to the side and spit an orange seed out onto the Oriental carpet.

Gurney shrugged. "The one time I saw Biggs on television his statements on the racial divide seemed mild and reasonable."

"Pretty wrapping on a box of scorpions."

"And you see me as some sort of solution to this?"

"I see you as a way to keep the levers of power out of the wrong hands."

"If I were to be elected with your help, what would I owe you?"

"Nada. The defeat of Maynard Biggs would be my payment."

"I'll sleep on it."

"Fine, but don't sleep too long. There's a filing deadline three days from now. Say yes, and I promise you you'll win."

"You really don't think Biggs has a chance?"

"Not against you. And I could always turn up a few students who might recall instances of inappropriate advances from their professor." Gelter smiled venomously.

Gelter's main course arrived, a colorful bouillabaisse, followed by Gurney's boeuf bourguignon. They ate, mostly in silence, and both declined dessert.

The subject of their meeting wasn't mentioned again until they were out in front of the restaurant, about to get into their cars.

"As soon as you say yes," said Gelter, "we'll put you on *NewsBreakers* and have Kilbrick and Kronck introduce you to the world. They're both dying to talk to you." When Gurney didn't reply, he continued. "Just think about what you could do with the power and influence of the AG title. All the right contacts. Whole new world. I know people who'd kill for that spot!"

"I'll let you know."

"Opportunity of a lifetime," Gelter added, flashing his adrenaline-charged grin one more time as he stepped into his red Ferrari.

51

Gurney sipped the cup of coffee he'd made the minute he'd arrived home from Lockenberry. Purple finches were busy at the feeder Madeleine had set up at the edge of the patio. She was at the sink island chopping onions for soup.

"So," she said lightly, "what did he want?"

"He wants me to run for attorney general."

The knife paused on the cutting board, but she didn't look as surprised as he'd expected. "In place of Dell Beckert?"

"Exactly."

She nodded thoughtfully. "I guess he wants a real law-and-order hero to replace the one that blew up in his face."

"That's pretty much what he said."

"He didn't waste any time."

"No."

"Clever, cold, and calculating."

"All of that."

"And it goes without saying that he has the connections to get you in the race?"

"Not just that. He told me I'd win."

"What did you say to that?"

"That I'd sleep on it."

"What were you thinking when you said it?"

"I was thinking that after two minutes of feeling flattered, I'd ponder the unknowns, imagine the problems, talk to you about it, then turn it down."

She laughed. "Interesting process. What does the attorney general do, anyway?"

"I'm sure there's a description of responsibilities on the state website, but what a real live person might choose to spend his time on is another matter. The last occupant of the office is rumored to have fucked himself to death with a Las Vegas hooker."

"So you're really not interested?"

"In jumping into a political shark tank? With the backing of a man I don't even like being in the same room with?"

Madeleine raised a curious eyebrow. "You did agree to have lunch with him."

"To find out why he wanted to have lunch with me."

"And now you know."

"Now I know—unless his agenda is more twisted than I realize."

She gave him one of her searching looks, and a silence fell between them.

"Oh, by the way," he said as he was finishing his coffee, "I crossed paths with Walter Thrasher at the crime scene in White River last night. He said he'd drop by around five today to talk about our archaeology project."

"What is there to talk about?"

Gurney realized he hadn't shared Thrasher's phone message with her. "He's done some research on the objects I found. His comments have been rather strange. I'm hoping he'll clarify the situation this afternoon."

Madeleine's silence eloquently conveyed her hostility to the project.

Thinking of Thrasher reminded him of the Jackson-Creel apartment. Madeleine reacted to the look on his face.

"What is it?"

"Nothing. Just . . . a little jolt from last night. I'm fine."

"You want to tell me about it?"

He didn't want to, but he'd learned over the years that describing something that was disturbing him loosened its grip on his mind. So he told her the story, beginning with his discovery on the hospital personnel list that Blaze Jackson and Chalise Creel shared an address and ending with the scene in the apartment—the decomposing bodies, the propofol hypodermics, the money, and the fingerprint link to Dell Beckert.

She smiled. "You must feel good about that."

"About what?" There was sourness in his voice.

"Being right about Beckert. You were uncomfortable with him from the beginning. And now you've amassed all this evidence of his involvement in . . . how many murders?"

"At least four. Six, if he killed those two women. Seven, if he set up Judd Turlock."

"If it wasn't for you, that Payne boy would probably be in jail."

He shook his head. "I doubt it. A good defense lawyer would have seen that the evidence against him was a setup. As for the evidence against Beckert, we got lucky out at the gun club."

"You're not giving yourself enough credit. You're the one who decided to go there and check it out. You're the one who turned the whole case around. You're the one who's gotten to the truth."

"We've had some luck. Recoverable bullets. Clean ballistics. Clear evidence that—"

She interrupted him. "You don't sound very proud of what you've accomplished."

"And you sound like you're talking to one of your clients at the clinic."

She sighed. "I'm just wondering why you don't feel better about the progress you've made."

"I'll feel better when it's all over."

Thrasher arrived at five twenty, negotiating the uneven lane up through the pasture with obvious care in his pristine Audi. After getting out of the car he stood for a few moments surveying the surrounding landscape, then came over to the open French doors.

"Damned construction workers on the interstate, busily doing nothing except impeding traffic," he said as Gurney let him in.

From his position in the breakfast nook he looked around the big farmhouse kitchen with an appraising eye. His gaze lingered on the fireplace at the far end. "Nice old mantel. Chestnut. Unique color. Style of the hearth appears to be early eighteen hundreds. You research the provenance of the house when you bought it?"

"No. Do you think there's some connection between this house and—"

"The remains of the house down by the pond? Lord, no. That predates this by more than a hundred years." He put his briefcase down on the dining table.

Madeleine, who'd been upstairs practicing a Bach piece on her cello, came in from the hallway.

Gurney introduced her.

"Asparagus," said Thrasher. "Wise choice."

"Excuse me?"

"I noticed your asparagus bed out there. Only vegetable worth the trouble of growing at home. Freshness. Huge difference." He glanced around again. "Might be a good idea to have a seat."

"How about right here," suggested Gurney, gesturing to the chairs at the table. He added, "We're eager to find out what this is all about."

"Good. I'm hoping your interest will survive the answer."

With curious frowns, Gurney and Madeleine took seats next to each other at the table.

Thrasher remained standing on the opposite side. "First, a bit of background. As you know, my vocation is forensic pathology, with a focus on determining the causes of untimely death. My avocation, however, is the examination of northeastern Colonial life, with a focus on its darker aspects, particularly the malignant synergy of slavery and psychopathology. I'm sure you're aware that slavery was not an exclusively Southern phenomenon. In Colonial New York City in seventeen hundred, nearly half the households owned at least one slave. Chattel slavery—the buying and selling of human beings over whom the owner had absolute control—was widely accepted."

"We're aware of the history," said Madeleine.

"A glaring defect of history as it is commonly taught is that the events of an era are often seen acting upon one another in only very large terms—for example, the interaction between advances in mechanization and the movement of populations to manufacturing centers. We read about these interactions and think we're grasping the essence of an age. Or we read about slavery in the context of agricultural economics and we think we understand it—when, in fact, nothing could be further from the truth. It's possible to read a dozen books about it and never *feel* the horror of it—never even glimpse the malignant synergy I mentioned a moment ago."

"What synergy?" asked Madeleine.

"The appalling ways in which some of society's ills combine with others."

"What are you getting at?"

"I wrote an article on the subject last year for a journal of cultural psychology. The title was 'Victims for Sale: Torture, Sexual Abuse, and Serial Murder in Colonial America.' I'm working on another right now—detailing the confluence of psychopathic disorders and a legal system that permitted one person to own another."

"What does this have to do with us?"

"I'm coming to that. The average American's image of Colonial America doesn't run much deeper than stolid-looking Pilgrims in big black hats, happy Indians, brotherly love, religious freedom, and occasional hardship. Colonial reality, of course, was something else entirely. Filth, fear, starvation, ignorance, disease, superstition, the practice of witchcraft and the torture and hanging of witches, heresy trials, cruel punishments, banishments, absurd medical practices, pain and death everywhere. And of course, all the major mental disorders and predatory behaviors—all rampant, all misunderstood. Psychopaths who—"

Madeleine broke in impatiently. "Dr. Thrasher . . ."

He ignored the interruption. "The convergence of two great ills. The desire of the psychopath to exert total control over another person—to use, to abuse, to kill. Imagine that urge combined with the institution of slavery—a system that enabled the easy purchase of potential victims at a public market. Men, women, and children for sale. Objects to be employed at the owner's pleasure. Human beings with hardly any more rights than farm animals. Human beings with virtually no effective legal protection against constant rape, and worse. Men, women, and children whose deaths, accidental or intentional, few authorities would bother to seriously investigate."

"Enough!" said Madeleine. "I asked you a question. *What does this have to do with us?*"

Thrasher blinked in surprise, then replied matter-of-factly. "The old foundation David uncovered dates, in my opinion, to the very early seventeen hundreds. There were no settlements in this part of the state at that time. This was a frontier wilderness, the essence of the unknown—a place of savagery, danger, and isolation. No one would have chosen to live here, this far from a protective community, unless they were under constraint."

"Constraint?"

"The people who came here would have done so for one of two reasons. One, they were engaging in practices that would have been considered abhorrent to their community and so came here to avoid possible exposure. Or two, they *were* exposed—and banished."

There was a silence, broken by Gurney.

"What kind of practices are you talking about?"

"The objects you found indicate some involvement with witchcraft. That may have been the reason they were driven out of their original community. But I believe that witchcraft was the least of their transgressions. I believe the essence of what was happening in that house by your pond three hundred years ago was what we would define today as serial murder."

Madeleine's eyes widened. "What?!"

"Two years ago I was called in to examine the buried remains of an early-eighteenth-century house over by Marley Mountain. I found some items related to sorcery rituals; but more significantly, there were iron shackles and other evidence of individuals having been held in captivity. There were several devices typically used in the torture of prisoners, including implements for breaking bones, extracting fingernails and teeth. An excavation of the grounds around that foundation uncovered partial skeletal remains of at least ten children. DNA testing of their extracted teeth traced their genetic lineage to West Africa. In other words, to the slave trade."

Madeleine's gaze was fixed on Thrasher with a growing revulsion.

Gurney broke the silence. "Are you suggesting a connection between the house you're talking about and what we found here?"

"The similarities between your excavation, even in this early stage, and the Marley Mountain site are striking."

"What are you suggesting we do?"

"I'm suggesting we bring in the appropriate archaeological equipment and personnel to explore the site with the thoroughness it deserves. The more hard evidence we can find to document the existence of psychopathic elements in the treatment of slaves, the more accurate the historical picture becomes."

Now Madeleine spoke up. "How sure are you?"

"About the abuse and murder of slaves? One hundred percent."

"No, I mean how sure are you that those things took place here, on our property?"

"To be absolutely sure, more digging will be necessary. That's why I'm here. To explain the research opportunity and enlist your cooperation."

"That's not my question. Based on what you've seen, how sure are you *right now* that the kind of horrors you described actually occurred *here*?"

Thrasher looked pained. "If I had to assign to my opinion a level of confidence, based only on what's been unearthed so far, I'd put it around seventy-five percent."

"Fine," said Madeleine with a brittle smile. "That leaves a twenty-five percent chance that whatever is down there by the pond has nothing to do with the serial murder of slave children. Is that right?"

Thrasher let out an exasperated sigh. "More or less."

"Fine. Thank you for the history lesson, Doctor. It's been very enlightening. David and I will discuss the situation, and we'll let you know what we decide."

It took Thrasher a moment to realize that he'd been dismissed.

52

The charged silence that followed Madeleine's final comment persisted long after Thrasher had departed. It reminded Gurney of the silence in their car on the way home from a medical appointment years earlier, during which he'd been informed that the results of an initial MRI had been inconclusive regarding a possible cancer and that he'd need to undergo additional tests.

Such a disturbing subject. Such a major unknown. So little to be said.

They hardly spoke at all during a brief dinner. It wasn't until Gurney began to clear the table that Madeleine commented, "I hope what I said to him, the way I said it, isn't going to create a problem in your professional relationship."

He shrugged. "It doesn't make much difference how he feels about me."

She looked doubtful. He carried their dishes to the sink, then came back and sat down.

"Twenty-five percent is a lot," she said.

"Yes."

"So there's a good chance he's wrong."

"Yes."

She nodded, appearing comforted that he'd agreed, even if he'd done so without much conviction. She stood up from the table. "I have some watering to do while it's still light out. The new delphiniums from Snook's were looking droopy today."

She slipped into a pair of clogs by the French doors and headed for the flower bed, calling back over her shoulder, "Leave the dishes in the sink. I'll take care of them later."

He remained where he was, immersed in dreadful images raised by Thrasher's comments on the "malignant synergy" between psychopathic obsessions and the availability of purchasable victims to satisfy them. There was a particular horror in the mundane practicality of buying human beings to torture or kill. He tried to imagine the unique terror experienced by those in that helpless position. The terror of being under the absolute control of another person.

His phone rang, a welcome distraction.

It was Hardwick.

"Shit, Gurney, I'm impressed that you took my call."

Gurney sighed. "Why is that, Jack?"

"According to RAM-TV, you're a man destined for greatness."

"What are you talking about?"

"*NewsBreakers* just did an interview with Cory Payne. He told the world you saved his life. But that was nothing compared to what Stacey Kilbrick said about you."

"What did she say?"

"I wouldn't dream of spoiling the surprise. All I can say is that I feel privileged to be speaking with a man of your caliber."

Gurney's customary uneasiness at any public mention of his name was amplified by the fact of its occurring on RAM-TV. It certainly wasn't something he could ignore, particularly after Marv Gelter's comments at lunch. He went into the den, accessed the site on his laptop, and clicked on that day's edition of *NewsBreakers*. He used the time slider on the video window to get past the promotional graphics to the point where Stacey Kilbrick and Rory Kronck, sitting at their studio news desk, frowning with concern, were addressing their top story. As the audio kicked in, Kilbrick was in the middle of a sentence.

". . . learned today that there have been two more suspicious deaths in White River. The bodies of Blaze Lovely Jackson, a leader of the Black Defense Alliance, and her sister, Chalise Jackson Creel, were found in their apartment by detectives Mark Torres and David Gurney—someone we'll have more to say about later in this program. The district attorney's office, which is overseeing the investigation, is calling the deaths possible homicides."

She turned toward Kronck. "The terrible carnage in White River just keeps going on. What do you think are the chances these 'possible' homicides turn out to be the real thing?"

"My guess would be ninety-nine percent. But so far the DA has released very little specific information. I suspect he wants to be absolutely certain before he has to acknowledge two more murders on his watch—two more murders in a case that was already bizarre."

Kilbrick nodded grimly. "On the other hand, Cory Payne, son of the mysteriously missing police chief, was *very* forthcoming with his own view of the situation."

"You can say that again, Stacey! I overheard your interview with him, and that young man certainly doesn't pull his punches. Let's show our viewers what we're talking about."

The scene shifted to the simple setting in which Gurney recalled seeing Kronck interviewing Kline. The most conspicuous difference now was the camera being positioned to include the interviewer's short red skirt and long, shapely legs.

Payne appeared somewhat academic in a brown tweed sport jacket, a pale-blue shirt open at the neck, and tan slacks. His hair was still pulled back in a ponytail, but it looked more carefully combed than Gurney remembered. His face looked freshly shaved.

"What are you watching?"

Madeleine's voice behind him at the den door surprised him. He hadn't heard her come in.

"Cory Payne. Being interviewed. On that *NewsBreakers* program."

She pulled a second chair over to the desk and peered intently at the screen.

Kilbrick was resting a clipboard and a pen on her crossed legs. She leaned forward with an expression of painful earnestness. "Welcome to *NewsBreakers*, Cory. I appreciate your coming here today. You've been at the center of the most disturbing criminal case I've ever encountered as a journalist. Among other horrible events, your own father accused you of murder on national television. I can't imagine how that must have felt. We sometimes use the term 'worst moment of my life' loosely. But in this instance, would you say that was true?"

"No."

"No?" Kilbrick blinked, evidently nonplussed.

"It was the most infuriating," explained Payne, "but far from the worst."

"Well . . . that does raise an obvious question."

He waited for her to ask it.

"Tell us, Cory, what *was* the worst moment of your life?"

"The moment at boarding school when I was told that my mother had died. That was the worst. Nothing has ever come close to that."

Kilbrick consulted her clipboard. "That was when you were fourteen?"

"Yes."

"Your father was already prominent in law enforcement at that time. Is that right?"

"Yes."

"And he made a number of public statements blaming illegal drugs, specifically heroin, for her death." She looked up from her clipboard. "Was that true?"

Payne's gaze turned icy. "As true as blaming a rope for the death of a hanged man."

Kilbrick looked excited. "Interesting answer. Could you expand on that?"

"Heroin is just a thing. Like a rope. Or a bullet."

"Are you saying there was more to your mother's death than a simple overdose?"

Payne spoke softly. "I'm saying that he killed her."

"Your father killed your mother?"

"Yes."

"With drugs?"

"Yes."

Kilbrick looked stunned. "Why?"

"For the same reason he killed John Steele, Rick Loomis, Marcel Jordan, Virgil Tooker, Blaze Jackson, Chalise Creel, and Judd Turlock."

She stared at him.

"They threatened his future, the way he wanted things to turn out."

"Threatened all of that ... how?"

"They knew things about him."

"What did they know?"

"That he wasn't what he seemed to be. That he was dishonest, cruel, manipulative. That he extorted confessions, tampered with evidence, and destroyed people's lives to build his own reputation. To ensure his own security. To prove to himself how powerful he was. He was a truly evil man. A killer. A monster."

Kilbrick was staring at him now in amazement. She looked down at her clipboard, then back at him. "You said ... I believe ... that he killed Judd Turlock?"

"Yes."

"The information we have from the DA's office is that the Gort brothers are being sought in connection with the Turlock homicide."

"My father has always used other people to do his dirty work. The Gorts were convenient tools for dealing with Turlock."

"We were told that Judd Turlock was your father's longtime friend. Why would—"

Payne cut her off. "Longtime tool and strong-arm man. Not friend. He had no *friends*. Friendship requires caring about another human being. My father never cared about anyone but himself. If you want to know why he would have arranged for Turlock to be killed, the answer is simple. He outlived his usefulness."

Kilbrick nodded, glancing up out of the frame as though checking the time. "This has been . . . remarkable. I have no more questions. Is there anything you'd like to add before we wrap this up?"

"Yes." He looked directly into the camera. "I want to thank Detective David Gurney with all my heart and soul. He was the one who saw through the framework of false evidence that made it look as though I'd killed those two police officers. Without his insight and persistence, the world might never have known the truth about Dell Beckert, the truth of what he is and what he always was. A destroyer of lives. A controlling monster, a corrupter, a killer. I want to thank Detective Gurney for the truth, and I want the world to know that I owe him my life."

Gurney grimaced.

The scene shifted back to the studio news desk.

Kronck turned to Kilbrick. "Wow, Stacey, astounding interview!"

"Payne certainly had a lot to say, and he wasn't shy about saying it."

"I noticed the name David Gurney came up again—in a very favorable way— just like it did in my interview with Sheridan Kline."

Kilbrick nodded. "I noticed that, too. And you know what I'm thinking right now? It's kind of a wild possibility . . . but I'm thinking David Gurney might be a great choice for our next attorney general. What do you think?"

"I think that's a fabulous idea!"

"Okay!" said Kilbrick, smiling, turning to the camera. "Stay with us. Our next guest—"

Gurney closed the video window and turned to Madeleine. "I have a creepy feeling that Gelter is using Kilbrick and Kronck to push his AG idea."

"You think he has that kind of influence at RAM-TV?"

"I suspect he may own it."

53

The weather the following morning matched Gurney's mood—gray and unsettled. Restless breezes kept changing direction, pushing the asparagus ferns this way and that. Even Madeleine seemed at odds. A mottled overcast was obscuring the sun, and Gurney was surprised to see by the old regulator clock on the kitchen wall that it was already past nine. As they were finishing their oatmeal, Madeleine frowned and tilted her head toward the French doors.

"What is it?" he asked. His hearing was normal, but hers was extraordinary and she was usually aware of approaching sounds before he was.

"Someone's coming."

He opened the doors and soon he heard it—a vehicle coming up the town road. As he watched, a large SUV came into view. It slowed and came to a stop between the barn and the pond. When he went out on the patio for a clearer view he saw that it was a dark-green Range Rover, its polish glistening even in the sunless light.

The driver emerged, a solid-looking man in a blue blazer and gray slacks. He opened the rear door, and a woman stepped out. She was wearing a khaki jacket, riding breeches, and knee-high boots. She stood there for a few moments, looking around at the fields and woods and up across the pasture to the Gurney house. After lighting a cigarette, she and her driver got back in the big green vehicle.

Gurney watched as it proceeded slowly up through the pasture to the house, where it stopped not far from his Outback, which by comparison seemed very small. Again the driver got out first and opened the rear door for the lady, who Gurney could now see was probably somewhere in her late forties. Her ash-blond hair was arranged in a short asymmetrical style that looked expensive and aggressive. After a final drag, she dropped her cigarette and crushed it into the ground with the tip of a boot that looked every bit as costly as her hairdo.

As she surveyed the property around her with a dour expression, her driver noticed Gurney standing on the patio. He said something to her, she glanced over, and then she nodded to him. She lit another cigarette.

He approached the patio. He had a hard, expressionless, ex-military look about him. For a heavy man his step was light and athletic.

"David Gurney?"

"Yes?"

"Mrs. Haley Beckert would like to speak with you."

"Dell Beckert's wife?"

"That's correct."

"Would she like to come into the house?"

"Mrs. Beckert would prefer to remain outdoors."

"Fine. We can talk right here." He gestured toward the two Adirondack chairs.

The driver returned to the Range Rover and spoke briefly to the woman. She nodded, crushed the second cigarette as she had the first, then made her way around the asparagus patch and flower bed to the patio. When they came face-to-face she looked at him with the same distaste with which she'd regarded the surrounding landscape, but with an added element of curiosity.

Neither offered to shake hands. "Would you like to sit down?" he asked.

She didn't reply.

He waited.

"Who's paying you, Mr. Gurney?" She had the syrupy voice and hard eyes of many a Southern politician.

He replied blandly, "I work for the district attorney."

"Who else?"

"Nobody else."

"So this story you've sold to Kline, this fantasy about the most respected police chief in America being a serial murderer—running around shooting people, beating people, God knows what else—all of that bilious nonsense is the product of an honest investigation?" Her voice was dripping with sarcasm.

"It's the product of evidence."

She uttered a bark of a laugh. "Evidence no doubt *discovered* by you. I've been told that from day one you did everything you could to weaken the case against that little reptile Cory Payne—and you constantly tried to undermine my husband."

"The evidence against Payne was questionable. The evidence that he was being framed was far more convincing."

"You're playing a dangerous game, Mr. Gurney. If anyone is being framed, it's Dell Beckert. I'll get to the bottom of this, I promise you. And you'll regret your part in it. *Deeply and permanently* regret it."

He didn't react, just held her gaze. "Do you know where your husband is?"

"If I did, you'd be the last person on earth I'd tell."

"Doesn't his running away strike you as peculiar?"

Her jaw muscles tightened. After regarding him venomously for a long moment she said, "I was told that a TV newsperson mentioned your name last night in connection with the election for attorney general. I don't suppose your interest in that position would explain your attacks on my husband?"

"I have no interest in that position."

"Because if that's what this is all about, I will destroy you. There will nothing left of you or your so-called supercop reputation. Nothing!"

He saw no point in trying to explain his position to her.

She turned away and walked quickly to the big SUV. She got into the rear seat, and the driver closed the door. A few moments later the Range Rover was heading silently down the uneven path toward the barn and the town road beyond it.

Gurney stood for a while on the patio, replaying the scene in his mind—the strained expression, the rigid body language, the accusatory tone. Having conducted thousands of interviews over the years with the family members of fugitives and otherwise missing persons, he had gotten good at reading these situations. He was reasonably sure that the fury Haley Beckert expressed was the product of fear, and that her fear was the product of being blindsided by events she didn't understand.

The cool, humid breezes, though still shifting direction, were growing stronger, creating the feeling of an impending thunderstorm. He went inside and closed the French doors.

Madeleine was sitting in one of the armchairs by the fireplace reading a book. She'd started a small fire, which was flickering weakly. He was tempted to rearrange the logs but he knew his interference would not be appreciated. He sat in the armchair that faced hers.

"I assume you overheard all that?" he said.

Her eyes remained on her book. "Hard not to."

"Any reaction?"

"She's used to getting her way."

He stared at the fire for a while, repressing the urge to fix it. "So. What do you think I should do?"

She looked up. "I guess that depends on whether you see the case as open or closed."

"Technically, the case remains open until Beckert is located, prosecuted, and—"

She cut him off. "I don't mean *technically*, I mean *in your own mind*."

"If you're talking about a sense of completion, I'm not there yet."

"What's missing—other than Beckert himself?"

"I can't put my finger on it. It's like trying to scratch an itch that keeps moving."

She closed her book. "You have doubts about Beckert's guilt?"

He frowned. "The evidence against him is substantial."

"The evidence against his son looked that way, too."

"Not to me. I had concerns about all of it. From the beginning."

"You have no similar concerns about the evidence against the father?"

"Not really. No."

She cocked her head curiously.

"What is it?" he asked.

"Could that have anything to do with your 'eureka' theory?"

He didn't reply. He knew not to answer too quickly when a question got under his skin.

54

On the occasions when he'd conducted seminars on criminal investigation, he'd always included a discussion of a subtle investigatorial trap he'd named "The Eureka Fallacy." Simply stated, it was the tendency to give one's own discoveries greater weight than discoveries made or reported by others, especially if the things one has discovered had been purposely concealed (hence the term *eureka*, Greek for "I have found it!"). A manifestation of the basic human tendency to trust one's own perceptions as objective and accurate and competing points of view as subjective and prone to error, it could derail an investigation and was responsible for an unknown number of wrongful arrests and prosecutions.

Even being fully aware of the phenomenon, Gurney resisted seeing it in himself. The mind has strong defenses against self-doubt. However, since Madeleine raised the question, he forced himself to take a closer look at it. Was he, in fact, applying a double standard of credibility to the evidence against Payne and the evidence against Beckert? He didn't think so, but that meant little. He would need to look at the evidence piece by piece to make sure he was subjecting all of it to the same level of scrutiny.

He got up from his chair by the fireplace, went to his desk in the den, took out the case files and his own notes, and began what he hoped would be a clear-eyed review.

By the time Madeleine interrupted the process a little after twelve to let him know she was leaving for an afternoon shift at the clinic, he had reached two conclusions.

The first, reassuringly unchanged from what it had been, was that every piece of evidence against Cory Payne could be explained away, and the switched toilet handle was as convincing proof of a frame job as one could imagine.

His second conclusion, somewhat disconcerting, was that the evidence against Beckert and/or Turlock had the same weaknesses as the evidence against Payne. It was all portable and therefore plantable. Even the items bearing fingerprints—the pen he'd found in the grass in back of the Poulter Street house, the plastic bag at Blaze Jackson's apartment—could have been acquired in an innocent environment for later use in an incriminating one. In short, although there was no proof of it—no equivalent to the switched toilet handle—it was *possible* that Beckert was also being framed. It was admittedly a rather farfetched scenario. But the evidence in hand against Beckert wasn't nearly as solid as it seemed at first glance. In fact, a clever trial lawyer might make it appear very shaky indeed.

For some time after Madeleine left, Gurney remained at his desk, staring out the den window, wondering about the advisability of raising the issue with Kline. It would not be a welcome subject. He decided to speak to Torres first.

The call was picked up immediately.

"Hey, Dave, I was just about to call you. Big morning here, lot of stuff coming in at once. Bad news first. There was no CODIS hit on the DNA from that used condom found near the Willard Park playground. So that's a dead end. But finding an eyewitness to what went down that night was always a long shot anyway. Now the good news. We got a report from the Albany computer lab on the laptop you found under a mattress in the cabin. Key discovery was a series of searches on brain structure, specifically something called the 'medulla oblongata' and the extent of protection afforded by adjacent bone structures. The kind of information—and anatomical diagrams—someone might need if they wanted to drive an ice pick into someone's brain stem. It looks like a solid link between Beckert and the attack on Loomis."

Gurney wasn't sure how solid it was, but it certainly was suggestive.

"And that's not all," continued Torres. "The lab sent us a report on the phone that was taped to the bottom of one of the footboards. The call record confirms Payne's explanation for why he was in the Bridge Street area the night Steele was shot. He claimed he'd gotten a series of texts, setting up a meeting behind the apartment building, then moving it to the other side of the bridge, then canceling it. Those texts were sent from that phone you found in the cabin."

"Interesting," said Gurney. "Kline have any reaction to that?"

"He's a happy man. He says it feels like we're finally tying the bow on the package."

Gurney's idea of a bow on the package would be a credible confession from Beckert. Kline's use of that wrapped-up image to describe the accumulation of a few extra pieces of portable-plantable evidence seemed to make the search for the perp a postscript. That could turn out to be a major mistake.

Gurney ended his call with Torres and entered Kline's number.

"David. What can I do for you?" The man's hurried tone suggested that 'nothing' would be the only welcome answer.

"I want to share a concern."

"Oh?" There was more anxiety than curiosity in that single syllable.

"I've been thinking about the evidence that appears to incriminate Beckert."

"Appears to?"

"Exactly. The evidence against Cory Payne had weaknesses that a defense attorney could have exploited at trial. Successfully, in my opinion."

"Your point being?"

"The evidence against Beckert has some of the same weaknesses."

"Nonsense. The evidence against Beckert is overwhelming."

"That's what you said three days ago about Payne."

Kline's voice was tight and cold. "Why are we having this conversation?"

"So you don't walk into a courtroom thinking you have more than you do."

"You're not suggesting that Beckert is being framed just like Payne was, are you? Tell me you're not that crazy."

"What I'm telling you is that your case isn't the slam-dunk affair you think it is. From an evidentiary point of view—"

Kline cut him off. "Fine. Point taken. Anything else?"

"Hasn't it occurred to you that there's *too much* evidence?" He could picture a half-angry, half-puzzled frown on Kline's face in the ensuing silence. He continued. "Framers want to make sure their targets look guilty as hell. So they overdo it. I can't prove that's what happened here, but you shouldn't dismiss the possibility."

"Your *possibility* is the craziest hypothesis I've ever heard. Just listen to yourself. You're saying that someone framed Cory Payne for the sniper attacks on Steele and Loomis, then framed Dell Beckert for the same attacks? Plus those on Jordan and Tooker? And Jackson and Creel? Have you ever in your life heard of any case remotely like that?"

"No."

"So . . . you just dreamed up the least likely scenario on God's earth? And decided to drop it in my lap?"

"Look, Sheridan, I'm not saying I understand what this White River mess is all about—only that it needs to be investigated further. We need a full understanding of who did what, and why. It's vital that Beckert be located and—"

"Hold on! Hold it right there! Our goal is not *a full understanding* of anything. I administer a process of criminal investigation, indictment, and prosecution. I'm not running the Ultimate Truth Psychology Club. As for finding Beckert, it's possible we never will. Frankly that wouldn't be the worst thing. He can be indicted in absentia. If the case were to end with him seen as a guilty fugitive, that would be an adequate conclusion. A well-publicized indictment can project the same sense of law-enforcement success as a guilty verdict at trial. I'll just say one more thing. It would be inadvisable for you to go public with your baseless double-frame theory. It would do nothing except create more chaos and controversy—not to mention a loss of credibility for this department and you personally. Our discussion of this topic is over."

In retrospect, Gurney found nothing surprising in Kline's reaction. Having the case careen around another curve was simply not acceptable. Kline's own public image was his ultimate concern. Procedural smoothness was a key goal. Surprises were unwelcome. Yet another course reversal was to be avoided at all cost.

If anyone were going to upend the case once again, Gurney realized he was the one who would have to find answers to the questions raised by his own unlikely hypothesis—the first of which was the most baffling.

Cui bono?

To whose advantage would it be to frame both Payne *and* Beckert?

55

Despite Hardwick's sometimes grating skepticism and verbal abuse, Gurney respected the intelligence and honesty that made him a valuable sounding board.

Rather than trying to explain his new concerns by phone, he decided, after checking with Hardwick to make sure he'd be home, to drive to his place in the hills above Dillweed later that afternoon.

The challenging grin that Gurney knew so well was already on the man's face as he opened the door. He was holding two bottles of Grolsch. He handed one to Gurney and led the way to the small round table in the corner of the front room.

"So, Davey boy, what's the story?"

Gurney took a sip of his Grolsch, set the bottle on the table, and proceeded to review the range of his own doubts and speculations. When he was finished Hardwick stared at him for a long moment before speaking.

"Am I hearing this right? You're suggesting that after someone framed Payne for the whack jobs on the cops, he also framed Beckert for the same shootings? What the hell for? As a backup if the first frame fell apart? That was his fucking plan B? And then he frames Beckert for the Jordan and Tooker murders as well? And for Jackson and Creel?"

"I realize it sounds a little off-the-wall."

"*A little?* It makes no fucking sense at all. I mean, what the hell kind of a plan is that? And who on earth would benefit from it?"

"That's my basic question. Maybe someone who hated them both and didn't care which one went down? Or maybe someone trying to drive the ultimate wedge between them? Or maybe someone who just considered them convenient scapegoats?"

"Maybe, maybe, maybe." Hardwick gazed long and hard at his Grolsch. "Look, I get the fact that somebody framed Payne. You can't argue with the toilet handle. But what makes you so sure that Beckert was framed, too? The fact that there's *too much* evidence against him? That's got to be the most absurd reason I ever heard for assuming a suspect is innocent."

"It's not just *too much* evidence. It's that it's all so convenient. Even the full-metal-jacket rounds with perfect ballistic markings. And the ease of . . ." Gurney's voice trailed off.

Hardwick looked up from his beer bottle. "What's the matter?"

"I'm thinking about the ease of recovering them. We've been thinking of that as a lucky break. But what if that was the shooter's intention?"

"His *intention*?"

"Remember the thing in the Steele video that bothered me? The laser dot?"

"What about it?"

"The delay. The two-minute delay between the sniper getting the scope dot on the back of Steele's head and the fatal shot. Why did he wait so long?"

"Who the fuck knows?"

"Suppose he was waiting for Steele to pass in front of that pine at the edge of the field?"

"For what?"

"To ensure that the bullet would be recoverable."

Hardwick's default expression of disbelief was on full display.

Gurney went on. "The same logic could apply to the Loomis shot, except in that case it was more rushed, with him coming out of his house and heading for his car. That shot happened with the front door post just behind him. Another easily recoverable round. I was there when Garrett Felder dug it out. Same thing again with the shot at the back of my house. Another intact round, easily recoverable from the porch post."

Hardwick made his acid-reflux face. "So you've got three situations with a common factor. But that's no proof of anything. In fact, it sounds like the kind of shit lawyers focus on to mind-fuck a jury."

"I know it's not conclusive. But it seems very convenient to have recovered three perfectly intact rounds with clean ballistics linking them directly to a rifle in Beckert's cabin." Gurney paused before going on. "It's like the plastic bag with the money. Why plastic? Well, unlike some paper, it just happens to hold a perfect print. Anyone with access to Beckert's home or his office could have taken a plastic bag he'd used for something else—then later put the money in it, and left it in Jackson's apartment."

"The killer just pops into Beckert's kitchen, takes a bag out of his refrigerator, makes sure there's a good print on it, than heads for Jackson's place and—?"

Gurney cut him off. "No. I'm thinking this whole White River thing was planned way ahead of time. There was nothing spontaneous or opportunistic about it. It was just made to look that way. Think about it. A white cop being shot at a racial demonstration. Followed by a pair of black men being beaten and strangled. Followed by another white cop being shot. The Black Defense Alliance being blamed for the shootings, along with Cory Payne. And the white-supremacist Gort twins, along with the so-called Knights of the Rising Sun, being blamed for Jordan and Tooker. Followed by our discoveries at the gun club—the rifle, the rope, the branding iron—suggesting that Beckert and Turlock carried out all four murders and framed Payne and the Gorts. But what if all that evidence at the gun club was planted there? The whole damn thing shows signs of having been meticulously constructed—layer upon layer of deception, all orchestrated in advance. We peel away one false layer, and we discover another false layer. I've never seen anything like it."

"Hell of a summation," said Hardwick sourly. "It's just missing a couple of details. Like *who* the fuck did all that orchestrating—and what the fuck was the *purpose* of it all?"

"I can't answer those questions. But I do know that if someone was trying to frame Beckert, he must have had access to Beckert's cabin. Maybe we could start with that."

"Oh, sure. Look into the least likely possibility first. That makes a shitload of sense."

"Humor me."

"Fine. Let's get it over with. Call his wife. She'd probably know who he was close to."

Gurney shook his head. "Haley Beauville Beckert sees everything that's happened in White River as a giant conspiracy with her husband as the victim and the rest of us as the conspirators. I doubt at this point she'd give us the time of day. But Cory might know some names."

Hardwick sighed impatiently. "Fine. Call the little fucker."

Gurney took out his phone. As he was looking for Payne's number he heard soft footsteps coming down the stairs from the second floor. A few seconds later Hardwick's on-and-off girlfriend, Esti Moreno, entered the room.

She was a strikingly attractive young woman—all the more attractive at that moment in remarkably abbreviated shorts, a tight tee shirt, and glistening ebony hair still wet from the shower. She was also a tough undercover cop.

"David! How nice to see you!"

"Hello, Esti. Nice to see you, too."

"Don't let me interrupt you. I just came down for one of those." Pointing at Gurney's Grolsch, she passed through the sitting room and went into the kitchen.

Gurney made the call to Payne.

"I have an urgent question, Cory. Do you know if your father ever brought other people out to the gun club? Other than you. Other than Turlock."

There was a short pause. "I'm pretty sure every hunting season he'd have his special people out there."

"Special people?"

"The people who could be useful to him. That's the only thing that ever made anyone *special* to him."

"And those people were . . . who exactly?"

"DA Kline, Sheriff Cloutz, Mayor Shucker, Judge Puckett."

"Anyone else?"

There was another short pause. "Yeah. Some rich guy. Marvin something. Obnoxious billionaire over in Lockenberry."

"Gelter?"

"That's it."

"How about people in the department? Anyone 'special' there?"

"Obviously Turlock. Also a captain and a couple of lieutenants who did pretty much whatever he wanted them to do."

"Like what?"

"Concocting phony cases against BDA members. Lying in court. Shit like that."

"How do you know this?"

"Some BDA people told me. That's the kind of stuff that Steele and Loomis were looking into . . . and Jordan and Tooker, too . . . which is obviously why they were all killed."

"I need their names—the captain and his lieutenants."

"Joe Beltz, Mitch Stacker, Bo Luckman."

Gurney made a note of the names. "Do you know anyone else who might have had access to your father's cabin?"

"I don't know. His wife, I guess."

"One more question. Did your father own any other real estate? Summer house, another cabin somewhere, anything like that?"

"Not that I'm aware of. But that doesn't mean anything. My father is an iceberg. Most everything about him is below the surface. Why do you ask?"

"It's a place he might be. Somewhere to stay out of sight. How about rentals? Leases? A place he might have used on hunting or fishing trips?"

"I don't think he liked fishing."

"Okay, Cory. Thanks for your help. If you think of anyone else who might have had access to his cabin, let me know."

"Absolutely."

Gurney ended the call.

Hardwick raised his Grolsch and took a long swallow. "That little fucker any help?"

"Yes and no. Apart from a growing list of unpleasant individuals—any one of whom could have seen where Beckert kept his cabin key—I'm not sure I know much more than I did before. I should get back to Mark Torres, see if he knows anything about Beckert's associates."

"Goddamn waste of time." Hardwick punctuated his comment by putting his bottle down on the table with noticeable firmness. "Focusing on people with access to the cabin isn't relevant to anything other than your double-framing idea—which is definitely on the batshit end of the hypothesis spectrum."

"You may be right. But there's no harm in asking the question." He took a sip of his Grolsch and placed the call to Torres.

"Mark, I'm trying to get a sense of the people Beckert was close to. I was given the names of three members of the WRPD command staff—Beltz, Stacker, and Luckman. What can you tell me about them?"

Torres's initial response was an uneasy hesitation. "Wait a second. Just making sure . . . there are no open ears nearby. Okay. I can't really tell you much, beyond the fact that they spent a lot of time in Beckert's office—more than most of the guys who report to him. Maybe it's my imagination, but they've been looking pretty nervous since he disappeared."

"They need to be questioned. Do you know if Kline's gotten to them yet?"

"I don't know. He's not telling us much."

"How many people does he have working on Beckert's disappearance?"

"Actively searching for him? None, as far as I know. His priority is totally on the physical evidence side. You think that's a mistake?"

"Frankly, yes. Beckert's connected to everything that's happened. And his role in the case may not be what it seems to be. Locating him could resolve some questions."

"What do you think we should be doing?"

"Everything possible to find him. I'd like to know whether he owns any other property in this part of the state. Someplace he might go if he didn't want to be found."

"We could have our county clerk check for his name in the property tax rolls."

"If you can free up a couple of uniforms, you could have them check the adjoining counties, too. They should also check the names Beauville, Turlock, and Blaze Jackson. She seems to have been involved from the beginning."

"Okay. I'll get someone on it."

"Before you go, a question about the silent alarm system at the cabin. You told me there was some password protection on the list of numbers it was programmed to call."

"Right—and computer forensics did get back to us on that. There were three cell numbers. Beckert's, Turlock's, and an anonymous prepaid. No way to track down that one."

"Not to its owner, but to its nearest cell tower when it received the alarm call. That could be helpful. In fact, you ought to get the receiving locations of the other two as well. Be interesting to know if Beckert was still in the area that morning when Turlock was killed."

"No problem. I'll get in touch with the phone company right now."

After Gurney ended the call, Hardwick asked, "Where do you think he is?"

"I have no idea, just a hope that he's still in the area."

"Kline's got an APB out on him?"

"Yes, but that's about it." Gurney paused. "I've been thinking about something you told me last week. About Beckert's family problems. You mentioned that the boot-camp school he sent Cory to was down South. Do you know where in the South? Or what the name of the school was?"

"I could find out. I know the state police guy who recommended it to Beckert."

"I was wondering if it might be in Virginia. Like Beckert's own prep school. And his wife's family. It's a state he might know well and head for if he wanted to disappear for a while."

Hardwick eyed Gurney over the top of his Grolsch bottle. "What are you suggesting?"

"Just thinking out loud."

"Horseshit. You're asking me to explore this Virginia possibility, start checking out all the places Beckert could be. Which would be an enormous pain in the ass."

Gurney shrugged. "Just a thought. While Torres is checking tax rolls in the towns around here, I'll be looking into rentals. There are no public records arranged by tenants' names, but Acme Realty might have a searchable database of renters in the White River area. I'll drop in on Laura Conway tomorrow morning."

"What's the matter with the phone?"

"Face-to-face is always better."

56

Gurney was the first one up the following day. He'd had his initial cup of coffee and put out the bird feeders before Madeleine appeared for breakfast. She had her cello with her, which reminded him that her string group was booked for a morning concert at a local nursing home.

While she was preparing a bowl of her homemade granola, he scrambled three eggs for himself. They sat down together at the breakfast table.

"Have you spoken to Thrasher?" she asked.

"No. I wasn't sure what to say. I guess we need to discuss it."

She laid down her spoon. "Discuss it?"

"Discuss whether or not to let him go ahead with his exploration of the site."

"You really think that needs to be discussed?"

He sighed, laying down his fork. "Okay. I'll tell him the answer is no."

She gave him a long look. "We live here, David. This is our home."

He waited for her to go on. But that's all she said.

The interstate portion of the drive was, as usual, relatively traffic-free. He pulled over just before the White River exit and entered Acme Realty's address in his GPS. Six minutes later it delivered him to a storefront on Bridge Street, less than a block from the first sniper location.

He found that fact interesting, then dismissed it as one of those coincidences that usually end up meaning nothing. He'd learned over the years that one of the few investigatorial mistakes worse than failing to connect crucial dots was connecting irrelevant ones.

He got out in front of the office and began to examine the listings that filled the windows. Most of them were properties for sale, but there were rentals as well—both single-family homes and apartments. The area covered by the listings extended beyond White River into neighboring townships.

The front door opened. A rotund man with a chocolate-brown toupee and a salesman's smile stepped out. "Beautiful day!"

Gurney nodded pleasantly.

The man raised a chubby hand toward the listings. "You have something in mind?"

"Hard to say."

"Well, you've come to the right place. We can make it easy. That's what we're here for. You interested primarily in buying or renting?"

"Actually, I've already spoken to Ms. Conway. Is she in?"

"She is. If you're already dealing with her, I'll leave you to it. She's one of our finest agents." He opened the door. "After you, sir."

Gurney walked into a carpeted area with an empty reception desk, a water cooler, a bulletin board with notes tacked to it, and two big tropical plants. Along the back of this area was a row of four glass-fronted cubicles with a name on each.

He'd been imagining someone young and blond. Laura Conway was middle-aged and dark-haired. She was wearing colorful rings on all ten fingers. A bright-green necklace drew attention to her already eye-catching cleavage. When she looked up from her desk, her earrings, gold disks the size of silver dollars, were set swinging. She greeted him with appraising eyes and a lipsticked smile.

"What can I do for you on this gorgeous day?"

"Hello, Laura. I'm Dave Gurney."

It took a moment for the name to register. The wattage of the smile dropped noticeably. "Oh. Yes. The detective. Is there a problem?"

"May I?" He gestured toward one of the two spare chairs in the cubicle.

"Sure." She placed her hands in front of her on the desk, interlocking her fingers.

He smiled. "I love the rings."

"What?" She glanced down at them. "Oh. Thank you."

"I'm sorry to be bothering you again, Laura. As you may have seen in the news, this crazy White River case just keeps getting crazier."

She nodded.

"Have you heard that we're trying to locate Dell Beckert, the former police chief?"

"It's all over the news shows."

"Right. So here's the thing. We suspect he might still be in the White River area. We're checking to see if he owns any local property. That's easy for us to do. But he might be renting a place, and there are no public records of renters for us to check. Then I recalled someone telling me that you folks manage most of the rentals around here. So I figured if anyone could help us out, it would be you."

She looked puzzled. "What kind of help do you want?"

"A simple tenant database search. Beckert may have leased a place himself, or he could be staying in a house or apartment leased by someone close to him. I'll give you a few names, you run them against your master file of tenants, and we'll see if you get any hits. Pretty straightforward. I already know about the apartment on Bridge Street and the house on Poulter, so I just need to know about any others beyond those." He added, "By the way, that necklace you're wearing is gorgeous. It's jade, right?"

She touched it gently with the tips of her fingers. "The highest quality jade."

"That's obvious. And it goes beautifully with those rings."

She looked pleased. "I believe appearances matter. Not everyone today agrees with that."

"Their loss," he said.

She smiled. "Do you have those names with you?"

He gave her a piece of paper listing Beckert, Beauville, Turlock, Jackson, and Jordan, plus the three ranking WRPD officers whose names Payne had provided. She placed the paper in front of her keyboard, frowned thoughtfully, and got to work. A quarter of an hour later, the printer came to life. A single page slid out, and she handed it to Gurney. "Beyond the two you mentioned, these are the only three rentals that come up in connection with those names."

The first property was a one-bedroom apartment on Bacon Street in the Grinton section of White River. It was on the top floor of a building owned by Carbo Holdings LLC. A one-year lease in the name of Marcel Jordan had begun four months earlier. The agent's name was Lily Flack. Her notes indicated that the full $4,800 annual rental had been paid in advance in cash by the tenant's representative, Blaze L. Jackson.

The second property was a single-family house in a place called Rapture Hill. It had also been leased four months earlier for one year—from the foreclosed properties division of a White River bank. The name of the lease-signing tenant was Blaze L. Jackson. The agent, Lily Flack, noted that Ms. Jackson had paid the full amount of the lease—$18,000—in cash.

The third property was an apartment in Grinton, leased to Marcel and Tania Jordan six years earlier and renewed annually every year since. That one didn't strike Gurney as having any relevance to Beckert's possible whereabouts. The other two locations, however, seemed worth looking into. He folded the sheet and put it in his jacket pocket.

Laura Conway was watching him carefully. "Is that what you wanted?"

"Yes," he said. He made no move to get up from his chair.

"Is there something else?"

"Keys. To the first apartment and to the house."

Her expression clouded. "I don't think we can give out keys."

"You want to ask your boss about that?"

She picked up her phone. Then she put it down and left the cubicle.

A couple of minutes later, the man who had greeted Gurney on the street appeared in the doorway, lips pursed. "I'm Chuck Brambledale, the manager here. You asked Laura for keys to two of our rentals?"

"We may need to enter them and we'd rather do it without causing excessive damage."

His eyes widened. "You have . . . warrants?"

"Not exactly. But I understand we have a cooperative agreement."

Brambledale stared into the middle distance for a few seconds. "Wait here."

While he was alone in the cubicle, Gurney got up and examined a framed award on the wall. It was a Tri-County Association of Real Estate Professionals certificate recognizing Laura Conway as Salesperson of the Year—ten years earlier.

Brambledale reappeared with two keys. "The silver one is for the apartment—top floor, 4B. The brass one is for the house up in Rapture Hill. You know where that is?"

"No."

"It's an unincorporated locality north of White River. You know where the gun club is? Well, it's just two or three miles farther up."

"Past Clapp Hollow?"

"Between Clapp Hollow and Bass River. Middle of nowhere." He handed the keys with obvious reluctance to Gurney. "Weird place."

"How so?"

"The property was once owned by one of those end-times cults, which is how it got named Rapture Hill. Then the cult disappeared. Right off the face of the earth. Got raptured up to heaven, some folks said. Other folks said the cult somehow ran afoul of the Gort twins, and they're all buried somewhere up there in the quarries. Only thing anyone knows for sure is that there was nobody to pay the mortgage, so now the bank's got it. Hard to sell with the isolation and the peculiar history, so they decided to rent it."

"The flowers are amazing!" Laura Conway appeared beside Brambledale. "The house itself is kind of plain, but wait till you see the flowers!"

"Flowers?" said Gurney.

"As part of our management service, we check on our rental properties at least once a month, and when we were up there two months ago we discovered that the tenant had Snook's Nursery put in these beautiful beds of petunias. And lots of hanging baskets in front of the house."

"Blaze Jackson hired Snook's Nursery to plant petunias?"

Conway nodded. "I guess to cheer the place up. After that disappearing cult business, it always felt kind of spooky up there."

Blaze Jackson? Petunias?

Mystified, Gurney thanked them both for their cooperation and returned to his car.

Although the Rapture Hill property was certainly more intriguing, it made logistical sense for him to visit the Bacon Street apartment first. He checked the printout Conway had given him and entered the address in his GPS.

He arrived there in less than three minutes.

Bacon Street had that universal quality of run-down areas—the brighter the day, the worse it looked. But at least it had escaped the arson outbreaks that had made some Grinton streets uninhabitable. The building number he was looking for was in the middle of the block. He parked in a no-parking zone by a hydrant and got out. It was a convenience when one was on police business, with the downside that it announced that one was on police business.

A man with tattooed arms and a red bandanna on his head was working on one of the ground-floor windows. He commented as Gurney approached, "Nice goddamn surprise." His voice was rough but not hostile.

"What's the surprise?"

"You're a cop, right?"

"Right. And who are you?"

"I'm superintendent for all the buildings on this block. Paul Parkman's the name."

"What surprised you, Paul?"

"In my memory, this is the first time they sent anyone the same morning we called."

"You called the police? What for?"

He pointed to a pried-apart security grating on the window. "Bastards broke in during the night. Vacant apartment, nothing to steal. So they shit on the floor. Two of them. Two separate piles of shit. Maybe you can get some DNA?"

"Interesting idea, Paul. But that's not why I'm here."

"No?" He uttered a sharp bark of a laugh. "Then what *are* you here for?"

"I need to check one of the apartments. Top floor, 4B. You know if it's occupied?"

"Yes and no."

"Meaning?"

"Yes, there's officially a tenant. No, they're never here."

"Never?"

"Not to my knowledge. What is it you want to check? You think someone's dead in there?"

"I doubt it. Any obstructions on the stairs?"

"Not to my knowledge. You want me to come up with you?"

"No need for that. I'll call you if I need you."

Gurney entered the building. The tiled foyer was reasonably clean, the staircase adequately lighted, and the all-too-common tenement odors of cabbage, urine, and vomit blessedly faint. The top-floor landing had been mopped in the not-too-distant past, and the two apartment doors on it were legibly marked—4A at one end, 4B at the other.

He pulled his Beretta out of its ankle holster, chambered a round, and clicked off the safety. He stood to the side of the 4B door and knocked on it. There was no response, no sound at all. He knocked harder, this time shouting, "Police! Open the door!"

Still nothing.

He inserted the key, turned the lock, and pushed the door open. He was struck immediately by the musty odor of a space whose windows hadn't been opened for a very long time. He clicked the safety back on and slipped the Beretta into his jacket pocket. He switched on the ceiling light in the small entry hall and began making his way around the rather cramped apartment.

There was a small eat-in kitchen, a small living room, and a small bedroom and a closet-sized bathroom—all looking out over a weedy vacant lot. There was no furniture nor any other sign of habitation. And yet Blaze Jackson, supposedly acting for Jordan, had paid cash for a yearlong lease.

Had the place already served some purpose and been abandoned? Or was it intended for some future use? He stood at the living room window pondering the situation. The view from that window included some of Grinton, some of Bluestone, a narrow slice of Willard Park, and—he'd almost missed it through the hazy glass—the front of the police headquarters building. As he watched, a uniformed cop came out the main door, got into a squad car in the parking lot, and drove off.

His mind jumped to the obvious explanation that the apartment had been leased as a third potential sniper site. Why the other two had been used instead was a question that would need more thought. At the moment, however, it was outweighed by his desire to visit Rapture Hill. Perhaps when they were considered together the purpose of each location would become clearer.

57

Gurney by nature tended to go where his curiosity drew him without being overly concerned about backup. Oddities and discrepancies attracted his attention, arousing a desire to examine them more closely, even under conditions that might give others pause. In fact, it was his intention to proceed directly to the house at the end of Rapture Hill Road and no doubt that's what he would have done, if Madeleine had not called while he was on his way.

She said she had no special reason for calling him, just a free moment and was wondering what he was doing. As he answered in some detail she was silent; he sensed the situation he was describing was making her uncomfortable.

Finally she said, "I don't think you should go there alone. It's too isolated. You don't know what you could be walking into."

She was right, of course. And while at another time he might have dismissed her concern, he was now inclined to be guided by it. At the next intersection he pulled over in front of an abandoned farm stand. The faded word "Pumpkins" appeared on a deteriorating sign.

He thought about the possibilities for backup. Any solution involving Kline, the WRPD, or the sheriff's department would create its own set of problems. He decided to try Hardwick.

"Rapture Hill? The fuck are you talking about?"

"I'm talking about a house in the middle of nowhere, where Dell Beckert might possibly be holed up."

"What makes this a possibility?"

"The house was leased by Blaze Jackson, who almost certainly had some sort of relationship with Beckert. She paid the eighteen-thousand-dollar annual rent in advance. I doubt she had access to that kind of money herself, but I'm sure Beckert did. And the house is just a few miles from the gas station where his Durango was sighted a day or so after he disappeared. So it's worth a look."

"If you don't mind wasting your time, go look."

"I intend to."

"So what's the problem?"

"A possible welcoming committee."

Hardwick paused for a moment. "You want Uncle Jack to ride shotgun again to cover your cowardly ass."

"Something like that."

"If the son of a bitch is there, maybe I could find a reason to pop him."

"I'd rather you didn't."

"You're taking the joy out of this. The only upside of riding shotgun is getting to fire the fucking thing."

"Well, there's a chance we might run into the Gorts."

"Okay. Where do I find you?"

The meeting place Gurney chose, after consulting Google Maps on his phone, was the intersection of a winding wilderness lane called Rockton Way and the starting point of Rapture Hill Road. When he got there he parked in a weedy space between the road surface and the evergreen woods.

According to his dashboard clock, a quarter of an hour had now passed since his call with Hardwick. He figured it would take Jack another half hour to make the trip from Dillweed. He fought an urge to proceed at least part of the way up Rapture Hill on his own. Not only would that defeat the purpose of having called Hardwick, it would increase the level of risk in return for no benefit other than learning thirty minutes sooner whatever there was to be learned.

He tilted his seat back and waited, occupying his mind with various permutations of who might have set up whom for each of the seven murders and why. He kept coming back to the question that had been haunting him for some time. Did the murders necessitate the apparent frame jobs, or were the frame jobs the goal that necessitated the murders? And did the same answer apply to each case?

After twenty-five minutes, he heard the welcome rumble of Hardwick's GTO pulling in behind him. He got out to meet him.

The man's favorite weapon, his Sig Sauer, was strapped on over the black tee shirt that had become as characteristic a part of him as those unsettling pale-blue eyes. In his left hand he carried a scoped AK-47 assault rifle.

"Just in case things get interesting," he said with a manic gleam in his eye that might have unnerved someone who didn't know him as well as Gurney did.

"Thanks for coming."

He coughed up a wad of phlegm and spit it onto the dirt road. "Before I forget to mention it—I got in touch with that boarding school Cory got sent to in Virginia, plus Beckert's old prep school. Nobody at either place had any idea if Beckert owned any property down there. I spoke to half a dozen county clerks in the areas around those schools and the areas around the Beauville family tobacco farms, but none of them would give me the time of day. So much for that—unless you want to spend the next week of your life in the ass end of that state going over tax rolls. Which I think would be an incredibly stupid idea."

"Nobody would tell you anything?"

"The psychologist at Cory's boarding school told me Cory was a lot like his father."

"In what way?"

"Strong-willed. Determined. Precise. Controlling."

"No details?"

"Confidentiality laws. Closest she came to anything specific was to say that his mother's death had a major impact on him."

"Nothing we didn't know already. Right now I'm more interested in Beckert. I presume he was involved in his son's intake interview. She say anything about him?"

"Strong-willed. Determined. Precise. Controlling."

"Okay. So much for that. Hopefully our visit here isn't another dead end."

Hardwick peered up the rutted road leading into the pine forest. "How far's the house?"

"Little over a mile, according to the satellite map. All uphill."

"We walk or drive?"

"Walk. Less chance of getting stuck, and it'll give whoever might be there less notice of our—" He stopped as his eye caught a tiny glint of reflected light in a tree not far up the road. "If that's what I think it is, we can forget about the element of surprise."

Hardwick followed Gurney's gaze. "Security camera?"

"Looks like it."

They soon discovered that the reflection had indeed come from a security camera—a sophisticated model mounted about twelve feet off the ground on the trunk of a giant hemlock.

Hardwick peered up at it. "Axion Five Hundred," he said with a combination of admiration and concern. "Motion-activated recording, satellite-based transmission. You want me to put a bullet in it?"

"No point. I drove into its field of view at least half an hour ago. If Beckert or anyone else is at the house, they already know we're here."

Hardwick nodded unhappily, and they continued moving forward.

As the ascent grew steeper and their progress slowed, a new theory began to take shape in Gurney's mind. He decided to talk it out with Hardwick as they trudged along.

"Suppose that Beckert was the target from the beginning."

Hardwick made a face. "You mean everyone was killed just so the sainted police chief could be framed for their murders?"

"I don't know about *everybody*. Let's say Steele, Loomis, Jordan, and Tooker. It may be that Turlock, Jackson, and Creel were just loose ends that needed to be cleaned up."

"If Beckert was the target, what about Payne? Why was he framed first?"

"Maybe the ultimate purpose of that had nothing to do with Payne himself. Maybe it was just a way of damaging his father."

"Damaging him how?"

"Politically. In that world, having a cop-killer son would seem to be a career-ender. Whoever engineered it couldn't have anticipated Beckert turning it around into a plus."

Hardwick looked unconvinced. "So what then?"

"Then, when the killer realizes the evil-son angle isn't working out as planned, he takes all the physical evidence related to the first four murders and plants it out at the cabin, making it seem not only that Beckert was the murderer, but that he'd attempted to frame his own son for Steele and Loomis and the Gort brothers for Jordan and Tooker."

Hardwick broke out in a sharp laugh. "You've got a hell of an imagination."

"I'm just saying *maybe* that's what happened. I have no proof."

Hardwick grimaced. "Seems . . . diabolical. If you're right, whoever set it up had no qualms about the murders and no qualms about the possibility of Cory spending the rest of his life in jail. All that just to mess up Beckert's life? Seems out of proportion."

"Even if I'm wrong about the motive, or about Beckert being the ultimate intended victim, the fact is that at least seven people have ended up dead, and some evil bastard killed them."

A silence fell between them, broken by the ringing of Gurney's phone.

The screen said it was Torres.

Gurney stopped where he was to take the call.

Torres's voice was low and rushed. "New ball game. Kline just heard from Beckert. He wants to turn himself in."

"When?"

"Today. The exact time depends on how soon we can make the arrangements he wants."

"Arrangements?"

"Beckert wants certain people to be present, people he considers trustworthy witnesses. He says he doesn't want what happened to Turlock to happen to him."

"Who are these witnesses?"

"His wife, Haley; a wealthy political donor by the name of Marvin Gelter; Sheriff Cloutz; Mayor Shucker; and the WRPD captain you asked me about."

"Quite a committee. Where is this surrender supposed to occur?"

There was a moment's hesitation. "At the location where he's been staying since he dropped out of sight."

"That's not exactly an answer."

"I know. I'm sorry about that. Kline briefed a few of us and said it was confidential and that absolutely no details were to go to anyone else. He mentioned you, specifically."

Gurney saw an opportunity to find out if he was in the right place. "Kline doesn't want me to know about the house on Rapture Hill Road?"

There was a moment of dead silence. "What did you say?"

"You heard me."

"But . . . how . . . how did you know . . ."

"Doesn't matter. The thing is, I'm approaching the house right now. Tell Kline I'm here—and that I want to know what his plan is, so I don't louse it up."

"Jesus. Let me go find him. I'll ask him to call you."

Gurney turned to Hardwick and filled him in on the situation.

"Beckert wants to turn himself in? And then what? Confess to seven murders, then run for AG anyway, based on the impressive honesty of his confession?"

"At this point, who the hell knows—"

His phone rang, Kline's name was on the screen.

"Gurney here."

Kline was nearly shouting. "How the hell did you know where Beckert was? And why didn't you notify me the instant you found out?"

"I didn't *know* where he was. I was following a hunch."

"Where the hell are you?"

"On Rapture Hill Road, not far from the house."

"Don't get any closer. In fact, don't do a goddamn thing. This surrender is a big deal. As big as they come. I'm running the operation personally. Nothing happens before I get there. You read me?"

"Things may happen that require a response."

"That's not what I mean. You are to take no initiatives. None. You understand?"

"I do."

"That's good. I repeat, *do nothing*. I'm on my way."

58

Gurney passed Kline's comments along to Hardwick.

He bared his teeth in disgust. "Kline's a pathetic little shit."

"But he's right about this being a big deal," said Gurney. "Especially if the surrender is accompanied by a confession."

"Which would knock your Beckert-as-victim theory on its ass."

"If it gets us to the truth, that's fine with me."

"So what do we do until the cavalry arrives? Stand here holding our dicks?"

"We get off this road, stay out of sight, get closer to the house. After that . . . we'll see."

As they made their way up through the woods, the terrain began to level out. Soon they were able to glimpse through the hemlocks what appeared to be a mowed clearing. Using the drooping branches as a screen, they moved forward until they had a good view of a plain white farmhouse in the middle of a bright-green lawn. Next to the house was a garage-sized shed. Almost all the space in front of the house was filled with mulched beds and hanging baskets of red petunias.

"So what now?" muttered Hardwick.

"We treat this as a stakeout. See if anyone enters or leaves."

"What if they do?"

"That depends on who they are."

"That's clear as mud."

"Like life. Let's take diagonal positions out of sight where we can watch the house without any cameras watching us." Gurney pointed through the woods. "You go around that way to a point where you can see the left side of the house and the back. I'll keep an eye on the front and right side. Give me a call when you've picked your spot."

He put his phone on Vibrate so there'd be no chance of the ring giving away his location. Hardwick did the same.

Gurney made his way through the trees to a place that gave him good cover while affording decent views of the house and the shed. From his position he could see a small, very new-looking satellite dish mounted on the corner of the house. He also became aware of the muffled drone of a generator. As his ears became accustomed to the hum, he realized that he was also hearing a voice. It was too faint to identify any words, but as he listened he concluded that what he was hearing was the cadence of a TV newscaster. Under the intense circumstances, it seemed odd that Beckert would be watching television—unless, perhaps, he was expecting some announcement of his impending surrender.

Gurney's phone vibrated. It was Hardwick.

"Reporting as requested. I just breathed in a goddamn gnat. Fucking thing is in my lungs."

"At least it wasn't a wasp."

"Or a bird. Anyway, I'm in position. Now what?"

"Tell me something. If you listen carefully, can you hear something that sounds like a TV news show?"

"I hear a generator."

"That's all?"

"That's all. But I do have a thought about your double-frame theory. Your idea that all this White River shit was ultimately devised to destroy Beckert raises a big cui bono question."

"I'm aware of that."

"You also aware of the answer?"

"No. But it sounds like you are."

Hardwick inserted a dramatic pause before replying. "Maynard Biggs."

Gurney was unimpressed. His recollection of Biggs as an honest, smart, compassionate man made him an unlikely multiple murderer. "Why Biggs?"

"He's the only one who seems to benefit in any practical way from the destruction of Beckert. Remove the famous law-and-order police chief, and Biggs wins the AG election without breaking a sweat."

It didn't feel right, but he was determined to keep an open mind. "It's a possibility. The problem is—"

He stopped speaking at the sound of a vehicle, maybe more than one, coming up the dirt road. "Hang on, Jack, we have visitors."

He shifted his position in the woods for a better view of the opening where the road entered the clearing. The first vehicle to appear was Mark Torres's Crown Victoria. The second was an unmarked black van, and that was followed by a dark nondescript SUV. They parked in a row at the edge of the clearing, facing the house. No one got out.

Gurney got back on the phone with Hardwick. "Can you see them from where you are?"

"Yeah. The van looks like SWAT. What do you think they're planning to do?"

"Not much until Kline arrives. And there are other invitees coming to this party, assuming he got in touch with them. Let me check with Torres and get back to you."

Torres picked up on the first ring.

"Dave? Where are you?"

"Nearby, but out of sight, which is the way I'd like to keep it for a while. Do you guys have a plan?"

"Kline's calling the shots. Nothing happens until everyone gets here."

"Who's with you now?"

"SWAT and Captain Beltz. The mayor and the sheriff are being driven by a deputy in the sheriff's car. Mr. Gelter is coming separately. Mrs. Beckert's chauffeur is bringing her."

"What about Kline?"

"He's on his way. By himself, far as I know."

"Anyone else?"

"No. Well, yes, in a way. The RAM-TV people."

"*What?*"

"Another of Beckert's conditions. More witnesses."

"Kline agreed to that?"

"*Agreed* to it? He *loves* it."

"Jesus."

"Another piece of news. You asked about the locations of the phones that received calls from the alarm system at Beckert's cabin when you and Hardwick were there. The calls went to Beckert's phone, to Turlock's, and to an anonymous prepaid. Beckert's was turned off at the time, which makes sense if he was already on the run, so we have no location on that. Turlock's was on, and the call was received through the Larvaton cell tower, which is the closest one to his house. It would explain why he showed up at the gun club that morning. No surprise there. The interesting one is the call to the prepaid. It was received through the White River tower, and thirty seconds later a call was made from that same prepaid to a phone registered to Ezechias Gort."

This was no surprise to Gurney, having assumed that someone with reason to believe that Turlock would be present had notified one of the Gorts, but having it confirmed was encouraging. "Thanks for pursuing that, Mark. It's a nice change of pace when something in this damn case makes sense."

At the sound of another vehicle coming up the hill, they ended the call.

A maroon Escalade entered the clearing and came to a stop next to the Crown Victoria. A sheriff's deputy got out of the driver's seat and tapped on Torres's window. After conferring for a few moments, he got back in the Escalade. For the ensuing quarter of an hour there was no other activity in the line of vehicles and no sound but the persistent hum of the generator and, at least to Gurney's ear, the almost subliminal intonations of a cable news program.

Then Kline arrived in his Navigator, got out with a brisk man-in-command air about him, and paid a quick visit to each of the other vehicles. He was wearing a too-large windbreaker made of the stiff dark-blue fabric favored by most law-enforcement agencies. Across the back in bold letters were the words DISTRICT ATTORNEY.

He returned to the Navigator and stood in front of it, feet planted wide apart—the image of a conquering hero, had it not been for the oversize jacket making him look unusually small. Gurney was watching closely from his spot at the near edge of the woods as Kline took out his phone.

Gurney's phone vibrated. He looked at the screen and took the call. "Hello, Sheridan. What's the plan?"

Kline looked around the clearing. "Where are you?"

"Out of sight, keeping an eye on the house."

"This is a surrender, not a battle."

"Has he confessed to anything?"

"To everything. Everything except the Turlock homicide."

"Why would he confess?"

"What difference does it make? The fact is, he did. We have it in writing."

"In writing? How—"

Kline broke in impatiently. "Phone text. Electronic thumbprint attached."

"Did you ever actually speak to him?"

"On the phone, briefly. There was noise in the background—probably that generator—which made it hard to hear him. I didn't want any future disputes over what was said. So I told him to spell it out in a text, and that's what he did."

"And in that text he confessed to six murders?"

"He did."

"You have no concerns about that?"

"I'm delighted with it. Obviously you're not. Is that because it makes your idea that he was a helpless victim, framed by some Machiavellian genius, sound totally ridiculous?"

Gurney ignored the snark. "I'm concerned about it for two reasons. First, whatever else Beckert may be, he isn't stupid. But confessing to multiple murders with no deal on the table is very stupid. It makes me wonder what's going on. Second, I've been thinking about what drew me into this case to begin with—that message on Steele's phone. I'm pretty sure it wasn't what it seemed to be."

Kline's voice on the phone was clipped and angry. "It was exactly what it seemed to be—a warning to watch his back, which turned out to be very good advice. He just didn't get it in time."

"Maybe he wasn't meant to."

"What's that supposed to mean?"

"The message was sent to his personal phone after he left for work—where he used the department-issued BlackBerry. So maybe the message wasn't meant to be found until after he was killed."

"*After?* For what purpose?"

"To point us toward the WRPD, and ultimately Beckert. Of course that would mean that the sender knew in advance that Steele would be killed. The so-called warning could have been the first subtle piece in the plot to incriminate Beckert."

"Very clever. That's what you're all about, Gurney, isn't it? One damn clever theory after another. Too bad this one is obvious nonsense. Maybe you didn't hear me. WE HAVE A CONFESSION! Do I need to keep repeating that?"

In the hope that he might be able to better communicate his concerns face-to-face, Gurney ended the call and made his way out of his concealed position in the woods—which was starting to feel a bit ridiculous—and made his way over to Kline, whose exasperated expression offered zero encouragement.

"Look, Sheridan, I appreciate your position," Gurney began, trying to sound as accommodating as possible. "I just think—"

He was interrupted by the deep growl of a finely tuned twelve-cylinder engine. It was Marv Gelter arriving in his classic red Ferrari.

The instant Kline saw Gelter he gave Gurney a dismissive wave of his hand and strode over to the Ferrari. When Gelter got out of the car, they engaged in a brief frowning discussion, Kline gesturing in an explanatory way toward the house. Then Gelter spotted Gurney and came over to him, leaving Kline staring after him.

His smile was as hard-edged as the scraping timbre of his voice. "Time flies, my friend. You owe me an answer. I hope it's the right one."

Gurney responded to the man's intensity with a bland shrug. "The truth is, I'm afraid I'd make a lousy candidate and an even worse attorney general."

"Hah! That's exactly the kind of statement that'll get you elected. The reluctant hero. No pretenses. Like a humble fucking astronaut. What a gift! And you don't even know you have it. That's the magic of it."

Before Gurney could articulate a more definitive refusal, a large satellite-transmission media van pulled into the clearing, followed by a big Chevy SUV, both bearing the same promotional identification in red-white-and-blue lettering:

RAM-TV—ON THE SPOT

WHERE NEWS IS BREAKING!

As Stacey Kilbrick stepped out of the SUV, Kline hurried over to greet her.

"Circus time," said Gelter. With a wink at Gurney he went over to join Kline and Kilbrick.

A restless breeze was beginning to stir. Gurney looked up and saw that a bank of clouds was slowly moving in from the west. The darkening sky lent a chilling visual effect to a situation that was making him increasingly uneasy. The fact that no one seemed to share his apprehension was only making it worse.

59

What went on for the next fifteen or twenty minutes looked to Gurney a lot more like the choreography of a media event than the securing of a site for a police operation.

As Kline, Gelter, and Kilbrick were conferring, one of her assistants was fussing with her hair, and a member of the TV crew was affixing a microphone to the collar of her blazer. Another crew member was working with the camera operator to pick a spot for her to stand that would show the house and the array of flower baskets in the background.

Meanwhile Mayor Shucker and Sheriff Cloutz had emerged from the Escalade and were standing next to it. Cloutz was rocking his white cane back and forth like a metronome. Shucker was eating a doughnut. Captain Beltz was leaning on the open door of his Explorer, smoking a cigarette with fierce inhalations.

Kilbrick took her place in front of the camera, adopted a highly energized and concerned expression, cleared her throat, gave the camera operator a nod, and began speaking.

"This is Stacey Kilbrick on location with a special edition of *NewsBreakers*. Due to a startling development in the White River multiple-murder case, we're delaying until this evening the celebratory Mother's Day interviews originally scheduled for this time slot. Instead, we're bringing you—live and unedited—the final bizarre twist in this sensational case. We've just learned that fugitive police chief Dell Beckert, allegedly responsible for at least six of the seven recent White River homicides, is about to turn himself in to District Attorney Sheridan Kline—who's here with me right now."

Kline straightened his large jacket and, following a crew member's silent direction, took a position on Kilbrick's right.

She turned toward him. "I understand the hunt for Dell Beckert may be over."

Kline produced a grim smile. "It looks that way. We've been closing in on him, and I guess he saw the writing on the wall."

"Is it true that you've secured a confession?"

"Yes. A bare-bones confession. We have the essentials, and we expect he'll be providing the details in the days to come."

"When do you expect him to come out of the house and be taken into custody?"

"As soon as his wife arrives. His agreement to surrender peacefully and make a full confession came with the request that it occur in the presence of trustworthy witnesses. It's quite an irony that this man who was willing to take the law into his own hands is now afraid that someone might do the same thing to him."

As Kline was speaking, two more vehicles entered the clearing. They were stopped by Torres, who conferred briefly with each driver and then directed them to the end of the row of vehicles already present. Gurney recognized Haley Beauville Beckert's imposing green Range Rover. The second car was a beige Camry. It had the look of a rental.

Cory Payne emerged from it, caught Gurney's eye, and raised his hand in an urgent gesture. They made their way toward each other and met beside the RAM-TV van.

Payne looked agitated, running on nervous energy. "I got this weird message from my father. It sounds like he's gone totally crazy."

He showed Gurney the text on the screen of his iPhone, reading it aloud at the same time. "I've done what I've done for a greater good. Men of principle must act. I will surrender and explain everything on the top of Rapture Hill at 3:00 PM."

Gurney found the message as disconcerting in its brevity as in its content. Before he could comment on it, Kline came striding over, demanding to know why Payne was there.

He showed him the text.

Kline read it twice and shook his head. His agitation level seemed to be rising by the minute. "Look, there's obviously something going on with him. Mentally. Emotionally. Whatever. But that's neither here nor there. The fact is he's surrendering. That's the part that matters. Let's not get distracted. Cory, I'd advise you to stay back out of the way. In fact, that's an order. I don't want any surprises." He took a deep breath and looked around the clearing. "The people Beckert requested have all arrived. In another few minutes we'll be gathering them in front of the house. At that point he should present himself . . . and this goddamn nightmare will be over!"

He took another deep breath and headed over to the Range Rover to greet Beckert's wife.

Kilbrick, meanwhile, was interviewing Dwayne Shucker in the area staked out by the TV crew about fifty feet from the house. Seeing Kline gesturing to her, Kilbrick concluded the interview and looked directly into the camera. "After these important announcements, we'll be back with the event we've all been waiting for—the dramatic surrender of the White River killer."

Kilbrick went to join Kline along with the three members of her crew. From their gestures and the way they were sizing up the large area in front of the house, Gurney concluded they were deciding on how the imminent appearance of Beckert, the positioning of the witnesses, and the actual movement of the man into Kline's custody should be stage-managed for maximum clarity and dramatic impact. At one point he overheard the camera operator questioning how much screen space should be devoted to the floral display.

At the same time, Torres was talking to Beckert's requested safe-passage committee—his wife, Haley; Sheriff Cloutz; Captain Beltz; Marv Gelter; and Mayor Shucker, fresh from his truncated interview with Kilbrick.

The four SWAT team members had come out of their unmarked van and were leaning against it with alert, impassive expressions. The sky was growing darker, and the petunia baskets were moving ever so slightly in the shifting breezes. The generator continued to hum in the background, nearly extinguishing that faint sound of a television voice.

There was something profoundly wrong about it all that had Gurney on edge.

The media aspect, of course, was surreal. But that was the least of it. The whole situation had a warped feeling about it—more like a bad dream than the culmination of a successful investigation.

Just then he overheard Kline telling Kilbrick and her crew that he was going to move his vehicle into a better position to receive Beckert when he was escorted from the front door of the house.

When Kline stepped away and headed for the Navigator, Gurney intercepted him. As disorganized as his thoughts were and as closed-minded as Kline had become, he felt compelled to share his concerns.

"Sheridan, we need to talk."

Kline eyed him coldly. "What now?"

"Listen. Tell me what you hear."

"What are you talking about?"

"Two sounds. The generator. And a television."

Kline looked furious. But he listened, then nodded impatiently. "Okay, I hear something. A radio, television, something. What of it?"

"I'm certain it's the sound of a television. And it's obviously coming from the house."

"Fine. What's your point?"

"Doesn't it seem odd to you that Beckert would be spending the last few minutes of his life as a free man watching television?"

"Maybe he's watching the news, seeing what's being said about him."

"That can't be very pleasant. He's being excoriated. Publicly ripped to pieces. Portrayed as a serial murderer, a self-righteous maniac, a framer of innocent people, a complete law-and-order fraud. The image that meant everything to him is being flushed down the toilet. The world is being told that Dell Beckert is a despicable criminal nutcase, and that his life was a total lie. You think that's what he wants to listen to?"

"Jesus Christ, Gurney. How should I know what he wants to listen to? Maybe it's a form of self-hatred. Self-punishment. Who the hell knows. I'm about to take this man into custody. End of story."

Kline brushed past Gurney and got into the Navigator. Easing it out of its position in the row of vehicles, he moved it to a spot where the camera could follow Beckert's progress from the front door through the floral area and across fifty or sixty feet of lawn to the Navigator's open rear door.

As he watched Kline making his preparations for his moment of televised law-enforcement glory, Gurney's uneasiness increased, and the what-ifs multiplied in his mind.

What if all this, including Beckert's confession, was some sort of elaborate ruse?

What if Kline's view of the case and Gurney's own view of it were both wrong?

What if Beckert wasn't even in that house?

As his list of what-ifs grew longer, he eventually came to a particularly troubling one that an early mentor in the NYPD had drilled into him. He could picture the man's hard Irish face and bright-blue eyes. He could hear the ironic challenge in his voice:

What if the perp intended you to discover everything you've discovered in order to lead you to where you are right now?

As Kline was making his way back to Kilbrick, Gurney stopped him again with a rising sense of urgency. "Sheridan, you need to reconsider the level of risk here. It may be higher than you think."

"If you're worried about your safety, feel free to leave."

"I'm worried about the safety of everyone here."

As they were speaking, Torres was ushering the chosen five witnesses toward the house. A concerned backward glance from Haley Beckert suggested she'd heard Gurney's comment.

"Christ," muttered Kline, "keep your voice down."

"Keeping my voice down won't diminish the risk."

Kline bridled visibly. "I have a fully equipped SWAT team here. Plus Captain Beltz. Plus Detective Torres. I have my own sidearm. I presume you do as well. I think we're in a position to handle any surprises." He started to walk away.

Gurney called after him. "Has it occurred to you that Beckert's main supporters are all here?"

Kline stopped and turned. "So what?"

"Suppose they're not here for the reason you think they are. Suppose you're dead wrong about the whole point of this."

Kline took a step toward Gurney and lowered his voice. "I'm warning you—if you sabotage our arrangements, if you do anything that impedes Beckert's surrender, I'll personally prosecute you for obstruction of justice."

"Sheridan, the confession makes no sense. The surrender makes no sense. Something god-awful is going on that we're not seeing."

"Damnit! One more word . . . one more syllable of this craziness . . . and I'll have you removed."

Gurney said nothing. He saw Haley Beckert watching him with an intensely curious frown. She detached herself from the group Torres had assembled in a semicircle around the entrance to the house and walked back across the lawn toward Gurney and Kline.

A second later, the world exploded.

60

It took Gurney a moment to grasp the nature of the event.

A deafening blast, a physical shock wave slamming the side of his body facing the house, the stinging impact of what felt like birdshot to the side of his face and neck, the air full of flying dirt and dust and the caustic odor of dynamite—all this at once—followed by a sharp ringing in his ears that made the cries around him sound far away.

As the dust began to settle, the horror gradually came into focus.

Across the lawn on the smoldering, flattened grass lay Dwayne Shucker, Goodson Cloutz, and Joe Beltz—recognizable mainly by the intact pieces of clothing that clung to their shattered bodies. Even from some distance away Gurney could see with a surge of nausea that Shucker's nose and jaw were gone. Beltz's entire head was missing. Cloutz's intestines were exposed. His right hand still gripped his white cane, but the hand was at least a yard from the bleeding stump of a wrist. Marvin Gelter, spread-eagled on his back, was covered with so much blood it was impossible to tell where it was coming from.

Torres was still on his feet, but barely so. He moved slowly toward the carnage, checking, it seemed, for signs of life like a medic on a devastated battlefield.

Haley Beckert was on her hands and knees about fifteen feet from Gurney. Her back, covered with dirt, was heaving with her rapid gasps. Her driver arrived at a run from the Range Rover and knelt beside her. He said something and she nodded. She looked around, coughing.

As more of Gurney's hearing returned, he became aware of half-stifled yelps of pain behind him. He turned and saw that the four SWAT cops who'd been leaning against their van had all suffered some damage to their vision. They'd apparently all been looking toward the group in front of the house at the moment of the explosion, and all were hit in the face and eyes by the propelled dirt and debris.

One had dropped his assault rifle, and, as Gurney watched, he tripped over it and fell to the ground, cursing. Another with no rifle in sight was bent over, grimacing, trying to clear his vision. Another was walking in circles, holding his rifle in one hand, the fingertips of the other hand against his closed eyes, alternately groaning through clenched teeth and calling out, "What the fuck happened?" The fourth was standing with his back to the van, blinking hard, wincing, stumbling, trying to hold his rifle in a ready position, shouting repeatedly, "Answer me! Someone answer me!"

Cory Payne was on his knees in front of his car, bent over, patting the ground, apparently feeling for something he'd dropped.

Gurney ran over to him. "You all right?"

He looked up, dirt on his face, eyes tearing and half closed. "What the hell happened?"

"Explosion!"

"What? Was anyone hurt?"

"Yes."

"Who?"

"Can't tell."

Cory was breathing fast, sounding panicked. "Can you see my phone?"

Gurney glanced around. "No."

"I have to find it."

Torres, in the midst of the human wreckage, called to Gurney in a shaky voice, "This one has a pulse! I can feel it. He's breathing, too. Shallow breaths, but breathing. Jesus!"

He was crouching next to Gelter's blood-soaked body, his fingertips on the side of the man's neck. "I can't tell where he's bleeding from. What should I do?"

"Call headquarters," cried Gurney. "Tell them to notify the local EMTs, state police, sheriff's department. Message is: major crime scene, use of high explosives, multiple homicides. Sheriff, mayor, and a police captain all down."

Torres straightened up, breathing hard, and took out his phone. Gurney could have made the call himself, of course, but he knew that following simple orders could steady a man, and it looked like Torres needed some steadying.

At that point Gurney noted that the front windows of the house had been blown in. He also realized that something was missing. The hanging baskets of petunias were gone. Obliterated. And most of the shepherd's crooks on which they'd been hung had been flattened to the ground. So now he knew where the explosives had been positioned. And why the request for the "trustworthy witnesses" had specified that they be brought to the front of the house.

After Torres completed his task, Gurney asked him to do one more thing—call the department's contact at the phone company and arrange for an immediate ping—a three-tower triangulation—to determine the precise current location of Beckert's phone.

Torres looked puzzled. "Wouldn't it have to be with him in the house?"

Gurney had no time to explain. "Just make that ping happen *now.*"

While Torres complied with the request, Gurney continued his rapid survey of the scene. Two members of the TV crew were holding on to the front door of the RAM van. Kilbrick's camera operator, however, was still operating his camera. He was prowling around the lawn with a war-zone reporter's intensity, panning here, panning there, zooming in on bodies and body parts, capturing it all. Kilbrick herself appeared to be rooted in one spot. The only movements Gurney could discern were small and tremor-like. She appeared to be looking wide-eyed at something in front of her feet.

That's when he heard the howling. It was somewhere out in the woods. Distance and direction were hard to pin down. Coyotes, most likely, disturbed by the blast. Or it might be the Gorts' pack of pit bulls, a more disconcerting possibility. He checked the Beretta in his jacket pocket. For one hallucinatory moment as he was scanning the edges of the clearing he thought he saw the Gort twins themselves in the dark shadows of the hemlocks—one tall, one short, both gaunt and bearded. But when he looked again there was no one there.

He returned his attention to what was in the clearing itself. In addition to the house windows, the explosion had blown in the door of the adjacent shed, revealing the Durango with its distinctive CBIIWRPD vanity plate. An acute moment of déjà vu intruded into Gurney's already overloaded consciousness. He was sure it had nothing to do with having seen the plate number displayed during Kline's recent RAM-TV interview. Whatever the connection was, it wasn't that direct. But there was no time now to figure it out. Figuring out the who and the why behind what had just happened was a hell of a lot more urgent.

He saw Kline coming toward him. Perhaps the explosion and resulting slaughter had finally opened the man's mind. There was a bewildered look in his eyes. "Have you called it in?"

"Torres did."

"Good. We'll get . . . get reinforcements, right?"

Gurney took a long look at him and realized he was in some kind of shock, and not entirely present. Maybe a sense of personal responsibility for what had happened had begun to dawn on him and something in his brain shut down. There seemed to be little use in engaging Kline in a discussion at this point.

When the EMTs arrived they could deal with Kline. In the meantime he suggested that Kline stay by his Navigator, so people could find him easily when they needed him. Kline seemed to think this was a good idea. In the meantime, Gurney had the feeling that lives were still at stake. He looked around, deciding on the next move.

A high-pitched whine drew his attention to Stacey Kilbrick, and he headed over to her. She was still transfixed by something on the ground—an object the size of a honeydew melon but uneven in shape. It was a mottled red with white patches. When he realized what he was looking at he stopped so suddenly he almost tripped.

It was Joe Beltz's head, looking up at Kilbrick. His uniform hat was still on, although it had been knocked sideways at a jaunty angle. One of the eyes was wide open. The other was closed, as though the head were winking at her.

Kilbrick, who appeared frozen in place, let out another piteous mewling sound. Gurney stepped forward between her and the object of her terror, gripped her upper arms, turned her away, and led her firmly over to the RAM-TV van. He got her into the front passenger seat and told the two crew members who were standing by the door with terrified expressions to make sure the EMTs checked her out.

He moved farther down the row of vehicles to the black SWAT van and the four cops who were trying to regain their vision. He quickly introduced himself as a senior member of the district attorney's investigative staff and announced that he and Detective Torres had assumed control of the site since they were both uninjured and the DA appeared disoriented as a result of the blast.

He told them he'd seen a garden hose and water spigot on the side of the shed. As soon as they could regain enough vision to function safely, they needed to take control of the house—and Beckert, if in fact he was there.

Nodding their agreement, they headed for the shed, led by the one whose vision was least impaired. Gurney then got on the phone to Hardwick, who answered immediately.

"What the goddamn hell is going on?"

"Good question. Where are you?"

"In the woods. I figured I'd stay out of sight. Element of surprise might turn out to be useful."

"Good. The scene here is an absolute horror show. I'm thinking there's only one way any of this makes any sense. The whole thing—from Steele's murder right up through this explosion—has been a giant manipulation."

Hardwick cleared his throat noisily. "Giant manipulations usually have giant goals. Any ideas about that?"

"Not yet, but—"

His comment was cut short by more howling in the woods, louder this time and more prolonged. Then it stopped as abruptly as it began.

As he ended the call, he felt a wave of jittery exhaustion pass through him. The cumulative horrors of the case were taking their toll. The widowed wives of Steele and Loomis. The gruesomely methodical murders of Marcel Jordan and Virgil Tooker. The ripped-apart body of Judd Turlock. Blaze Lovely Jackson and Chalise Creel, dressed for a night out, dead and rotting on their couch. And now this—this gory devastation on Rapture Hill.

Counting the latest, there were now ten dead in all.

For what?

When detectives looked for murder motives, they often settled on one of the big four: greed, power, lust, envy. One or more of those was almost always present. But there was a fifth motive that Gurney had come to believe was the most powerful of all. Hatred. Pure, raging, monomaniacal hatred.

That was the hidden force that he sensed was driving all this death and destruction.

This was not, however, the sort of practical insight that immediately identifies a prime suspect—since hatred at such a pathological level is often well concealed.

Looking for a simpler way forward, he decided to try a process of elimination. He began with a mental list of everyone who had a significant connection to the case. The first eliminations naturally were the ten murder victims themselves—plus Marvin Gelter, who was unlikely to have triggered the explosion that now had him close to death.

He was about to eliminate Haley Beckert for a similar reason, but he hesitated. Her stepping out of the fatal area of the explosion a moment before it occurred was probably just a lucky coincidence. However, at least for the moment, she should probably be left on the list.

Dell Beckert, as far as Gurney knew, was still alive. If the texted confession

Kline had received was, in fact, from him, he was the prime suspect and then some. But that was a big *if*. Gurney still considered it quite possible that Beckert was being framed. And if he were guilty of the earlier murders, killing off the few people who might still be on his side would make no sense.

Cory was alive and at the scene, and the injury to his vision wouldn't get him off the list of potential suspects. What did get him off the list was the fact that he'd been framed for the first two murders, and Gurney was convinced that the same mastermind behind those two was behind all those that followed.

Kline was alive and at the scene, but Gurney found it impossible to see the moderately dishonest, moderately intelligent, anxiety-prone DA as an evil genius.

Torres also was alive and at the scene. Gurney found him a more interesting potential suspect—but only because he seemed so honest, harmless, and naïve.

The Gort twins, on the other hand, would never be accused of being honest, harmless, or naïve. They had almost certainly been involved in the bloody demise of Turlock; they were the likely source of the dynamite; and that intermittent howling in the woods was likely from their dogs. But Gurney was reasonably certain they were acting as the instruments of the same unknown manipulator who had planted the KRS evidence in their compound in an effort to frame them for Jordan and Tooker, and at the same time set up Judd Turlock as the one who framed them. It was the only scenario that made sense.

Maynard Biggs, as Hardwick had pointed out, was the person who appeared to have the most to gain from the whole affair—especially if Beckert ended up being prosecuted for some or all of it. In fact, if there was one clear answer to the cui bono question, it was Maynard Biggs. However, Gurney resisted the possibility of the man's guilt—probably because it would destroy whatever confidence he had in his ability to read character.

And, finally, there was the rector of Saint Thomas the Apostle Episcopal Church, the Reverend Whittaker Coolidge—the man who provided posthumous exonerations for Jordan and Tooker, who was a major defender of Cory Payne, an enemy of Dell Beckert, and a huge fan of Maynard Biggs. He was also the individual connected to the case who Gurney found the least knowable.

Having made his list, he discovered that it did little to illuminate the playing field. No one seemed to leap out in a clearly persuasive way. Perhaps the basic motive-means-opportunity screen could narrow it down a bit—especially the means and opportunity parts, since they were more easily discernible.

He had started to think about his list from that angle when he was interrupted by the return of the SWAT cops from the shed faucet, their faces and jacket fronts dripping wet. Red-eyed and squinting, they indicated they were ready.

Gurney hoped their vision had been sufficiently cleared. "Priorities right now are, one, making sure no one enters or leaves the site without my authorization; two, establishing a no-go zone around the immediate area of the explosion and casualties; three, searching and securing that house. That's the tricky part. We don't know if Beckert is in there or not, or what his intentions might be."

The cop closest to Gurney replied, "The tricky part is what we're good at."

"Fine. Just let me know what you're going to do before you do it."

The four, conferring in low voices, went to their van.

Torres, frowning at his phone, approached Gurney.

"The phone company pinged Beckert's phone. But I don't know if we can trust the result. The ping coordinates show the phone being outside the house."

Gurney was more excited than surprised. "Do you know what kind of phone he uses?"

"BlackBerry. Like everyone else in the department."

"Where outside the house did the ping put the coordinates?"

"Pretty much where we're standing."

"Be more specific."

"I can't. Given the distance between cell towers out here, they said the placement resolution would be defined by a twenty-foot radius around the center point of the coordinates. So, a circle with a forty-foot diameter, which includes that whole row of vehicles and this area around us."

"Okay. So now we know that someone else has Beckert's BlackBerry. So we know that the messages Kline received from that phone came from someone other than Beckert—including the so-called confession, the offer to surrender, and the list of the people who were supposed to witness the surrender—three of whom are now dead."

Torres was staring at him. "You look like you're on the verge of understanding Einstein's theory of relativity."

"Better than that. I think I finally understand this whole wretched case. Come with me."

Gurney half ran to the SWAT van. The four team members were there. Three were checking the magazines on their assault rifles. The other was hefting a battering ram out of a storage case.

"You're not going to need the artillery," said Gurney. "You'll find Beckert in the house in whatever room the television is in. He'll be watching RAM-TV. And you won't need the battering ram." Gurney reached into his pocket and handed the cop the key he'd been given at the real estate office that morning. "Don't go into the house until I give you the word. I need to locate something first."

The SWAT cops looked as baffled as Torres.

"Just wait till I give you the go-ahead," said Gurney, "and everything will be fine."

He turned to Torres. "We need to find a missing phone."

"The BlackBerry?"

"No. Payne's iPhone."

Gurney led the way down the row of cars to the beige Camry. Payne was down on his hands and knees, peering and feeling underneath it.

"You haven't found it yet?" asked Gurney.

Payne looked up, wincing. "No. With this grit in my eyes—"

Gurney cut him off. "Is there something in particular you need it for?"

"I want to try to reach my father."

"I didn't think you were on speaking terms."

"We're not. At least, we weren't. But I thought . . . maybe . . . if he was responsible for that explosion . . . maybe I could find out what's happening."

Gurney made his way around the car. Then again. And once again, in widening circles. The fourth time around he finally spotted a shiny rectangle about ten feet back from the side of the car, close to the edge of the clearing. He picked it up and saw that it was indeed an iPhone. He went over to Torres and said matter-of-factly, "Go tell the team in the van to proceed immediately."

Torres nodded and left.

Gurney held the phone up so Payne could see it. "This what you were looking for?"

"Yes, that's it!" Payne scrambled to his feet, reaching out for it. "I must have been confused about where I was standing when that blast went off."

Gurney regarded the phone curiously. "Mind if I take a look at it?"

Payne said nothing.

Gurney studied the screen and pretended to press one of the program icons.

"Don't do that," said Payne sharply. "I have things set up a certain way. Just the way I want them."

Gurney nodded. "Do you think your father set off that explosion?"

"I . . . well . . . it's possible, right? I mean, his message to me did sound pretty crazy." He hesitated, squinting toward the wreckage and bodies on the ground in front of the house. "You said that people were injured. Was anyone killed?"

"Yes."

"Who?"

"Not your stepmother. She's fine. In case you were worried."

Payne showed no reaction. He wiped his eyes with the back of his hand. "Can I have my phone now?"

Gurney ignored the request. "So . . . if I open your address book . . . which phone number would I choose . . . to set off the final charge of dynamite?"

"What?"

"The final charge of dynamite. If I wanted to set it off—"

"What the hell are you talking about?"

Gurney shrugged. "It worked for the dynamite in the petunia baskets, so I figure it should work for the dynamite in the house."

Payne stared at him, the emotion in his expression not quite readable.

"You almost got away with it. John Steele . . . Rick Loomis . . . Marcel Jordan . . . Virgil Tooker . . . Judd Turlock . . . Blaze Lovely Jackson . . . Chalise Creel . . . Dwayne Shucker . . . Goodson Cloutz . . . Joe Beltz . . ."

"What are you talking about?" The question was oddly calm, almost perfunctory.

"Ten murders. You almost got away with them all. Such careful planning. Such meticulous execution. Such control. And then you forgot to close your eyes. Such a silly oversight after all that attention to detail. If you hadn't gotten all that dirt blown into your eyes, you wouldn't have lost your phone. And if you hadn't lost your phone, you could have blown your father to pieces by now."

Payne shook his head. "You're the one who saved my life. You're the one who proved I was innocent."

"I didn't prove you were innocent. I proved that you were framed."

"You're playing with words. They mean the same thing."

"For a while I thought they did. That was *my* stupidity. Those toilet handles had me fooled. It never occurred to me that you might have been the one who switched them. It was the proof that someone had tried to frame you. Which made you appear to be an innocent victim of the real killer. And it instantly threw into doubt all the other evidence against you. It may be the cleverest criminal trick I've ever run into."

As Gurney was speaking, he was watching Payne's eyes. He'd learned long ago that any sudden physical movement is telegraphed first by the eyes. He saw no evidence of anything physical about to happen, but what he did see was more disturbing. Payne's relatively normal range of expressions had deadened into something not quite human. The word "monster" tended to be overused in descriptions of murderers, but it seemed a conservative description of the unblinking creature returning Gurney's gaze.

As he tightened his grip on the Beretta in his jacket pocket, an unnerving guttural shriek came from somewhere behind him, and a body hurtled past him, smashing Payne against the side of the car. It took Gurney a moment to realize that Haley Beauville Beckert was wildly punching and kicking Payne in an animal fury, screaming, "You filthy little bastard!"

Gurney drew his weapon, made a fast assessment of the situation, and decided that holding back for the right moment would be a safer option than trying to subdue Payne immediately.

That decision turned out to be a mistake.

After letting Haley exhaust her burst of furious energy, Payne turned her around, threw his arm around her neck, and dragged her backward with startling speed away from the car toward the edge of the clearing—a nine-millimeter Glock appearing simultaneously in his free hand.

Gurney remained where he was, steadying his Beretta on the roof of the Camry, waiting for a clear shot at Payne's head. "It's over, Cory. Don't make it worse."

Payne said nothing. He seemed well aware of Gurney's goal. He was doing a good job of keeping his body safely behind Haley's and repeatedly yanking her head from side to side in jerky movements that made taking a shot at him unacceptably risky.

Gurney called out to him again. "Let her go, Cory, and drop the nine. The longer you wait, the worse it'll be."

Astoundingly—or perhaps predictably, given the nature of RAM-TV—the roving camera operator took up a position forming a triangle with Gurney and Payne as the other two points. After a quick shot of Gurney, he panned in slowly on Payne and his hostage.

Gurney tried once more. "The longer you hold on to her, the nastier things will get."

Payne burst out laughing. "It's all for the best. All for the best." He wasn't talking to Gurney. He was talking to the camera. Which meant he was talking to Beckert via the TV in the house.

The ugly truth that Gurney had assembled from a number of observations, including the brand-new satellite dish on the corner of the house, was that while

Payne was holding Beckert captive on Rapture Hill, he was forcing him to watch RAM-TV and witness the spectacle of his own ruination.

"All for the best!" Payne repeated, his mouth in a rictus of a grin aimed at the camera, his gaze as dead and cold as a shark's. "All for the best. That's what you said after you killed my mother. You called her a worthless addict. You said that her death from the drugs you gave her was all for the best. Then you replaced her with this vile, stinking bitch. You dared to *replace* her with *this*—this rotten, cancerous whore. All for the best!"

He gave Haley's head a vicious jerk before going on with his speech to the camera. "You framed weak, frightened people to get them off the streets. *Your* streets. You sent helpless people to die in prison. All for the best. You put the girlfriend I loved in a hellhole where she was raped and killed. All for the best. You had nickel-and-dime drug dealers shot on the street for 'resisting arrest.' All for the best."

He looked into the camera with those inhuman eyes. "So I'm thinking that I'll do the same. Like father, like son. I'll put a bullet in this whore's head. All for the best. Happy Mother's Day, bitch!"

Gurney jumped out from behind the Camry, firing his Beretta in the air and shouting, "Over here, scumbag!"

As the Glock swung away from Haley's temple toward Gurney, a hard metallic impact rang out almost simultaneously with the sharp report of a rifle shot from the woods across the clearing, and the Glock flew out of Payne's hand. After an instant of surprise, he shoved Haley toward Gurney and with a sprinter's speed disappeared among the dark hemlocks. Less than a minute later that sector of the forest was filled with an eerie howling that increased steadily in volume and ferocity, then devolved suddenly into deep savage growls—until a high-pitched whistle produced an absolute silence.

It was then that the SWAT team emerged from the house with a drawn, hollow-eyed Dell Beckert. He had three sticks of dynamite with a cell phone detonator duct-taped to his stomach. The team leader placed a call to the NYSP to make sure an explosives expert was among the troops on the way. In the meantime, Beckert's semireunion with his wife was conducted at a distance with desperately fraught expressions on both faces.

Hardwick stepped into the clearing from the nearby woods, cradling his AK-47. When he got close enough, Gurney asked casually, "So what was that Western-movie show-off shit all about?"

Hardwick looked offended. "Beg pardon?"

"Shooting the gun out of Payne's hand. Nobody does that."

"I know."

"So how come you tried it?"

"I didn't. I was aiming for his head and I missed."

Soon the sound of approaching sirens reached the clearing. They seemed to be coming from all directions. Hardwick grimaced. "The classic clusterfuck is about to begin."

The sun had long since been blotted out by a lowering bank of clouds. There was a gust of cold air across the clearing, and then the rain began to fall, turning the pulverized petunia blossoms that covered the ground into a million crimson specks—as though the rain itself was turning to blood.

EPILOGUE

The classic clusterfuck predicted by Hardwick did indeed take place. In the narrative that subsequently took hold in the media, the White River case and its messy denouement had no clear heroes. "Colossal Law Enforcement Fiasco" was a typical headline. One of the punchier news blogs called it a "Fatal Fuckup." Focusing on the bloody final events, the RAM-TV news shows spoke of "the Rapture Hill massacre."

District Attorney Kline came out of it badly. He was widely portrayed as the man whose repeated mistakes led to the catastrophe. Uniformly negative press coverage, rumors that he'd suffered a breakdown at the crime scene, and a growing public outcry led to abandonment by his political allies and soon thereafter to his resignation.

Cory Payne's ill-advised alliance with the Gort twins ended badly. His scattered remains, torn apart by the Gort pit bulls, were found in a pine thicket at the foot of Rapture Hill. In his manipulation of the twins to kill Turlock—and to provide him with the dynamite for his plan to blow his father and all his father's enablers to kingdom come—he'd evidently overestimated the Gorts' trust in him. Daytime TV psychologists opined for weeks on Payne's wounded life and dark motivations. A book titled *Blind Revenge* was written about him. It was optioned for a film.

•

The Gorts and their dogs vanished. The unanswered questions surrounding their disappearance and their ill-fated relationship with Payne provided fodder for many tabloid articles. There were claims of occasional sightings by backwoods hikers, and stories about them could give overnight campers gooseflesh, but there was no tangible evidence of their presence. It was as though they had melded like a malignant force of nature into the wilderness that had always seemed so much a part of them.

The Rapture Hill death toll rose to four when Marvin Gelter died in the hospital a week later of a massive infection.

Members of the Black Defense Alliance, temporarily leaderless, declined to make any public statement. So did Carlton Flynn, who apparently couldn't come up with a sufficiently provocative political slant on the case.

Gurney's role in the affair was treated in a muted but generally positive way. His accurate final assessment of the situation and his fearless confrontation of Cory Payne were acknowledged. Haley Beckert in particular lauded his attempts to warn Kline of the truth of what was happening at Rapture Hill.

As Gurney was falling asleep one night, the déjà vu experience he'd had when he looked at Beckert's CBIIWRPD license plate suddenly became clear. The CBII part, standing for Cordell Beckert II, had prompted the half-conscious recollection that Cory Payne's real name was Cordell Beckert III. Which would make his equivalent initials CBIII. Which looked very much like "C13111." A severely injured person on a stretcher trying to scribble a note might very well end up making a *B* that looked like *13*. So Rick Loomis's note, which said in its entirety "T O L D C 1 3 1 1 1," was an effort to let Gurney know that he'd told Cory Payne something. It raised questions that Gurney knew he'd never get the answers to. But that wasn't unusual in a murder case. Too often the only people who knew the entire truth were dead.

•

Lines of grief became a permanent part of Kim Steele's face. The weight of sadness in her was palpable. But she kept functioning.

Heather Loomis, on the other hand, seemed more deeply damaged. After learning of her husband's death, her condition declined from a depressed state to a near-catatonic one. She was transferred to a major New England mental hospital for long-term treatment. She gave birth prematurely, and the baby was put in the care of her brother and sister-in-law. She showed no interest in the baby or the arrangements made for it.

Mark Torres confided to Gurney that he intended to resign from the WRPD to pursue a degree in social work. Gurney suggested he give the department another year. He believed it was cops like Torres who could brighten the future of policing.

Tania Jordan left White River without a word to anyone.

Dell Beckert, for the first time in his adult life, persistently refused all contact with the media. He appeared to have aged years in the days of his captivity—and the stress promised to continue as investigators from the U.S. Department of Justice and the New York State Attorney General's office launched an extensive review of his personal involvement in alleged civil rights violations, evidence tampering, and obstructions of justice.

Within a month of replacing the late Goodson Cloutz, acting sheriff Fred Kittiny was arrested and charged with seven counts of suborning perjury.

A specialist in turning out instant books on sensational crimes, disasters, and celebrities created one titled *Lovely* that focused on Blaze Lovely Jackson's fatal alliance with Cory Payne. The cover depicted a helmeted leather-clad figure on a red motorcycle—just like the one belonging to Judd Turlock that Jackson rode away from the Poulter Street sniper site as part of Payne's elaborate framing scheme.

The statue of Colonel Ezra Willard was quietly transported from the public park to the private estate of a self-described Civil War buff. The man made no secret of his sympathies for the Confederate cause, which left a lingering discomfort in the minds of many about the solution to the controversy. There were those who would have been far happier had the thing been pulverized and dumped in the county landfill. But the majority of the city council was content to approve the less dramatic transfer and be rid of at least one racial flash point.

Maynard Biggs was appointed by the governor to serve as acting attorney general until the upcoming special election, which he was now favored to win.

The Reverend Whittaker Coolidge delivered a series of well-received public lectures on the destructive power of hatred. He described hatred with a phrase that Maynard Biggs had used to describe racism: *a razor with no handle that cuts the wielder as deeply as the victim.* His other description of it: *a suicidal weapon of mass destruction.* And he always managed to work into his lectures an eight-word summary of Cory Payne's life and death: *His hatred drove him. His hatred killed him.*

• • •

For some time after the bloody culmination on Rapture Hill, followed by Gurney's extensive debriefing by the state and federal investigators who descended on White River, he and Madeleine seemed to have little appetite for discussing the case.

There was often a preoccupied look on her face; but he knew from long experience it was best not to ask about it, that she'd share what was on her mind in her own time.

It happened one evening in early June. They'd just finished a quiet dinner. The French doors were open, and the warm summer air carried the scent of the season's fading lilacs. After a period of silence, she spoke.

"Do you think anything will change?"

"You mean the racial situation in White River?"

She nodded.

"Well . . . things are happening that weren't happening before. The rotten apples are being removed from the police department. Old cases are being scrutinized, particularly the Laxton Jones incident. A more transparent citizen complaint process is being installed. The statue is gone. Discussions are under way to create an interracial commission that would—"

She stopped him. "I know all that. The announcements. The press conferences. I mean . . . doesn't it sound like just another example of rearranging the deck chairs on the *Titanic*?"

Gurney shrugged. "That's what deckhands do."

"What do you mean?"

"Isn't that what most of the people we elect to solve our problems really do? They don't *solve* anything; they just rearrange the details to relieve the political pressure and make it look like something significant is being done. Real change doesn't happen that way. It's less manageable, less predictable. It only happens when people see something they never saw before—when the truth, for whatever reason, hits them hard enough, shockingly enough, to open their eyes."

Madeleine nodded, seemingly more to herself than to him. After a while she got up from the table and stood in the open doorway, looking down over the low pasture toward the barn and the pond. "Do you think that's what Walter Thrasher wants to do?"

The question surprised him.

He thought about it for a moment. "Yes, I think so. He has a natural fondness for bringing things to light, for discovering the truth, even when it's ugly—maybe especially when it's ugly."

She took a deep breath. "If we let him do what he wants to do . . . he might not find anything at all."

"That's true."

"Or he might find dreadful things."

"Yes."

"And then he would write about those dreadful things."

"Yes."

"And people would read what he wrote ... and some of them would be horrified."

"I would think so."

She gazed down toward the area of the excavation for a long minute or two before saying, almost inaudibly, "Maybe we should let him go ahead with it."

ACKNOWLEDGMENTS

As the Dave Gurney series of mystery-thrillers grows, so does my gratitude to the people responsible for its success.

My thanks first to my wonderful agent, Molly Friedrich, and her superb associates, Lucy Carson and Kent Wolf. Their keen insights, close reading of my manuscripts, creative suggestions, and wholehearted support have been invaluable.

My thanks also to my remarkable editor, Dan Smetanka, whose fine instincts for dramatic structure, character, and pacing—along with a talent for deft pruning—have made my stories better, leaner, stronger. And my thanks to my copy editor, Megan Gendell, whose eye for the crucial details of language, tone, and consistency resulted in countless improvements.

My thanks to my wife, Naomi, who makes everything possible.

And finally, my thanks to all the readers of the Dave Gurney novels. Your enthusiasm for these books is one of the brightest elements in my life as a writer.

Author photograph by Naomi Fisch

JOHN VERDON is the author of the Dave Gurney series of thrillers, international bestsellers published in more than two dozen languages: *Think of a Number, Shut Your Eyes Tight, Let the Devil Sleep, Peter Pan Must Die,* and *Wolf Lake.* Before becoming a crime fiction writer, Verdon had two previous careers: as an advertising creative director and as a custom furniture maker. He currently lives with his wife, Naomi, in the rural mountains of upstate New York—raising chickens, tending the garden, mowing the fields, and devising the intricate plots of the Gurney novels. Find more at johnverdon.net.